T he three Harper judges waited impatiently for the sage to continue. Elminster rose to his feet and circled around the table till he stood directly before the tribunal. "Three things . . ." he began. Then suddenly his face went pale. He gasped and clutched at his chest.

"Elminster?" Morala cried, rising to her feet.

"Are you all right, sir?" Breck asked, leaping from his seat to come to the aid of the sage. Some invisible force, though, repelled the young ranger. He bounced backward onto the dais at Kyre's feet.

In the span of three breaths, Elminster's body seemed to turn to clear crystal. Then, in a flash of bright light, the sage was gone. In his place stood a huge, hideous beast.

The creature stood as tall as a hill giant, towering over the three Harpers. The long red robe and fur cape it wore couldn't hide the inhumanness of its form. It was covered with sickly green scales, and its eyes glittered red in the torchlight. Two sharp ivory horns sprouted from its head, and a third, even longer, horn rose from the tip of its long snout. Around the back of its head grew a bony frill, edged with spikes and decorated with arcane magical symbols. A muscular tail curled up from beneath the hem of its robe and swished back and forth like an angry snake.

In one clawed appendage, the beast clenched an iron staff tipped with a yellow orb, and in the other claw it held out a small blood-red object vaguely resembling a large chess rook. The red object began to glow, and the Harpers could feel heat emanating from it.

Kyre shouted, "Kill it!" Without a second's hesitation, she drew a dagger from her boot

Also by Novak and Grubb:

AZURE BONDS
THE WYVERN'S SPUR

FANTASY ADVENTURE

SONG
OF THE
SAURIALS

KATE NOVAK AND JEFF GRUBB

Cover Art
CLYDE CALDWELL

TSR, Inc.

To my sisters, Sharon and Beth

K.N.

To Frank, Jeff, Dave, Joe, and all the other
denizens of the CMU and Purdue Dungeons
who walked Toril so long ago

J.G.

SONG OF THE SAURIALS

Distributed to the book trade in the United States by Random House, Inc., and in Canada by
Random House of Canada, Ltd.

Distributed in the United Kingdom by TSR Ltd.

Distributed to the toy and hobby trade by regional distributors.

FORGOTTEN REALMS is a registered trademark owned by TSR, Inc.

PRODUCTS OF THE IMAGINATION and the TSR logo are trademarks owned by TSR, Inc.

First printing: March, 1991
Printed in the United States of America.
Library of Congress Catalog Card Number: 90-71497

9 8 7 6 5 4 3 2 1

ISBN:1-56076-060-5

TSR, Inc.
P.O. Box 756
Lake Geneva, WI 53147
U.S.A.

TSR Ltd.
120 Church End, Cherry Hinton
Cambridge CB1 3LB
United Kingdom

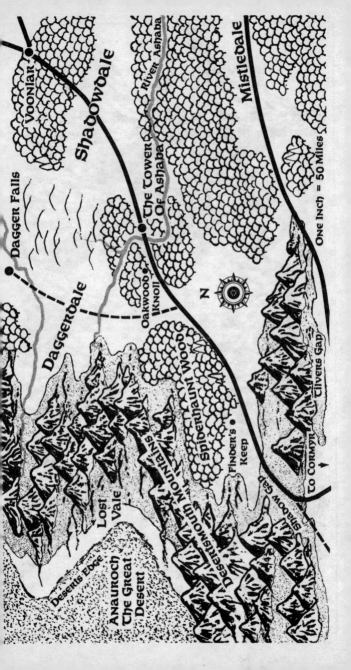

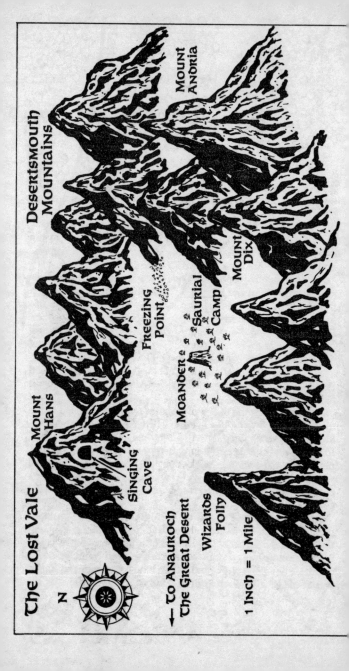

❦ 1 ❦

The Nameless Bard

"Hear what you've denied the Realms, what you've denied yourselves," the prisoner muttered as he raised the chordal horn to his lips. His breath flowed through the instrument's chambers with the steady force of a trade wind, and his fingers danced gracefully over the horn's holes and keys. Sweet music filled the prison cell, slipped through the iron bars set in the cell door, swirled down the hallways of the Tower of Ashaba, and entered, unbidden, into the courtroom.

The tune echoed along the bare stone walls of the chamber and danced about the Harpers' courtroom. There, seated at a table before a tribunal of three Harpers, sat Elminster the Sage, about to offer his own counsel concerning the prisoner. Elminster paused before beginning his opening statement and closed his eyes to listen to the tune. It took him only a moment to catch the gist of the spell it was meant to weave. Ah, Nameless, will ye never change? he thought. A penitent man would plead for his freedom, a righteous man demand it. Is seduction all ye knowest?

Morala of Milil, the eldest of the three judges, scowled at the musical interruption. Her eyes nearly disappeared in the wrinkles that creased her face. A lock of her snow-white hair fell forward, and she shoved it impatiently back into the gold hairnet at the nape of her neck. She, too, recognized the spell wrapped within the melody, and when she caught Elminster's eye, she folded her frail arms across her chest and smiled coldly.

Elminster smiled back, as if oblivious to the ancient priestess's hostility. He thought with some annoyance, Why did the Harpers have to choose thee for this tribunal? Ye could hardly be considered unbiased. Ye never liked Nameless.

Morala had been one of the judges who had sentenced Nameless at his first trial. Of course, Elminster knew that was exactly why she was here now. Someone had to represent the past, someone who knew the Nameless of old and recognized his tricks, tricks such as the one Nameless was engaging in at this very moment.

"It wouldn't kill thee to enjoy the melody, Morala," the sage muttered under his breath. "A mere tune could hardly corrupt a pillar of stone like thyself."

Morala gave the sage a harsh glare, as if she'd heard his remark. Uncertain just how good her hearing was, Elminster shuffled a stack of scrolls across the table as if he were preoccupied with his defense and did not hear the music. When he sensed that Morala had turned her attention away from him, the sage sneaked a glance at the other two judges.

Not surprisingly, Breck Orcsbane, the youngest of the three judges, seemed delighted with the music. The ranger's head bobbed in time with the music, setting his long plait of yellow hair swaying like a pendulum. Elminster half-expected the brawny woodsman to get up and dance a jig. Morala had already expressed her displeasure that someone of Breck's simplicity had been chosen for the tribunal, but Elminster was relieved to discover that at least one of the judges knew how to enjoy life.

Only the bard, Kyre, displayed a completely neutral reaction to the music. The beautiful half-elven woman tilted her head to listen, but Elminster suspected that her technical analysis of the tune precluded experiencing it on any emotional level. The sage wished he could tell what she thought of it. He wished he could tell what she thought of anything. Kyre was so remote and stiff whenever he addressed her that Elminster felt as if he were speaking with the dead, an experience with which he was not unfamiliar. As if to compensate for her reserved nature, Kyre wore a vivid red orchid in her lustrous black hair. To bloom in this climate, the sage realized, the orchid had to be enchanted, but who, he was left to wonder, was she trying attract with it?

"Heth," Morala said, addressing the tower page assigned to the Harpers. "Request the captain of the guard to do something about that noise," she commanded, "and close the door on your way out."

"Oh, that won't be necessary," Breck said. "The music's not half bad."

Heth hesitated at the doorway.

Morala's eyes narrowed as she looked to Kyre for support.

Kyre shrugged, indifferent to the priestess's annoyance.

"The sound does not disturb me," the half-elf said flatly.

"Elminster? Aren't you distracted by the noise?" Morala asked, hoping the sage would at least have the decency to admit the inappropriateness of the music at the trial. They had already agreed that Nameless should not appear before the tribunal. Morala feared he might charm the younger Harpers with his wit, while Elminster feared he might disgust them with his ego. It certainly did not seem appropriate to the priestess that the man's music should be heard. It was just such music that Nameless had used to justify his crimes, and the Harpers had not yet repealed their original judgment that all the prisoner's music be banished from the Realms.

"I'm sorry, Morala," Elminster replied. "My hearing's not what it once was. Didst ye ask if I heard boys?"

Morala let her breath out in a huff. She motioned the page to sit. "Please, continue with your argument, wise Elminster," Morala prompted.

Having gained the upper hand with Morala on so small a matter, Elminster hesitated before moving on to the more important issue at hand. Do I really dare speak on Nameless's behalf? he wondered. Nameless's ordeals don't seem to have humbled him any. Is he any wiser for all his suffering? The sage sighed to himself and shook his head in an attempt to clear away his doubts. He had said he would speak on the prisoner's behalf, so he would. He could only hope that the collective decision of the tribunal would prove at least as wise as his own uncertain counsel.

The sage rose to his feet and cleared his throat. "At my request," he explained, "the Harpers have agreed to reconsider the case of the Nameless Bard. They have chosen ye from among their ranks to represent them and serve on this tribunal. For the benefit of Kyre and Breck Orcsbane, who were not yet born when Nameless was first tried, I will review the circumstances of his trial and the outcome. If it please thy grace," the sage said, nodding politely in Morala's direction, "feel free to add to or correct me at any point. Ye knew Nameless as well as I."

Morala nodded politely in return, but Elminster realized it

was unlikely she would interrupt him. His report would be scrupulously accurate, and Morala was astute enough to know she would only look like a fussy old woman if she began correcting him.

Elminster began his tale. "The Nameless Bard was born three hundred and fifty years ago in a small village in one of the northern nations, the second son of local gentry. At an early age, he completed his training at a renowned barding college and graduated with highest honors. He chose the life of a wandering adventurer, and his songs became popular wherever in the Realms he roamed. While he relished his fame, he also put it to good use, attracting other young adventurers to help in any cause he felt worthy. Thus he and his companions became the founding fathers of the Harpers.

"With the blessings of his gods and such aid as magic can give, he lived well beyond the natural span of years given to a human, yet there came a time when his mortality began to prey greatly on his mind. The bard became obsessed with preserving his songs for posterity. He was never satisfied with any other person's performance of his works, so he would not settle for the tradition among most bards of passing the work on orally or leaving a written record. He began to experiment with magical means of recording his work and thus created a most marvelous piece of magic—the finder's stone."

Elminster paused a moment and glanced at Morala, wondering if she would object to his mentioning the name of the magic device. Morala, however, chose to ignore Elminster's mischief and waved her hand impatiently for him to proceed.

"The stone was originally a very minor artifact that would serve any person as a compass of detection. Basically its wielder needed only to think of a person, and the stone would send out a beam of light indicating a path to that person," the sage explained. "It also protected itself from theft as well as it could with a blinding light spell. Occasionally it was known to direct its wielder without instruction, as if it had a mind of its own, so that the stone was said to help the lost find their way.

"The Nameless Bard experimented with altering the artifact's nature, something only the most skilled or the most foolish magic-wielder would dare to try. Into the crystal's heart he inserted a shard of enchanted para-elemental ice. Having survived such a risky undertaking, Nameless reaped a great reward. In his hands or those of his kin, the stone acted as a rechargeable wand holding those spells Nameless had acquired. Like the blank pages of a journal, the stone could store other information as well. Nameless claimed it could recall for him an entire library of tomes. It could also recall his songs and 'sing' them, as it were, in Nameless's voice, exactly as he sang them. He added other enchantments so it could project the illusion that he was actually sitting there, singing the song."

"A little stuck on himself, wasn't he?" Breck noted with a grin.

Morala huffed in agreement.

"More than a little, good ranger," Elminster replied, smiling at Breck. The sage was pleased that the young man wasn't afraid to speak out and even more pleased that the failings of others amused rather than annoyed the ranger. "Despite all that he had accomplished," Elminster went on, "Nameless still was not satisfied. The stone's illusion of himself needed to be commanded when to sing and told what to sing. It had no vital force to sing of its own will, or judgment to choose a song appropriate to the moment, or ability to gauge an audience's reaction and build upon their emotions. So Nameless abandoned the stone as a failure. He planned next to build a powerful simulacrum of himself. The creature was to have Nameless's own personality as well as all the knowledge Nameless had placed in the finder's stone. So that none would shun it as an abomination, Nameless researched ways to make it indistinguishable from a true human. Finally, he intended to give it immortality."

Breck gave a low whistle of amazement. The priestess Morala shuddered, even though she was already familiar with the story. Kyre's expression remained neutral—interested, but emotionless. The tune from the prisoner's cell swelled into a bold fanfare.

Elminster continued. "Having found it useful in his alterations of the finder's stone, Nameless obtained another shard of para-elemental ice for the heart of the simulacrum." The sage paused. It was easy enough for Elminster to speak of Nameless's brilliance and daring, and even his obsession and vanity, but the sage's heart ached to recall the bard's crime.

It was better he should tell it, though, than let Morala give the account. "Yet, for all his brilliance and natural ability with magic," Elminster explained, "Nameless was a bard, not a trained magic-user. He recognized his own limitations and tried to enlist the aid of several different wizards, but without success. There were not many people whom he had not offended with his arrogance. Among those mages he counted as friends, many thought his project silly, a waste of time and energy. Some did not believe it would even work. Others thought the creation he proposed to be a heinous act. A few pointed out that the creation could be copied and used by malicious beings for evil purposes. They tried to convince him that he should be satisfied with the finder's stone's recreation of his music. Whatever their opinion, every mage he spoke with told him the project was too dangerous. It would prove fatal to himself or some other."

"He went ahead and did it anyway, didn't he?" Breck asked, as eager as a child to hear the outcome of Elminster's story.

The sage nodded. "Yes, he did. With the aid of his apprentices, he built the simulacrum's body in his own home. As he began casting the spell that would animate the creature, however, something went wrong. The para-elemental ice exploded. The simulacrum was destroyed, and one apprentice died instantly. Another lost her voice, and all attempts to heal her failed."

"She killed herself later," Morala interrupted with a trace of anger.

"Yes," Elminster admitted, then hastily added, "but that was after the time of which I speak. When Nameless summoned help for his wounded apprentice, he freely admitted how she had sustained her injuries. The other Harpers were appalled that he had risked his own apprentices in so dangerous a task, all for the sake of his obsession with his music. They summoned him to judgment and found him guilty of slaying one apprentice and injuring another. They determined a punishment to fit his crime.

"His music and his name were to be banished from the Realms. To keep him from thwarting them in this goal, and also to keep him from trying his reckless experiment again, the Harpers removed the bard's own name from his memory and banished him from the Realms, exiling him to a border region of the positive plane of life, where, due to the nature of that region, he would live in good health and relative immortality. He was condemned, however, to live in complete solitude." Elminster paused again.

Nameless's tune switched to a plaintive minor key as Morala, Orcsbane, and Kyre sat contemplating their fellow Harper's crime and his punishment. It almost seemed as if Nameless was aware of what point in his story Elminster had reached. Morala glanced suspiciously at the sage, but he seemed not to notice the tune at all.

Actually Elminster's attention at the moment was attracted to a fluttering shadow behind the tribunal. The sage made no sound or movement to call attention to the small figure he spotted skulking along the courtroom wall. It was only the halfling, Olive Ruskettle. Elminster could see no harm in her unauthorized presence. After all, she knew Nameless's story already. The sage made a mental note, though, to chide Lord Mourngrym about the quality of the tower guard. In the courtroom, the halfling was nearly impossible to spot, adept as she was at hiding in the shadows, but she should not have been able to pass through the tower's front gate in broad daylight unchallenged by the guards.

Unaware she had been observed by the sharp-eyed sage, the halfling sneaked out of the courtroom and down the corridor toward the prisoner's cell.

If ye have plans to visit thy friend Nameless, ye little sneak thief, ye are in for a surprise, Elminster thought, suppressing a grin. He focused his attention again on the judges. "Two hundred years have passed since the exile of the Nameless Bard—"

"Excuse me, Elminster," Kyre interrupted, "but are we to continue calling this man Nameless throughout this hearing? Surely we can be trusted with his name. It would simplify things, would it not?"

"No!" Morala objected. "It is we who made him Nameless. Nameless he will remain."

Elminster sighed at the old priestess's vehemence. "It is the purpose of this tribunal to decide not only whether or not to free Nameless, but whether or not Nameless's name should be restored to the Realms. Morala and I have both taken an oath not to reveal the name unless the Harpers decide otherwise. So we must continue to refer to him as Nameless, at least until the end of this trial."

"I see," Kyre replied, nodding her head slightly. "Excuse my interruption."

Elminster nodded and once again began the second half·of his tale. "Nameless remained in exile for two centuries. Then certain evil powers deliberately sought him out and freed him from his place of exile."

The tune coming from the bard's prison ceased abruptly. Morala's lips curled ever so slightly in satisfaction while Elminster stroked his beard thoughtfully, wondering just what Nameless was up to now.

* * * * *

In his prison cell, Nameless lowered the chordal horn and glared at his cell door. Something was jiggling in the lock. Elminster had given the guards specific instructions to show the prisoner every courtesy possible, including always knocking before opening his door. The prisoner scowled in anticipation of delivering a scathing reprimand to whichever guard had been so foolish to interrupt him in the middle of his composition.

The door swung open slowly. A female halfling stood in the doorway. Her hazel eyes sparkled, and she winked conspiratorially as she slid a copper wire into her russet hair. "Nice ditty," she quipped. "Has it got any lyrics?"

"Naturally," the prisoner replied, relaxing his angry face. "Would you like me to write them down for you, Mistress Ruskettle?" he asked.

"That'd be great," the small woman said, stepping into the cell. She pushed the door almost, but not quite, closed behind her. Her furry bare feet padded silently across the plush wool Calimshan carpeting. She slipped off her knapsack and her wet cloak and checked to be sure the back of her tunic and pants were dry before seating herself on a tapestry-covered footstool.

The Nameless Bard lay the chordal horn down on the table. "Come in, Mistress Ruskettle. Have a seat and make yourself at home," he said, though he knew sarcasm was wasted on halflings in general and on Olive Ruskettle in particular.

"Thank you, Nameless," Olive replied. "Nice quarters you have here," she said as her eyes inspected the polished furniture, the velvet drapes, the brass-bound clothes chest, the silk bedspread, the gold candelabrum, the crystal wine decanter, and all the other luxuries Nameless's captors had provided for his cell. "You're looking well," she added, grinning at the fine silken shirt, fur-trimmed tunic, wool pants, and leather boots he wore.

Nameless grinned back as he seated himself cross-legged on the bed. He never could remain annoyed with Olive for long. She had, after all, rescued him from the dungeon of the cruel sorceress Cassana and also helped him free his singer, Alias, from Cassana. It wasn't just gratitude, however, that made him fond of the halfling thief; Olive's brash nerve amused him. It reminded him of himself.

"What have you been up to?" the bard asked. "It's been over a year since I've seen you last."

"Yes. Sorry about that. This summer's been rather chaotic, as you've probably heard. I was staying with friends in Immersea, who talked me out of traveling until the trouble died down. If I'd known you were wasting away in prison, I would have come sooner," the halfling said. From a silver bowl piled with fruit, she plucked a large, juicy plum and ate the delicacy in several dainty, but quick, bites.

"My imprisonment is a mere formality until the new trial is over," Nameless said. "That door wasn't even kept locked until that old bat Morala arrived and caused a stink."

"She's the priestess of Milil?" Olive asked. "The one who has it in for you?"

"You've met?" Nameless asked.

"I've seen her around."

"Have you seen Alias?"

"Actually, I came to see you the moment I hit town," Olive said. The halfling didn't care much for Alias. Olive realized, however, that Nameless thought of the singing swordswoman as a daughter, so in an effort to be polite, she asked the bard, "How is dear Alias?"

"I don't know," Nameless huffed. "She and Dragonbait arrived in Shadowdale a day after Morala, and Morala won't allow me any visitors. How did you get past the guard at the tower gate?"

"You know," the halfling said, pulling out a silver pin from her cloak pocket, "it really is amazing how much respect the local constabulary has for this silly harp-and-moon symbol, even when it's pinned to the breast of a short person with no visible weapons."

Nameless grinned at the irony. He'd given the halfling thief his old Harper's pin. According to custom, Olive would need him to vouch for her until she was accepted by the other Harpers, but he was a disgraced Harper. Now she'd used the pin to break a rule made by Morala—a Master Harper. There was nothing like the chaos a halfling—or a woman—could cause, Nameless thought, and Olive is both. "You realize," Nameless asked aloud, "you'll have some problems being accepted by the Harpers until I have reestablished myself?"

"You realize," Olive retorted, "that I'll have some problems accepting the Harpers if they don't get off their high horses and forget this banishment business. In the meantime, you can't stay in this dump. I've got a horse and provisions for you hidden at the edge of town."

"Why, that's awfully thoughtful of you, Mistress Ruskettle."

"So let's go," Olive said, hopping up from the footstool and standing beside the bed, tapping her foot in mock impatience.

Nameless leaned forward, reached out a hand, and stroked her hair. Ordinarily Olive couldn't stand having humans patting her on the head, but Nameless hadn't actually patted her, and she liked him more than any other human she'd ever met, so she could forgive him a good deal. She looked up at him, puzzled that he'd even touched her at all.

"Oh, Olive," he said with a rueful smile.

"What's wrong?" she asked, not failing to note he had used her given name, something he'd never done before.

"Did you think me incapable of arranging my own escape, Olive?" Nameless asked.

"You're still here, aren't you?" Olive pointed out, growing annoyed.

"Yes, but not due to any lack of skill with locks," Nameless said, holding out his hand and presenting the halfling with the copper wire he'd just slipped from her hair. Dexterously he twirled the shining metal strand through his fingers, then made it vanish so quickly that Olive couldn't be certain if he'd flipped it away or slipped it up his sleeve.

"All right, I'm impressed. Can I have my pick-bone back?" the halfling asked.

"It's in your hair, Olive, right where you put it," replied Nameless.

Olive ran her fingers through her hair and found the wire lodged behind her ear exactly where she'd put it. "An illusion, right?" she guessed.

Nameless did not reply. Instead, his eyes twinkled with mischief.

"I hate it when you do things like that," Olive huffed.

"You love it when I do things like that," Nameless countered. "You just hate that you can't do them yet."

"All right. So you didn't need my help to escape. Why are you still here?" she demanded.

"Because I have no desire to become a hunted fugitive when I don't have to. The Harpers will come to their senses and release me."

"That's what you thought when you turned yourself over to them two hundred years ago," Olive argued. "What makes you think this trial's going to end any different from the first one?"

"Elminster is speaking in my defense this time," Nameless replied confidently.

"You put a lot of store in that old coot."

"The Harpers have grown accustomed to abiding by Elminster's counsel."

Olive sniffed. "And you expect them to forgive all, to take you back into their fold and restore you to your position as a Master Harper?"

"Naturally," the bard said coolly.

"What then?" Olive snapped. "Engagements at all the royal courts? A few noble titles granted in honor of your talents? Wizards begging for your secrets? Flocks of apprentices ready to serve under you?"

"Why should it be any different than it was before?" Nameless asked with a cocky grin.

"You're dreaming, pal!" Olive shouted, completely frustrated with his vanity and unrelenting certainty. "Wake up and smell the bacon! Not even the great Elminster is going to bring Morala around. As for the other two, the ranger might take pity on you, but that half-elf bard's got all the compassion of an iron golem. You need—" Olive halted, alarmed at the way her voice echoed through the cell and annoyed that this stupid human had made her lose her self-control. "You need a contingency plan," the halfling whispered. "Just in case I'm right and you're wrong."

"I have too much to lose if I flee now and you're wrong," Nameless retorted heatedly.

"You have too much to lose if you don't. Security isn't going to get any more lax if they condemn you, you know. Since you've already broken out of the Citadel of White Exile, they'll have to find some place even worse—if you can imagine any place worse than that."

Nameless fought to control a tremor in his lip. For two centuries, he'd lived in the Citadel of White Exile, able to scry on the happenings in the Realms but completely unable to participate. It had been torture for him, but he could imagine worse things. He had other objections to trying to escape, though. "You forget we're talking about the Harpers," he said. "They'll have no trouble tracking me down. "

"You're a Harper yourself," Olive pointed out. "If you weren't so eager to rest on your laurels, you could keep a step ahead of them. I've got a place where you could hide, too—somewhere you'll be welcome, and no one would ever be able to detect you magically."

"You want me to hide behind Alias's shield," Nameless replied, referring to the misdirection spell cast on the swordswoman, a spell which made her and anyone she traveled with completely undetectable by magical means. "Forget it," Nameless said vehemently. "I'm not getting her involved in this."

"I wasn't talking about Alias," Olive said. "Give me credit for some sense. She's too obvious. I wasn't talking about a magic dead zone, either. That's too obvious, too; besides, there's too much riffraff in places like that. I have someplace even better in mind. With any luck, the Harpers will waste their time checking out Alias and the dead zones and miss us altogether. The Harpers aren't perfect. They make mistakes. Why do you give them so much power over you?"

"Because," Nameless hissed angrily, "they have my name."

Olive shrugged her shoulders and helped herself to another plum. "Big deal. So do I. It's Finder. Finder Wyvernspur, from the clan Wyvernspur of Immersea, in Cormyr," she said nonchalantly. She stifled a mock yawn before adding, "Your older brother was Gerrin Wyvernspur. Your mother's name was Amalee Winter, and your father was Lord Gould. Your grandfather was *the* Paton Wyvernspur. Sound familiar?"

The bard leaned back against the wall, staring at the halfling with undisguised amazement. Silently, with his eyes closed as if he were reciting an oft-repeated prayer from childhood, the bard mouthed the names Olive had given him .

"Surprised?" Olive asked, unable to keep from grinning.

The bard looked at the halfling and nodded, still dumbfounded.

"I've got something else for you, Finder," Olive said, pulling something from her cloak pocket. She laid it down on the bed in front of the bard. "Recognize this?"

Finder looked down at the halfling's gift. It was a sparkling yellow crystal, multifaceted and roughly egg-shaped, somewhat larger than a hen's egg. The bard gasped. Then he whooped once with pleasure, leaped from the bed, snatched Olive up in the air, and swung her around, laughing with delight. "You stole the finder's stone! You incredible halfling! I could kiss you!"

"Well, I suppose I deserve it," Olive said, turning her head and pointing to her cheek. Finder pressed his lips against her flushed face. Then he laughed and spun around again, with Olive still in his arms.

"I'll lose that plum I just ate if you don't set me down," Olive threatened.

Finder lowered the halfling gently to the bed. Olive bounced once on the mattress and snatched up the crystal. "Is this thing still loaded with magic? " she asked, tossing the stone to the bard.

Finder caught the crystal with one hand. He sang a short, clear G-sharp and peered into the stone's depths. "Yes!" he announced. "I don't believe it. Elminster didn't give this to you, did he? You *did* steal it, didn't you?"

Olive grinned. "No and no. Elminster gave it to Alias last year. Maybe he felt she had some right to it, seeing how she's related to you. We lost it outside of Westgate, but I ran into the man who found it and convinced him to part with it."

"And my name? Who parted with that?" Finder asked.

"That's a longer story. Why don't we save it for later? Let's go, huh? "

Finder sat down on the footstool. "There's no hurry now," he insisted. "We can leave anytime. There's a teleport spell in the crystal."

"Which won't work if Elminster's cast some sort of anti-magic shell around this cell," Olive argued.

"The finder's stone is an artifact. Not even Elminster's magic can stop spells cast from it," Finder declared. He picked out a plum from the bowl and took a bite, slurping noisily. "I want to give Elminster the chance to argue my case before the Harpers as he should have done the first time. If he fails to convince them to pardon me, then we'll leave."

"I have a bad feeling about this, Finder. Let's go now, please," Olive pleaded.

"Relax, Olive. I have everything under control. Here, have another plum." Finder held out the silver fruit bowl toward Olive.

Olive crossed her arms, determined not to encourage her friend's indifference to his own peril.

Finder waved the bowl enticingly under her nose. Unable to resist the smell, the halfling chose a second plum.

"Finder. Such a proper name," the bard mused as he set the bowl back on the table The halfling suppressed an unexplainable shiver and bit into her plum.

* * * * *

While Olive Ruskettle was trying her best to convince the Nameless Bard that Elminster might fail to get him freed, the sage himself was explaining to the Harpers how the alliance of evil beings that had freed Nameless had managed to trick the bard into building a new version of his simulacrum for them.

Morala shook her head and bit her tongue, but she could no longer hold back her annoyance. "This is just what I warned him would happen when he was planning the first simulacrum. Evil cannot disguise itself from good unless good looks the other way. Nameless's own arrogance blinded him to their nature."

"That may be, thy grace," Elminster replied, "but he did not hesitate to act against these evil beings when he finally recognized their true nature. He did his best to keep them from gaining control of the simulacrum. He freed her so that she and her companions were able to return and destroy all of the members of the consortium, the sorceress Cassana, the lich Prakis, the Fire Knives Assassins Guild, the Tarterean fiend Phalse, and even Moander the Darkbringer."

"She? You mean the simulacrum?" Breck asked.

"He succeeded in animating it, then?" Morala asked with a defeated sigh.

"Actually, she's more than animated. She's very much alive and possessed of her very own soul and spirit. Not even ye, thy grace, could tell she was unborn."

"Impossible!" the priestess declared.

"Impossible for Nameless and the evil beings who backed him, but not impossible for a god."

"Moander is the Darkbringer. He could not give her a soul," Morala insisted.

"I did not speak of Moander," Elminster said.

"What god, then, Elminster?" Kyre asked.

"I'm not certain. The fiend Phalse kidnapped a paladin from another world to supply the simulacrum with a soul, but the paladin still lives. Somehow his soul doubled, and a shard of his spirit broke off. Both grew inside Nameless's creation. It is possible one of the paladin's gods made this possible. I also suspect that the goddess of luck, Tymora, may have interfered in the creation. Nameless still invokes her name on occasion, and the simulacrum seems to have an affinity for Lady Luck. Perhaps it was a joint effort of these gods. Whatever the case, the woman lives."

"Why did Nameless make this creation a woman?" Breck asked.

"For her own vile reasons, the sorceress Cassana insisted it be made in her image," the sage explained. "Perhaps that was for the best. Nameless gave the simulacrum much of his personality, but in an effort to make her a more 'ideal' woman, in his own view, he created in her a tender and nobler side Nameless himself had never displayed. She has already made a name for herself as a brave and clever sell-sword. The paladin I mentioned before, a noble saurial known here in the Realms as 'Dragonbait,' travels in her company, totally convinced of her goodness."

Breck gasped. "You don't mean Alias of Westgate!"

"The very same, good ranger," Elminster replied. "You have met the lady, then?"

"Well, not exactly," Orcsbane admitted. "I've seen her down at The Old Skull tavern, though, and listened to her sing. She has a voice like a bird—sings some of the most moving songs I've ever heard."

"She sings!" Morala shouted angrily. "She sings *his* songs, doesn't she, Elminster? And you've done nothing about it!"

"What could I do, thy grace? She is a free woman who has committed no crime. The people of Shadowdale consider her a hero. The time is long past when the Harpers could intimidate ordinary folk into obedience, let alone demand it of heroes."

Elminster could tell Morala was struggling to control her rage. The priestess was breathing deeply, with her eyes closed and her jaw set. The sage had no desire to anger Morala, but he would not be reprimanded for behaving in a civilized fashion.

"Perhaps we should meet this woman," Kyre suggested calmly. "Will she speak with us if she is summoned forth?"

Elminster nodded. "She is eager to speak if there is a chance it will help Nameless."

"Ah-ha!" Morala cried. "She is his creature indeed."

"No, Morala," Elminster snapped back, fighting hard to keep his own anger in check. "She is her own creature. She is fond of Nameless, though, as any generous and good woman would be of a father who nurtured her as best he could."

Morala looked down at her hands, fearing that she had aroused the sage's wrath. As old as she was, Elminster was many years her senior, and he was the Harpers' most powerful ally and advisor. "We should hear her speak," she agreed softly.

Kyre signaled the page and ordered him, "Find Alias of Westgate and request that she come before this tribunal."

Heth stood up, bowed before the tribunal and hurried out of the courtroom to fetch the Nameless Bard's singer, Alias.

❦ 2 ❦

The Singer

The patrons of The Old Skull applauded enthusiastically as the singer finished her song. Even the innkeep, Jhaele Silvermane, paused a moment from her duties at the bar to show her appreciation. The singer bowed once to her audience and then to the songhorn player who had accompanied her.

The rustic common room was full of farmers who only half an hour ago had been grumbling and cursing the rain that kept them from the season's haying. Now, instead of nursing their first drink for two hours and worrying about how they were going to feed their livestock all winter on moldy hay, the farmers were ordering their second pint and cheering for the singer to give them another song.

The singer, the sell-sword Alias of Westgate, also known as Alias of the Azure Bonds, smiled gratefully. She sang to keep herself occupied, since the Harpers would not let her visit her father, the Nameless Bard, and she sang to defy the Harpers, who had tried to wipe out the bard's music. Mostly, though, she sang because she knew the bard would want her to, no matter what happened to him. Secretly, though, she was struggling to think of a graceful way to decline singing any further this day.

"Please, Alias," the songhorn player whispered to the singer. "They need something to keep their minds off this weather."

"Han, I . . . I think I'm losing my voice," Alias whispered back.

"Your voice sounds just fine," Han insisted.

"One more at least," a deep voice rumbled from a table beside the musicians' platform, "or I'll have to have the watch haul you off for denying the happiness of the good people of Shadowdale."

Alias laughed good-naturedly at the threat. The speaker was Mourngrym Amcathra, lord of Shadowdale, and the swordswoman counted him among her friends. She tossed her red hair behind her shoulders and flapped the bottom of her green woolen tunic in an effort to cool off. "Then I suppose I'd have to sing for the watch, wouldn't I?" Alias asked Mourngrym.

"That's right," Mourngrym replied with a twinkle in his eye. "And then," he added, "I'd have to sentence you to sing lullabies to my son for a year." His lordship bounced the aforementioned baby on his knee and asked him, "You'd like that, wouldn't you, Scotty?"

Although he was far too young to understand the question, Mourngrym's heir responded to his father's enthusiastic tone of voice by laughing and clapping his hands.

"A fate worse than death," Alias said with mock terror.

The farmers laughed and Scotty shrieked happily. Still Alias hesitated. She'd been singing at the Old Skull for three days in a row, and the audiences loved every song she sang. Four times since spring, however, she'd lost control of her voice and had begun singing strange words and changing Nameless's melodies. She was sure it was only a matter of time before it happened again. Here in Shadowdale, though, she risked more than shocking her listeners. If Nameless heard about it, he would be greatly displeased with her.

From the back of the room, she caught Dragonbait's eye. The saurial paladin motioned encouragingly with his hands. Alias sighed inwardly. Nothing's going to go wrong, she told herself. Stop being such a ninny and face the music.

Trying to focus her thoughts on her audience, Alias chose a farming song, the lyrics of which were an old folk rhyme that Nameless had set to music. Han knew the rhyme, but he was unfamiliar with the tune, so he stood silently beside Alias, listening carefully, hoping he could pick up the melody with his horn by the second or third verse. Alias sang out clear and strong:

> *"We till the soil, we spread the grain,*
> *We shoo the birds, we pray for rain.*
> *The rain comes down, the shoots spring out,*
> *But so do weeds, and then comes drought.*
> *We haul the water till our backs are sore;*
> *The weeds grow richer, but the crop stays poor.*
> *Then one day Chauntea ends our strife,*
> *And our grain takes root in the river of life.*

"The river of life, the river of life:
Every woman's man, every good man's wife.
We should all drink deep from the river of life.

"The river of life, the river of life:
Every woman's man, every good man's wife.
We should all drink deep from the river of life."

Everyone joined in singing the repeat of the chorus. Han played softly, not wanting to spoil anything should he guess a note wrong, as Alias began the second verse:

"We scythe the grains, we pluck the fruits,
We gather the nuts and dig up the roots.
The days grow cool, the birds fly away,
The beasts grow fur, the pastures turn gray.
We eat our fill and store what's left,
Then the snow comes down and the fields rest.
The darkness grows inside our souls,
And our labor's turned to evil goals."

Han fumbled with his fingering. The songhorn player had never heard the last two lines before. The version he knew told of preparation for midwinter revels. But something disturbed Han even more than the unfamiliar words Alias sang. The young singer had suddenly switched to a new, eerie-sounding key. Then, without a repeat of the chorus, the swordswoman launched into a third verse with still more lyrics Han did not recognize.

"We hack the vines, we cut the trees,
We trample the roots and burn the seeds.
When the rain comes down, the soil washes away,
Leaving barren rock and heavy clay.
We wear chains of green till our bodies rot;
The corpses still move, their minds without thought.
Soon the great dark will devour the Realms;
Death is the power that overwhelms."

At the first four lines, the farmers began scowling and muttering among themselves. This certainly wasn't farming as they practiced it. It might be the way of those in lands under the sway of evil, like those to the north, controlled by the Zhentarim, but here in the dales they tried their best to live in harmony with the land. At the last four lines, the farmers shifted nervously in their chairs and peered into their ale, confused by the direction the song had taken.

Although Alias had failed to note that Han had ceased accompanying her, she recognized now that she no longer held her audience's attention. She knew all too well what was wrong, and her voice failed. Oh, gods, she thought, shaking with fear. I've twisted this song the same way I twisted the others.

She felt Han's hand on her shoulder. "Alias, are you feeling well?" the songhorn player asked quietly.

"I'm sorry," she whispered. "I'm so tired. I've forgotten the words," she lied. "I think I'd better go sit down."

Han squeezed her shoulder reassuringly and patted her on the back as she walked away. Anxious to spare her from the stares that followed her, Han raised his horn back to his lips and began playing a reel to distract the audience.

Equally protective of the singer's feelings and eager to break up the unpleasant atmosphere the song had created in the common room, Jhaele nudged her son Durgo and whispered for him to get up and dance with his sister Nelil. Durgo, a middle-aged farmer with little sense of rhythm, had as much love of dancing as he had of crows and weevils, but he was a dutiful son. He grabbed Nelil's hand and tugged her to her feet. The other farmers shook off their uneasiness and began clapping to the beat. A few joined Durgo and Nelil in the energetic dance.

As Alias threaded her way through the tables to the back of the common room, she kept her eyes on the floor, too embarrassed to look at anyone. She wanted to rush up the stairs to her room and lock herself inside, but before she could get past the table where Dragonbait sat, the saurial paladin grabbed her wrist. He pulled her toward him, slowly but firmly. Alias yielded to his strength and sat down heavily beside him.

"That's the fifth time this has happened," she growled through her clenched teeth, made angry by her own fear. "I'm not singing again. You shouldn't have encouraged me."

Ordinarily the pair communicated with a sign language that Alias had taught Dragonbait. It was a variant of the thieves' hand cant, which the swordswoman had learned magically from the assassins who had helped create her. The visual language was capable of conveying quite complex ideas, but it still was inadequate when the paladin needed to comfort the swordswoman. Dragonbait reached out and stroked the inside of Alias's sword arm with his scaly fingers. It was far easier to remind her how much he cared for her by touching the magical blue brand on her forearm—the brand which had bound his life to hers.

Alias felt her brand tingle at the paladin's touch, and her irritation subsided somewhat. His touch there always filled her with the paladin's own inner calm. Alias laid her fingertips on the front of Dragonbait's tunic, where a similar brand scarred his chest scales beneath it. Alias knew that, despite the layer of fabric, he would experience the same tingling sensation she felt. Considering the misery she still felt, though, she couldn't help but worry that her touch would only disquiet him.

"What's wrong with me, Dragonbait?" she whispered, struggling to keep from crying. "Why can't I sing a simple song without ruining it?"

The saurial paladin shook his head. He didn't know.

Alias sniffed and caught a whiff of the odors the saurial emitted in response. The sell-sword smiled ruefully. She knew the scent of honeysuckle was Dragonbait's expression of tender concern. The honeysuckle scent, however, was intermingled with the tang of baked ham, an odor that indicated the saurial was worried. Like a human's body language, the saurial's odors often gave away more of his true feelings than he would have chosen to reveal.

Someone nearby coughed politely, and the sell-sword and her companion looked up. Lord Mourngrym stood before their table with his son squirming under one arm. His lordship looked down at Alias quizzically and asked, "Is something wrong, Alias?"

"Nothing important, your lordship," Alias said hastily. "I'm sorry I spoiled the song. I've just got a lot on my mind, I guess."

Mourngrym would not be put off so easily, however. Alias looked pale and frightened. With Nameless in jail and no one to care for her but the peculiar lizard-man, his lordship felt protective of the sell-sword. He sat down beside her, balancing Scotty on the table before him. "I'm the one who insisted you sing," Mourngrym reminded her. "I'm the one who should apologize. Now, show that you forgive me and tell me what's wrong," he said, patting her hand.

"I don't know," Alias said, trying to hide her fear with a shrug of her shoulders. "Sometime this spring I just started to sing strangely. I can sing a few songs just fine, and then one song suddenly turns into something about death and decay and darkness. I don't even know I'm doing it until . . . until people start to stare at me as if I'm a monster. I thought I might be cursed or possessed, but three different priests told me there was nothing wrong with me—except that I was arrogant, headstrong, and disrespectful."

Mourngrym smiled. "Well, they got that part right," he teased.

Scotty reached out and grabbed a lock of Alias's shiny red hair. The swordswoman picked the child up off the table and helped him stand on her thighs. Scotty bounced up and down, chortling with delight.

"I don't know what I'm going to do," Alias said quietly. "What will Nameless think?"

"Alias, it wasn't a bad song," Mourngrym argued. "Just, um . . . different."

Alias lowered her eyes guiltily. "I was upset that the Harpers wouldn't let me see Nameless, but to tell the truth, I was a little relieved, too. I'm afraid the next time he asks me to sing for him, I'll change the song, and he'll be upset. He doesn't like the least little change in his songs."

"Alias," Mourngrym replied, "you can't spend the rest of your life doing everything exactly the way Nameless wants you to. You have to live your own life."

"I know that," Alias said unhappily, "but I don't want to disappoint him by ruining his songs. If I was improving them, I could argue with him about it, but I'm only making the songs ugly and grotesque."

Despite her claim to the contrary, his lordship didn't believe Alias understood his advice. The bard's enchantment of her went deeper than any magic. She loved Nameless, and she sang to please him. Trying to reassure her, Mourngrym said, "Sometimes we need frightening songs, whether we like them or not. They remind us what we stand for or against and give us the incentive to take action."

"But I don't know even know what these new songs are about, even though they're coming out of my own head," Alias objected. "How am I supposed to take action? Against what?"

Mourngrym had no answer. These were questions for sharper minds than his own. "Have you discussed any of this with Elminster?" he asked.

Alias shook her head. "I don't want to bother him until he's finished helping Nameless."

Mourngrym shook his head. Alias was losing control of her voice, something that obviously frightened her, but she was more concerned about Nameless's plight. His lordship wanted to tell Alias to forget Nameless for once, but he knew the sell-sword would not heed his words.

Dragonbait chirped and pointed toward the doorway. Alias turned to see a group of travelers entering the inn. There were a dozen or more of them, pulling off their rain-drenched cloaks and shouting requests for drinks and food and rooms to the inn's staff. From their clothing, Alias guessed they were merchants and caravan guards from Cormyr. One man, however, had to be from much farther south. His skin was the dusky hue of a southerner. He wore silken red-and-white-striped robes, and a golden cord banded his curly brown hair. He stood taller than the other merchants and many of the guards.

"It can't be," Alias muttered. She craned her neck impatiently until the man turned around. In the manner of a Turmishman, he sported a square beard, and to indicate he was married, he wore a blue sapphire in his earlobe. The three blue dots on his forehead indicated he was a scholar of reading, magic, and religion. But these things hardly registered on Alias now. It was the familiarity of the man's face that excited her. "It's him!" she gasped. "Dragonbait, it's Akabar! He's come back to us!"

Alias rose to her feet, thrusting Scotty back at his surprised father, and ran to the door of the inn, crying out the Turmishman's name.

A few heads swiveled to see who the swordswoman was calling to, but most of the inn's occupants kept their attention on Han's songhorn music and the dancers on the floor.

Akabar Bel Akash held his arms out to greet the sell-sword in a traditional handclasp, but Alias threw herself into his arms and embraced him like a long-lost brother. From where he sat, Mourngrym could tell from the look of surprise on the Turmishman's face that Akabar hadn't expected quite so warm a reception.

Mourngrym exchanged glances with Dragonbait. The saurial shrugged and turned back to watch the newcomers. His scaly brow knit with concern when he spied a woman standing behind Akabar.

Tugging on the southerner's arm, Alias led Akabar back to her table. She didn't seem to notice the heavily veiled woman who followed several paces behind them. Mourngrym did, however, and he rose to his feet with Scotty seated in the crook of his arm.

"Mourngrym, you remember Akabar bel Akash?" Alias asked. "He was a member of my party when I first visited Shadowdale."

"The 'mage of no small water,' " Mourngrym said, recalling the phrase Akabar had often used.

Akabar bowed low. "I'm honored you remember me, your lordship," the Turmishman said.

Mourngrym grinned. In his experience, it was seldom that a mage lived long enough to prove his boasts. Alias had told his lordship the story of how the Turmishman had defeated the evil god Moander. Akabar was indeed a 'mage of the first water,' as his people would say. "And who is the lady?" Mourngrym asked, finally drawing Alias's attention to the woman standing behind Akabar.

Akabar stepped to one side. "Your lordship, Alias, Dragonbait," Akabar said, "may I present, Zhara, Priestess of Tymora."

Zhara took a step forward. She was as tall as Alias, but her green eyes and slender brown hands were the only parts of her body not covered by the blue robes of her calling or the long blue and white veil draped across her face. "I am honored to meet you," Zhara said softly. She curtsied low, but she did not remove her veil.

Mourngrym bowed and Dragonbait nodded, but Alias eyed the priestess with annoyance. She didn't like clerics or priests. Dragonbait was always trying to convince her that she felt this way because Cassana and the swordswoman's other evil makers had enchanted her, but Alias rejected that idea. She didn't like members of the clergy because, as far as she was concerned, they were a nearly useless bunch of fools—even those who served Tymora, Lady Luck, the goddess of adventurers. Why in the world is Akabar traveling with a priestess? she wondered.

As if he read her mind, Akabar explained, "Zhara is my third wife."

Anger and disappointment stabbed at the pleasure Alias had felt at seeing Akabar again. A moment ago, she had imagined their reunion would be just like old times, but the presence of one of his wives put a damper on that hope. With the exception of Dragonbait, Akabar was the swordswoman's oldest friend in the world. He had helped Alias on her quest to discover her origins, but if Alias had had her way, she'd have never met this woman.

To avoid just such a meeting, Alias had once claimed that she was unable to stand the heat of the south and declined an invitation to accompany Akabar to his home in Turmish. The swordswoman hadn't wanted to face the scrutiny of his wives. Though she'd never been south, Alias had heard how insufferably proud southern women were of the way they lived: their modest dress, their subservient soft speech, their efficient households and businesses, their innumerable children. They were all greengrocers, Alias's term for boring nonadventurers, and Alias couldn't imagine them welcoming a wandering sellsword with no real family. Even more unbearable than the thought of their disapproval had been the thought of sharing Akabar's company and attention with women he was closer to than he was to her.

"I was under the impression that southern women didn't travel away from home," the sell-sword said coolly as she sat down at the table and motioned for Akabar to take the seat beside her.

"My sister-wives, Akash and Kasim, have charged me to protect our husband from the barbarians of the north," Zhara replied matter-of-factly, slipping herself into the chair that Alias had intended for Akabar. Akabar seated himself between Zhara and Dragonbait.

Uneasy because of the tension he sensed, Lord Mourngrym turned toward the door of the inn. "If you'll excuse me," his lordship said, "I think I'd better head back home before the rain starts falling harder. I'll leave you to rehash old times." He bowed once again to Akabar's wife, then strode off, with Scotty balanced on his shoulder.

Akabar sighed inwardly as he glanced from Alias to Zhara. He hadn't expected Alias to get along with Zhara. Although the sell-sword was too proud to admit it, he believed she was jealous of his wives. He hadn't expected Zhara to show jealousy, though, but then Alias was special to him, and Zhara knew that. At least the women's coolness toward one another would give him time to explain about Zhara to Alias.

Akabar glanced at Dragonbait, who was watching Zhara curiously. The saurial paladin gave Akabar an inquiring look. He can smell what Zhara is, the Turmishman thought. Will he have the wisdom to keep it to himself? he wondered.

Dragonbait shrugged and looked down at his teacup. Akabar, he realized, thought Alias loved him and would become enraged with jealousy if she knew all that Zhara was. The paladin knew Alias far better than the merchant-mage, and he knew that Alias did indeed love Akabar, but not the way Akabar thought she did.

Despite Alias's adult body and brilliant mind, Dragonbait had come to understand that her emotions were no more mature than a child's. The paladin suspected that the Nameless Bard, who denied his own emotions as a matter of pride, had been unable to give Alias skill controlling her feelings when something upset her. Like a child, Alias grew jealous easily, and it wasn't easy for her to accept that she couldn't always be the center of attention. Akabar was right to worry about her reaction when she learned of Zhara's true nature. What the merchant-mage did not realize, however, was that Alias wouldn't react as a woman but as a child.

Still, it would be bad to put off explaining about Zhara, the paladin thought. He would give Akabar a day to work up to it, but no more.

From the unpleasant, but fortunately weak, stench of brimstone that wafted from Dragonbait, Alias could tell there was something about Akabar's wife that interested the saurial. Nevertheless, Alias ignored Zhara and focused all her attention on Akabar. "So what brings you this far north so late in the year?" she asked the Turmishman.

Instead of answering Alias's question, Akabar asked one of

his own. "Have you been well since I saw you in Westgate last year?"

Alias's brow knit in puzzlement. "Of course. Why shouldn't I be? Akabar, what's wrong? Why are you here?"

Akabar drew a deep breath. "I came to Shadowdale to seek Elminster's advice. I also hoped to find you here, in order to warn you."

"Warn me?" Alias asked, more confused than alarmed. "What about?"

"The return of the Darkbringer," Akabar said.

"The Darkbringer! You mean Moander?" Alias asked.

Akabar nodded.

"Akabar," Alias reminded the mage, "after you destroyed Moander's body, most of its worshipers killed themselves. Cassana had the Fire Knives assassinate those who didn't, so she wouldn't have to share me with them. Dragonbait and I spent the past two summers checking out all the Darkbringer's temples. They've all been abandoned. Without worshipers in the Realms, it could be centuries before Moander can regain enough energy to make a new body and return here from the Abyss."

"I have been troubled by nightmares of late," Akabar explained. "Zhara tells me they are warnings from the gods of light."

Alias sighed in exasperation. "Akabar, after all Moander put you through, of course you're going to have nightmares about it for a while. It's only natural. The gods don't have anything to do with it."

"The dreams did not begin until this past spring, nearly a year after Moander's death," Akabar countered.

Alias shrugged. "Spring is when you destroyed Moander. Maybe the weather just reminded you of him," she suggested.

"Spring weather in Turmish is nothing like spring weather in the north or even in Westgate, where Moander died," Akabar persisted.

Dragonbait rapped on the table for attention. Alias watched the saurial's paws flutter about the tabletop, then move to his lips. Finally he pointed at her and Akabar.

Alias shook her head. "They're not related at all," she told the paladin.

"What's he trying to say?" Akabar asked curiously.

"Nothing important," Alias said.

Dragonbait shoved his elbow into Alias's side. The sell-sword glared at her lizard companion, and Dragonbait glared right back at her. The contest of wills lasted only a few moments, but it astonished Akabar. He'd never seen Dragonbait challenge Alias before. When the mage had traveled with the pair, Dragonbait had been as submissive to Alias as a Turmishwoman was to her husband in public. Obviously the relationship between the saurial and Alias had changed in the past year. Alias looked away from Dragonbait, muttering, "All right. Think what you want, but you're wrong."

"What is it?" Akabar demanded.

"Dragonbait thinks I should tell you that it was last spring when I started singing strangely."

"Singing strangely? I don't understand," Akabar said, his eyebrows arching.

"Somehow the melody and the lyrics of songs I was singing came out twisted. And I didn't even realize I was doing it," Alias explained, obviously disturbed.

"Do you have dreams about Moander?" Akabar asked.

"I wouldn't know," Alias replied. "I never remember my dreams when I wake up. Dreams are for sleeping."

"You remembered the dream you had about Nameless in Shadow Gap," Akabar reminded her.

"That was different. That was a magical dream caused by the witch Cassana, sent in order to distract me from the ambush she was laying."

Akabar stroked his beard thoughtfully, then suggested, "Since you do not remember your dreams, it could be that the gods are trying to warn you through your songs."

"Akabar, why should the gods go to all the trouble to send you dreams and ruin my songs when they could just send a letter?" Alias asked skeptically.

"If you do not believe Zhara and you do not believe me," Akabar said, "you certainly would not believe a letter, Alias. The gods know the way to your heart is through your music."

Alias sighed. She'd known, of course, that Akabar was a scholar of religion, but this sudden devout belief that the gods were speaking to him and her made her uneasy. It was this new wife's influence, she was sure. "Well, if the gods are causing me to sing this way," Alias said, "they certainly have lousy taste in music. And they could work on making their lyrics a little less obscure, too."

Zhara, who had been silent for a long time, spoke out suddenly, with anger and passion. "You cannot expect the songs of the gods to be of the same simple sort you northern barbarians delight in," she said.

Alias glared at the priestess. "My songs are the best in the Realms," she growled.

"They are nothing compared to the words spoken by the gods," Zhara replied heatedly. "Our prayers to them are the most suitable music we can make."

Realizing that it was futile to argue with a religious zealot, Alias turned her attention back to Akabar. "I don't suppose the gods have given you any details about what you're supposed to do about this return of Moander," she said.

"Yes, they have, as a matter of fact," Akabar replied, and his face looked suddenly haggard. "I must find Moander's body in the Realms and destroy it again. Then I must find its body in the Abyss and destroy it there. Only then will Moander be destroyed forever," he explained.

Alias looked at her friend with astonishment and fear. He was absolutely serious. He meant to fight the god again. If Dragonbait hadn't recruited the help of an ancient red dragon, who had died battling Moander, she and Akabar would still be under the god's domination now, unable to fight the abomination's awful power to control their minds. Now Akabar not only wanted to fight Moander in the Realms, but also in the Abyss, where it would be surrounded by numbers of powerful minions. The swordswoman was sure the mage couldn't have come up with such a dangerous idea on his own. She glared across the table at Akabar's new wife, and as she so often did, she channeled her fear into anger.

"This is all your doing, isn't it?" Alias snarled at Zhara. "You lousy priests are always trying to convince some nice, noble soul to go out and get killed trying to destroy some great evil that no one in their right mind would want to run into. Not even the mighty elven kingdom of Myth Drannor, in the height of its powers, could destroy Moander. You softened Akabar up with sweet talk and then start blowing his nightmares out of proportion. I'll bet you even used your priestly magic to set him on this stupid quest, didn't you?"

Alias looked back at the Turmishman. "Don't be a fool, Akabar," she pleaded. "You've done more than your share. You should never have married this priestess. She doesn't care about you. She's only interested in what you can do for the glory of her goddess."

Akabar's jaw trembled and his face went livid. Instinctively Alias backed her chair away from him. Zhara laid one of her slender hands on her husband's arm and said something in Turmish that Alias didn't understand. Akabar closed his eyes and calmed his temper with several long, slow breaths.

Beneath the table, Dragonbait's tail slapped warningly at Alias's knee. The swordswoman shot an angry glance at the paladin. Dragonbait was rubbing his chin. He was asking her to apologize to Zhara, but Alias remained adamant. She didn't care how Akabar felt about Zhara. Zhara was obviously using him.

A youth dressed in a page's uniform, his hair dripping wet from the rain falling outside the inn, interrupted the uneasy silence that had settled over the table. "Excuse me, lady," the boy said timidly.

Alias looked up. She knew the boy. His name was Heth, and he was one of Lord Mourngrym's pages. She smiled to put the boy at ease. "Yes? What is it, Heth?"

"Alias of Westgate, the tribunal of Harpers requests that you come come before them," Heth said formally.

Alias started. For a short while, she'd forgotten her anxiety about Nameless. Now it returned with double force. Her face went pale and her lips trembled. Nameless's fate was in her hands. If she said or did the wrong thing, they would exile him again, send him away from the Realms, away from her.

"What tribunal?" Akabar asked.

"The Harper tribunal that is rehearing Nameless's case," Alias said, rising to her feet. "I asked to speak to them on his behalf."

Despite his offended pride and the insult she had just delivered to his wife, Akabar couldn't help but feel sympathy for the warrior woman. Alias had always had difficulty trusting other people and growing intimate with them, but she had accepted Nameless as her father. Akabar didn't like to think of the grief she would suffer should the Harpers be so merciless as to recondemn the bard.

"I would have thought the Harpers had taken care of that last year," Akabar said. "What's taken them so long?"

"It took Elminster all last year to convince them that they should rehear the case," Alias explained. "Now I have to go."

Akabar stood up in front of the sell-sword. "I'll go with you," he said. "I, too, will speak on his behalf, for he saved my life."

The page looked confused for a moment, uncertain how to respond to this stranger.

"Heth," Alias explained to the page, "this is my friend, Akabar bel Akash. He knows all about Nameless. May he come with me?"

"He is welcome to accompany you, lady," Heth replied, "but I do not know if the tribunal will hear him."

"Then I shall speak very loudly," Akabar said.

Alias looked up at Akabar with a grateful smile. At least Zhara's influence was not so complete that the Turmishman could not spare time from his insane quest to help a friend.

Dragonbait chirped, and Alias turned her head to watch him sign. "Dragonbait says he'll look after Zhara for you," she explained to Akabar. Though I'm sure the shrew can handle herself, she thought, but she managed to resist saying so aloud. She wished the paladin would come along with her instead of remaining with Zhara, but she didn't want to argue with him in front of Akabar.

Akabar motioned for the page to go ahead. Alias went to speak to Jhaele for a moment, then grabbed her cloak from a hook and joined Akabar and Heth at the door. The swordswoman and the Turmishman followed the boy from the inn out into the drizzling rain. They walked in silence down the main road that led west toward the Tower of Ashaba. Over the tops of the trees, they could make out the tower's peculiar off-center spire, which gave it the nickname "the Twisted Tower."

Despite its notoriety, Shadowdale was a small town, but the Tower of Ashaba was a massive and impressive structure nonetheless. It served as a home to not only the Lord of Shadowdale and his family, but also to most of his court and household staff, not to mention numerous adventurers friendly to his lordship. Mourngrym had invited Alias to winter there, but Alias could only think of the tower as Nameless's prison, and she had declined. She wouldn't have accepted at any rate. As much as she liked Mourngrym, becoming his guest would have meant giving up some of her independence. She felt more comfortable paying Jhaele for a room at the inn.

As they passed Elminster's tower, Akabar glanced sidelong at Alias. She looked nervous. Having already swallowed his anger at her earlier behavior, the mage was determined to reestablish their friendship. He began with what northerners called "small talk."

"Have you heard anything of Mistress Olive Ruskettle since she took her leave of us in Westgate?" the Turmishman asked.

Alias looked at Akabar and grinned. Olive, at least, was something the two of them had always agreed upon. The halfling thief had attached herself without invitation to their adventuring party the previous year, only to make a tremendous nuisance of herself, betraying them to Alias's enemies and only at the last moment helping to rescue them from fates worse than death. Olive hadn't actually taken her leave of them at the end of their adventure. She'd left in the middle of the night with a good deal more than her share of the treasure they'd taken from the sorceress Cassana's dungeon. To the halfling's credit, she at least left them all the gold and silver coin, preferring the more portable gemstones and jewelry for herself.

"I believe she's in Cormyr," Alias said. "Travelers who have passed through there speak of a halfling bard who sings some of the best songs they've ever heard and who claims to have been the mastermind behind the destruction of the Fire Knives assassin guild, the Darkbringer, a red dragon, a lich, an evil sorceress, and a fiend from Tarterus. She was aided, naturally, by her faithful assistants, an anonymous southern mage, a little-known northern sell-sword, and a mysterious lizardman."

"That sounds like our Olive Ruskettle, all right," Akabar agreed.

"I almost wish she were here now," Alias said. "If anyone was able to talk her way around this Harper tribunal, it would be Olive."

Akabar chuckled, "Remember the saying, 'Be careful what you wish for.' " He sensed the nervousness in her voice, and made an effort to reassure her. "Alias, Elminster is speaking on Nameless's behalf. The Harpers will be influenced by the sage's wisdom. Even if they are not, the Harpers are good people. They couldn't be so cruel as to return Nameless to exile after what he has suffered. They may not forgive him, but they will realize that isolating him serves no further purpose. Don't worry."

"I can't help it," Alias replied in barely more than a whisper. "I know what you say is true, but I have this tremendous foreboding that something awful is going to happen to Nameless, that someone wishes him harm."

The mage shuddered inwardly at the woman's words. Alias had rejected so fiercely his quest to destroy Moander that Akabar had been reluctant to tell her any more about his dreams. She would learn soon enough, though, that he was not the only one chosen to battle the evil god. Nameless, too, was destined to be caught up in the final confrontation with the Darkbringer.

❦ 3 ❦

The Beast

While page Heth was fetching Alias, the Harper tribunal continued to discuss the matter of the Nameless Bard.

"Even if this Alias is the paragon you say, Elminster," Morala said to the sage, "her existence does not mitigate the bard's initial guilt. You would not speak on Nameless's behalf at his first trial," she reminded him. "What has changed between then and now?"

What indeed? Elminster wondered. "As ye know, thy grace, I was a good friend to Nameless, but when he proceeded with his experiment against my advice, I felt . . . betrayed. I was angry with him, so I did nothing to defend him. I now believe I was wrong to do nothing."

"It is a master bard's sworn duty to protect his apprentices," Morala continued. "Nameless was found guilty of recklessly endangering his apprentices, resulting in the death of one and injury to the other. What can you possibly say in his defense?" Morala asked.

"Nothing, thy grace," Elminster said.

"Nothing?" Breck asked with surprise.

Kyre tilted her head in confusion, but Morala's eyes narrowed suspiciously. The sage had some trick up his sleeve; she was sure of it.

"Nothing, good ranger," Elminster said. "But then," he added, "there is also nothing I can say in defense of the punishment meted out by the Harper tribunal that sentenced the bard." Elminster's tone deepened with anger and contempt. "How long did they sentence Nameless to exile?" The sage answered his own question. "Forever. Two hundred years he has spent alone. Like barbarians who slice off the hands of a thief, the Harpers have given him no opportunity to atone for his crime. And what was done with the best part of the man, the beautiful music he composed despite his vanity and thoughtlessness, music which might have proven there was some good in him? The Harpers tried to wipe it out, just as barbarians wipe out the innocent children of their enemies."

Kyre raised her eyebrows at the sage's analogies, and Breck blushed with shame, but Morala rose angrily to her feet.

"Nameless knows nothing of atonement!" Morala insisted. "He was adept at charming others into spending their lives on his schemes. Not even the deaths of his apprentices stopped him from attempting to build a second singing simulacrum. If not for the intervention of others, who knows what evils Cassana and her consortium would have set this Alias to accomplish? We exiled Nameless alone so he could never again harm another with his recklessness. As for his music, he was unwilling to have his songs passed from one generation of bards to the next, so we honored his wish."

"It is not justice to imprison someone for what he might do, Morala," Elminster replied. "Tomorrow you or I might cause some great harm. Should we then go into exile this very day? And as for his music, if the Harpers had only imprisoned Nameless for a few years but allowed his songs to be passed on in the natural way, Nameless might have learned to accept the way his music would evolve and change. Instead, the Harpers exascerbated the bard's fears."

"We could not afford your fine sense of justice, Elminster," Morala said. "We had to protect others from Nameless. A few years would not have changed his attitude. I doubt that two hundred years has done so. Even now that he has his singer, Alias, is he any less likely to use people? Can you offer any proof that Nameless himself has changed?"

Elminster considered the question carefully, searching his memory for any speech or action by Nameless that would demonstrate the bard's redemption. "Yes," he said finally.

The Harpers waited impatiently for the sage to continue. Elminster rose to his feet and circled around the table till he stood directly before the tribunal. "Three things . . ." he began. Then suddenly his face went pale. He gasped and clutched at his chest.

"Elminster?" Morala cried, rising to her feet.

"Are you all right, sir?" Breck asked, leaping from his seat to come to the aid of the sage. Some invisible force, though, repelled the young ranger. He bounced backward onto the dais at

Kyre's feet.

In the span of three breaths, Elminster's body seemed to turn to clear crystal. Then, in a flash of bright light, the sage was gone. In his place stood a huge, hideous beast.

The creature stood as tall as a hill giant, towering over the three Harpers. The long red robe and fur cape it wore couldn't hide the inhumanness of its form. It was covered with sickly green scales, and its eyes glittered red in the torchlight. Two sharp ivory horns sprouted from its head, and a third, even longer, horn rose from the tip of its long snout. Around the back of its head grew a bony frill, edged with spikes and decorated with arcane magical symbols. A muscular tail curled up from beneath the hem of its robe and swished back and forth like an angry snake.

In one clawed appendage, the beast clenched an iron staff tipped with a yellow orb, and in the other claw it held out a small blood-red object vaguely resembling a large chess rook. The red object began to glow, and the Harpers could feel heat emanating from it.

Kyre shouted, "Kill it!" Without a second's hesitation, she drew a dagger from her boot and hurled it. The dagger struck the red object in the beast's hand, knocking it to the stone floor, where it landed with a soft plop.

The beast looked up at Kyre and growled menacingly.

"Kill the monster, Breck!" Kyre cried. "Kill it before it's too late!"

The ranger lost no time in picking himself up from Kyre's feet, drawing his long sword, and charging the beast.

The creature was just as quick, holding out its staff with both clawed appendages to block Breck's blow. Sparks flew where the ranger's steel sword ground along the length of the iron staff. The beast's heavy tail lashed forward, struck Breck's left shoulder, and knocked him backward. Breck stumbled back into the dais, grunting from the pain that shot down his arm and back.

Meanwhile, Morala rose to her feet, drew a vial of holy water from the sleeve of her robe, and began singing a series of increasingly higher-pitched musical scales, praying to Milil, the god of bards, for his aid. Kyre stepped from the dais, circling cautiously around the beast until she stood at the periphery of its vision. Then she began a magical chant of her own, one far more harsh and guttural than that of the priestess.

Breck recovered enough to close in on his opponent again, searching for an opening in the beast's defenses. The creature grabbed Breck's injured arm and lifted the ranger several feet off the floor. Breck heard a pop as his arm dislocated from its shoulder joint, and he howled in agony. In a fury, he brought his sword down on the beast's head, but the blade got caught on the bony frill protruding from its skull.

Crimson blood oozed from the skin covering the beast's frill, and the creature roared. It hurled Breck through the air, straight into Morala, knocking her off balance.

The ranger and the priestess tumbled from the dais. Breck's head hit the stone floor with a sickening thud. Morala was able to soften her own landing with her hands, but her vial of holy water smashed on the floor, and her concentration shattered with it. Her spell, which would have sent the beast back to whatever foul plane it had come from, was ruined. "You may just have destroyed our only hope, ranger," the priestess snapped.

When Breck failed to reply, the priestess turned to face him. The ranger lay still on the floor. Morala knelt to examine him. He was still breathing, but the impact to his head had knocked him unconscious.

Indifferent to the fate of her fellow Harpers, Kyre completed her own spell before the beast could turn its full attention to her. A fan of flames shot out from the half-elf's fingers. The assault caught the beast in its midsection, and immediately its robes burst into flames. The creature roared, dropped to the ground, and rolled to extinguish the flames.

Kyre drew her own sword and approached the beast until she stood over its prone form. She raised her blade up to strike, but she, too, neglected to watch out for the beast's tail. The serpentine appendage lashed out suddenly and slapped her legs out from under her. As she fell to her hands and knees, she lost her grip on her sword. Her weapon slid across the stone floor, but quickly she rolled toward it and grabbed it.

The beast picked itself off the floor, leaning heavily on its staff, and lumbered from the courtroom and down the hallway.

Kyre stood up and turned to Morala. "Alert the guard!" the half-elf ordered. "I'm going after the monster!"

"Breck's injuries are serious!" Morala called to her. "Alert the guard while I tend to him." Morala looked up when Kyre did not reply. The half-elf was already chasing after the beast. "Kyre! Come back here!" the priestess shouted after her, but the half-elf did not return.

Morala set her jaw angrily. "Foolish girl," she muttered. As the priestess of Milil laid her hands on the ranger's pale face and began humming a healing spell, she noted a peculiar mixture of odors wafting through the room. The smell of burning cloth, she realized, was the result of Kyre's burning hands spell. But where, Morala wondered, did the smell of fresh-mown hay and baking bread come from?

* * * * *

Olive stood at the door to Finder's cell, fidgeting nervously. "I know what I heard!" she insisted. "Something roared out there."

"Olive, this is the Tower of Ashaba," Finder reminded the halfling. "The home of Mourngrym, Lord of Shadowdale. The guards aren't going to allow any wild beasts to roam the halls."

"How do you know? After all, they let me roam the halls," Olive argued.

Finder grinned at the halfling's indirect comparison of herself to a wild beast. "Come away from the door, Olive," he said patiently. "We don't want the guards to see you in here."

"I'm just going to take a peek," Olive insisted, opening the door a few inches more. She tried to slip out of the cell, but an invisible barrier across the threshold blocked her escape. "It's blocked!" Olive hissed angrily. "It's a one-way door. Why didn't you tell me I was walking into a trap?"

Finder raised his eyebrows in surprise. "I didn't know, Olive. Really." He began to laugh.

"What's so damned funny?" Olive demanded.

"The irony of it all," Finder explained. "I thought Elminster trusted me, but he knew me well enough to take extra precautions. He must have made the door one-way to catch anyone who might try to help me escape from the cell."

"I still fail to see any humor in it," Olive said coldly.

"Olive, Olive, Olive. I told you. The finder's stone can get past any barrier Elminster may have cast to try to prevent me from leaving this room. In his wildest dreams, the sage couldn't have imagined you'd find the stone and bring it to me."

"You could put my mind to rest by using the stone to get us out right now," Olive said.

Finder shook his head from side to side. "We'll leave after the Harpers have made their decision. Not a measure sooner or later," he said. He laid the finder's stone down on the table and picked up his chordal horn.

Olive leaned back against the wall beside the prison cell door and slumped to the floor. Finder began playing a soldier's marching melody.

Olive sniffed the air. Although exit from the prison cell was magically blocked, the smell of fresh-baked bread wafted into the cell. The halfling's stomach rumbled in response. "I should have eaten a bigger breakfast," she muttered.

Something in the hallway clomped toward the door. "Would the guards be bringing you something to eat about now?" Olive whispered.

Finder lowered his horn from his mouth. "What are you talking a—" The bard halted in midword as the door of the prison cell flew open. A huge green lizard in charred robes bent low and squeezed through the doorway. The creature was dripping blood from a shallow wound on its head, and the scales on its hands were black and blistered.

Olive stood cautiously, trying not to attract the beast's attention, while Finder grabbed the finder's stone from the table and backed away from the door.

"Don't come a step farther!" the bard ordered the beast.

The smell of baking bread was overwhelming. Olive gasped. A flicker of memory burst into enlightenment.

Alerted to the halfling's presence by Olive's gasp, the lizard turned to face her. It pointed a clawed finger at her.

"Don't touch her!" Finder barked sharply. "Back away from it slowly, Olive," he whispered to the halfling.

"It's all right," Olive said, showing more courage than Finder would have ever credited her with possessing. "At least, I *think* it's all right," the halfling added softly. She reached out slowly with one hand and touched the beast's robes. "Are you a friend of Dragonbait's?" she asked tentatively.

The beast looked down at the halfling as if it were concentrating on trying to understand her, but it made no reply.

Olive sighed. "Of course. Dragonbait could only understand us because of his link to Alias." The halfling turned to Finder. "I don't suppose you speak any Saurial, do you, Finder?" she asked.

Finder eyed the creature suspiciously. "What makes you think this monster's a saurial? He doesn't look anything like Dragonbait."

The halfling raised her eyes to the heavens and muttered, "Humans!" She looked back at Finder with disappointment. "I don't look anything like you, either," she pointed out. "And you don't look anything like Alias, yet we're all from the Realms. What makes you think all saurials have to look like Dragonbait?"

Finder conceded Olive's point with a slight nod. "I grant you that it could be a saurial. What makes you think it is?"

"Only two things smell as good as fresh-baked bread," Olive explained. "Fresh baked bread and angry saurials."

"Because that's the smell they use to communicate their anger," Finder said, recalling now all that Alias had told him about Dragonbait's scents.

"He doesn't smell quite so much like bread anymore. I hope that means he's calming down," Olive said.

"Yes, but what got him angry in the first place?" Finder asked. "And what's he doing here?"

"It looks like someone tried to roast him," Olive said, indicating the beast's charred clothing and hands. "I imagine that could make him pretty mad."

From the sleeve of his robe, the beast pulled out a silver medallion on a silk cord and handed it to Olive.

"For me?" Olive asked, her eyes glittering with delight.

The beast tapped the medallion with a claw.

Olive's eyes widened in astonishment at the design inscribed into the shining metal. "Finder, the picture on this medallion—it's Dragonbait!" Olive declared, holding out the medallion for the bard to see. "It looks just like him. And that's his sword—well, the sword he had last year before Alias lost it in the battle with Phalse. This guy knows Dragonbait," she added, poking a finger at the beast.

"Dragonbait's at The Old Skull with Alias," Finder said. "If this overgrown saurial is Dragonbait's friend, why isn't he down there raising a mug with Dragonbait? What's he doing here with us?"

"Maybe Alias and Dragonbait sent him here to rescue you," Olive suggested as she casually slipped the creature's medallion into a pocket of her tunic.

Finder looked exceptionally doubtful. "Wait a minute!" the bard said, slapping himself in the forehead. "We don't have to play guessing games. I have a tongues spell in the stone." Finder laid his chordal horn on the table and held the finder's stone out before him. He sang a scale in A-minor. Olive watched, fascinated, as the stone glowed in Finder's hands and surrounded him with yellow light.

The bard and the lizard stood staring at one another for what seemed to Olive like an eternity, though it was actually no more than a minute. She could detect a collage of scents rising from both the beast and Finder, but she grew bored not knowing what they were discussing. "Well?" the halfling prompted, reminding the other two of her presence.

"The creature's name is Grypht," Finder explained finally. "He's been looking for Dragonbait, but he was unable to locate him magically."

" 'Cause Dragonbait's with Alias, and they're both hidden by her shield of magical misdirection," Olive said.

"No doubt," Finder said, nodding. "Grypht knows you're a friend of Dragonbait's, so he's come looking for you, hoping you can tell him where to find his friend. Grypht teleported into the tower directly from his native dimension, but apparently someone here took him for an enemy and attacked him. He's put up a wall of ice in the corridor to keep anyone from following him."

"Then let's take him to Dragonbait before the ice melts," Olive suggested.

"No hurry," Finder said. "I can explain to the guards that he means no harm."

"Suppose they don't believe you?" Olive asked anxiously.

Finder waved impatiently for Olive to remain silent as he resumed his "conversation" with the saurial Grypht.

Olive huffed and slumped back against the wall, wishing fervently that this strange friend of Dragonbait's could talk Finder into leaving, and leaving soon. She was growing increasingly more nervous, though she couldn't say exactly why. Just to be on the safe side, she pushed the door closed and relocked it with her lockpick. If she was unable to escape, she was going to make it just as difficult as possible for anyone or anything else to get in.

* * * * *

Following the trail of blood drops from Grypht's wounds, Kyre nearly ran into the wall of ice that the creature had cast to block the corridor. She was especially susceptible to injury from cold—something that, unfortunately, Grypht knew only too well. She backed away from the ice carefully, shivering uncontrollably.

The half-elf didn't know precisely what had brought Grypht to the Tower of Ashaba, but it was doubtful he'd come here looking for her. He'd seemed as surprised to see her as she'd been to see him. She had to capture or destroy him before it was too late.

After a minute, Kyre had warmed sufficiently to think clearly and control her movements. She replaced her sword in its scabbard and pulled a magical scroll from one of the pockets of her tunic. She'd meant to use the scroll to break the Nameless Bard out of his cell, but dealing with Grypht had a higher priority. She unrolled the scroll and held it out to read from it. At that moment, Lord Mourngrym and three armed guards came running up behind her. All four fighters had their swords drawn.

"What's going on?" Mourngrym demanded. "I heard something roaring!"

"It's a denizen of the Nine Hells, your lordship," Kyre said. "Somehow it teleported Elminster from the courtroom and appeared in his place."

"That's impossible. No monster from the lower planes can enter this tower. Elminster has it warded against such evil," Mourngrym scoffed.

"Nothing is impossible, your lordship," Kyre replied. "I know this monster. It is called Grypht, and it is very powerful, a master of lies. It works for the Zhentarim. It attacked Breck; Morala is tending him in the courtroom. I chased the monster down this corridor. It has sealed itself behind this wall of ice."

"Caitlin, go make sure Morala and Breck are all right," Mourngrym ordered one of the guards.

The guard ran down the corridor toward the courtroom.

"Is there another passage leading to the corridor beyond?" Kyre asked.

"No," Mourngrym replied. "This hallway comes to a dead end. That's why Elminster put the Nameless Bard in the room at the far—" Suddenly his face went white. "Nameless! He's locked up in there . . . defenseless!" his lordship gasped. "We have to get through this wall of ice! Thurbal, fetch a mage. Sar, get torches and axes!" Mourngrym demanded.

As the two guards hurried to obey their lord, Kyre held out her magic scroll. "You must get through as quickly as you can, your lordship," the half-elf said, "but I cannot wait. I must use a magical door to get myself to the other side of the wall."

"You can't go alone," Mourngrym argued.

"I must," the half-elf insisted. "Someone must protect the Nameless Bard from that creature."

Lord Mourngrym nodded. There was no other choice. His lordship watched as Kyre chanted aloud the words on the magical scroll she held in her hands. She read quickly, but it took her a full minute to complete the spell. The instant she had finished reading it, the scroll burst into flames, and Kyre was swallowed up by a dimensional door and disappeared.

His lordship pulled out his dagger and began chipping away at the wall of ice, unwilling to waste time waiting for an axe while the brave half-elf faced Grypht alone.

* * * * *

At the front gate of the Tower of Ashaba, Alias and Akabar halted as Heth announced them. "Alias of Westgate and her friend Akabar bel Akash," the page informed the four guards who stood at the entrance. The announcement was a mere formality. The guards all knew Alias, and they weren't likely to challenge anyone who accompanied her. She had served in the tower guard herself the previous winter, and she was a trusted friend of Lord Mourngrym.

Just as Alias and Akabar stepped across the threshold, a balding, burly man-at-arms came racing across the entrance hall toward the gate. Alias recognized him as Captain Thurbal, the warden of the town of Shadowdale. Thurbal looked anxious and distracted, and in his haste, he ran into Heth.

"Captain," the boy squeaked, "what's wrong?"

"Heth! Good—you're just the person I need!" the captain exclaimed as he grabbed the page's shoulders. "Run to the inn and bring back any mages who may be staying there! Hurry!" He pushed the page toward the door, then turned to Alias. "Alias, it's good you're here. We may need you."

Heth looked annoyed and began to protest. "But, Captain, his lordship said that today I was to page only for the trib—"

"No buts, boy!" Thurbal shouted. "This is an emergency!"

"Excuse me," Akabar said. "I'm a mage. What's wrong? Can I be of some assistance?"

"Thank Tymora!" the captain exclaimed. "Come with me, please." He took the Turmishman's arm and hustled him across the front hall toward the tower's main staircase.

Hurrying behind them, Alias asked anxiously, "Thurbal, what's wrong, anyway?"

Without breaking his stride, Thurbal explained, "Some fiend from a lower plane has broken into the tower."

"That's impossible," Alias interrupted. "Elminster has warded the tower against—"

"So we all thought," Thurbal said. "The Harper bard Kyre says the creature is from the Nine Hells, however, and it's barricaded itself behind a wall of ice. The creature is in the same passage where the Nameless Bard is imprisoned. Harper Kyre transported herself beyond the wall magically to help Nameless, but the rest of us are stuck on this side of the wall. We may need a mage to take it down."

At the mention of Nameless, Alias looked alarmed and began to race up the staircase. Akabar and Thurbal had to take the steps two at a time to keep up with her.

"Head for the west tower room," Thurbal huffed as they reached the third story.

Alias dashed off ahead of the two men, running past the doors to the Harpers' courtroom. As she turned the corner of the hallway, she was forced to halt abruptly to avoid running into the wall of ice.

The thing was dismally cold; it made the corridor feel like a fen in winter. Two guards were piling burning torches at its base, but there was no indication whatsoever that the wall was melting.

Mourngrym was hacking at the ice wall with a great axe. He

had managed to chip away several inches, but it had taken its toll on him. His face and ears were flushed from the cold, his hands were red and raw, and the tips of his fingers were white from frostbite. He looked exhausted. As Alias watched, the axe slipped from his grasp and clanged to the floor.

"Mourngrym!" Alias cried, taking hold of his shoulders and pulling him away from the wall. "You've got to stop before you lose your hands."

Mourngrym looked back at the swordswoman with grim determination. "I can't, Alias. Nameless and Harper Kyre are trapped behind there with an evil monster," he said.

"I know," Alias said, trying to keep her voice calmer than she felt. "I've brought Akabar. He'll dispel the wall."

Just then Akabar and Thurbal turned the corner of the corridor. Akabar's eyes widened at the sight of the wall of ice, and he swallowed uncertainly. The wall was obviously very thick, indicating that it had been cast by a spell-caster far more powerful than he. Without much hope, he began a chant to dispel the magic ice.

Mourngrym, Alias, and the two guards moved away from the wall as the mage raised his clasped hands over his head. Akabar finished his disenchantment spell by unlacing his fingers with a flourish. Sun-yellow motes of light sparkled toward the wall and scattered across the ice.

The specks of light faded, but the wall of ice remained. Akabar lowered his arms and looked troubled. "I'll have to try to melt the wall with a fireball," the mage said. "It's quite dangerous. The explosion will release very hot steam. You must all take cover."

"What about you?" Alias asked.

"I cannot cast the magic from behind a wall," Akabar said.

* * * * *

Back in Finder's cell, Olive began to fidget with the straps of her pack as the bard's expression grew more serious. Finder shook his head at something Grypht was "telling" him.

Olive's sharp ears caught the sound of someone out in the hallway picking at the door lock. "Someone's coming!" she whispered anxiously.

Grypht spun about and growled. Finder tossed Olive the

finder's stone. "Take this and your cloak and knapsack and stay out of sight," he ordered the halfling. "Now!"

Olive picked up her gear and slipped behind the velvet drapes. Hastily she poked a tiny peephole in the fabric with her dagger.

As the door swung open, Finder took a position at Grypht's side, prepared to reprimand the guards for attacking the creature without provocation.

He was not prepared, however, for Kyre. The lovely half-elf stood in the doorway holding out a rather large but innocuous-looking walnut.

"I'm afraid we haven't had the pleasure of being introduced," the bard said, turning on his most charming smile. Kyre's face contorted in disgust, and she turned her gaze impatiently on the giant lizard. Grypht hissed and raised his staff.

"Darkbringer!" Kyre shouted. The round nut in her hand began to radiate a sphere of darkness, which within the span of five heartbeats, grew as large as a pumpkin, concealing Kyre's hand and forearm in an inky black ball.

Finder stepped protectively in front of the large saurial. "No," he said calmly. "There's been a misunderstanding here. He's a foe of the Darkbringer, not an agent."

Kyre ignored Finder. "Grypht," she said flatly. The sphere of darkness about her hand began to shimmer like hot tar, then reached out a vinelike tendril of glassy black that shot over Finder's head. The end of the tendril struck Grypht in the face. The saurial stood motionless, paralyzed by the magic, as the dark sphere around the nut oozed along the tendril toward its prey. When it reached Grypht, the darkness poured down him like oil, covering every inch of his body until the great lizard was nothing but a black silhouette. Then the darkness constricted and shrank about Grypht until he was squeezed into a tiny black, marble-sized sphere.

From behind the curtain, Olive watched in horror as the dark tendril contracted back into the walnut, taking Grypht along with it. Then the darkness about the nut dissipated, leaving the walnut as clear as glass.

"That wasn't necessary," Finder insisted angrily. "I told you he meant no harm."

Kyre pocketed the walnut and then turned her attention to the prisoner. "Master Nameless, I'm so pleased to meet you at last," she said, smiling at Finder.

Behind the curtain, Olive shuddered. The halfling couldn't put her finger on it, but there was definitely something creepy about the way the half-elf smiled.

❧ 4 ❧

The Half-Elf

Kyre took another step into Nameless's prison. "I've been so eager to meet you," the half-elf said to Finder.

"That's some sort of soul-trapping gem you used on the saurial, isn't it?" Finder asked, ignoring Kyre's pleasantries. "I demand you release him at once."

"I'm afraid I can't do that. You see, he's a very dangerous creature," the half-elf replied. "But useful—not unlike yourself." Kyre reached her hand into her pocket and pulled it out again. She held a second walnut. "Darkbringer," she said. Once again a sphere of darkness emanated from the nut, just as it had before. "The Nameless Bard," Kyre pronounced slowly.

The sphere shimmered, and a tendril of black began to rise from it. Suddenly the tendril collapsed in on itself, and the darkness dissipated. Having failed to suck up the bard's essence, the magical nut shattered, and shards of its shell flew in all directions. The half-elf didn't even flinch. Instead, she stared up at the Nameless Bard with interest, waiting for him to explain.

Finder sneered. "I am Nameless no longer, but you, woman, whoever you are, will answer to the Harpers for this attack!"

Kyre laughed confidently. "I think not. You see, I am the Harper Kyre, and Nameless or not, you, bard, are in no position to threaten me."

"Elminster would never approve of the cowardly way you've treated that saurial," Finder retorted hotly. "Have the Harpers degenerated so far in the past two centuries that they attack innocent creatures and helpless prisoners?"

As Finder spoke, Olive could see Kyre slip a wand out of her tunic sleeve. The halfling couldn't contain her anxiety a moment longer. She burst out from behind the curtain, shouting, "Finder! Look out!" and hurled herself at Finder's legs, knocking him to one side.

A beam of green light shot out from the tip of Kyre's wand, missing Finder by inches. The light struck the silver fruit bowl on the table behind him, enveloping it and the fruit in a sparkling green mist. After several seconds, the beam of light went out and the mist dissipated. The silver bowl was unharmed, but the plums, pears, and apples within had turned completely brown from rot and their skins had collapsed on the decayed flesh within.

Finder's face registered fear now that he was finally aware of the danger he was in. He stared wide-eyed at Kyre.

Olive took quick aim and hurled her dagger at the half-elf. The weapon hit Kyre's wrist, causing her to drop the deadly wand. Kyre's eyes flashed angrily, but she made no sound or movement to indicate the weapon had hurt her hand.

Olive shuddered at the woman's indifference to pain. "Would you get us out of here now?" the halfling shouted, shoving the finder's stone at the master bard.

Finder grabbed the stone with one hand and Olive's shoulder with the other, then sang an E-flat. Olive sighed happily as a yellow light began glowing around her body.

The halfling's relief was short-lived. Though the light continued to glow, she and Finder didn't vanish from the cell as expected. Olive felt as if something was pulling her in two, and she screamed in pain.

Across the room, Kyre laughed and held out her arms. Long, slimy green tendrils shot out from her sleeves toward Finder. Olive cried out once more, this time in fear. There was something terrifyingly familiar about Kyre's tendrils.

The tendrils reached over Olive's head just as Finder sang a second E-flat, this time an octave lower than the first. The yellow light shimmered with the deep resonance of the bard's voice and then glowed so brightly that Kyre, her tendrils, and the room faded from his and Olive's view.

* * * * *

Alias, Mourngrym, and his guards waited anxiously around the corner of the hallway as Akabar chanted his fireball spell. The mage's voice rose sharply, then a great explosion shook the floor and walls around them and echoed through the corridors. A second later a burst of steam came rushing down the corridor, past the side passage in which they stood. Clouds of hot, moist air billowed around them.

Anxious about Akabar, Alias rushed around the corner and into the steam. The floor was covered with water and the walls were dripping with moisture. Alias spied Akabar in the dispersing mist. Not even the darkness of the mage's skin could hide the flush of his face from the scalding he'd received, but he still stood. He was drenched from the steam, and when he shook himself, drops of water scattered from his beard, hair, and robes.

"Are—are you all right?" Alias asked.

"I think so," Akabar replied. "As a mage I have more immunity from the power of magic than you. At any rate, the wall is melted," he said, gesturing at the clear passage ahead.

Mourngrym and Thurbal and the two tower guards rejoined the mage and the swordswoman.

"Good work, Akabar," his lordship said, clapping the mage on the back.

Assured that the Turmishman was all right, Alias prepared herself for combat. Having brought no weapon with her, she retrieved the great axe that Lord Mourngrym had been using to chip at the wall of ice. Then she started down the corridor, silently hoping that Nameless was unharmed and swearing vengeance if he was not.

His sword drawn, Mourngrym took the lead with Alias. Akabar, Thurbal, and the two guards brought up the rear. A shadow fell across them, framing the doorway at the end of the corridor. Mourngrym and Alias halted and raised their weapons, poised to charge into combat.

A slender half-elven woman appeared in the doorway. She wore a silky yellow tunic and fine elven boots; a sword in a scabbard hung from the black belt at her hips, and a bright red orchid hung in her long, dark hair. The half-elf stepped into the corridor.

"Kyre!" Mourngrym gasped. "Are you all right?"

The half-elf looked up at Mourngrym. "You broke through the wall of ice?" she asked. There was a hint of confusion in her voice.

"What happened?" Mourngrym demanded, ignoring her question. "Kyre, where is Grypht? Where is Nameless?"

Kyre lowered her head. "I'm afraid I've failed, your lordship.

I could not stop Grypht from reaching the Nameless Bard. Grypht grabbed Nameless and teleported away with him."

* * * * *

For what seemed an eternity, Olive felt as if she were trapped in a golden web. When the light from the magical stone finally dimmed, she and Finder stood looking out over a grassy meadow on a sloping hillside.

Olive quickly sank to the ground, exhausted by the magical teleportation.

"Admit it, Finder," she murmured, "whatever spell Elminster used to keep you inside that cell, it was almost a match for your rock, artifact or no."

Finder cursed angrily under his breath. The halfling looked up at the bard. His face was drenched with sweat, and his complexion was pale. "What's wrong?" she asked. "Are you all right?"

"Kyre snatched the finder's stone away from me just before we teleported," Finder growled with rage. "That bitch has my stone!"

"Oh," Olive said uncertainly. "Well, at least we escaped."

"But she has my stone!" Finder snarled irritably.

"She could have *you*, like she got Grypht," Olive snapped back. If you hadn't been so stubborn about waiting for the Harpers' blessing, you would have escaped before she arrived, Grypht wouldn't have been captured, and you'd still have your precious rock."

"She said she was a Harper," Finder said incredulously. "She couldn't be a Harper."

"She is," Olive said. "I told you—she's one of the tribunal judges."

"I can't believe she tried to kill me," Finder said. "She never would have gotten away with it."

"She didn't care," Olive said. "You said something to her about Grypht being a foe of the Darkbringer. That's Moander, the Darkbringer god, right?"

"Yes. Grypht said he was looking for Dragonbait because Moander was threatening their tribe."

"Oh, great!" Olive muttered, slapping her hand against her forehead.

Finder looked at her blankly. "I don't see the connection," he said.

"Don't you get it? Kyre's one of Moander's servants."

"That's impossible. No Harper would aid the Darkbringer."

Olive huffed in frustration. "I recognized those slimy tendrils Kyre used to grab the finder's stone. They're just like the ones Moander had all over its body. Moander was probably controlling her mind, the same way it controlled Akabar's mind last year."

"Akabar," Finder mused. The bard recalled the southern mage, Akabar bel Akash, who had befriended Alias the previous year, and how he had been captured by the Darkbringer when he had tried to free Alias from the god's clutches. "But Akabar destroyed the body Moander used in the Realms," Finder argued. "There's no way Moander could have possessed Kyre."

"Suppose Kyre visited a world outside the Realms?" Olive asked.

Finder considered the halfling's suggestion and frowned darkly. "It's possible," he admitted.

"We have to get back to Shadowdale and tell Dragonbait so he can rescue Grypht," Olive said. "Where are we, anyway?" she asked, tossing a pebble at a thistle.

"Home," Finder said.

"Home? It doesn't look like Immersea," Olive replied.

"It's not. Were you under the impression I lived at Redstone Castle with my family?" Finder asked.

Olive grinned, thinking of all the Wyvernspurs she'd met and trying to imagine Finder getting along with them. "I guess I should have known better."

"What's that supposed to mean?" Finder asked.

Olive chuckled at his defensiveness. "Did they kick you out?" she asked.

Finder's eyes narrowed to slits. "I left them. They never took me seriously."

"Never a prophet in your own land," Olive teased. Finder's face darkened, and the halfling realized she might be pushing him too far. She decided to change the subject. "So where is this home?" she asked.

Finder made a sweeping motion with his arm, indicating something behind Olive. "Finder's Keep," he said.

The halfling turned around abruptly. The walls of a crumbling manor rose behind her. Thistles and grass grew between cracks in the stone. Kudzu covered the chimneys. Moss and fungus grew from the fallen roof beams. "I think you need a new decorator," Olive quipped.

"The underground complex was sealed. It should be in good condition," Finder said.

"Are we still in the Dales?" Olive asked.

Finder nodded. "The southern edge of the Spiderhaunt Woods."

"That's not too far from Shadowdale," Olive said, her mind racing. "We can walk to the road connecting Shadowdale and Cormyr. There should be plenty of traffic on it this time of the year. Then we can get a lift from a caravan going north. We should be able to reach Shadowdale in about four days."

"Olive, you've been trying all morning to convince me to flee Shadowdale," Finder reminded the halfling. "Now you want me to go back and turn myself in to the Harpers. Suppose Kyre isn't the only one in Moander's possession?"

"You are a problem, aren't you?" Olive sighed. "All right. When we get to the road, we'll go south to Cormyr, and we'll send a message back to Dragonbait with the first caravan we meet that's heading north to Shadowdale."

"No," Finder said. "I don't want to do that."

"Then how are we ever going to tell Dragonbait about Grypht?" Olive asked, exasperated.

"We're not," Finder said simply. "If Dragonbait finds out about Grypht, he'll try to help him."

"That's the idea, isn't it?" Olive asked.

"Alias, in turn, will want to help Dragonbait," Finder explained. "And I don't want her going anywhere near Moander or Moander's minions. Moander wants her for a servant. I won't have the god using her again."

"That's Alias's business, not yours," Olive replied.

"She's my daughter. I'll protect her as I see fit," Finder retorted sharply.

"Then don't you think you should warn her that Moander might be after her again?" Olive asked.

"Moander can't detect her if she doesn't go looking for the god," Finder said. "What she doesn't know can't hurt her."

Olive shrugged. "Whatever you say. No note to Dragonbait.

We still want to get to the road before dark. We'll catch a caravan going south to Cormyr. That place I told you about, where we can't be detected magically, is in Cormyr."

Finder shook his head. "I'm not hiding anywhere. I've decided you were right. I've credited the Harpers with too much power. Once I get access to my workshop, they'll never capture me again."

Olive sighed. She had planned to send a note to Dragonbait anyway. It didn't look as if she'd get a chance unless she left Finder.

The halfling didn't really want to leave the bard, though. Olive genuinely liked Finder. He knew more about her than anyone in the Realms, yet he didn't condemn her for her greed or her cowardice or her minor jealousies. He'd shown a lot of patience in teaching her more about music in one month than she'd learned during the rest of her whole life. In addition, he'd offered her a passage to respectability by giving her his Harper's pin.

"You know," the halfling said, rubbing her chin, "I'm beginning to worry that I might be a bad influence on you."

Finder chuckled. "Don't worry. I'm not influenced easily." He turned and headed up the hill toward the crumbling manor house.

That's what I'm afraid of, Olive thought, but she held her tongue and followed.

* * * * *

When Alias heard that Nameless had been kidnapped, the blood drained from her face and she swayed alarmingly. Akabar put his hand on her elbow to steady her.

"Don't worry, Alias," the mage said softly. "We'll find him."

"Kyre, this is Alias of Westgate," Mourngrym explained to the half-elf. "Alias, this is the bard Kyre, one of the members of the Harpers' tribunal."

After taking a few deep breaths, Alias had recovered from her shock enough to nod politely to the Harper bard. Kyre nodded back at the swordswoman, but it was Akabar who held the half-elf's gaze.

"This is Alias's friend, Akabar bel Akash," Mourngrym added, noting how Kyre stared at the mage. "Akabar used his magic to destroy the wall of ice for us."

"A pity that your effort, though great, came too late," Kyre said to Akabar.

"I don't understand how anything from a lower plane could have gotten into the tower," Alias said impatiently. "Elminster had it warded against entry by that sort of creature."

"Elminster also had a no-exit spell cast on Nameless's room," Mourngrym said. "How could Grypht teleport past that?"

"Such wards and spells sometimes deteriorate, your lordship, or they can be broken by powerful magic," Kyre replied. Though she addressed Mourngrym, the half-elf's attention was still fixed on Akabar. "As you saw, I just left the room without any trouble."

Mourngrym frowned. "I've never heard of any spell of Elminster's deteriorating or breaking. He's the most powerful mage in the Realms."

"Excuse me, your lordship," Akabar replied, "but the lady is quite correct. Such things do happen on occasion. In fact, there is considerable evidence of many spells having failed this past summer when the gods walked the Realms."

"Elminster took extra care to reset all the wards on the tower after that," Mourngrym interposed.

"Yet we cannot deny the evidence of our eyes," Akabar said.

"Speaking of Elminster, where is he?" Alias asked suddenly.

"He disappeared before our very eyes. Grypht appeared in his place," Kyre explained. "Perhaps his absence weakened his spells."

That didn't sound likely to Mourngrym, but he had no training in magic. He turned to Thurbal and the two guards. "Better have the tower searched, in case something else has managed to sneak in."

Thurbal nodded and ushered the two guards off with him.

Still unconvinced, Alias asked Kyre, "What type of monster was it? What did it look like?"

"Grypht is not a type of monster but one unique unto itself," Kyre replied calmly. "Grypht is a duke of Caina, in the Nine Hells. The Zhentarim often use Grypht for their evil schemes. It stands ten feet tall. Its hide is covered with green scales. It has horns, claws, and a tail."

Alias walked into Nameless's former cell. Sigils and symbols were scrawled on the walls and the windowsill and even the doorsill, evidencing the wards protecting the room from entry by creatures from the lower planes. They looked all right to her. "Akabar, what do you think?" Alias asked, motioning the mage into the room.

Akabar stepped into the cell and began to study Elminster's wards. As she watched Kyre's eyes follow the mage, Alias wondered if the half-elf recognized the Turmishman from somewhere, but when the half-elf reached up to adjust the orchid behind her ear, Alias realized that Kyre was physically attracted to the merchant-mage. Akabar was, after all, a handsome man. Even Cassana, a connoisseur of men, had lusted after him.

Alias turned around to survey the rest of the room. Elminster had sworn to her that he had made Nameless as comfortable as possible. The old sage hadn't lied. Everything about the room was lovely—the furniture, the curtains, the carpeting. A well-crafted songhorn lay on the table beside a silver fruit bowl. "Oh!" Alias cried out suddenly in disgust, revolted by the sight of the rotting, moldy plums, pears, and apples within the silver bowl.

"What is it?" Akabar asked, hurrying to her side. Mourngrym was close behind him.

Alias pointed at the bowl of fruit. "Is this some sick joke to taunt Nameless?" she asked.

Mourngrym scowled angrily when he saw what had upset the swordswoman." I can't imagine who would do such a thing," he said curtly, "but I guarantee I will find out who is responsible."

"The sign," Akabar whispered.

"What?" Alias asked, looking up at the Turmishman. Even beneath his dark skin, the swordswoman could see that the blood was draining from her friend's face. Akabar's body trembled visibly.

"Akabar, what's wrong?" Alias asked.

"It's the sign of danger. From my dreams. The bowl of rotting fruit marks its coming," Akabar said.

Alias shivered, momentarily frightened by Akabar's words. With a deep breath, she cast off the ridiculous idea that Akabar's dreams were rooted in reality.

From the doorway, Kyre called Akabar's name. The half-elf's face was clouded with concern. When Akabar looked up at her, she spoke a word to him that neither Alias nor Mourn-grym could comprehend, though it sounded to Alias as if it was in Turmish.

Akabar didn't appear comforted by whatever the half-elf had said. He reeled around and was forced to lean heavily on the ta-bletop to keep from falling over. He began muttering, "The sign . . . the rotting," over and over again.

"Get hold of yourself, Akash," Alias demanded, placing her hands on Akabar's shoulders.

"I think your friend is not well," Kyre said, hurrying into the room and taking Akabar's hands in her own.

"What is it?" Mourngrym asked Kyre. "What's wrong with him?"

"He's in shock. He should lie down. Here, Akabar Bel Akash," the half-elf said softly. She tugged gently on Akabar's wrists un-til she'd led him to the bed. "Sit here," she ordered.

As if he were in a trance, Akabar obeyed wordlessly.

"Now lie down," Kyre said.

Akabar swung his feet up on the bed and laid his head down on the pillow.

"Perhaps we should fetch Morala," his lordship suggested, alarmed by the mage's glassy-eyed stare.

"There's no need to trouble the priestess, your lordship," Kyre said. "I'm sure he'll recover soon."

"I'm sure she's right," Alias said. "Akabar's been having these strange dreams," she explained. "I'm afraid he takes them a lit-tle too seriously."

"Perhaps I can help," Kyre said. "I have made a study of dreams. If he will speak to me about them, perhaps I can tell him what they mean."

"Alias," Mourngrym said from the bedside, "I think he's try-ing to say something to you."

Alias knelt by the Turmishman's side. "I'm here, Akabar. What is it?"

Fighting to get the words out, Akabar whispered slowly, "Take . . . me . . . to . . . Zhara." His eyes glittered and his breath-ing was too quick.

Alias looked up at Kyre.

"I don't think you should move him," the half-elf said softly. "Who is Zhara?"

"His wife," Alias said reluctantly. She stood up again and explained more to Kyre in a whisper. "His third wife, a priestess. She's got him believing his dreams are real."

"Dreams are only real in our heads," Kyre said.

"Can you convince him of that?" Alias asked hopefully.

"Perhaps. If you and Lord Mourngrym will leave me alone with him for a time, it will be easier to speak with him about it," Kyre suggested.

Alias looked down anxiously at Akabar. Perhaps this attack of nerves, or whatever it was, was a blessing in disguise, she thought. Kyre was a beautiful woman, and Alias found herself hoping that if the half-elf was left alone to care for Akabar, he would find Kyre as attractive as Kyre obviously found him. If Akabar liked Kyre enough, Kyre might break Zhara's spell on him and convince him that Zhara was wrong, that his dreams of Moander weren't some godly command to place himself in the path of evil, but only the memories of old terrors.

Alias nodded her consent. "Summon me if you need me," the swordswoman said.

"I will let his wife know he is in my care," the half-elf said. "Where is she?"

"The Old Skull Inn. I asked Jhaele to put Akabar and his wife in the Red Room," Alias said. "There's no hurry. Zhara won't be expecting Akabar to return right away."

Kyre nodded as she laid her slender hand on Akabar's forehead.

Mourngrym put a comforting hand on Alias's shoulder as they left the room. "He'll be fine," his lordship said, pulling the door closed behind them. "I'm told Kyre is quite clever."

"She seems very sensible," Alias said, but she couldn't keep from adding, "Do you think she's right that this Grypht is a duke from the Nine Hells?"

Mourngrym shrugged. "I really don't know. You heard what she said about its working for the Zhentarim. Whatever Grypht is, the Zhentarim would certainly like to get their hands on Elminster. Still, I can't imagine that Elminster is in any real danger. He has an evasion spell to take him to safety if his life is ever seriously threatened."

"But Nameless doesn't have such a spell," Alias said. "The Zhentarim could be holding him to force Elminster to stay with them. Nameless and Elminster were once close friends. Elminster wouldn't abandon him. Suppose the Zhentarim heard some rumor about me and decided to try to coerce Nameless into creating another creature like me so they could use it as an agent? They might try to force Elminster to help him."

Mourngrym's face clouded over with concern. Alias's theory was too sensible to be discounted. "Why don't you pay a visit to the sage's scribe? If anyone knows anything about Elminster, it would be Lhaeo. In the meantime, I'll try to find some spell-casters who could scry for Nameless and Elminster."

*   *   *   *   *

Immediately after Alias and Mourngrym left Nameless's former cell, Kyre crept to the doorway and listened for a few moments as the swordswoman and the lord of Shadowdale moved away down the hall. When their footsteps and voices had faded into the distance, Kyre whispered a chant to hold the door closed so that nothing would interrupt her talk with the Turmishman. With Elminster gone and Akabar indisposed, it would take Mourngrym some time to scare up a mage capable of forcing the door. By then she would be gone and Akabar would be gone with her.

The half-elf crossed back to the bed and sat down beside Akabar. The Turmishman rolled his head and shook, as if he were in the midst of a bad dream. It must seem to him as if he were, Kyre realized. She had stunned him with a power word right in front of the lord of Shadowdale and the swords-woman, but since Kyre had spoken the word in Turmish, nei-ther Mourngrym nor Alias had the slightest suspicion that the merchant-mage's state of shock had been brought on by a mag-ical attack. Like most northerners, they had never bothered to learn Turmish or any of the related southern tongues, and now the half-elf would reap a great reward because of their ignorance.

For a brief moment, when Akabar had found the strength and wits to ask Alias to take him to his wife, the half-elf had feared her scheme would be ruined. Fortunately Alias had been more willing to trust a stranger than accept the Tur-mishman's trust in his priestess wife. Cassana had done a good job conditioning the swordswoman to dislike members of the clergy, Kyre thought with satisfaction.

Kyre ran her finger down the sleeve of Akabar's robe. After

she had spent months of fruitless searching for the Turmishman, he had brought himself to her, and now he lay here completely at her mercy. Before he regained his senses, she would have to put him under a stronger enchantment. She could place him in a gem of soul-stealing to carry him off to her master, but it would be easier and far more amusing to convince him to come with her of his own free will.

"Please forgive me for casting a spell on you, Akabar," she said in his native tongue, "but I can't permit you to tell everyone about your dreams." The mage's brow furrowed in puzzlement. Kyre pulled a glass vial out from her tunic pocket and unstoppered it. "Drink this down," she told him, raising the vial to his lips. "It will help clear your head."

In his confused state it didn't occur to Akabar to resist Kyre's suggestion. Dutifully he swallowed the liquid she poured in his mouth.

Kyre leaned over and kissed the mage gently on the lips. "Lie still a few minutes and you'll feel better," she said in flawless Turmish.

"Zhara," Akabar sighed. Then, with more agitation, he cried out, "The bowl of rotting fruit! Zhara, beware!"

Kyre frowned slightly. Aside from having too great a hold on the mage's heart, this Zhara probably knew too much. Fortunately Alias had told the half-elf all she needed to know to deal with the priestess.

Kyre stood up, padded over to the window, yanked open the curtain, and threw back the shutters. "The rain has stopped for the moment. How convenient," she declared.

From her tunic pocket, the half-elf pulled out a bit of thistledown with the seeds still attached. "Darkbringer," she murmured in Realms common. The thistle seeds in her hand began to glow. "Zhara, wife of Akabar Bel Akash, in the Red Room at the Old Skull Inn," she whispered. Then she held the thistledown up to her mouth and blew it out the window. The silky, seed-bearing strands danced away from the window toward the heart of Shadowdale, moving against the wind.

Kyre stood at the window, staring blankly at the greenery surrounding Shadowdale Akabar, hearing his wife's name spoken, turned his head in the half-elf's direction. He began studying her profile with fascination. Her silky black hair contrasted sharply with her fair skin, and her figure was lithe and muscular like a dancer's. She's really very beautiful, he thought. Not to mention well educated. She speaks Turmish well, with a soft-spoken voice like a true lady. And her touch is tender, as a woman's should be.

Why, though, the mage puzzled, did she have to stun me just to keep from speaking of my dreams? Akabar sighed to himself. No matter, he thought. She said she was sorry. I must give her a chance to explain. She must have a good reason.

A few minutes later, just as the half-elf had predicted, his head felt much clearer, his body felt rested, and the strength returned to his limbs. His heart still beat a little too quickly, but he didn't notice. He sat up and took a deep breath.

Kyre turned away from the window and smiled gently. "I'm pleased to see you feeling better," she said softly, still speaking in Turmish. "You will forgive me, I trust, for being so forward, but I must tell you, you are the most attractive man I've ever met."

Akabar blushed deeply. Usually the immodest advances of northern women annoyed him, but he felt inordinately pleased that someone as attractive as Kyre should find him appealing. Still, he wasn't the sort to leave mysteries unsolved. "Why don't you want me to tell about my dreams to anyone?" he asked.

Kyre crossed the room to his bedside, her walk graceful and sinuous. "I'm not sure who can be trusted," she replied as she sat down again on the edge of the bed.

"You can trust Alias," Akabar said. "She's a good friend."

"But I don't think I can trust Lord Mourngrym," Kyre replied. "However, I know I can trust you, Akabar. You've been chosen." The half-elf ran her finger along the curve of the Turmishman's ear and down along the artery in his neck.

Akabar felt his heart begin to pound and his blood throbbing in his head. "What do you know of my dreams?" he asked.

Kyre slid her hands up inside the loose sleeves of Akabar's robe, lightly touching the inside of his arms with her fingertips. "They are of the Darkbringer's return to the Realms, are they not?" she asked.

"Yes," Akabar admitted. "They are." He grasped the half-elven woman's elbows, and rubbed his thumbs along the silky sleeves of her tunic.

"And in your dreams, you must find the Darkbringer. Correct?" Kyre asked.

"Yes," Akabar said.

"I will help you," Kyre said. "Would you like that?"

Akabar pulled the woman closer to him. With amusement, he noted how the orchid behind Kyre's left ear was held in place. Some magic, elven no doubt, had coaxed the stem's tendrils to twist about several strands of her hair. The mage buried his face in the half-elf's hair and breathed in the orchid's intoxicating scent. "I would like that very much," he whispered, but something about the orchid's scent left him feeling anxious. The perfume tickled at some unpleasant memory that would not surface readily.

Kyre blew her warm breath into his ear. "I will take you to Moander's place of resurrection," she breathed. Leaning heavily against Akabar's chest, the half-elf forced him to fall back against the bed pillows. She placed her right ear directly over his heart.

Akabar knew she could hear his heart pounding. "How do you know these things?" he asked.

"The master told me," Kyre said. She raised her head and kissed the tip of his beard, then his chin.

As the woman's lips moved toward his own, the Turmishman suddenly caught sight of her orchid's tendrils, which twisted not about her hair but into her ear canal. Others had pricked her temples. The tendrils twitched and writhed beneath her skin, as if they were trying to get purchase on her brain. Akabar's stomach churned with revulsion, and his heart began pounding with fear. Finally he recalled where he'd smelled the orchid's perfume before. It was the scent of one of Moander's sleeping drugs. Akabar cried out and thrust Kyre away from him.

Three tendrils shot out from Kyre's mouth like snakes lashing out at their prey. These tendrils, tipped with pea-sized pods, were far longer than the orchid tendrils. As the green shoots curled and undulated in the air before the merchant-mage's face, he realized with horror that they might have easily slithered past his lips and down his throat if he had closed his eyes in anticipation of the half-elf's kiss. Suddenly the pods at the ends of the tendrils burst open, shooting tiny black seeds at Akabar's face. Then the tendrils collapsed as Kyre sucked them back into her mouth.

"Those seeds were meant for you to swallow," the half-elf said when her mouth was clear of the tendrils, "but don't worry. There are more."

Akabar sat up, shaking with terror, and tried to push Kyre away, but the woman had an iron grip on his elbows. As he struggled to free himself, Akabar felt other tendrils, incredibly slimy and as strong as rope, reaching inside his sleeves and entwining his upper arms.

"There's no use resisting, Akabar," Kyre said, still speaking in Turmish, only now her tone was cool and authoritative. "Your destiny is sealed." The half-elf slid her hands out of Akabar's sleeves. Her victim remained trapped by the plant appendages, which stretched from her wrists up his arms. The tendrils grew steadily longer, giving Kyre the freedom to move her hands up to Akabar's face. The merchant-mage closed his eyes, revolted at the way the tendrils protruded from beneath the skin of her forearms.

"The Darkbringer desires to possess your body again and once more gaze into the sharp-edged crystal of your mind," Kyre said mesmerizingly as she stroked his beard. "You should feel honored."

"No!" Akabar shouted. He managed to rise to his feet, pulling Kyre along with him. Terrified, he screamed, "Alias! Help me!"

Kyre cut off his cries with a choke hold to his throat. "The Darkbringer would prefer that I deliver you alive," the half-elf snarled, "but if that is not possible, the Darkbringer will be pleased enough with your corpse." She released Akabar's throat, and, as the mage gasped for air, she drew out a slender dagger from her sleeve and pressed its point against his neck.

"You wouldn't dare," Akabar whispered hoarsely. "If you murder me, Alias will cut you to pieces."

"Alias will never know," Kyre said. With her free hand, she pulled out an object and held it up to Akabar's eyes. It resembled a crystal the size and shape of a walnut, colorless but for a flickering dark flaw at the center. "Behold, Akabar," Kyre said. "Inside this stone is entrapped an enemy of the master, a mage far more powerful than you. If you continue to resist, I will slay you and carry you to the Darkbringer within just such a stone. If, instead, you cooperate and come with me of your own free will, you will be rewarded well. Moander will grant you such power as few men in the Realms have ever known."

Akabar stared into Kyre's eyes, thinking what a fool he'd been. Zhara had warned him he would be in danger the moment he saw the bowl of rotting fruit, yet, for all his faith, he hadn't acted quickly enough to defend himself. To add to his folly, he'd trusted Kyre, a complete stranger, and allowed her liberties with his body. Now he was tainted by her touch and helpless in her grasp. He was doomed—worse, he had doomed all he loved and all who dwelt in the Realms.

"You will behave now, won't you?" Kyre asked sweetly, pricking painfully at his throat with her dagger.

The mage's shoulders slumped and his arms went limp. With a deep sense of shame, he realized he wasn't prepared to give his life just to keep Moander from possessing his body and invading his mind again. He nodded his agreement to the half-elf.

♣ 5 ♣

The Young Priestesses

Zhara closed the door to the Red Room of the Old Skull Inn and motioned for Dragonbait to have a seat at the table. The paladin had agreed to join Akabar's wife for lunch in the privacy of her room. The priestess of Tymora crossed the room and sat down opposite her guest.

After all that Akabar had told her about Dragonbait, Zhara felt the paladin was like a brother to her. Showing her face to a brother would not be immodest, she decided, pushing back the hood of her robe. She removed her veil and laid it on the table.

Dragonbait studied Zhara's face curiously.

"You do not seem shocked or surprised," the priestess said.

Dragonbait motioned with his hands.

"Yes, I can understand your sign language," Zhara answered.

Dragonbait motioned with his hands that he could smell what Zhara was.

"Oh," Zhara replied, remembering Akabar had also mentioned the paladin's refined sense of smell.

Let's eat, Dragonbait signed. *Then we can talk.*

Zhara nodded in agreement. She said a short prayer in Turmish in thanksgiving for the food laid out before them and began serving the meal. They ate in silence, but it was a comfortable silence. After the paladin had eaten his fill of the venison and potatoes and peas, all northern dishes that were strange to Zhara, the saurial leaned back in his chair and signed that he was full.

The priestess shook her head at the saurial's plate "You haven't eaten very much," she said. "I thought warriors all had ravenous appetites."

With his fingers, the paladin explained that saurials preferred many small meals to a few large ones.

"Akabar said saurial paladins have something called shen sight—that you can see into a person's soul. Is that true?" Zhara asked.

Dragonbait nodded.

"I want you to look into my soul," Zhara said. "Tell me, am I not a virtuous woman?"

Dragonbait lowered his eyes, and the scent of vanilla wafted from him. Fortunately, Zhara didn't realize it was a sign that he was amused by the priestess's self-righteousness. Despite his amusement, the saurial paladin complied with her request and summoned his shen. He saw in Zhara exactly what he had expected to see—a soul of pure blue, which indicated grace, the state of being sanctified and loved by her goddess. He also sensed that the priestess's spirit was strong and arrogant. She was not so very different from Alias.

Do you have reason to doubt your virtue? Dragonbait signed, teasing the priestess.

Zhara shook her head. "I only want to know if you believe, as Alias does, that I could be so evil as to lie to Akabar about his dreams? That I don't love him and I'm only using him?" she asked.

Dragonbait shook his head and signed to Zhara. *Do not be offended by the swordswoman. She is still frightened by the Darkbringer, and her fear always makes her angry.*

"Your Alias has no respect for the clergy," Zhara noted coolly.

She was created that way, Dragonbait signed. *She cannot help herself.*

"Only a barbarian would belittle the gods as she does," Zhara said contemptuously.

Barbarians also belittle beautiful music, as you did, Dragonbait pointed out.

Zhara looked momentarily flustered. She hadn't expected the paladin to chide her about her behavior. She replied defensively, "Akabar has told me much of Alias. For instance, I know she practically worships Nameless and his music. That is wrong," Zhara insisted. "Nameless is only a man, and his music is but the creation of a man. Neither the man nor his creation can compare to the gods or their works."

Dragonbait sighed. *I'll tell you a little story,* he signed. *It's a story I've never told anyone else. A story with a lesson.*

Zhara leaned forward and watched curiously as the paladin's hands motioned over the table.

Once there was a paladin who served the god of justice,

the saurial explained. *The paladin loved a priestess who served Lady Luck. The paladin was proud of himself and his service to his god. He felt there was no cause more noble than justice. He felt everyone should feel as he felt. Lady Luck was not always just, however; sometimes she was fickle. Occasionally she bestowed her favor on those who did not deserve it, and withheld her favor from those who did. The paladin demanded that his priestess lover serve his god instead of Lady Luck. The two argued about it, and the paladin insulted Lady Luck and the priestess, but the priestess would not leave her goddess.*

Because the paladin loved the priestess very much, he knew that if he remained near her, he would soon grow to accept her decision and remain her lover despite her refusal to do as he wished. He thought that if this happened, he would be tainted by the priestess's love for her goddess. In his anger and pride, the paladin was determined that these things should not happen, so he left his tribe to serve his god's cause in the dark and evil region of Tarterus.

There the paladin was captured by a fiend who intended to sacrifice the paladin for a very evil purpose. As the paladin hung from chains in a dank dungeon, very close to death, he had a vision, or perhaps it was just a dream, in which Lady Luck appeared before him. The goddess said that she did not care if she ever saw him again, but the god of justice had asked for her help in sparing the paladin's life. If the paladin would agree to perform a service for Lady Luck, she would free him from the evil creatures who intended to kill him.

The paladin wished to live, of course, and since his god had intervened on his behalf, it would be arrogant to turn down the goddess's offer. The paladin had learned that even the cause of justice cannot always win against evil without Lady Luck's blessing. He agreed to perform the service, and Lady Luck sent a human to free the paladin and tell him what service he must perform. So the paladin lives yet to serve the god of justice, but he pays homage, too, to Lady Luck or to any other god or goddess who can further the cause of justice.

Dragonbait leaned forward in his chair. Zhara thought he was finished and was about to speak when the saurial began motioning once again with his hands. *The paladin,* Dragonbait signed, *learned that the god of justice is also served by other worldly beings—merchant-mages, halfling thieves, arrogant* bards—and even by the creations of worldly beings—commerce and government, history and tales, music and song. Thus the paladin learned to respect worldly things. Is it not possible that the goddess you serve is served by such things as well?

Zhara huffed. "Even if Alias's music serves the gods, it does not make it right for her to belittle them," the priestess insisted.

Dragonbait nodded in agreement. *She has reason, though,* he signed.

"What reason?" Zhara snapped.

Her taunts help her fight her fear of the gods, the paladin explained.

"If she were virtuous, she would have no reason to fear the gods," Zhara declared.

If you had ever lain helpless in the Darkbringer's power, as she has, you would know better, the paladin replied.

Zhara lowered her eyes, chastened.

After pausing several moments, Dragonbait chucked her gently under her chin. *You've had a long journey,* he signed. *You should rest now.*

"Before I rest, I want you to tell me one thing," Zhara said. "Will the paladin in your tale ever return to the priestess he loved?"

When he has finished his service to Lady Luck, Dragonbait signed.

"When will that be?" Zhara asked.

When the Darkbringer is destroyed for all time, Dragonbait signed, *and the paladin's sister need never fear becoming helpless again. Rest now. We will talk again.* The saurial rose to his feet.

Zhara smiled up at the lizard. "Do you promise?" she asked.

The paladin laid his hand on his chest, bowed, and slipped out of the Red Room as quietly as a cat.

The priestess sighed. Although she vowed to think more kindly of Alias, she doubted she'd ever really like her. The swordswoman was still a northerner and an adventuress, synonymous, in the priestess's mind, with a barbarian. Zhara felt honored, though, that the paladin had divulged his story to her.

She yawned. Dragonbait was right. She should rest. The priestess reached over to the window, unfastened the shutter latch, and pushed the shutter open. Cool, moist air wafted into he room, carrying a number of tiny tufted seeds. As Zhara stared sleepily out across the gray landscape, the rain started falling once again.

She pulled off her sandals and threw them at her clothing trunk, listening with satisfaction to the thumping noises they made. Then she picked up her veil from the table and, for good measure, threw it in the direction of the trunk. It landed several inches short, but she was too tired to bend over to pick it up. Stupid veil, she thought. Let it lie there.

Pushing herself out of her chair, Zhara shuffled exhaustedly across the room and flopped onto the bed. Before they'd arrived in Shadowdale, she and Akabar had spent several days on the road with the caravan, camping in the open on the hard ground. As she lay back on the plump pillows, she anticipated the pleasures of sharing so large and private a room with her husband again. While she missed Akash and Kasim, her co-wives, there was no denying that she enjoyed having Akabar's company all to herself.

Thinking of Akash and Kasim, Zhara uttered a quick prayer for their safety and health. Then she drifted off to sleep to the sound of the pattering rain and a vision of her handsome husband leaning over her, whispering her name.

A bad dream troubled her sleep. In the dream, Alias was closing her inside a coffin lined with daggers. The darkness of the coffin frightened Zhara as much as the idea of the daggers, and she was struggling with all her might to resist, when suddenly she awoke with a start.

The priestess wasn't sure how long she'd been asleep, but the room about her was much darker than it had been; twisting shadows played on the walls all about her. She reached into a pocket of her robe for one of the stones she had enchanted with a continual light. Something pricked at her elbow when she moved her arm. She reacted automatically, rolling on her side, away from whatever she'd brushed against.

Instead of rolling to safety, she rolled into worse stabs—painful and itchy. She rolled onto her back once more and yanked out her light stone. She gasped in horror. The room was choked with a thicket of greenery, sprouting needle-sharp daggers from every stem and leaf. She was buried in the center of the thicket, unable to move without lancing herself on the needles. As if she were still dreaming, a scream caught in her throat and would not escape.

Attracted by her light stone, the plants closed in toward her, stabbing at her flesh. Zhara cringed from the pain and threw her arms up to protect her bare face. She could feel a dagger plant coiling under the hem of her robes, stabbing at her bare calves.

Zhara felt panic wrapping about her as tightly as the plants. This had been one of Akabar's dreams. The Darkbringer had gained the advantage of first attack. Once it finished with her it would take Akabar. It would devour his soul before his spirit was strong enough to resist.

"No!" Zhara growled through clenched teeth at the purple flowering pods pricking at her lips, trying to thrust their way into her mouth. "You'll never get my husband!" A burst of anger forced the panic away from her. She thrust her left hand into another pocket of her robe and grasped at a handful of bark there, meanwhile clutching at her throat with her other hand for the silver disk that was the holy symbol of her goddess. Ignore the pain! she ordered herself as the needles pricked into the back of her knee. Concentrate! Zhara began a prayer to Tymora asking for the goddess's aid. The oft-repeated lines helped calm her nerves until she was able to summon the power for her spell. Crumbling the bark in her fist, she whispered, "Oak sister."

Zhara squeezed her eyes tightly shut, concentrating on the numbness creeping up her left hand into her arm, across her torso, up her throat, down her other arm and into her legs. She took a deep breath and sat straight up in the bed. The dagger plants resisted her movements with their woody stems, but she could no longer sense their sharp prickers. Her spell had transformed her skin into bark that was hard enough to protect her but also smooth and supple enough so she could still move. She fought back the attacking greenery with her arms as if it were nothing deadlier than hay.

Her eyes were still vulnerable, so she was forced to keep them closed. The spell wouldn't last long. It wasn't panic that caused her to seek help, she assured herself, and she did so, shouting, "Dragonbait!" at the top of her lungs. She pushed herself off the bed and stomped on the plant stems, crushing them under her bark-covered heels until the floor was smeared with sticky pulp.

All around her, the plants kept growing faster than she could crush them. They began winding around her ankles and wrists, restricting her movements until finally they held her fast. Another plant twisted tight around her throat, and she knew that when the bark skin faded, she'd either be strangled or have her jugular vein pierced by the thorns.

She screamed for Dragonbait again and again, until a flowering pod thrust itself into her mouth. The prickles stung like a hundred bees, and the plant forced itself deeper, choking her.

Unable to get her hands to her mouth, Zhara bit down on the plant and ripped the flower from the stem with her teeth. She chewed, despite the agonizing pain, until she'd worked the flower into a wad small enough to spit out.

Something thumped on the door. "Help!" Zhara screamed. "Hurry!"

The door opened just wide enough for Dragonbait's arm to slip through. He held out his sword and growled. The sword glowed, then burst into flame, illuminating the room in a brilliant light. Dagger plants swayed instinctively toward the light, only to be scorched by the fire. The saurial slashed blindly at the greenery until he'd cleared the way enough to thrust the door open all the way. He hacked at the stems, setting them alight and filling the room with an acrid, black smoke. Then he slashed at the base of the plants that held Zhara until he could pull her from the room.

The saurial stood in the doorway, brandishing his flaming weapon. The plants hesitated to approach now, as if warned that the glowing weapon was deadly. Dragonbait hissed once and pulled the door shut.

Very gently the saurial pulled away the prickly shoots and flowers still wrapped around Zhara. Now that they'd been separated from their roots, the plants were no longer able to move, but they still clung ferociously to the priestess.

Zhara's skin was reverting to normal, and it was an effort to keep from wincing as the paladin freed her from the plants. Her mouth and tongue were numb and so swollen she could hardly talk. "Akabar—" she gasped, and began to weep hysterically.

Dragonbait pulled her into his own room across the hall and forced her to sit on his bed, holding her firmly by her shoulders.

Zhara smelled woodsmoke all around her, and then she felt calmer. Her mouth tingled, but at least it no longer ached. She took a deep breath. "You healed me, didn't you?" she asked.

The lizard nodded, brushing her reddish-brown hair out of her eyes and stroking her cheek gently with one of his scaly fingers.

"Alias was the one who sent those things after me," Zhara said.

Dragonbait looked down at the priestess with widened eyes, as if she'd lost her mind.

"She did. I dreamed it."

The saurial paladin shook his head vehemently.

"I have to find Akabar! He's in terrible danger! You must take me to him! You must!" Zhara cried.

Dragonbait nodded. He pulled a scarf from his pack and handed it to her, signing that she could use it as a veil.

While the paladin couldn't believe that Alias had anything to do with the attack on Zhara, he never doubted for an instant that Zhara was right about her husband's being in danger. The deadly enchanted thistles smelled of the Darkbringer's magic, and Dragonbait shuddered to think what other sorts of plants and creatures the god would send after the merchant-mage.

* * * * *

Satisfied that she had broken Akabar's spirit, Kyre slid her dagger back up her sleeve and set the crystal nut down on the table. She kissed the mage on the lips, more passionately than she had the first time, tugging on his lips with her own.

Akabar shuddered, too terrified of the tendrils in the half-elf's mouth to risk unclenching his jaw, but he made no verbal complaint. He could feel the tendrils about his arms loosening and then falling away.

"Now, prove to me your sincerity," Kyre demanded as she slid the tendrils out from his sleeves. "Embrace me," she ordered.

Akabar slid his arms around the woman's shoulders and pulled her close to him. She wrapped her arms around his waist and ran her fingers up and down his spine. The tendrils from her arms slithered about his ankles and lay bunched on the floor like pythons. The merchant-mage's feelings warred between revulsion and desire.

"That potion you had me drink was a philter of love, wasn't it?" Akabar asked.

Kyre looked up at the Turmishman with surprise. "Yes," she admitted, laying her head against his chest. "The master made a perfect choice. You are very clever."

Akabar's eyes fell on the crystal soul trap lying on the table. If an enemy of Moander's was trapped within, Kyre must have used it on Elminster, he thought. Then she had Grypht appear in his place to distract the other two Harpers before it occurred to either of them that she might be responsible. Grypht fled from the Harpers' court and Kyre followed, making herself appear the monster's foe. No doubt she assisted it in the capture of Nameless and then gave it the opportunity to escape.

"I shall be your first reward," Kyre whispered, pressing her slender body against his own. "The potion still courses in your blood. You know you desire me."

"I know," Akabar replied flatly. He had never loved anything so hateful in his life. Only another mage could dispel the love charm to which he'd fallen prey. Elminster could do so without batting an eye, but Elminster was as trapped as Akabar was. Suddenly a glimmer of hope flickered in the Turmishman's heart. If Elminster were to be freed, the old sage could do more than dispel Kyre's evil magic: Elminster could destroy Kyre as well.

On the table, beside the crystal soul trap and the bowl of rotting fruit, lay a chordal horn, a northern woodwind instrument, which must have belonged to Nameless. It was beautifully crafted of black wood and decorated with gold, but Akabar was only interested in its length and weight. It would make a reasonable club if he could just get hold of it.

Steeling himself to the task of distracting Kyre from his efforts to reach the horn, the merchant-mage bent over the woman and began kissing her all about her throat. The half-elf moaned softly. Akabar squeezed her tighter, forcing her back against the table, and ran his right hand down her back until he felt the tabletop. He closed his fingers around the instrument, but as he began lifting it from the table, he accidentally struck it against the rim of the silver fruit bowl.

Kyre started at the clanging sound and twisted around in Akabar's arms. Akabar grabbed the half-elf's right hand in his left and aimed the chordal horn over the soul trap gem on the table.

Realizing the mage's intent, Kyre looked alarmed. She screamed, "No!" and snatched for the crystal nut with her left hand.

Akabar slammed the chordal horn down hard on the table. The top of the instrument smashed into the crystal nut, shattering it into pieces, but the middle of the instrument smashed into Kyre's wrist with a sickening sound. Blackness oozed and billowed over the table where the soul trap had lain, but Akabar could not tear his eyes from the half-elf's injured wrist.

Beneath Kyre's skin, which had burst open like the rind of an overripe melon, there were no sinews or muscles or bones; instead, her arm was packed with rotting, mold-encrusted tendrils. Akabar gagged on the stench of decay that rose from her wrist. Most of the tendrils had been smashed by the chordal horn, and Kyre's hand hung from the end of her wrist like a piece of dead meat.

The tendrils lying about Akabar's ankles whipped upward and lashed about Akabar's wrists, cutting off his circulation. Kyre yanked her uninjured right wrist out of the mage's grasp. Akabar tried to club Kyre with the chordal horn, but Kyre pulled the instrument out of his hand and threw it to the floor.

Akabar turned his attention to his last hope of escape—the blackness over the table, which was now coalescing into the shape of the being that had been trapped within the crystal. Akabar gasped. He'd been expecting Elminster to appear, but although the being standing on the table wore the robes of a spell-caster, it looked nothing like the sage. It was huge, with horns and green scales and claws and a tail.

Akabar suddenly made a wild guess. "You transformed Elminster into that beast!" he accused Kyre.

Kyre didn't answer the merchant-mage's charge. With her uninjured hand, she had already pulled an empty soul trap out from her pocket. She held it out in the beast's direction and triggered it by shouting, "Darkbringer!"

Akabar threw himself into Kyre, knocking them both to the floor. Kyre lost her grip on the walnut-shaped crystal, and the magical device rolled across the carpeting.

The beast pulled out a crystal cone from his sleeve and pointed it at the bard pinned beneath the merchant-mage.

A freezing blast of cold hit the tangled bodies on the floor, covering them with rime. Akabar's skin felt as if it were on fire, and his heart and lungs ached as though they'd been stabbed. Unable to cope with such terrible pain, he lapsed into unconsciousness.

The beast Grypht watched with satisfaction as Kyre's tendrils and the orchid in her hair withered from the frost that covered them. Kyre lay as still as Akabar, but Grypht was taking no chances. With his staff, he pried the merchant-mage off Kyre. Then he set the half-elven bard's body alight with bursts of magical flames shot from his fingertips.

As the corpse crackled and sizzled, a horrible stench filled the room. Grypht made a face, but decided the smell could be borne. He climbed down from the tabletop and bent over his rescuer. He realized with a start that he recognized Akabar. Like the thief Olive Ruskettle, this creature was a friend to Champion—or Dragonbait, as people called the paladin in this strange world.

Unfortunately the Turmishman didn't appear to have weathered the cold spell very well. He wasn't breathing. Grypht's people could breathe even when they fell into a torpid state, but the saurial had no idea what was normal for these chirping apes.

He sighed to himself. Killing Kyre had been far more important than worrying about who got in the way—even if that person had been responsible for freeing him and was a friend of Champion's. Champion, however, would probably not see it that way. The paladin is always so damned idealistic, Grypht thought.

Grypht pulled a small bottle out of the sleeve of his robe. There was a chance it would prove unsafe for the creature on the floor, but he had to risk it. He unstoppered the bottle and poured its contents between Akabar's lips.

Akabar coughed back some of the thick liquid, but he must have swallowed some, for a moment later, he breathed a shuddery breath, then another and another. He did not regain consciousness, but his complexion turned from gray to his normal brown, a change that seemed like a good sign to Grypht. The saurial turned his attention back to the remains of Moander's servant.

There was nothing left of Kyre but ashes. Grypht used his

staff to stir through them and knock aside the unburnt items Kyre had carried and worn—a dagger, a sword, a belt, a scabbard, three more walnut-shaped soul traps, two gold rings, a silver pin of a crescent moon and harp, and her boots. Always a careful scavenger, Grypht turned her smoking boots upside down. A silver ankle bracelet tumbled from one boot, and from the other a large yellow gem—the one the ape Finder had used to cast a tongues spell.

Grypht pocketed the yellow gem. He crushed the soul traps in his bare paws, but no other beings rose from the broken shards. The traps had been unused. Remembering the last trap Kyre had triggered, the saurial searched the floor until he discovered it under a chair and smashed it with his staff.

Time to leave this vermin-infested ape lair, he thought, rising to his feet. He looked down at the Turmishman. He'd have to take the creature with him. It had freed him from Kyre's trap; it stood to reason it was an enemy of the Darkbringer, and leaving it here would endanger it further. If it recovered, it might be able to help him find Champion. He bent back down, swaddled Akabar in his cape, and slung him over his shoulder.

Unbowed by the weight of the merchant-mage, Grypht strode over to the window and stuck his head out. There was a river to his left, and beyond that a temple, but beyond the temple lay a forest. He looked long and hard at the tree line, first estimating its distance, then checking to be sure there were no other apes nearby.

Exuding the scent of fresh-mown hay, Grypht shifted himself and his burden through a dimensional portal. A moment later, he stood at the edge of the tree line across the river. He glared back at the twisted tower of Ashaba, glad to be free of it, and then turned and lumbered into the forest.

* * * * *

As Grypht carried Akabar Bel Akash from the Tower of Ashaba, he failed to note he was being observed. He was tired and wounded and preoccupied with how he would find Champion. Even if he had been fresh and alert, the saurial wizard might not have sensed the eyes watching him, for those eyes spied upon him with magic from over a hundred miles away.

The Mouth of Moander, high priestess of the Darkbringer, regarded Grypht's fleeing image in an enchanted pool of water. Moments after Moander had used the possessed body of the Harper Kyre to stun Akabar, the god had sent the Mouth of Moander to the pool to cast a spell to scry upon the half-elf. It was important to the Darkbringer that the high priestess see this Turmishman whom the god desired to possess beyond all others.

The previous year when Moander had possessed Akabar, the god had been so pleased with the mage's well-trained mind and talents that it had taken special care with the mage's body so the possession could be permanent. The god had made the error, though, of using Akabar in a battle against his own friends, and the paladin Dragonbait had managed to free the mage. Afterward, Akabar succeeded in destroying Moander. Now, though, the god had possessed new minions and had forced them to built it a new body. Moander demanded that Akabar be brought to the body to witness its resurrection.

Akabar had proven difficult to find, though. He had left Turmish, and some powerful misdirection spell made it impossible for the Mouth of Moander to discover the mage with scrying magic. Moander suspected Akabar was in Alias's company, so Kyre had been sent to Shadowdale to discover if the Nameless Bard knew of Alias's or the mage's whereabouts. Kyre had succeeded in discovering Akabar and separating him from Alias or whatever had protected him from scrying magic. Moander was too pleased with the half-elf's successes to be annoyed by the inconvenience of her violent death.

The images of Grypht and Akabar began to blur and fade as the scrying spell cast on the pool of water wore off, but not before the Mouth of Moander had time to note that Grypht fled west from Shadowdale.

"Kyre recruited other servants on her way to Shadowdale," the Mouth of Moander said. "It will be a simple matter to send flyers to alert them to intercept Grypht and Akabar. The Turmishman will not escape the destiny the Darkbringer has assigned to him."

The two saurial priests who attended the priestess nodded.

"The flyers are too weak to travel so far," the priestess cried suddenly with vehemence.

The two priests shifted uneasily. The priestess's habit of arguing with herself frightened all her people who witnessed it.

"They only need to fly away," the priestess answered herself with a cooler tone of voice. "It matters not if they return."

The Mouth of Moander glared at her reflection on the dark surface of the pool of water. A female saurial with pearly white scales glared back up at her with disgust. Before Moander had possessed her, her name had been Coral, and she had served the goddess of luck. Then she had protected all her people, but now, because she had been too weak to resist Moander, there was no evil the god could not force her to perpetrate on even the smallest or most innocent saurial.

For the moment, Moander had loosened its hold on her mind, as it always did after having used the priestess's body to cast a powerful spell such as scrying. Coral fought against the control of the Darkbringer so strongly that the god was forced to withdraw so their battle of wills did not use so much energy that the tendrils of possession controlling the priestess were destroyed.

Moander lurked in the back of Coral's consciousness, though, ready to pounce on her thoughts should she try to act against the god. In the meantime, the god savored with a cruel delight the anguish and horror Coral felt at every action it forced her to perform. Most especially, the Darkbringer enjoyed controlling the priestess and forcing her to speak aloud its evil thoughts. Unable or unwilling to keep her emotional outbursts in check, Coral always argued aloud with what the god had made her say. Hence the priestess appeared to be arguing with herself.

None of Coral's people understood what was really happening. Although all the members of her tribe who had been captured by Moander were infected with its tendrils of possession, most were only controlled physically. The Darkbringer had no need to control the minds of ordinary saurials; however, the god had magically shackled the thoughts of any spell-casting saurials it caught. The ordinary saurials thought the priestess had turned evil and insane, while the spell-casters, who had been enchanted to love the Darkbringer, thought the priestess was merely insane.

"If Grypht cannot be captured," Moander said, addressing the priests through Coral's mouth, "he must not be left alive. He might yet find allies to interfere with our plans. He searches now for Champion, the paladin whom people of this world call

Dragonbait. If our servants discover Champion, however, they must bring him to me alive. In order to enslave the servant Alias to the master's will, Champion must be sacrificed with special ceremony. Mine will be the hand that destroys the paladin."

"No!" Coral shouted with anguish. "I want no part of his destruction!"

The priests shook their heads disapprovingly.

With a complete sense of hopelessness, Coral envied Kyre her death. It was horrible enough to Coral that she was forced to slaughter sacrifice after sacrifice to further strengthen Moander's new body. She didn't wish to live to arrange the conquest of Grypht or the Darkbringer's reunion with Akabar, but most especially the priestess would rather die than spill the blood of her former lover. "Lady Luck," she called out to the goddess she had once served, "please let me die!"

Moander's tendrils of possession used the priestess's mouth to argue with herself. "No," Coral was forced to say. "I have something to live for: vengeance. Champion's insults cannot be forgiven. I must see him humbled. "

As the priestess spoke these words, the scent of roses and baked bread and mint all wafted from the glands at her throat. She felt anger and grief and shame, for she was not able to argue with Moander's words. She had struggled to forgive the paladin for leaving her, but she had never really succeeded, and imagining him humbled was a source of perverse pleasure to her. Unfortunately this feeling was Moander's foothold in her mind. The god had twisted and perverted it to seduce her from her natural feelings of compassion. Should Champion actually be brought before her, Coral feared that Moander would have little trouble goading her into harming the paladin.

"Champion despised me when I worshiped the goddess of luck," Moander made Coral say aloud.

"No," Coral insisted, trying desperately to keep from growing angry with the paladin. "He merely disapproved. He never despised me."

"Now that I am Moander's priestess, he will be horrified and repulsed by me. I will kill him gladly to wipe that look from his face," Moander said through Coral's mouth.

The two priests nodded with approval.

Coral thrust her hand over her mouth to stop the god's hateful words. Inside her head, she heard the god think, *And after you slay him, I'll release your mind to relish your guilt and grief.*

Coral clawed at the fin on top of her head in a futile attempt to sweep Moander from her brain.

You only live to serve and amuse me, priestess, he reminded her in her thoughts.

Coral shrieked like a madwoman and crumbled to the ground, sobbing hysterically.

The two priests stood beside Coral, annoyed at her peculiar behavior, unable to understand why someone who was insane had been granted the honor of serving as the Mouth of Moander. Why hadn't one of them been chosen? they both wondered resentfully.

Moander gathered up all the tendrils of possession inside Coral's mind, like a rider taking up a horse's reins, and drove her back to her duties as the Mouth of Moander.

❦ 6 ❦

The Old Priestess

Morala the Harper, priestess of Milil, leaned over the table in the Harpers courtroom and stared into the silver basin she had filled with holy water. When she was satisfied that the water was completely still, Morala began singing a wordless melody. The silver basin and the surface of the water began vibrating with the power of the priestess's voice and the magic she summoned with her spell.

After several minutes, the water began to sparkle and shine from a source of magic beneath its surface. Morala ceased singing and concentrated on the colors swirling in the water. Gradually the colors coalesced into solid shapes.

"I see him," the priestess whispered.

"Is he alive?" Breck Orcsbane asked eagerly, moving toward the priestess.

Lord Mourngrym held the ranger back with a hand on his shoulder. Before Morala had begun her scrying spell, she had cautioned them not to distract her or touch the table on which the silver bowl rested. Breck was a veteran fighter, but too inexperienced with magic to realize the danger of disregarding the priestess's warning.

Morala squinted at the images that had formed on the surface of the water. The gangly figure with the flowing gray hair and beard was unmistakably Elminster, but Morala had never seen anything quite like the scenery in the field of vision afforded by her scrying spell. Blue-green ferns, lavender horsetails, and green-and-yellow-striped mushrooms towered over the sage. Great trees, their trunks bare but for a small crown of red and green fronds, waved behind the sage like grasses in the wind.

Elminster stood in the strange forest, apparently alone and uninjured. His lips moved, but Morala's spell did not allow her to hear what he said, or any other sound about him. The sage's head was tilted back, and he gazed alertly at something high overhead. Morala brought her hands together over the surface of the water and then pulled them away. The view in the water widened to include more of Elminster's surroundings. The sage appeared as a blot of gray on the water's surface, but now the priestess could see what held his attention.

Five winged creatures, as exotic to Morala as the plants, flew in a **V** formation over Elminster's head. Each was as large as an ancient dragon and had a vaguely dragonlike silhouette. They were covered with frayed, almost featherlike scales, and they were as brightly colored as any bird. Their heads were bright scarlet, their throats orange, their long serpentine necks yellow, and their bodies hues of blue and green. As the group watched in horror, the creatures dove toward the sage.

Elminster motioned with his hands, and a bright light flared from the surface of the water. Morala gasped.

"What is it?" Breck demanded anxiously.

"Elminster just cast a meteor swarm," the priestess said. "He battles monsters such as I have never seen before!"

The lead creature fell from the sky, knocking down several trees as it crashed to the earth. Its companions pulled up just as Elminster released a second meteor swarm.

From her magical vantage point, Morala could see a great cat stalking the mage, sneaking up behind him. The beast was twice the size of a tiger, with a mottled orange and brown hide. It halted ten yards from Elminster. The muscles in its haunches tautened and twitched as the cat prepared to leap.

"Elminster, behind you!" Morala cried out instinctively, though she knew the sage could not hear her.

Something alerted the sage to the danger, though, for he spun about with his hands spread out before him, thumbs touching, and sent a fan of fire shooting from his fingertips.

The cat twisted in midleap, trying, without success, to avoid the sage's fiery barrage. One side of the beast burst into flame, and it fell to the ground and rolled in the dirt to smother the fire burning its pelt. Before the cat had a chance to rise to its feet, Elminster pointed at it, and the beast crumbled to dust.

Elminster turned his attention back to the remaining feather dragons, who had circled and returned. As the dragons dropped down and soared over the sage, great plumes of sparkling dust shot from the maws of all four monsters, but when the dust had blown away, Elminster remained standing, apparently unaffected. The sage cast a wall of fire across the feather dragons' flight path. Two of the beasts were unable to pull up in time to avoid passing through the curtain of flame. They plunged through it and immediately crashed to the earth like meteors.

Watching the sage do battle while unable to hear any of the accompanying sounds felt unnatural and eerie to Morala, yet she kept her eyes fixed on the water. She wished the blessings of Milil on the sage, though she suspected her god might have little power over events in the strange world where Elminster was now.

As the last pair of feather dragons came swooping down on the sage, talons extended, prepared to tear him to pieces, Elminster cast a forked bolt of lightning. Before the scorched bodies slammed into him, the sage winked through a dimension door, emerging some fifty feet away, where he could not be crushed in the monsters' death throes. Witnessing Elminster's unscathed emergence from the battle, the priestess breathed a sigh of relief. Elminster turned in Morala's direction and seemed to look right at the priestess. His eyes twinkled with mischief, and he gave a little theatrical bow. Then he turned away again and walked off into the strange forest.

The colors in the water began to swirl in a chaotic pattern and then fade. The water began to bubble; then, in a great burst of steam, it evaporated away. Morala stepped away from the table and swayed, exhausted from the effort of scrying.

Lord Mourngrym stepped forward and helped the frail, elderly woman to a chair.

Morala leaned back, her eyes closed. "Elminster is alive and well," she said weakly. "The moment before my spell wore off, he had just defeated several monsters the likes of which I have never seen in the Realms. He appeared in no immediate danger. His instincts were sharp enough to note that he was being scried upon. He does not seem to be anyone's prisoner."

"Then why doesn't he return?" Breck asked.

"I do not know," the priestess answered. "He travels on foot in a strange world, and I couldn't perceive his goal. Perhaps some other wizard has summoned the sage to perform some service and he cannot return until it is completed. Perhaps he does not realize we have need of him here."

Alias stood in the doorway to the Harpers courtroom. She had returned from speaking with Elminster's scribe, Lhaeo, just in time to hear the priestess report what she had seen in her scrying.

"What of Nameless?" Alias asked from across the room.

Morala thrust out her neck and squinted, trying to focus on Alias. The priestess motioned for the swordswoman to come closer.

Alias strode across the courtroom until she stood a few feet from the small old woman.

"Your grace," Mourngrym said to Morala, "this is—"

"Alias of Westgate, Nameless's singer," Morala finished the introduction herself. "I could tell by her resemblance to Cassana. I am Morala of Milil, child."

"I know. I could tell by your garb," Alias said. The priestess's crimson robe, elaborately embroidered with gold dragons, was standard ceremonial garb among those who served the patron god of bards.

"Alias, this is ranger Breck Orcsbane," Mourngrym added, motioning toward a brawny young woodsman in leather armor. The ranger's face was clean-shaven, but he wore his blond hair in a plait that reached his waist. Alias recognized his face; she had seen him in the Old Skull Inn last night listening to her sing.

The swordswoman nodded briefly, then turned back abruptly to Morala. "Did you see Nameless?" she asked. Although her eyes shone hopefully, her heart pounded with fear.

Morala shook her head. "No," she replied. "He was not with Elminster. I shall have to scry for him separately."

"Then what are you waiting for?" Alias asked impatiently.

Lord Mourngrym laid a hand on the swordswoman's shoulder. "Scrying is a most difficult spell, Alias," his lordship said softly. "Morala must rest for a while."

Alias clenched her fist. It was frustrating enough having to rely on spell-casters to find Nameless, but being forced to wait was maddening.

Mourngrym sensed the swordswoman's tension. As a fighter himself, he understood how she felt. She wanted to act, to hunt for Nameless, to kill anything that threatened him, to rescue him. She knew, though, that she couldn't run off without an inkling of a direction to run in, but that realization didn't make the waiting any easier. "What did the sage's scribe say?" he asked the swordswoman, trying to keep her mind occupied.

Alias huffed out some of her anger, then replied, "Lhaeo said Elminster's evasion spell hadn't been triggered, so the sage definitely wasn't dead, wounded, mindless, or desperate to leave wherever he is, but you already knew that from scrying or him. Since Elminster hadn't planned to leave, he didn't give Lhaeo any instructions about how to contact him. Lhaeo said a few other things, too," Alias added, glancing at Morala and Breck, uncertain how they would receive what she had to say.

"What?" Mourngrym asked.

"First off, from what Kyre said—that Elminster disappeared and Grypht appeared in his place—Lhaeo suspects that Grypht used a variation of a teleport spell called transference. By switching places with another mage who's already standing in a safe place, it guarantees that a mage can teleport without ending up too high off the ground or inside a stone wall. It's a rare spell. According to Lhaeo, you could count the mages in the Realms who know it on the fingers of one hand. According to Lhaeo, there aren't any creatures from the lower planes that can use it. Lhaeo also said that there was no way anything from the Nine Hells or the Abyss could have gotten past Elminster's wards on this tower. He'd bet his father's sword that Grypht is a wizard, not a monster."

"If Kyre says Grypht is from the Nine Hells, then that's where it's from," Breck insisted. "Kyre would never make a mistake about something like that. She's very accurate."

"Just how well do you know her?" Alias asked curiously.

"She brought me into the Harpers," Breck explained. "We've worked together often in the past."

"I see," Alias said. If Kyre had been Breck's sponsor for the Harpers, the swordswoman realized she'd never convince Breck that Kyre was capable of error. She looked to Mourngrym to support Lhaeo's opinion.

His lordship looked uncertain. "Grypht did break Elminster's one-way spell on Nameless's cell," Mourngrym pointed out to Alias.

"That's not the same thing as a ward against evil creatures," the swordswoman argued.

"That's true," Morala agreed. "There are important differences. A protection ward is very cut-and-dried, but Elminster's one-way spell required provisions so that the servants and guards and the sage could enter and leave Nameless's cell unhindered. I suppose the spell would have also allowed Nameless to leave if the room was burning, say, or in the case of some other emergency that threatened the bard's life. If Elminster's wording had been ambiguous on some provision, the spell might have broken from the strain of determining whether or not the provision was met."

"Excuse me, your lordship," a voice said from the hallway.

Mourngrym turned toward the voice. A tower guard stood at the door to the Harpers' courtroom.

"Yes, Shend? What is it?" his lordship asked.

"Captain Thurbal has finished checking the tower security. He said to tell you everything seems in order, except for two things. First, he can't get into Nameless's cell; the door's locked.

"Akabar Bel Akash felt unwell, so he's resting in there," Mourngrym said. "Harper Kyre is tending him. No need to disturb them. I'll check with them later. What's the second thing, Shend?"

"When I was on guard duty early this morning, I let someone pass through the gate without announcing her. She said it wasn't necessary. Now we can't find her, and no one saw her leave the tower. Captain Thurbal thought it a little strange, so he wanted me to report it to you personally."

"Who was it, Shend?" Mourngrym asked.

"That halfling Harper," Shend replied.

"What halfling Harper?" Morala asked.

Shend's eyes wandered up to the ceiling, as if the halfling's name might be written there.

Alias felt her heart skip a beat. It can't be, she thought.

"You know the one, Lady Alias," Shend said. "The bard what helped you and Dragonbait kill the kalmari two years back. Tree name she 'ad . . . Peach or Maple or—"

"Olive," Alias supplied, rubbing her temples with her fingers.

"That were it. Olive Rustiepan."

"Ruskettle," Alias corrected.

"Who?" Breck asked.

"There aren't any halfling bards," Morala pointed out.

"She's a rogue," Alias explained. "A thief . . . a minstrel . . . an adventuress."

"Olive Ruskettle," Breck murmured. "I don't recall any Harpers by that name. Who was her sponsor?" he asked.

Alias swallowed. "Nameless," she said softly.

"Nameless!" Morala exclaimed. "You mean he gave her a Harper's pin?"

Alias nodded.

"Of all the reckless, arrogant— The man is impossible!" the priestess declared.

"Olive freed him from Cassana's dungeon in Westgate, then helped him rescue Dragonbait and me," Alias explained.

"She could be the Princess of Cormyr and we still wouldn't accept Nameless's sponsorship of her," Morala insisted. "Nameless was exiled in disgrace. He has no business—"

"Excuse me, your grace," Breck said, "but we might yet reverse our decision, in which case this Ruskettle might be of some use to us—that is, providing she wasn't involved with this Grypht creature. Is it possible she might have allied with Grypht in the hope that it would rescue Nameless?" the ranger asked Alias.

Alias paused to consider. After the close call Olive had had with the pseudo-halfling Phalse, who had turned out to be a fiend from Tarterus, one would have thought that the halfling had learned her lesson about dealing with strangers. Still, Olive could be awfully unpredictable. She might do something truly foolish if she believed it would help Nameless. She had seemed exceptionally fond of the bard last year in Westgate.

On the other hand, Olive's affection might work the other way. Alias had also noted that as long as Nameless's attention had been fixed on her, the halfling had seemed to behave with unusual civility and honor. "She wouldn't suggest a plan to Nameless that she knew he'd disapprove of," Alias answered.

"Where could she have gone?" Mourngrym asked.

"She would have tried to see Nameless," Alias said.

"She would have been trapped inside Nameless's cell, then," Mourngrym said. "She could still be in there, hiding behind the curtains or something."

"Unless Grypht took her along with Nameless," Breck suggested.

"Kyre didn't mention seeing a halfling," Mourngrym pointed out.

"A halfling could easily hide behind such a beast," Breck replied. "Kyre might have missed seeing her in the excitement of the moment."

"Or perhaps Kyre mistook Olive for an imp," Alias said with a hint of sarcasm.

Breck glowered at the swordswoman. "Grypht *was* a denizen of the Nine Hells," the ranger growled. "It had horns and scales and claws and a tail."

"I think," Morala interjected calmly, "that whatever Grypht is, it is not as important as where it took Nameless."

"If your grace will excuse me," Mourngrym said, "I'm going to have a second look at Nameless's cell. Alias, do you want to come along to see how Akabar is doing?"

Alias glanced anxiously at Morala.

As if she could read the swordswoman's mind, the priestess said, "I think Alias should stay here to keep me company until I recover sufficient strength to scry for Nameless. Breck, why don't you accompany Lord Mourngrym? Maybe the halfling left some tracks you could follow or something."

Breck sensed Morala was dismissing him, but he shrugged indifferently. Searching for a halfling would be far more interesting than watching the old priestess fuss and chant over a bowl of water.

The ranger and the guard, Shend, followed Lord Mourngrym out of the courtroom.

When the two of them were alone together in the room, Morala motioned for the swordswoman to have a seat near her.

As Alias pulled out a chair from behind the table, the priestess sat with her eyes closed, absentmindedly humming an A-minor scale, at the same time brushing her fingertips along the golden embroidery of her robe. Alias noticed specks of gold flaking from the robe. Suddenly Morala started visibly and snapped her eyes open, as if she'd been napping. Alias wondered if perhaps the ancient priestess's wits weren't beginning to flake away like the embroidered decorations on her ceremonial robe.

"How much longer until you're rested enough to scry again?" Alias asked the priestess.

"Not long," Morala replied, smiling at the swordswoman's impatience. "Perhaps, in the meantime, you could tell me if you know anything about these disappearances."

Alias stiffened. "You think this was a plan of mine to rescue

Nameless, don't you?" the swordswoman asked, unable to keep the anger from creeping into her tone.

"No . . . not really. I've been told you are a good woman. However, we must investigate every possibility before we can rule it out," Morala replied calmly. "So tell me, child, did you have anything to do with Elminster's or Nameless's disappearance?"

"No, I didn't," Alias answered hotly. "If I had wanted to free Nameless, I certainly wouldn't have involved Elminster, and I wouldn't have needed help from some wizard or whatever this Grypht is. And I wouldn't admit it to you, anyway."

"Yes . . . I can believe that," Morala said with a chuckle. "But then, I've cast a detect lie spell on you."

Alias's eyes narrowed angrily. She was unaccustomed to having her word questioned, let alone magically analyzed. She was even more annoyed that she hadn't caught on to Morala's spell. The old priestess hadn't been drifting off to sleep after all; she'd been concentrating on her spell. "I should have realized. Milil is the lord of all songs. Music is a language, too. That humming was actually your spell chant, wasn't it?" the swordswoman asked.

Morala nodded. "Nameless taught you well," she said. For a few moments, she studied Alias's face. "You may look like Cassana, but there is nothing of her in you," she said.

"Did you know Cassana personally," Alias asked, "or are you merely comparing me to the character in the opera about her and her lich lover Zrie Prakis?"

Morala chuckled. "I knew her. I wrote that opera."

Alias's eyes widened. "You did? I . . . I didn't know. I've never heard it sung. Elminster told me about it. Why did you ever want to write an opera about Cassana?"

"At the time, Cassana's evil was a danger to us all," the priestess explained, "but she had many powerful friends, and the Harpers didn't have the strength to drive her from the north. The opera made the details of the sorceress's life common knowledge. Cassana couldn't stand ridicule. The gossip following the opera's performance caused her sufficient embarrassment to leave the region," Morala said. A grin lit up her wrinkled face.

Alias grinned back. She found herself liking the foxy old woman, even if she was a priestess and one of Nameless's judges.

"I have something else I want to show you," the priestess said, holding out a lump of what appeared to be ordinary red mud. "I picked this up from the floor. Grypht held it when he first appeared. It's clay—of very high quality and rare color."

"Maybe this duke of the Nine Hells is a potter," Alias joked.

Morala smiled gently. "The clay was glowing when Grypht first appeared . . . as would a spell component," she explained.

"Don't creatures from the lower planes have a natural ability to cast magic without spell components?" Alias asked.

"That's what I've always been told," Morala answered. "Unfortunately, or perhaps fortunately, Kyre knocked the clay out of the beast's hand and ruined its spell before it was cast, so we don't know what the beast intended. In clerical spells, clay is a component that affects stone, though I'm sure it has other uses in spells for wizards. Elminster might have been able to identify such spells for us. Could your friend Akabar Bel Akash do so?"

"Akabar's pretty clever," Alias replied. "When he recovers, we can ask him. So you think Kyre made a mistake?"

"In elvish, Kyre means 'flawless,' " Morala said, shaking her head. "She has a reputation for not making mistakes. I think it more likely she wanted us to believe that Grypht was something evil." Morala smiled slyly.

"You mean you think she lied?" Alias asked with surprise. "Why would she do that?"

"She may have put some personal goal ahead of her duties as a Harper," Morala suggested. "Kyre is a bard, after all."

"You think *she* planned Nameless's escape!" Alias guessed. "Grypht is just a smoke screen. Then Nameless is all right!" Alias said excitedly. "You don't have to scry for him!"

"But I do," Morala insisted. "Kyre might have made a foolish alliance. Grypht may not be from the Nine Hells, but he still could be an evil wizard. He might be holding Nameless against his will, threatening his life."

"But suppose Nameless is all right?" Alias asked.

"He must still be brought back here for his trial," Morala said.

Alias's face fell. "Don't you think Nameless has suffered enough?"

"You misunderstand, child. The Harpers did not send Nameless to the Citadel of White Exile to make him suffer. We sent him there in order to protect other innocents from his reckless behavior."

"But you don't have to send him back," Alias insisted. "He's sorry about the apprentice who was killed and the one who was hurt. He wouldn't do anything like that again. Besides, now that he's done creating his singer, he's satisfied."

"Is he?" Morala mused. She leaned forward and stroked Alias's hair with a withered hand. "He would be a fool not to be pleased with you, child. Tell me, do you love Nameless?"

Alias lifted her chin and answered proudly, "Yes, I do."

"As a daughter loves a father?" Morala asked.

Alias nodded.

Morala pursed her lips together and shook her head sadly. Alias could see that the old woman's eyes were moist with tears. "He does not deserve your love," the priestess whispered.

"Love is something people give freely," Alias argued. "It's not a commodity to be earned or forfeited."

Morala sighed and clasped her hands together in her lap. "Yes. That's the problem, all right. It doesn't have to be earned, and it is not easily forfeited." Morala was silent for several moments. Then she said coldly, "Maryje loved Nameless, though not as a father. Maryje was one of Nameless's apprentices . . . the one who was wounded."

"She lost her voice, then she committed suicide," Alias recalled from Nameless's tale. "Is that why you can't forgive Nameless . . . because Maryje was a friend of yours?"

Morala took Alias's hands in her own and squeezed them hard. "I cannot forgive Nameless because he lied, and his lie bound Maryje to her wounds, and her wounds bound her to her shame, and her shame bound her to her death. The truth would have set her free, and she would not have killed herself."

"What lie?" Alias demanded. "What are you talking about?"

"Ask him," Morala demanded. "Ask Nameless to tell you the truth—the truth he would not admit to Elminster, the truth he would not tell the Harpers, the truth about himself that even he is ashamed of. If he will do that, he will set himself free and even I will forgive him."

Alias pulled her hands away from the priestess and backed her chair away. Her heart was racing wildly, and despite her wool tunic, she felt chilled. "Suppose I don't want to hear this truth?" she asked.

"I thought you loved him," Morala said. "Would you have him

bear the burden of his guilt to his grave?"

"All right, I'll ask him," Alias said defiantly, "and he'll tell me, and I won't love him any less, whatever it is he says."

"I did not think that you would," Morala replied.

"Why won't you just tell me what it is?" Alias asked with a growing sense of frustration.

"I intend this test to remind Nameless of what he has already taught you about love but seems unable to remember for himself," the priestess explained. Morala's mood became suddenly businesslike. She slapped her hands down on her thighs and said, "First, though, we must find Nameless. I am rested enough, now." She held her hand out.

Alias rose hastily to her feet and helped the old woman rise from her chair and return to the table. The swordswoman watched curiously while Morala cleaned out the silver bowl and refilled it with more holy water.

A growl came from across the room. Alias looked up. Dragonbait stood in the courtroom door with Akabar's wife, Zhara. The saurial paladin pointed at a spot on the floor directly before him. He wasn't in a patient mood.

"Excuse me," Alias said to Morala. "I have to see what my friend wants."

Morala nodded without looking up from her silver bowl. Alias hurried toward the lizard. Dragonbait thrust a dead, singed thistle at her and signed furiously.

"What do you mean, you were attacked by thistles?" Alias asked with annoyance. "What were you doing? Walking through Korhun Lherar's old pastures?"

Dragonbait signed again.

"In her room?" Alias asked. "Of course I didn't send them. What do I know about thistles?"

Where's Akabar? the saurial signed.

"Resting," Alias said. "He . . . uh, he wasn't feeling very well," she explained briefly, not wanting to give Zhara the details of Akabar's attack. She'd heard enough of the priestess's interpretations.

Take us to him, Dragonbait demanded.

"Morala is about to begin to scry for Nameless," Alias explained. "He's missing. He may have been kidnapped. Can't you wait?" she asked impatiently.

No. Immediately, Dragonbait signed.

Alias huffed angrily, but from the garlic scent the saurial emitted, she could tell he wasn't going to give in. "All right," she growled. Just in case Kyre hadn't yet made any progress in convincing Akabar of the folly of his priestess wife, Alias suggested, "Zhara, maybe you'd like to wait here."

Dragonbait shook his head.

"She'll be fine here," Alias said, signing to Dragonbait that Zhara must stay in the courtroom.

The saurial ignored her. He stomped his foot.

"Fine," Alias whispered angrily. "Have it your way." The swordswoman looked back at Morala. The elderly priestess had aleady begun her chant, so Alias didn't dare disturb her. "Follow me," she said, striding purposefully out of the courtroom.

Morala was vaguely aware that Alias had departed, but she was too wrapped up in her spell chant to find out where the swordswoman had gone. Several minutes later, the water in the silver bowl began to sparkle and shine, and the priestess ceased her chant.

Squinting into the water, Morala could just barely discern the features of the Nameless Bard. His face was illuminated by a flickering torch, but everything else about him was masked in darkness. The priestess sighed. The bard could be anywhere—in a cave somewhere on the same world as Elminster, in the tunnels beneath Waterdeep, in a closet in the tower of Ashaba—anywhere.

Morala motioned over the water with her hands. Now she could see a second torch, held by a small figure walking beside Nameless. "Well, well. It must be our little halfling Harper," the priestess muttered. As she turned her attention back to Nameless, an angry look swept over the bard's face. "What's wrong, Nameless?" Morala mused aloud. "Where are you, and what are you up to?"

❧ 7 ❧

Beneath Finder's Keep

Finder cursed under his breath as he and Olive turned a corner of the underground tunnels and were forced to another halt. Olive sighed with resignation. Their way was blocked by a wall of rocks, dirt, and mud where the ceiling had caved into the passage. It was the fourth such obstacle they'd encountered. The first had been at the base of the stairs that led from the ruined manor house to the underground tunnels. It had taken them an hour to clear a hole through it. The second collapse hadn't been as severe, and within half an hour they'd wriggled their way through. When they came upon the third collapse, Finder had decided to backtrack to the stairs and try a different route through the maze of twisting tunnels. Now they had no choice but to start digging again.

"If I hadn't lost the stone, we could have taken a dimensional door into the workshop," Finder growled, kicking at the base of the pile of rubble.

Trying to keep Finder from dwelling on the loss of his stone, Olive remarked, "Unless the roof in the workshop collapsed, too. Then we'd be transported beneath a pile of rubble and dead."

"No," Finder replied, shoving his torch into the base of the rubble. "Then the dimension door would leave us in the astral plane. The workshop will be fine, though," he said. "Nothing could have gotten in there."

"Half a ton of rock doesn't need a key," Olive pointed out, setting her own torch beside Finder's.

"True," Finder said. "but these ceilings haven't collapsed from anything natural." He pointed to a portion of the arched ceiling that was still intact. It was lined with quarried stone, perfectly fitted. "We haven't found any of the quarried stone in the piles," he said.

"It would probably be at the bottom of the pile," Olive replied.

"We haven't dug that deep."

Finder shook his head. "Some of it would be on the edges. It's impossible for an arch to collapse unless some of the stone is removed." The bard pointed to the top of the collapsed portion. "It wasn't pried or chipped out, and it didn't fracture in a straight line. See how circular the collapsed parts are—making an arc right through the stones?"

"Yes," Olive said hesitantly, feeling a little nervous.

"It's been disintegrated," Finder explained.

"Oh, great!" the halfling muttered.

"Recently, too, I'd say, judging from the lack of water damage," the bard added. "Probably by the same person or creature who dispelled the continual light enchantments that used to be on the archway keystones."

"Marvelous," Olive replied sarcastically. "And we're digging our way right toward whoever did it. Did it ever occur to you that this person or creature might have blocked the passages because he, she, or it wanted to be left alone?"

"I don't care," Finder snapped. "If it's there, it's in my home, and I'm going to get rid of."

"Right," Olive said without enthusiasm. "Suppose you get disintegrated first?"

"There's enough magic in my workshop to demolish an army. I created the finder's stone there," he said. He began pulling small boulders out of the rubble.

Olive scrabbled up the pile and began digging out dirt and mud with her tiny pack shovel. Finder had broken the handle using it as a wedge on a boulder in the first pile of rubble they'd dug through, so now only Olive could use it comfortably. "You mean," she corrected the bard, "that that's where you altered the stone's already magical nature with a piece of enchanted para-elemental ice."

Finder looked up at the halfling with a hint of surprise. "And where did you learn that?" he asked.

"Elminster was explaining it to the Harper tribunal when I . . . uh, passed through," Olive said.

"He was, was he? Well, that stone was one of the most brilliant ideas of the century," Finder said, tossing more rocks into the passageway behind them. "Para-elemental ice is far colder than ordinary ice," he explained as they worked. "It keeps the finder's stone from overheating no matter how much lore or how many songs or spells are stored inside it. The cold also helps the stone retrieve any information I've put into it as fast as a human mind could."

Olive recalled that Finder had once compared his own memory and voice to polished ice. "Did you use another piece of this magical ice in Alias?" she asked.

"Yes," Finder replied. "The most talented wizards of the era told me it couldn't be done, that it wouldn't work, but they were all wrong. Alias lives, and she will never forget anything I taught her. She's even better than the Finder's stone, since she can learn new things without my help. She amazes even Elminster," the bard boasted.

"I think Elminster likes her more than he's amazed by her," Olive said.

"Don't let the sage's grandfatherly act fool you. Alias is the most remarkable piece of craftsmanship Elminster has ever seen, and he knows it. She's a constant reminder that I was right and he was wrong. He'll always regret that he turned me down when I asked for his help trying to create the first singer."

Olive strongly doubted that Elminster felt any such thing. She was beginning to feel less tolerant of Finder and his vanity. She was hungry and tired and dirty and, quite frankly, afraid of whatever it was that had disintegrated the ceiling. Finder had failed to recognize the danger Kyre presented, and Grypht had paid the price. The halfling had no desire to become a casualty of the bard's scheme to recover his home. It was time, she decided, to prick his ego, to bring him back to reality and get him to reconsider heading back to civilization.

"So," Olive said, "what went wrong with the first singer?" she asked casually.

"I was careless," Finder replied, rocking a large stone loose from the pile. "I inserted the enchanted ice too quickly, and it exploded."

"That's what you told Elminster. But what really happened?" Olive asked.

"Why would I lie to Elminster?" Finder asked, without denying that there was more to the story.

Olive grinned. "I'll know that when you tell me what happened," she replied.

"What do you know about it, Olive girl?" the bard asked with a light tone, but the halfling could tell she'd made him nervous.

"I know that Flattery came to life," Olive said, "but even though he looked just like you, he didn't turn out to be as dutiful a child as Alias. He didn't want to go into the family music business. He took up magic instead."

Finder stopped working and stepped away from the blockade, looking up at Olive with astonishment, perhaps even fear. "How did you know that?" he gasped.

Olive sat down on a boulder. She laid down her shovel, pulled off her gloves, and ran her fingers through her hair, trying to brush out the dirt. "It's nothing special. I just happened to run into him—Flattery, that is."

Finder rolled his eyes to the ceiling, muttering, "Halfling luck!" He made it sound like a curse.

Olive laughed. "You don't believe in that silly superstition, do you?"

Finder leaned back against the passage wall. "Of course I do. You're living proof. Why do you think Cassana and Phalse tried so hard to get you to turn against Alias?"

Olive's eyes narrowed. It was embarrassing just remembering how close she had come to betraying Alias, Akabar, and Dragonbait. "Because they were vicious sadists," she snapped, "who wanted to see just how frightened they could make me."

"The truth is, they were afraid of you. You and all your race never follow the score. You're always improvising without the composer's consent. You destroyed all their plans with one decision and your halfling luck. I'm beginning to know how they must have felt," Finder said with an embarrassed grin. "And just what do you mean, you 'just happened' to run into Flattery?" he asked curiously.

Finder's sudden interest in her luck made Olive nervous. It was bad luck to talk about luck. "You tell me first. What went wrong when you created Flattery?" Olive asked.

Finder shrugged. "He didn't want to sing. We argued about it, and he got angry. I had two apprentices with me at the time, Kirkson and Maryje. Flattery killed Kirkson and injured Maryje. Then he ran off. By the time I'd gotten help for Maryje, the trail was cold. Then the Harpers brought me to trial and exiled me. I tried scrying for Flattery all these years, but he kept himself hidden with his magic."

"Did you name him Flattery?"

Finder's face turned stormy. "That was Kirkson's fault," he said. "A practical joke to tease me. Once he told the creature that was its name, it wouldn't accept a different one."

"What were you going to name it?"

"I hadn't decided yet."

"Hadn't decided or hadn't even considered giving it a name?" Olive guessed.

Finder looked contrite. "I remembered to give Alias one," he said defensively.

"Alias. Some name," Olive replied. "I still can't figure out why you lied to Elminster."

"I was afraid the Harpers might hunt down the crea— Flattery. I hoped if he was free, he might relent and sing my songs after all."

"Not a chance," Olive said. "Flattery hated your guts. He wanted to destroy you and wipe out the whole rest of the Wyvernspur clan, too."

Finder turned away from the halfling. In the torchlight, Olive couldn't tell what emotion he was concealing. With his back to her, the bard asked, "So how did you meet him?"

"I was in Immersea," Olive explained. "You know the wyvern's spur—your family heirloom that turns the bearer into a wyvern and protects him from magic and—"

Finder spun around and interrupted her. "I know all about the spur," he said with annoyance. "I watched my idiot brother use it often enough. Get to the point, please."

"Well, Flattery didn't know all about it. Fourteen years ago, one member of your family, Cole Wyvernspur, Giogi Wyvernspur's father, discovered that Flattery was slaughtering people. Cole figured out that Flattery was a member of the family and challenged him to a duel to keep the family honor intact, so to speak. Flattery killed Cole, but Cole, using the spur, nearly killed Flattery. So Flattery tried to steal the spur, thinking he could use it against you and the rest of the clan. Giogi stopped him, though."

"Giogi? Giogi Wyvernspur? That ridiculous fop whom Alias nearly killed last year?" Finder asked.

"That's the one. Grown some since then. Nice boy."

"What happened to Flattery?" Finder demanded impatiently.

"Giogi had to kill him," Olive said softly. "Even if Flattery couldn't use the spur, he would have wiped out the Wyvernspur family. He was powerful enough and certainly crazy enough."

Finder looked down at the tunnel floor and gave a resigned sigh. Olive thought he might be grieving, but when he looked back up, she saw a look of relief on his face.

"If it hadn't been for Dragonbait, Alias would have been just as bad as Flattery," Olive said. "Maybe worse."

"No, she wouldn't!" Finder answered vehemently. "I didn't make the same mistake with her."

"What mistake?"

Finder didn't answer. Instead, he bent over and resumed pulling stones from the debris that obstructed the passageway.

Olive reached down and grabbed one of the bard's fingers. "What mistake?" she repeated.

"Nothing," Finder said. "You're right. Dragonbait made all the difference."

Olive couldn't think of anything that could make Finder relinquish any credit for his success with Alias, but she was certain he was lying. However, she wasn't sure she really wanted to know why. She did know that she didn't want to see the workroom where Flattery had been created.

Olive released Finder's finger and patted him gently on the wrist. "Finder, let's leave. I told Giogi about you. He said you're welcome in his home anytime. That's where I was going to take you."

The bard looked up and laughed. "Giogi? That's who you expected to protect me from the Harpers? Ruskettle, have you taken leave of your senses?"

"Giogi has a friend called Cat who can keep you hidden. I thought you'd want to meet her."

"Why?"

"She's one of the copies that Phalse made of Alias," Olive explained.

Finder reached up and grabbed Olive's wrists. "What?" he shouted.

"You know—one of the twelve copies he made," Olive explained. "I found another one—Jade. We were friends, but Flattery killed her. He thought she was Cat. He was mad at Cat because he thought she'd betrayed him. She was his apprentice for a while, since she's a mage. Jade was a pickpocket—a good one, too. Anyway, Cat sided with Giogi against Flattery. He was horrible to her—Flattery, that is."

Finder sat on the pile of rock he'd been shifting. "Olive, I think I'm getting too old to keep up with you. If you have any more revelations, give them to me now, while I'm sitting down."

"Cat's going to have Giogi's baby next spring. So you'll be a grandfather, sort of, besides being an eleventh-generation great-granduncle."

Finder closed his eyes and began to rub his temples with his fingers.

"So how about heading for Immersea?" the halfling asked, hoping Finder would be more open to the suggestion in his shocked state.

Finder shook visibly and rose to his feet. "I need to get into my workshop first. Then we can discuss what to do next."

"Suppose whatever's set up housekeeping down here is between us and the workshop?" Olive protested.

"I'm not going to let some squatter keep me from my own home," the bard answered angrily.

"Finder, you've been in exile for two hundred years. It's not as if whatever it is didn't wait a decent interval before moving in."

The bard grinned slyly. "It's getting awfully late to be on the road, Olive," he said. "Wouldn't you rather have a bath and spend the night in a comfortable bed before we leave? I can get you that with the magic in my workshop."

Olive tried to fend off the temptation by imagining a ray of disintegration coming toward her.

"The door to the workshop is only about another hundred feet down this passage," Finder said.

Olive pictured the green ray of disintegration Flattery had used to destroy her friend Jade and did not reply.

"Then we wouldn't have to walk at all." Finder added. "I have copies of my spellbooks in my workshop. I can teleport us to Immersea."

Olive sighed at her own weakness. She slipped on her gloves, picked up her shovel once again, and started shifting dirt. Finder began to sing a dwarven mining tune as he returned to digging out the rocks. In spite of her annoyance with the bard's stubbornness and her fear of whatever lay beyond the obstructions, Olive hummed along in harmony. It was too hard to resist the power of Finder's voice.

They were both growing tired, so they worked more slowly. They'd been at it nearly an hour when Olive felt a flutter of air waft through her hair. "Got it!" she whispered down to the bard.

"Do you see anything?" Finder asked.

The halfling put her face near the flow of air and squinted. "It's too dark," she reported. Her talent for seeing in the dark had never been as well developed as most of her folk, but her other senses were sharp enough. "It feels warmer," she said, "and—phew! Your home's new tenant isn't much of a housekeeper. It smells like garbage."

Finder started working faster, excited by the nearness of their goal.

Olive slipped down to the floor to give the bard room to work. He piled stones up on either side of the tunnel to shore up the ceiling as he dug into the dirt. Olive watched him wriggle like a snake into the hole he'd created and disappear. If he wanted to go first, she had no objections. If there was something waiting on the other side, Finder was a bigger target and made a good shield.

"I need the torch," his muffled voice called out.

Olive took up Finder's torch and scrambled up to the hole. She thrust it through as far her halfling arm could reach and leaned it against the stones the bard had positioned. Finder reached back carefully and pulled it the rest of the way through. Olive slipped her shovel into her knapsack and slid back down the rubble to fetch her own torch. "Damn!" Finder growled from the other side of the rubble.

"What is it?" Olive called out with alarm.

Finder did not reply.

Olive froze in horror. "Finder?" she whispered. From the other side of the rubble, she heard the sound of rattling iron. Olive snatched up her torch and scrabbled to the hole. "Finder!" she shouted.

"No need to shout, Olive girl," Finder called back. "I can hear you."

"Why did you say 'damn'?" she asked angrily, thrusting her torch into the hole.

"Someone's put an iron grate across the passage," the bard explained. "Nothing I can't handle, though."

As Olive crawled through the hole toward the light, she heard the sound of a wire jiggling in a lock. As she poked her head out of the hole, she saw the iron grate ten feet away. There was a door with a simple-looking lock set in it. The bard was bent over it, picking at it with a bit of wire. Why, Olive wondered, would anyone seal the passages with cave-ins and then put up an iron grate with a door in it? That is, unless they had some insidious reason to want someone to open the door. . . . "Finder, wait!" the halfling cried urgently. "Let me have a look first!"

A distinct click echoed down the passageway. Finder pushed on the grate. It swung open on squeaky hinges. The bard turned around, grinning at Olive with amusement. "I told you I could handle it," he said.

Olive rolled her eyes. "You can never have too many people check a lock," she snapped. "Suppose it had been trapped?"

Finder shrugged. "It wasn't. No harm done," he said. "Let's get going."

Sometimes, Olive thought, he's just like a little boy. She slid down the pile of dirt and stone on the other side and picked up her torch.

"After you, my dear," Finder said, motioning for her to go through the doorway.

Olive eyed the passage cautiously. It was too dim to pick out any really well-hidden traps. "Age before beauty," she replied.

A rueful look flickered across the bard's face, but he turned and stepped across the threshold into the passage beyond.

Olive understood that look. Now that Finder was no longer living on the boundary of the plane of life, his body was feeling his great age more, and Finder had never liked anything that reminded him of his mortality. The younger halfling couldn't bring herself to tease him about it. She remembered all too well her mother's own groaning complaints when her body began to fail. No doubt, Olive realized, I'll be just as annoyed when I get old—providing I live long enough, she amended, though she suspected the odds of that decreased the longer she stayed with Finder.

She trotted after the bard anyway. "So, where's this workshop?" she asked when she caught up with him.

"Straight ahead, Olive," Finder said, pointing down the dim corridor.

Olive held her torch higher and peered into the darkness. Two dim torchlights shone somewhere farther down the passage. "Someone's coming," she hissed, halting in her tracks.

Finder chuckled. He moved his torch up and down, and one of the lights ahead of them rose and fell as if in reply. "It's just our reflection, Olive. The door is enchanted, made of polished steel. Keeps it from being disintegrated."

Olive paced behind Finder. Halfway down the passage, a strand of her hair blew across her face. Olive halted again and turned sideways. From a gap in the wall large enough for a human to pass through, warm air, stinking of garbage, blew into the corridor. The quarried stone that had covered the gap lay smashed in pieces about the passageway floor, crunching under their feet. Beyond the gap was a tunnel stretching farther than the torchlight could reveal.

"This must be where whatever it was that disintegrated those arches broke in," Olive said.

Finder turned and walked back to inspect the gap. "Yes," he said slowly. "The hillside is riddled with natural caves and galleries. I had this gap sealed off to keep cave monsters out. I should have filled in the tunnel behind the gap, too. Well, it can't be helped now," he said with a shrug and continued down the corridor, intent on his goal.

Olive stared down the tunnel behind the gap, wondering what sort of creature, possessing the power to disintegrate things, would live with that smell. Something without a nose, she thought, an idea that did not comfort her any. For a brief moment, she thought she saw tiny points of red light, but they blinked out immediately. She stepped closer to the hole.

From down the corridor Finder had followed came the rattle of another iron grate. With a start, Olive realized they had fallen into a trap—one undoubtedly set by the unknown thing that had disintegrated the ceilings. Her heart pounding with fear, she raced down the corridor toward the bard. Ten feet from the steel door to his underground workshop, someone had set up a second iron grate with a door. Finder had wedged his torch in the grating and was already bent over the door's lock with his wire pick.

"Must be something to keep the children out," the bard muttered disdainfully, but Olive could see at a glance that the lock on this second door was far more complicated than that on the first.

"Finder," she whispered nervously, tugging on his sleeve, "it's a trap. Something's coming from the caves back there. We have to get out of here. Now!"

"Don't be silly, Olive," the bard said. "I'll only be a moment; then we can seal ourselves in the workshop. Ouch!" Finder drew his hand up to his mouth and sucked on his knuckle. "Scratched myself," he said with a touch of embarrassment.

Olive's eyes widened with horror. "Spit!" she ordered him.

"What?" the bard asked with amusement.

"Spit, you idiot! You've been jabbed by a poison needle! Don't swallow!"

Finder's brow wrinkled with concern. He turned his head and spat on the floor while Olive pulled out a flask and shoved it into his hands.

"Rinse your mouth and your hand," she ordered, looking back down the corridor anxiously.

Finder took a swig from the flask and spat it out, gagging and coughing. "What is this?" he asked.

"Luiren Rivengut," the halfling said. "Best whiskey there is."

"Tymora! If the poison doesn't get me, this stuff will!" Finder muttered.

"Wash out the scratch," Olive ordered.

Finder splashed some of the whiskey on his knuckle.

"Let's go," Olive said.

"Olive, now that I've sprung the trap, we've nothing to lose," Finder said, bending back over the lock with his pick. "It will be a snap to get this grate open and get into the workshop."

"No, it won't," the halfling insisted, growing more frantic with each passing moment. "This is a tee-trap," she explained. "The first lock had a silent alarm. This lock will be so complicated it will detain us long enough for guards to reach us from that tunnel back there. We'll be trapped long before we can get the door open."

"No, we won't," Finder insisted, jiggling his wire in the lock, but a moment later, he fumbled the wire and it bounced through the grate. He slid his arm through the grate in an unsuccessful attempt to reach it.

Something crunched on the broken stone in the passage behind them. Finder froze, his lockpick forgotten. Very slowly the bard pulled away from the grate, rose to his feet, and turned around.

In the passageway near the tunnel behind the gap in the wall stood three shadowy human-sized figures. Their beady red eyes reflected the light of the bard's and the halfling's torches.

With his left hand, Finder grabbed Olive's wrist and thrust her behind him, while with his right, he drew a dagger from his boot.

One shadowy figure drew closer to the torchlight. It was a male creature with a jutting forehead, a snout, long canine teeth, pointed ears, and green skin covered with coarse hair.

Orcs, Olive thought with a disgusted shudder. Tymora, why couldn't it have been something cleaner or nicer, like giant rabid rats?

The other two orcs stepped into the light just behind the first. Each wore a pair of trousers, a vest of dirty yellow cloth, a necklace decorated with dried human ears, and a belt with a holstered axe, and each held a loaded crossbow pointed at Finder's middle. They carried no torches; they apparently could see well enough in the dark without them.

"S'render 'r die," the first orc ordered in slurred, barely intelligible common.

"Such unappealing options," Finder replied glibly. "I surrender. Here," he said, offering his dagger, hilt first, to the orc, but Olive could tell from the way his left hand tightened about her wrist that he was tensed for a fight.

The orc squinted his eyes suspiciously, but he was too tempted by the sight of the emeralds and topazes set in the hilt of Finder's dagger to order the bard to throw the weapon to the floor. Moving a step closer, the orc reached out to take the weapon from Finder.

More quickly than Olive would have thought possible, Finder's right leg shot up from the floor, kicking the orc's crossbow hand. The orc howled and fired his weapon, but the bolt discharged harmlessly toward the ceiling, then clattered to the floor. Finder charged between the other two orcs, pulling Olive with him. The halfling threw her torch into the face of one of the creatures as she passed it. Hurriedly the bard raced down the dark passage, dragging Olive behind him as though she were a rag doll.

Olive heard the orcs chasing after them, then the twang of another crossbow. The bolt thunked into something soft. From the grunt Finder made and the way he stumbled, the halfling guessed the bard had been hit, but he regained his balance and ran on. He smashed into the iron grate at the other end of the corridor. Something cackled beside them. It was a fourth orc, Olive realized, sent to relock the door leading to escape! The damned orcs weren't as stupid as they looked. In the dark, she couldn't see the creature, but she heard him breathing beside her.

Finder tugged on the iron grate door, but it held fast. A rough, hairy hand grabbed Olive's left arm and began pulling her away from the bard. Olive shrieked. Finder tightened his grip on the halfling's right wrist and tugged back. Olive felt like a wishbone at a feast. She sensed Finder slashing at the orc with his dagger, then something warm and sticky gushed over her head—orc blood. The orc released her arm and fell heavily.

"Get the lock!" Finder ordered, pushing Olive toward the door. He used his own body to shield her from the rest of the orcs, who had to be moving stealthily toward them.

Olive felt her way to the lock, slid a wire from her hair, and jiggled it in the iron mechanism. She couldn't believe how easily she got the bolt to turn over. If she'd been the one to open it the first time, she would have realized much sooner that this was a trap. As she pulled open the grate, she heard more crossbows twanging in the darkness and the sound of another bolt burying itself in flesh.

Tugging at Finder's sleeve, the halfling got the bard through the door, pushed it closed, and, within moments, relocked it with her wire. As she turned to hurry down the corridor, a hand slipped through the grate and grabbed her hair.

"Let go!" Olive shouted. She felt Finder near her, stabbing through the grate. She felt the hand go limp as it released her.

"Through the hole," Finder shouted. "Go! Go! Go!"

Olive scrambled up the pile of dirt and stone in the dark, all the while concentrating on locating a trace of the cool air on the other side of the cave-in. "Finder! Here!" she called out when she felt a bit of cooler air blowing through the tunnel. The bard scrambled up the slope beside her and pushed her through the opening.

Olive crawled as fast as she could to clear the tunnel so Finder could get through. After a full minute, when he still didn't emerge from the opening, Olive started back through to see what was keeping him. She found his body lying in the tunnel, motionless.

"Finder, you've got to get moving!" she shouted, shaking him by the shoulders. She grabbed his hand, thinking, quite unreasonably, that she might drag him through. His hand was warm, but it was puffed up to the size of an grapefruit.

It's the poison from that damned needle trap, Olive thought. He didn't get just a little scratch; he got stabbed good. "I should have realized he'd lie about it," she muttered to herself as she rummaged through her knapsack, searching in the dark for the one potion that might help the bard. In the dark, she had to identify the correct vial by its shape. She pulled it out, then shook the bard some more. "Finder, you've got to drink this. Wake up!" she insisted.

The bard groaned softly.

That might be the most reaction I get out of him, the halfling thought. Quickly she turned his head sideways, unstoppered the potion, and poured it past his lips. "Swallow," she ordered. To her great relief, he did.

After a few moments, Finder stirred, then croaked, "What?"

"Finder, come on!" Olive implored.

The bard shook himself and wriggled forward slowly. Olive backed away, tugging on his tunic encouragingly. Finally they both reached the other side and rolled down the pile of rubble.

Olive could hear the orcs arguing among themselves in some unintelligible tongue. Then the grate rattled loudly.

"I'll light a torch," Olive said. "It'll just take a mo—"

"We don't need one," Finder muttered.

Olive felt the bard take her right hand in his left. With his poisoned right hand, he felt along the wall, leading her through the maze of passages. She could sense he was limping.

The next cave-in was easier to crawl through, but it took Finder several minutes to negotiate it. Olive put her hand on his back after he'd managed to pull himself through. His shirt and tunic were drenched with perspiration.

"Do you want to rest for a minute?" she asked.

"No," the bard growled. "Keep going."

By the time they reached the cave-in below the stairs, Finder's breathing was strained and shallow, and his skin was cold and clammy. Olive wasn't sure he'd make it up the slope of the tunnel they'd dug. When she finally crawled out into the shaft of sunlight pouring down the stairway, Olive was exhausted, but perhaps the knowledge that it was the last stretch gave the bard more strength. He clambered through the tunnel and, with a great beastlike roar, tore up the stairs, passing the startled halfling.

Olive muttered as she was forced to use her hands to help her scrabble up the steep steps. Once she'd reached the top, she slammed the stairway door closed and threw the dead bolt. Her companion had a key to lock it as well, but he was in no condition to use it.

Finder lay on the stone floor of his ruined manor house, silent and motionless. Olive bent over the bard and shook him gently, whispering his name. The bard didn't answer. He had a bolt in the back of his right shoulder and another in his left thigh. He was either very lucky, or the orcs were lousy shots, Olive thought. Very gently she eased the weapons from his flesh. Blood seeped from the wounds, but at least it didn't gush out profusely. The wounds weren't serious enough to have made him pass out.

It's still the damned poison from the damned needle trap, Olive thought. The potion she'd given him wasn't strong enough to counteract the poison. All she'd accomplished by pouring it in him was to prolong his dying for a few hours.

❧ 8 ❧

Grypht

As Alias was leading Dragonbait and Zhara from the Harpers' courtroom to Nameless's former cell, Dragonbait halted suddenly and sniffed the air. No doubt, the swordswoman realized, the saurial can smell Grypht. She turned around and explained to him. "Something teleported into the tower—some creature, probably a wizard—and kidnapped Elminster and Nameless, maybe Olive, too."

Dragonbait shook his head as if confused, and his tail twitched with nervous excitement. Alias didn't notice. Her attention was attracted to the sound of thumping coming from the corridor that led to Nameless's cell. She hurried through the passages, anxious to see what was going on.

Lord Mourngrym and Breck stood outside the door to Nameless's cell. Breck was hacking furiously at the door with a battle-axe, but for all the ranger's strength and the weapon's sharpness, the door wouldn't give.

Alias heard Lord Mourngrym say, "It's no good, Orcsbane. The door's made of ironwood."

"What's wrong?" Alias asked as she and Dragonbait and Zhara hurried toward the two men.

"Akabar and Kyre aren't answering," Lord Mourngrym replied. He turned the door handle and pulled on it, but the door remained closed. "The door's unlocked, but it won't budge. It feels as if it's being held shut by magic."

Remembering Morala's suspicion that Grypht could be an evil wizard and that Kyre may have made an alliance with him, the swordswoman suddenly felt nervous and foolish. She hadn't believed the half-elf's claim that Grypht was a denizen of the Nine Hells, yet she had been so eager for Kyre to break Zhara's hold on Akabar and talk him out of his belief in Moander's return that she had trusted the half-elf anyway. "Maybe Kyre and Akabar just don't want to be disturbed," Alias suggested hopefully, without believing it herself.

Breck lowered his axe and fixed her with a cold stare. "Kyre isn't shy. If she wanted to be alone with a man, she'd have no qualms about telling us all to go away," he replied. "Something is wrong," he insisted. "We need a spell-caster to break in the door."

Zhara pushed her way past Alias. "Stand back," she ordered everyone. In her hand, she held a lump of clay fashioned just like the stone arch surrounding the door to Nameless's cell. With her fingers, she pushed one side of the clay arch away, then touched the clay to the stone arch in front of them, whispering, "Sculpture."

Alias gasped as the rock of the wall beside the door curled back like a potato peel, forming a gap large enough to walk through.

Zhara slipped into Nameless's cell before anyone else could stop her. She looked around in confusion. "He isn't here!" she whispered. "Where's Akabar?" Turning to face Alias, she demanded angrily, "Where's Akabar? What have you done with him?"

Alias slipped into the room and looked around, equally confused. Akabar and Kyre were nowhere in sight. The songhorn lying on the table was cracked and some of its keys were broken off. Bits of broken crystal lay on the table. Something crunched in the carpeting beneath her foot. Alias looked down. Walnut shells lay scattered about on the floor.

Then she spotted the ashes, and her face went pale. Gray ashes formed the unmistakable shape of a person. A pair of elven boots, a dagger, a sword, a belt, and a scabbard lay off to one side. Two gold rings, a silver ankle bracelet, and a Harper's pin were on the other side of the ashes.

"Mourngrym!" Alias called back into the hallway. "You'd better come and see this."

"What is it? What's wrong?" Breck demanded, squeezing his way into the room. When he saw the ashes and equipment lying on the floor, his eyes widened in fury. "Kyre! No!" he shouted. "She's dead! He killed her, didn't he? That fiend Akabar killed Kyre!"

* * * * *

In the Harpers' courtroom, Morala had grown bored scrying on Nameless and Olive Ruskettle beneath Finder's keep. She abandoned her watch on the bard and his halfling cohort while the pair was still digging through the piles of rubble. Now the priestess stood over her silver scrying bowl a third time. It had occurred to her that she might learn more if she turned her attention to the creature who had been responsible for Elminster's and Nameless's disappearances. She drew out the piece of clay Grypht had dropped and envisioned the huge creature.

The colors in the water of Morala's bowl swirled into Grypht's shape. The beast was bent over beneath a monstrous oak tree, yanking a handful of oak seedlings out of the ground. He straightened and munched absentmindedly on the seedlings as he studied a yellow gem he held in his hand.

Suddenly a beam of light shot out from a facet in the gem. Morala gasped, recognizing immediately that Grypht held the finder's stone. The Harpers had entrusted Elminster with the artifact's safety, but somehow this scaly creature had gotten hold of it. Is that why Elminster and Nameless had been abducted? the priestess wondered. Just to obtain Nameless's toy?

Grypht shook his head, and the first beam of light from the crystal faded away and a second beam burst out of another facet of the stone, aimed downward at the ground. Morala pulled her scrying view back until she could see more. At Grypht's feet lay a dark-skinned, bearded man dressed in striped robes, with the blue dots of a southern scholar and mage tattooed on his forehead. The light from the finder's stone struck the man's eyes, but although his chest rose and fell, he did not move. Apparently he was unconscious. Morala's brow furrowed. Who is he? she wondered.

Grypht nodded at the finder's stone with satisfaction.

He's experimenting with it, Morala realized.

Grypht shook his head, and the light on the southerner's eyes faded. Then the creature closed his eyes, and the crystal stone began to glow all over, but this time no beam shot out. Grypht squeezed his eyes tighter, as if he were concentrating hard. The stone glowed even brighter, but it gave no indication of the location of the person the scaly creature was thinking of. Grypht sighed and opened his eyes; the stone ceased glowing.

"How deliciously ironic!" Morala muttered. "You've gone to all this trouble to steal the finder's stone, and it can't find whoever it is you're looking for."

Grypht bent over and began pulling more oak seedlings from the ground. Suddenly a beam of light shot out from the yellow crystal in the direction of the setting sun. Grypht started with surprise and straightened up. After scanning the horizon for a few moments, he bent over and shouldered the unconscious southerner.

"Who are you after?" Morala mused as Grypht straightened and began trundling away toward the setting sun.

* * * * *

Mourngrym looked over the ashes lying beside Kyre's equipment and shook his head regretfully. "It doesn't look good, Alias," he said softly.

"I can't believe Akabar would do such a thing," the swordswoman said. "Something else must have attacked them."

"Then why isn't Akabar's body in a pile of ash on the carpeting?" Breck snarled. He was shaking with anger and barely controlled grief.

"How do you know those aren't his ashes mingled in with Kyre's?" Alias retorted hotly.

Zhara moaned and sank to the bed. Dragonbait glared at the swordswoman, but Alias ignored him. She couldn't afford to be tactful for Zhara's sake. She had to clear Akabar's reputation.

"If he was incinerated along with Kyre, too," Breck said, "his boots would be here."

"He was wearing rope sandals," Alias argued.

"And he didn't carry a single piece of metal with him?" Breck asked.

That, Alias realized, was hardly likely. She changed her tack. "Whoever killed Kyre could have carried Akabar off," she stated. "Grypht might have returned and eaten him, for all you know."

Zhara gave a keening wail. The swordswoman shot an annoyed look at Akabar's wife. Dragonbait nudged Alias angrily with his elbow.

"I believe Grypht has indeed carried off Akabar," a voice said, "but the beast appears to prefer greenery to human flesh. Akabar is still alive."

Everyone looked around. Standing in the new entrance to

the room that Zhara had fashioned with her magic was Morala. The old priestess leaned heavily on Captain Thurbal's arm, but she was smiling.

"I have just been scrying upon Grypht. He was carrying a southern mage dressed in a red-and-white-striped robe," Morala said.

"Akabar!" Zhara cried out eagerly. "His robes are red and white!"

"Then he is in league with Grypht!" Breck declared.

Mourngrym exchanged a distressed look with Alias. "Was Akabar being carried off by force, Morala, or using the beast as a mount?" his lordship asked.

"Akabar was unconscious, so I couldn't tell his wishes," Morala explained, shuffling into the room with Captain Thurbal beside her.

"What about Nameless?" Alias asked anxiously. "Was he with Grypht? "

Morala shook her head. "No, " she said. "Nameless appears to be in an underground tunnel of some sort, digging his way through, though whether he is trying to escape the tunnel or burrow in farther, I could not tell. There is a halfling woman with him. They both appear uninjured, but their location remains a mystery. I think we best concentrate on tracking Grypht," Morala said. "Grypht has the finder's stone, and with that, he can track both Elminster and Nameless."

"A finder's stone?" Alias asked. "Like the one Elminster gave to me?"

"*The* finder's stone," Morala corrected her. "There is only one. It's an old artifact that Nameless made to store his music and his spells," the priestess explained. "For anyone else, it worked as a compass."

"But we lost it in Westgate, battling Moander," Alias said.

The wrinkles in Morala's forehead doubled as she tried to think of how the stone got from Westgate into Grypht's hands. Unable to come up with a satisfactory explanation, the priestess huffed in frustration. "Well, Grypht has found it somewhere, somehow," she said. "When I last saw him, he was using it. He was standing atop a hill covered with many small oak trees and crowned with a single immense oak, laden with mistletoe and ivy and moss."

"That would have to be Oakwood Knoll, your lordship," Captain Thurbal said. "East of the river."

"A monster that size will be easy to follow," Breck said, heading for the door.

Mourngrym's arm shot out and caught Breck's tunic, pulling him back. "Hold on a minute there, man," his lordship said. "This . . . thing's already attacked you once today. You can't go after it alone. The dale's full of hiding places. You could be tracking it for days. Let me get a party of guards and provisions together. It will only take a few hours."

"A few hours!" Breck shouted. "Kyre's been murdered, and you expect me to wait a few hours? I'm going to bring this creature's head back on a pike—and Akabar's, too, if I find he's in league with it."

Zhara rose quickly and rushed at Breck, pushing him back against the table with a surprising show of strength. "My husband," she hissed, "is a man of honor, a scholar and a mage." The young priestess's voice rose in fury, and her eyes flashed with fire. "How dare you suggest such a thing?" she shouted. "If you harm one hair on his head, I will bring Tymora's curse down upon you!"

Breck looked stunned by the veiled woman's verbal attack. It took him only a moment to recover, however. "You could be in league with him, too, for all I know," he said to Zhara.

Zhara called Breck one of the few Turmish words Mourngrym knew. His lordship blushed. Fortunately, Breck didn't realize he'd been insulted.

Dragonbait gently pulled Zhara away from the ranger. Then he signed to Alias. She nodded.

"Your lordship," Alias announced to Mourngrym, "Dragonbait and I can be ready to leave in a quarter of an hour. If you can wait that long, Breck Orcsbane, we will join you."

"He can wait that long," Mourngrym said firmly. "Try to keep in mind, Orcsbane, that if you bring nothing but heads back, we may never find Elminster or Nameless or Olive Ruskettle. I understand how you feel about Kyre, but we have to think of those who are still alive. I want you to try to capture the beast."

"Capture a denizen of the Nine Hells?" Breck shouted. "That's impossible!"

"Try," Lord Mourngrym said. "It may not be a fiend."

"Kyre said that it was!" Breck hissed angrily.

"Try to capture it anyway," Mourngrym insisted. "And return

Akabar Bel Akash alive, whether he resists or not."

"I will go, too, to see that this man obeys," Zhara said.

"Oh, no, you don't!" Breck insisted. "Your lordship, this woman is the man's wife. I want you to arrest her."

"I can't arrest a woman for being a man's wife," Mourngrym said, barely able to contain his own annoyance with the ranger.

"But she could warn him that we're coming and foil our attempts to capture him," Breck argued.

"Lady Zhara," Morala said softly, "it would be best if you remain here in the tower. As you said, your husband is a man of honor. The least we can do is keep you safe until his return."

"Keep me hostage, you mean!" Zhara exclaimed hostilely.

"We're riding into the wilderness, and we'll probably end up having to fight this Grypht," Alias said with annoyance. "You'd only slow us down and get in the way."

"I am following my husband," Zhara insisted angrily.

"No, you aren't!" Breck shouted.

"Please stay here, Lady Zhara," Morala coaxed.

Dragonbait made two short, sharp signs to the Turmishwoman, which Alias did not see. Zhara bit her lip and took a deep breath. "I will stay," she said softly. "Show me to my room."

"Captain Thurbal, would you escort this lady to my wife's quarters and ask Lady Shaerl to look after her?" Mourngrym asked.

"Yes, your lordship," the captain said, nodding. "This way, lady," he said, motioning for Zhara to follow him.

Akabar's wife laid her hand on Dragonbait's chest and looked into his eyes. The paladin ran a clawed finger down the sleeve of her robe and nodded. Then Zhara turned and followed Thurbal from the room, as meekly as a child.

Dragonbait signed to Alias that he would fetch their things from the inn.

Alias nodded. "I'll gather some provisions together if Harper Breck will take care of saddling our horses," she said.

"I'll be waiting for you at the bridge," Breck replied. He strode from the room. Dragonbait followed him out.

"You have your work cut out for you," Mourngrym warned Alias. "If you think you need help handling Breck, I can ride along with you."

"No, thank you, your lordship," Alias said. "I'm sure Kyre was wrong about Grypht's origins, but if she was correct about his working for the Zhentarim, the Zhentarim may be planning an attack on Shadowdale. The dale folk need you here. As a favor to me, however, please see that Akabar's wife stays here."

"We'll keep her safe," Morala promised.

"Just keep her out of my way," Alias muttered.

Mourngrym pursed his lips with disapproval. Alias never seemed to get along with clergy. It was lucky Dragonbait had so much influence over the Turmishwoman. His lordship wondered what it was the saurial had signed to the priestess to make her obey so readily. "I'll be sure the guards know she's not to leave the tower, Alias," Mourngrym said. "I'll take you down to the storeroom to help you collect provisions."

"I think I'll stay here to rest awhile," Morala said. She stepped closer to the swordswoman. "We should say our good-byes now, Alias of Westgate. If you happen to meet Nameless before we meet again, remember to ask him to tell you the whole truth."

"I'll remember," Alias replied.

Morala reached up and laid a hand on Alias's shoulder. "Grief and pain lie in your path. May sweet music and brave songs bring you strength to endure them until you know joy again." Morala removed her hand from Alias's shoulder.

Alias sighed. She didn't believe prayers did any good, but at least Morala's blessing hadn't been too silly. "Good-bye, Morala," the swordswoman said. "It's been . . . interesting meeting you."

Morala smiled wryly.

Alias turned and strode from the room, and Mourngrym followed after her.

* * * * *

Grypht looked with a great deal of satisfaction down the ravine that cut across his path. It was quite deep and long, but far too wide to leap across. It was just what he needed to slow down any would-be trackers. He walked north along the edge for a hundred yards, then halted. The scent of fresh-mown hay rose again from his body as he summoned another dimensional portal to take him across the ravine with his burden. Once he stood on the other side, he moved as carefully as possible so as not to leave a trail that could be easily spotted from across the ravine. Then he turned once again toward the sinking sun, following the beam of the yellow crystal.

*   *   *   *   *

Dragonbait loped back to the tower carrying two sacks in addition to his pack and Alias's. One sack was full of Alias's weaponry and armor, both old and new; the other contained leftover dried rations he'd had stored in his room. The saurial nodded politely to the guards as he passed through the tower's front gate once again. He crossed the entrance hall quickly, then dashed up the stairs and raced through the corridors. He didn't have much time. He stood before the door to Lady Shaerl's quarters and took a few deep breaths to steady his nerves.

He was about to engage in a deceit, something which always made him uncomfortable, even when he believed it was for a good cause, such as allowing Zhara to accompany her husband's rescue party. Without Alias's support, Dragonbait knew he'd never break down Breck's opposition to the priestess's presence. The paladin needed time to persuade the swordswoman to accept Zhara, but things were happening too quickly. He didn't want to defy Lord Mourngrym, Breck, or most especially Alias, but he had no other choice.

The saurial knocked on Lady Shaerl's door.

From within, Lady Shaerl called out, "Come in."

Dragonbait opened the door and stepped inside. Zhara sat on a couch beside Mourngrym's wife, Shaerl, who held a sleeping Scotty in her arms. The saurial signed very quickly to her ladyship.

Shaerl understood the signing immediately and laughed. "Certainly, Dragonbait. Any time you wish to be alone with a lady in my quarters, just ask," she said lightly.

The paladin raised his eyes to the ceiling. Her ladyship's teasing could be most inappropriate at times. But then what else could one expect of a Cormyte noblewoman who understood the thieves' sign language? Not even motherhood, Dragonbait noted, had dampened the woman's taste for mischief and adventure. Obviously she did not intend her future to be any less colorful than her past. The saurial signed that his business was urgent.

"Excuse me, Zhara," Shaerl said, "while I go put this little monster to bed." Her ladyship rose and carried Scotty into an adjacent room and closed the door behind her.

"I did as you asked," the priestess said in low tones once the two of them were alone. "I pretended to submit. But I will not remain here while Akabar is in danger."

Dragonbait signed to Zhara that he was sure that Akabar had nothing to fear from Grypht; Grypht was his friend. Hastily the paladin signed his plans for her escape; then he began pulling pieces of Alias's armor out of the sack. A few minutes later, the pair of them descended the stairway into the front entrance hall. "This will never work," Zhara whispered, tugging at the uncomfortable studded leather collar she now wore around her throat. "Even if I look like Alias, my skin is too dark," she argued.

Dragonbait made a wheezing noise. Zhara realized he was chuckling. *They won't see your skin*, he signed, *only your flesh.*

Zhara shuddered and clutched the bundle that held her robes closer to her chest. Dragonbait stepped in front of her, and Zhara halted. The saurial forced her arms down from her chest, revealing a healthy cleavage between her breasts that Alias's enchanted chain armor did not cover.

Carry your bundle under one arm, the saurial ordered with his fingers. *Hold your head up higher. Don't look modest. Gods know, Alias isn't.* Dragonbait reached up and arranged a lock of Zhara's hair over the scholar's tattoo of three blue dots on her forehead. *Don't rest your hand on the sword hilt*, he added. *That's for swaggering amateurs.*

Zhara moved her hand from the blade's handle, and Dragonbait continued to instruct the priestess as they made their way down the staircase. *Just nod to the guards when you go past. Pay attention to my signing, and they'll realize you're too busy to chat.*

When they reached the entrance hall, the saurial began to encourage Zhara with a steady banter. *Remember, you're Alias, the warrior who defeated the Iron Throne's hired kalmari and the evil fiend Phalse. They all admire your courage. You're probably the most talented singer in the Realms. They all love your singing. You are very beautiful. The young women want to be like you and the young men want to be with you.*

Zhara's eyes met with those of one of the guards at the door. The guard nodded politely. Zhara nodded in return and hastily averted her eyes back to Dragonbait's signing hands. She could feel herself flushing. She had never before appeared in public without her veil, let alone without her priestess's robes. Only her husband had ever seen this much of her body before, and the priestess felt more than embarrassed. She felt ashamed, as though she'd been unfaithful to Akabar.

Once they'd stepped through the tower's front gate, Dragonbait clutched Zhara's arm and hurried her toward the stable. They passed an ornamental rose arbor, and the saurial dodged into it, yanking the priestess after him. The arbor protected them from the rain that continued to fall as well as from curious eyes.

Give me the sword, but put your robes back on over the armor. You may need its protection, Dragonbait signed.

"How much protection can it possibly offer?" Zhara asked, unstrapping the sword's sheath from the metal girdle about her waist. "There's nothing to it. Besides, what will Alias wear?"

Don't be fooled by the chain mail's looks. It's heavily enchanted, Dragonbait explained. *Alias can wear her spare armor. Remember what I told you*, he warned as she donned her robes, *once you are across the bridge, hide in the woods until you see us pass. Wait awhile longer before you follow. Look for strips of white or blue cloth. Here, take this cloak*, he ordered, handing her one of Alias's old cloaks. *Cover your head with the hood—a veil will attract too much attention.*

Handing her a small sack of dry rations, he signed, *This is all the food I could collect, but we will pass several farm fields. The farmers will not object if you glean from them. Take care, lady, until we meet again.*

Zhara grabbed Dragonbait's tunic. "All those things you said about Alias in the tower . . . I am not like her. I'm not nearly so brave or so talented or so beautiful. I do not think I can do this," she whispered anxiously.

Dragonbait stroked Zhara's arm, and the priestess felt the blue brand on her arm tingle just as it had when he had touched it before. It was an oddly comforting feeling.

You are different from Alias, the paladin signed, *but you can do this. You must and you will.* The smell of garlic surrounded them, the scent of the saurial's determination. Without another word, Dragonbait gave Zhara a light shove toward the road. The woman hurried toward the bridge and passed by the sentries stationed on the near side. In the drizzling rain, they didn't find it unusual that a traveler should keep her face covered under the hood of her cloak. When Zhara had reached the opposite side, the lizard strode back to the tower, carrying his and Alias's packs and the sack containing the swordswoman's spare armor.

The guards at the gate exchanged confused looks as Dragonbait returned to the tower. "Forget something, Dragonbait?" one of them asked.

The saurial nodded and strode past quickly.

The guards shrugged as Dragonbait raced down the hall toward the tower storerooms.

The paladin followed the trail of Alias's scent until he found her standing beside Mourngrym in the armory, examining longbows. Dragonbait shook the sack of armor to attract her attention.

"Just a minute, Dragonbait," Alias said, choosing a hornwood bow and handing it to Mourngrym.

"You change," Mourngrym said, picking up a quiver of arrows. "I'll take this out to your horse and make sure Breck doesn't bolt off without you." His lordship left the storeroom.

When they were alone, Alias asked the saurial, "What took you so long?"

Dragonbait set the sack of armor down and signed, *I went to say good-bye to Zhara and to try to reassure her about Akabar.*

"Tymora! You are so naive," Alias chided. "Zhara doesn't need any comforting. That woman doesn't care anything about Akabar. As far as priests are concerned, gods come first; husbands and wives place a poor second," she declared.

You are wrong, Dragonbait signed. *She is a good woman.*

"She's a fanatic," Alias countered.

So are you, the paladin signed. *You denied everything she and Akabar said without considering it carefully.*

"Moander is *not* coming back," Alias snapped.

You argue from emotion, not reason, Dragonbait signed. *You cannot change the truth by denying it. Moander is returning,*

Alias, and Akabar must destroy him.

"Why Akabar?" the swordswoman cried. "Why should he have to fight Moander again? Why not someone else?"

I don't know, the paladin signed, *but you are not helping him by insulting his wife and his faith.*

Alias lowered her eyes, realizing uneasily that Dragonbait could be right but unwilling to admit it. "We have to hurry or Breck will try to leave without us," she said, bending over and dumping out the contents of her sack of armor. "Where's my other chain shirt?" she asked.

Dragonbait shrugged and signed that he hadn't been able to find it.

"Dragonbait!" the swordswoman cried with annoyance. "It was lying across the chair. Are you certain you didn't just choose not to bring it?"

Dragonbait shrugged.

For months the paladin had tried to talk Alias out of wearing the chain shirt she'd gotten from the evil sorceress Cassana. The piece of armor was exceedingly immodest and consequently earned Alias a good deal of unlooked-for attention from men, but it also carried powerful enchantments that protected her far more than a full breastplate could. After she'd worn it for over a year, Dragonbait had ceased objecting to it. Alias thought that he had finally surrendered to her logic. Until now.

"You are such a stick-in-the-mud!" Alias grumbled. "Next thing I know, you'll try to get me to wear a veil like Zhara."

It would be easier to get Zhara into Cassana's armor, the paladin signed.

Alias laughed. "There's no time to argue about it now." She picked up her old chain shirt and slipped it over her tunic, then picked up the breastplate. "Well, now that I have no choice but to wear this awful, bulky plate, you could at least help me get into it."

Dragonbait helped the swordswoman attach the breast and back plates of her old armor about her torso and fastened the shoulder plates to the chain.

"Forget the rest of the pieces," Alias said. "I'm not used to that much weight. Leave them here." She strapped on her sword and shouldered her pack as Dragonbait placed the rest of her armor on an empty shelf.

The swordswoman stepped up behind the saurial. When he turned around, she lowered her head meekly and said, "I'm sorry I was so rude to Zhara. Forgive me?"

Dragonbait looked very stern and signed, *It is Zhara you need to apologize to.*

"I will," Alias promised. "Later. The next time I see her. Don't be angry with me now . . . please?"

Dragonbait ran his claw along her sleeve, so that her brand tingled comfortingly.

Alias could sense from the saurial's smell that he was still disturbed by something. "What's wrong?" she asked.

Grypht isn't from the Nine Hells, the paladin signed.

"I know that," Alias agreed. "He couldn't be, but there's no sense arguing with Breck about it. Kyre said he was, and Breck worshiped Kyre."

Grypht is a friend, Dragonbait signed. *He is one of my people.*

Alias's jaw dropped. "You mean he's a saurial?"

Dragonbait nodded.

"Why didn't you say something?" Alias asked.

Breck wouldn't trust Zhara because she was Akabar's wife. He would not trust me if he knew I was Grypht's friend. Breck is too angry, Dragonbait signed.

"Of course he's angry. Wouldn't you be if you found me in ashes like Kyre?" Alias asked.

Breck's anger is dangerous. He cannot be trusted. Grypht and Akabar could not have murdered Kyre, but Breck is too angry to consider any other possibility.

"He'll cool off on the trail," Alias replied.

Only bloodshed will cool him off, the paladin signed, but Alias was distracted by the sound of Heth calling her name.

The page appeared in the armory door all out of breath. "Lord Mourngrym asks that you hurry," the boy said. "He says it would be easier to hold back the tide than to keep the ranger waiting any longer."

"We're coming," Alias said.

Let's leave by the kitchen door—it's closer to the stables, Dragonbait signed.

Alias nodded, and they hurried to join Breck Orcsbane.

* * * * *

Grypht laid Akabar down on a bed of crushed grass and sank to the ground beside him. His burden had begun to stir, and the lizard decided the ape would probably prefer to waken in a less awkward position then slung over the shoulder of a stranger. Actually, Grypht was grateful to find an excuse to rest. He'd grown unaccustomed to trekking up and down hills for long stretches of time. Not wanting to waste time, Grypht laid his staff across his lap and studied the notches and lines cut into it. He would need to relearn the spell Kyre had prevented him from casting when he first arrived in this world.

The ape's sleep grew more and more restless. He began to toss and turn and mutter. When Grypht finished studying his magic staff, the saurial turned his attention back to the creature he'd rescued. The ape began to shout in his sleep. Grypht couldn't understand his language, but the creature seemed quite upset, so the saurial shook him gently.

Akabar came awake with a start, but he quickly realized he was too weak to sit up. His eyes darted about in confusion. The creature he'd freed from Kyre's soul trap sat beside him. "Elminster?" he whispered.

Grypht shook his head. He understood the word "Elminster," and that certainly wasn't him. The lizard pointed to himself and said, "Grypht" in saurial, but of course the ape could not comprehend.

Grypht pulled out a lump of red clay from his pocket and began fashioning it into a series of five short cylinders, each with a smaller circumference than the previous one. He piled one on top of the other until he had formed the model of a ziggurat.

A clay ziggurat is the component of a tongues spell, Akabar realized. In his excitement, he found the energy to sit up. He fidgeted impatiently for Grypht to finish casting so that they could communicate.

The scent of fresh-mown hay filled the air about them, and the miniature tower balanced on the lizard's palm glowed as if it were sitting in a kiln. Then the tower shattered into several pieces. Grypht turned his hand upside down, spilling the shards of baked clay into the grass. "I am Grypht," he said in a deep, low voice.

"I am Akabar Bel Akash," the Turmishman replied. "I presume you are not a creature of evil as Lady Kyre told us."

Grypht shook his head. "I am a saurial."

"A saurial!" Akabar said excitedly. "Like Dragonbait?"

Grypht chuckled. He couldn't wait to find Champion and ask how he'd picked up such a bizarre nickname. "In our tribe, the one you call Dragonbait is known as Champion. He is the sworn protector of our people. I must locate him."

Akabar nodded. "He's here in Shadowdale."

"Shadowdale?" Grypht asked.

"The town we're in—" Akabar paused and looked around. "The town we *were* in. Where are we now?"

"I fled the tower with you after I destroyed Kyre."

"Kyre," Akabar whispered. "You killed her?" he said.

Despite his relief at having escaped the half-elf's clutches, the Turmishman was unable to control the feeling of misery that swept over him upon learning she was dead.

"She was a minion of Moander," Grypht said, disturbed by Akabar's expression. "She would have drained your spirit and fed you to her master."

"I know," Akabar said, "but I loved her."

Grypht shook his head. Love makes such fools of mages, he thought. "When I last scried Champion, you and he and a halfling traveled on the back of a red lair-beast—what you call a dragon, I believe—but I have been unable to locate Champion magically for over a year now. Are you certain Champion is in the town we left?"

Grypht waited for several moments for Akabar's answer, but the only noise to fill the silence was a cricket in the brush. Finally the saurial poked the Turmish mage and growled, "Forget Kyre and answer my question."

Akabar looked up with a start. Realizing it was imperative he communicate with Grypht while the tongues spell still functioned, he shook off his misery and answered the saurial mage. "You probably couldn't find Dragonbait because he travels with Alias. She's a warrior with a powerful misdirection spell cast on her, which protects her companions, too."

"I could not detect you magically, either. Were you with them all this time?" Grypht asked.

"No," Akabar said. "My wife is also enchanted with a charm of misdirection, but she's back in Shadowdale. If you couldn't locate Dragon—er, Champion, how did you know to come to Shadowdale?"

"I chose it because Olive was there. Since she had once been a companion of Champion's, I hoped she could tell me where to find him," Grypht explained.

"Olive? Olive Ruskettle is in Shadowdale?" Akabar asked in amazement.

"She was in the tower," Grypht explained. "I teleported there, prepared to cast a tongues spell to explain my presence, but Kyre disrupted the spell and convinced others to attack me, so I fled. I managed to find Olive, but I was unable to speak with her. I talked with her friend—a bard, as tall as you are, very arrogant. He would not tell me where Champion was. He professed he needed proof that I was a friend of Champion's, but I think he did not want me to find Champion at all. Kyre interrupted us and scooped me into her soul trap. I thought she must have killed Olive and the bard, but now I believe they escaped, for this stone points out the halfling's location." The saurial held out the yellow crystal.

"The finder's stone!" Akabar said. "Dragonbait lost it in Westgate. How did you find it?"

"The bard had it. I found the stone in Kyre's boot, so I assumed she had killed the bard and Olive. I was using the stone to search for Champion, but it could not discover him for me. By accident, I thought of Olive, her clever fingers and brash nerve, and the stone sent out a directional light immediately. I couldn't believe my luck, or the halfling's, either. She had escaped from Kyre, something I would not have managed without your help."

"But how did the bard get the finder's stone?" Akabar asked.

"He said he created it. He used its magic to speak with me," Grypht explained.

Akabar's brow furrowed. The bard had to be Nameless. It was possible that he did create the stone. He was known as the Crafter as well as the Nameless Bard. Then Akabar found himself wondering why Nameless had kept Dragonbait's location from Grypht. Did he have some reason to distrust Grypht? Then it occurred to the Turmishman that he still hadn't found out about Elminster. "What did you do to Elminster?" he demanded. "He disappeared before you left."

"I transferred him to my tower and took his place," the saurial explained. "It was the only way I could absolutely guarantee my safe magical arrival here."

"Do you know the trouble you caused? Everyone thought

he'd been kidnapped," Akabar said.

"My apprentices were instructed to greet him and apologize for the inconvenience. He was free to leave at any time. He is a great wizard, with the power to travel between planes. I scried for Olive for some time, waiting for her to approach such a one so that I did not strand anyone in my world."

"If Elminster was free to leave, why hasn't he returned yet?" Akabar asked.

"He hasn't?" Grypht asked in return.

Akabar shook his head.

"Oh, dear," the saurial said softly.

"Oh, dear!" Akabar exclaimed. "Is that all you can say? You snatched Elminster from his home to another dimension just to guarantee you had a safe arrival and could find Dragonbait."

"It is imperative that I find Champion. Our people's very existence is imperiled. I must have his help if I am to save them."

"Why? What's wrong with your people?" Akabar asked suspiciously.

"The minions of Moander from the Abyss have come into our land and enslaved them all. Only my three apprentices and I remain uncaptured. The others have been marched forcibly through the plane of Tarterus and into this world. The Darkbringer is using them to recreate a body to use in the Realms."

"Moander," Akabar whispered and shivered. "So my dreams did not lie. It is returning."

"You, too, are an enemy of the Darkbringer?" Grypht asked.

"I have come north to destroy it," Akabar said with a quavering voice.

"Then you tread a dangerous path, Akabar Bel Akash," the saurial said. "For of the Darkbringer's minions in your plane, Kyre the bard was the least, and yet she nearly destroyed you."

❧ 9 ❧

Finder's Workshop

Olive knelt down beside the bard's unconscious body on the cracked stone floor of Finder's ruined keep. She pulled a vial of healing potion from her knapsack and uncorked it. Though the draft would have no effect on the poison in Finder's body, it would take care of his bleeding crossbow bolt wounds. There was a chance it would even bring the bard to consciousness. She waved it under Finder's nose, and he stirred slightly. She poured it past his lips and ordered him to swallow.

Instinctively Finder obeyed. In a few moments, he opened his eyes. "I dropped my dagger," he said.

Olive laughed. The bard was dying, and he was still fussing about a lost dagger. "I'll buy you another for your birthday," she said.

Finder shook his head from side to side. "My grandfather gave me that dagger."

Olive sighed. "Well, if you were thinking about going back to get it, forget it. I've given you a potion to slow the poison, but we've got to get you to a healer before the potion wears off. If we can just get you to the road, we should be able to get help from travelers. Do you think you can walk?"

With Olive's assistance, Finder rolled over and struggled to sit up. He couldn't use his injured hand at all. It was the size of a small melon and streaked with red and white lines, which ran up his wrists beneath the sleeve of his shirt. He was shaking slightly, though it was a warm afternoon. "I've got potions to neutralize poison in my workshop," he said. "It would be easier to get back down there."

"Are you crazy?" Olive shouted. "The place is crawling with orcs with crossbows! You nearly died down there!"

"We saw only four orcs. You probably blinded one with your torch, and I killed the two that grabbed you. If I hadn't panicked like an idiot, I would have realized that left only one for

me to handle while you took care of the other lock. The on
that's left will get bored soon and go back to its warren. B
then, I'll be rested, and we can try again. Instead of trying t
show off this time, I'll let you take care of the locks. An exper
of your caliber should be able to open them without setting of
the silent alarm or catching the poison needle."

Olive wanted to grab the bard and give him a good shaking
but in his condition, she didn't think he could take it. She trie
to remain calm, to reason with him. "First," she argued, "orc
breed like rabbits, and where there's four there's forty. An
don't forget, they still have a pal somewhere who disintegrate
ceilings. Suppose they set up a guard in the passage just in cas
we turn out to be really stupid and come back? Secondly, I'm
good with locks, but no one is perfect; there's no guarantee
can bypass the alarm on the first lock or open the second loc
fast enough in case I fail with the alarm."

"The orcs would all rather be snug back in their warren than
standing guard in a cold tunnel," Finder argued. "They've come
to rely on their alarm. It worked this time. They'll assume i
will work again. They won't set a guard. As for your talent
with locks you're too modest, Olive girl. I know you can do it.
He turned his most charming grin on the halfling.

Olive fought the urge to please him. "Finder, I don't want t
stay here," she insisted. "I want to get to the road before dark.

Finder glared at Olive. "All right. Go," the bard said coldly.

Olive looked at him with astonishment. She couldn't believe
he'd send her away. "Finder, I'm not leaving you. You can't stay
here. You have to try to get to the road with me."

Finder's chill expression thawed, and a rueful expression
crossed his face. He reached out with his uninjured hand and
pushed a stray strand of the halfling's hair out of her eyes. "Ol
ive," he said softly, "I don't want to die by the side of a road wait
ing for rescue. This place is my home. I'd rather be here when
that potion wears off."

"You aren't going to die waiting beside a road," Olive snappe
angrily. "There are plenty of grain caravans and adventuring
parties and soldiers traveling on the road this time of year
Most of them travel with healers, or at least with potions."

"It's half a day's walk to the road, Olive. I'd never make it. I'm
too weak. You'd better go now, in case there are any orcs
searching aboveground."

Olive dug her fingernails into her palms, trying to keep from screaming—or crying. "Oh, sweet Selune!" she said. "You have to try, Finder!"

Finder chuckled dryly. "You sound like my mother," he said. "She used to say that all the time—'sweet Selune.' "

Olive started. Invoking the goddess of the moon was a habit she'd picked up from her stay with Giogi and Cat Wyvernspur. She'd never be able to face the young man or his wife if she had to tell them she'd let their ancestor die out in the middle of nowhere. She'd never be able to face herself, either. Olive gave a deep sigh, unable to understand how she managed to get into these predicaments.

"I guess I'll have to go down to your workshop, then," she said with a false cheery tone.

"Good. Let's go," the bard said, trying to rise to his feet.

"Oh, no, you don't!" Olive exclaimed, holding him down with her hands on his shoulders. "I'm going alone. You'll only slow me down. Give me the key to your workshop and tell me where to find the potions we need."

"There is no key. Music unlocks the door to the workshop," Finder said.

"Like the finder's stone," Olive guessed. "What note?" she asked.

"It's more complicated than that. It takes a phrase from a song." Finder sang out an allegro melody Olive had never heard before: " 'When Lady Luck lies with Grim Justice,/ The soaring stars will be man's auspice.' "

"Now, that's right pretty," Olive said. "You never sang that one before."

"It's not finished," Finder said.

"When did you start it?"

"Before I finished building Flattery," the bard said. "Now sing it back," he ordered the halfling.

Olive obeyed.

"Lower it an octave," Finder ordered.

"Finder, I'm too small. My voice doesn't go down that low."

"Yes, it does. Do it."

"Whose voice is it, anyway?" Olive squeaked.

"I trained it. It's mine," the bard replied.

Olive laughed. "You've got to get this possessive streak under control," she said.

"Olive, you have a fine voice. You can't afford to waste it by constantly saying 'I can't, I can't.' Now try, for me, please."

Olive flushed deeply. She forced her voice down to the first note.

"Good," Finder said. "Now the words."

" 'When Lady Luck lies with Grim Justice—' "

"Two notes in 'Grim,' " the bard corrected. "G to F-sharp."

Olive sang the the line over.

"Good. Now both lines."

" 'When Lady Luck lies with Grim Justice,/The soaring stars will be man's auspice;' " the halfling sang.

"Again."

Olive repeated the phrase three more times before Finder seemed satisfied. He smiled and wrapped a curl of her hair around his finger. "I might make a bard out of you yet," he said, tugging playfully at the strand of hair.

"I'd settle for not ending up a corpse," Olive cracked.

"Never settle for anything, Olive girl. You're too good for that," the bard insisted, releasing her hair.

The compliment was lost on the halfling, who had begun to notice a forced sound to the bard's cheery tone. She could hear him wheezing, and he had to use his good hand to shift the injured one.

Olive pulled out one of her light cotton tunics from her sack, bunched it up, and poured what was left of her whiskey on it. She reached over and wrapped the wet cloth around the bard's swollen hand, then handed Finder her water jar. "When the bandage gets warm, pour some more water on it," she instructed. "Try drinking the water, too. It might help."

Finder nodded. He struggled to take a deep breath before he said, "You'll find the potions in the mahogany wardrobe. They'll be alphabetized. Look for the one labeled 'neutralize poison.' Also, bring the spellbook on the marble-topped desk and the sack of gems in the hidden compartment under the worktable bench." The bard drew in another wheezy breath before continuing. "The door will lock behind you when you close it. You only need the music key from the tunnel side. You can unlock it from the workshop side by tracing your finger over the treble cleft carved into the doorframe."

Olive nodded.

"You'd better take this," the bard said, twisting one of the plain gold rings on his injured hand. "It's a ring of protection."

"You'll never get that off," Olive said, flinching instinctively. "Better forget it."

"No," Finder replied. He hummed a high B-flat, and the ring expanded until he could pull it off his swollen finger. He slipped it on Olive's tiny fifth finger, and the ring shrank magically until it fit snugly.

"I'll be back soon," Olive promised, rising to her feet and shouldering her backpack.

Finder nodded, too tired to reply.

Olive drew the bolt, opened the door to the underground tunnels, and crept down the staircase. When she reached the first cave-in, she pulled a flint and a fresh torch out of her sack, but she debated mentally with herself before lighting the torch. She couldn't hide in the shadows if she carried a torch, but a torch would at least keep her from bumping into any orcs in the dark. If only she could see in the dark like the orcs could. "Why did I just inherit Grandmother Rose's singing voice? Why couldn't I get her nightvision, too?" she muttered.

With several strikes of the flint, she had the torch blazing. She began crawling through the first cave-in tunnel. It was more difficult crawling with a torch in one hand, and the knowledge that she was crawling toward orcs didn't compel her to move any faster.

She tried concentrating on how heroic the deed would sound when she told it later, but she couldn't help thinking that the entire ugly situation could have been avoided. It was all Finder's fault. "If you'd left the tower when I asked, we wouldn't have lost the finder's stone to Kyre," she muttered as she crawled. "If you'd only accepted Giogi's offer to stay in Immersea, we wouldn't have had to dig and crawl through dirt for four hours like moles. And if you hadn't been such a show-off with the locks, we wouldn't have been discovered by the orcs, we'd have probably made it into your lab, I wouldn't be covered with orc blood, and you wouldn't be dying from a poison needle trap."

Olive reached the other side of the first cave-in tunnel and slid down to the floor. She sighed. She'd gotten what she had to say out of her system. It hardly mattered that she hadn't said it to Finder's face. It wasn't as if he would pay any attention to her anyway. She padded silently down the stone passageways.

After wriggling through the second cave-in tunnel, Olive proceeded more cautiously toward the third and last cave-in. She considered putting her torch out before going through it. No, she thought, it's better to see what I'm afraid of than to be afraid of what I don't see. She crawled up the mound of dirt and stone and into the tiny tunnel. About halfway through, where Finder had collapsed the first time they had come through, Olive found the bard's dagger. As she slipped it into her pack, she imagined how she might wrap it and give it to him as a birthday present.

You'll have to get out of here alive with a neutralize poison potion first, she chided herself, or Finder may not make it to his next birthday. She emerged through the other side of the tunnel.

She paused several minutes, peering into the darkness beyond the iron gate, looking for the telltale red gleam of orc eyes. When her head began to hurt from the strain of not blinking, Olive decided it was time to get going. She slid as quietly as possible down the pile of dirt and padded up to the iron gate.

Without touching the gate or the lock, the halfling examined them for several minutes before she discovered a string between the gate and a hole in the wall nearby. Olive presumed that the string went all the way to the orc warren, where it triggered some sort of silent alarm. At any rate, the string was very well concealed. If she hadn't been certain that it was there, she might not have looked hard enough to find it. She checked for a second string, but didn't find one. Apparently the orcs weren't as paranoid as she was. Fortunately the alarm string was near the floor, so she could work on it comfortably. She wedged her torch in the grate, put her pack down, and pulled out the equipment she would need. She used a bit of putty to hold the string taut against the bottom bar of the iron grate. With a pair of scissors, she clipped the string where it was connected to the door.

It took her only a few seconds to unlock the door. Then she spritzed the hinges of the gate with oil and pushed the gate open a foot.

"So far, so good," she whispered, picking up her torch and pack and slipping through the gap. She pushed the gate nearly, but not quite, closed. Then she tiptoed down the corridor.

When she reached the gap in the wall that led to the tunnel the orcs had come from, Olive dashed across the open space, then pressed herself against the wall on the other side and waited a minute.

She listened carefully, but she heard neither voices nor footfalls. Finder must have been right about the orcs relying on their alarm, she thought as she crept down to the second iron grate.

The second lock was a masterful piece of workmanship, of fairly recent design. It definitely was not the kind she'd expect to see in an orc warren. The orcs' friend who possessed the disintegrate spell must have installed it, Olive decided. After setting her pack down again and disengaging the alarm, the halfling examined the other mechanisms with more care.

The needle trap was especially nasty. It refilled and retriggered itself automatically. Olive pulled out an especially long pick. Holding it awkwardly from a position above the lock, with her hand safely out of the way, she twisted it in the keyhole and watched the trap spring. It was a very long, very sharp needle. Olive sprang it several more times, but the reserve of poison didn't show any signs of running low. Judging from its effect on Finder, Olive suspected it was too potent a poison to risk receiving even a trace dose.

Olive turned and looked behind her, just to be sure there weren't any orcs watching her work. Assured that she was still alone in the hallway, she wedged her torch in the iron grate and turned her attention back to the trap.

She drew out Finder's dagger. It was heavy, just right for bending needles. It took her three tries, but she managed to bring the blade down on the needle after it sprang out and before it retracted. It bent, but the force of the spring connected to it pulled it back into the mechanism. Once inside the retriggering box, however, the needle was jammed tight and couldn't spring out again. Olive sniffed once with pride, then spat on Finder's blade a few times and wiped it off on her cloak so as not to risk leaving any poison on it.

After checking over her shoulder once again for any stray orcs, she began work on the lock. It was a heavy one, and she broke two wire picks in it. She wondered momentarily whether it had been welded shut. She began to examine miscellaneous keys from her key collection. When she thought she had a near match, she wriggled both it and another wire about in the hole. She tried to put Finder's poisoned hand out of her mind. She couldn't allow anything to distract her.

Olive had no idea how long she'd been fiddling with the gate, but when the lock finally gave way, her torch was burnt to a nub. When she pushed on the gate, the burning stick fell to the ground. The flame immediately went out, leaving only glowing cinders at her feet.

The halfling picked up her pack and pushed the door open farther, not bothering to oil the hinges. They didn't squeak, suggesting that the door was probably used often. Olive tried to put that idea out of her mind. If the only key was Finder's unfinished melody, there wasn't an orc in the world who could open the door. She'd heard orcs singing several times, and she had been anything but impressed.

Olive ran her hand along the polished steel door. There was no handle or lock. "Listen up, door," she whispered. She sang the lyrics to the melody Finder had taught her as softly as she could. Something in the door made a clicking noise. Olive pushed on the door gently, and it swung open. Bright light flooded into the corridor from the workshop within. Olive slipped into the room and pushed the door closed behind her. It clicked again. She was locked safely inside. The halfling sighed with relief and leaned back against the door.

"Hello, Father," a voice said from inside the workshop.

Olive stood bolt upright. A figure stood before her, dressed in black robes. He looked just like Finder, only younger, when he was in his prime. When he said the word "Father," his voice dripped with sarcasm.

"Flattery!" Olive gasped. "But—but you're dead! Giogi killed you!"

"I've been hoping you would escape the Harpers' prison someday and return here," Flattery said.

Since Flattery seemed unaware that she was not Finder, Olive realized she was seeing only a magical image of the evil mage, a message Flattery had left behind for Finder. Flattery had assumed his creator would be the only other person who could open the workshop door.

"After the weeks you spent trying to force me to sing your songs," the image of Flattery said, "I hope you'll be pleased to learn that I finally broke down and sang the key to the workshop door. Naturally I did not sing it to please you. When you struck me that first time, only three days after I was 'born,' I realized there was no pleasing you. Even if my new voice hadn't been weak and immature, even if it had been identical to yours, you would have found something else to criticize me for. Knowing that enabled me to endure your violent threats and your pitiful apologies."

Olive clenched her fists, digging her nails into her palms, trying to deny the truth behind Flattery's evaluation of Finder.

"It is now three years since my escape from this place, this hell hole you chose as my nursery," Flattery's image explained, indicating the workshop with a wave of his hand. "The Harpers have destroyed your reputation so fast that even I am impressed with their power. I haven't heard one of your stupid little tunes for nearly a year and a half now. Your name is truly forgotten.

"I shall never forget, though, the look of surprise and fear on your face the day you came down to this room and found me free. Your apprentice, Kirkson, had taken pity on me—something you and your fawning Maryje never possessed. Kirkson used to come down late at night to comfort me as best he could. It was he who gave me some of your books to read. By mistake, he gave me your spellbook. When I realized what it was, I used its magic to escape from my cage and stole the disintegration ring from your desk. Then I waited. It wouldn't have mattered that day whether you intended to plead with me or to beat me again. Either way, I intended to kill you and Maryje. Kirkson alone would be spared. It was unfortunate that it was he who leapt into the path of my disintegration ray in order to save your miserable lives.

"Since then, however, I've had my revenge on Maryje. She went mad after they exiled you, and last night she killed herself. It was I who drove her to it. It wasn't very difficult. I sent her constant nightmares about my pain and suffering, along with telepathic suggestions that she was worthless."

Olive felt sick to her stomach. She was trembling with grief and rage. She hadn't wanted to see the workshop where Flattery had been created, and she'd been right.

"That leaves only you, Father," Flattery's image said, spitting out the word "Father" like an epithet. "I returned here to my birthplace to claim my inheritance. I've left you nothing. You might as well be dead."

From the center of Flattery's image, a dozen green rays shot out like spokes from a wheel and whirled around until a single green plane of light shimmered three feet above the floor. Then just as suddenly, the green rays disappeared along with Flattery's image.

Olive reached up and touched the top of her head. A large clump of her hair came off in her hand, shaved off near the roots by the strange green light. A line of black scorch marks ran along the walls and furniture of the workshop.

The halfling walked about the workshop like an automaton. The room was well lighted with magical stones set in the walls and ceiling. Everything was tidy and dust-free. Olive looked at the marble-topped desk. There was no spellbook there. There were no books anywhere in the room. The shelves that lined the walls stood empty. She went over to the mahogany wardrobe on the wall behind the well and opened the doors. The shelves within were empty, too. There not only were no neutralize poison potions, but there were no potions at all.

Olive sat down on the bench at the worktable without bothering to check for any secret compartment holding a sack of gems. It just didn't matter anymore. Nothing mattered. She pulled her knees up to her chin, wrapped her arms around her legs, lowered her head, and wept uncontrollably.

* * * * *

Finder awoke from his nightmare shouting in fear. It took him several moments to remember he was in the ruins of his manor house. He was still having trouble breathing, and he was drenched in a feverish sweat and shivering from the cooling air. The sun was beginning to set, and the moon was cresting the horizon.

The bard had been dreaming of Flattery, something he thought was long past him. He'd told the lie of the creature's destruction so many times that he'd almost come to believe it himself. Leave it to Olive, he thought, a lying thief herself, to discover the existence of Flattery.

Finder had always believed that Tymora, Lady Luck, favored the halfling rogue, but now it seemed that Tyr Grimjaws, the Even-Handed, God of Justice, had made Olive his agent. If she told Elminster that she knew Flattery hadn't died, Elminster would know Finder had lied about the ice shard exploding in order to cover up a worse secret. If Olive knew anything about how he had treated Flattery and told Elminster, the bard's reputation would be ruined. Finder wondered whether Tymora had made Olive loyal to him because Lady Luck still favored him, or if Tyr was testing him somehow with the halfling's presence.

In his dream, Finder had opened the door to his workshop, just as he had two centuries ago, and discovered Flattery standing there, pointing a ringed finger at him, prepared to disintegrate him. In Finder's dream, though, it was Olive, not Kirkson, who leapt in front of him to save his life from the green death ray, but the halfling was too short, so the ray hit Finder anyway, and he died.

If Finder hadn't been feverish with poison, he might have chalked the dream up to memories brought on by the attempt to visit the scene of his failure. He might also have scoffed at the idea that the gods took any interest in him whatsoever. Finder, however, was feverish with poison, and his vivid imagination found other reasons for the dream. He thought it must be the gods' way of telling him he would die no matter what. "Why should I die?" he muttered to the sky. "Elminster hasn't. Morala hasn't."

The bard wondered what was taking Olive so long. He estimated she'd been gone over an hour. He had no doubt the halfling could handle the locks and the traps, and he grinned with pride at the memory of how easily she'd mastered the melody for the door lock. There was nothing in the workshop that could give her any trouble, he reassured himself. He dismissed the dream as having no basis in reality. After all, according to Olive, Flattery was dead.

Of course, he could have been wrong about the orcs. They may have decided to post a guard after all, and were lying in wait to grab Olive when she passed the tunnel that led to their lair. The longer the shadows lengthened, the more uneasy Finder grew. She'd saved his life twice already today, yet he'd had the nerve to convince her to go past an orc warren alone to save his life a third time. Here he was, a master bard, a Harper, a full-grown human male, relying on a tiny halfling female to pull his fat out of the fire. Female! Sweet Selune! He hadn't even considered what the orcs would do to her if they captured her.

Finder caught sight of the sun and the moon just as they were equally distant from the horizon, like Tyr's scales, balanced in the sky. Then the sun sank lower and the moon rose higher. The bard sighed. If Olive didn't return with a neutralize poison potion soon, he would die anyway. With a deep sense of shame, he realized there was no sense in letting her die, too. He twisted his tunic into a sling for his injured arm and forced himself to his feet. His head spun, and glittering dots danced before his eyes, but he did not change his mind. As the sun sank, the bard climbed down the stairs into the underground passages in search of the halfling.

* * * * *

After Olive had cried herself out, she stared for a while at the wall of the brightly lit workshop, blinking like an owl in daylight. Part of her kept telling her to hurry back to Finder. If she couldn't get him to the road, she could at least be with him when he died. Another part of her didn't want to watch him die. That part must have been stronger, because she didn't move until something heavy thumped against the door.

Olive started and nearly tumbled from the bench. She padded over to the enchanted steel door and pressed her ear against it. From the hallway on the other side came harsh, unintelligible cries. The orcs had returned and discovered the unlocked gate, Olive realized.

Fortunately there was a second door out of the workshop, but if she used it, she'd have to find her way through strange tunnels and dig her way through Tymora knew how many more cave-ins. Then it occurred to Olive that the other door might also lead to a T-trap guarded by orcs. The thought paralyzed her with fear.

From near the door, she heard another cry—an unmistakably haughty voice demanding the orcs back away.

"Finder?" Olive whispered to herself, confused by the bard's presence. Why hadn't he stayed put?

From the hallway, Finder shouted, "You have no business here. This is my home. Leave now or face the consequences."

Has he gone mad? the halfling wondered. There was a

slurred sound to his speech and a tremor in his deep voice. That's just great. He's delirious, she thought wearily.

The orcs in the tunnel outside shouted and screamed. There was another thump at the door, like a spear or a crossbow hitting against it. Then suddenly there was silence. A new voice, sharp and high-pitched, spoke in the common tongue. "Release him," the voice ordered calmly, in the manner of a being accustomed to being obeyed. Olive couldn't tell if it was male or female.

Someone else was out there, someone who ordered orcs around. Someone, Olive suspected, who had the power to disintegrate ceilings and other things.

"Don't try anything foolish. I can kill you in an instant. You are the Nameless Bard?" the voice asked.

"Yes," Finder replied with a croaking sound in his voice.

Olive bit her lip, wondering what she could do to rescue her friend.

"I'm pleased you returned," the sharp voice said. "I was sorry to have missed you the first time. The orcs were sure you'd fled for good. It seems that I came to investigate this tunnel in the nick of time. Now that you've gone to all the trouble to pick the lock on the gates, you might as well open the door to your workshop for me," the voice demanded.

"Why should I?" Finder replied. His tone was haughty, but Olive could hear him wheezing even through the workshop door.

"Because if you don't, these orcs will kill you," the voice explained.

"I'm already dying," Finder said. "I was caught by the poison needle trap in this gate."

"Show me," the sharp voice ordered.

There was a short silence, then the sharp voice said, "My, my. How inconvenient for you, nameless one. You can hardly play an instrument with that hand. Corx, the antidote!"

"He's not dying yet," an orc replied in common. "Let him open the door first."

"I need this hand to open the door," Finder lied.

"Corx, obey me!" the sharp voice insisted.

There was the sound of grumbling among the orcs, and a moment later, Olive heard Finder say, "A good year for antidotes. A youthful bouquet, fruity and light." His voice still sounded weak.

"My name is Xaran," the sharp voice announced, "and I have just saved your life. I think that deserves some consideration, don't you?"

"Consideration, certainly," Finder replied, "but not license to loot my workshop."

"I can still kill you without blinking an eye," Xaran pointed out.

"But then you'll never get into my workshop," Finder replied. "you've gone to such trouble to set up a trap to capture me before I got inside. What is it you're after? Perhaps we can come to some sort of agreement."

"Well, naturally my associates, these orcs, are interested in whatever wealth you might have been hoarding in there for the past two centuries," Xaran said.

"I'm flattered," Finder replied.

"I doubt it. Your monstrous ego is well known. Perhaps, though, your pride is justified. Certainly I can think of many uses for your renowned skills."

"You won't get much out of me if all you intend to offer me is my life," Finder said.

"But suppose I were to offer you immortality?"

"I already have that," Finder boasted, "through my music."

"But does that truly satisfy you?" Xaran asked. "Think of all the adventures you could yet experience, all the tales still untold, all the songs unfinished. People not even born could one day benefit from your wisdom and tutelage—singers and musicians, adventurers and Harpers, wizards and kings. You haven't even lived as long as Elminster the Sage. He has yet to surrender to death. Why should you?"

Listening behind the enchanted steel door, Olive tapped her foot nervously. This Xaran knows Finder too well, she thought. Who is he, anyway? How did he learn the bard's weaknesses? And most importantly, what in the Nine Hells does he want? The outline of a plan came to Olive, and she began pulling light stones out of the wall as she listened to the voices filtering through the door.

"Were you thinking of offering me an unlimited supply of elixirs of youth?" the bard asked. "Or did you have something more devious in mind, like depositing me in a magic jar or turning me into a lich?"

"No," Xaran said. "I had in mind a new spell, one that will

make your body immortal."

"I see," Finder said. "And what do you ask in return?"

"I am interested in your advanced knowledge of simula-crums."

"So is every evil tyrant in the Realms," Finder retorted.

"But I'm the evil tyrant who holds your life in his hands, so to speak."

"True enough. Is that all you want?"

"No. There is one other little thing. You must bring me Aka-bar Bel Akash. I believe you are acquainted with the gentle-man."

"Akabar?" Finder asked with surprise, echoing Olive's own thoughts. "What do you want with him?"

"He has in his possession something I desire. You must convince him to visit you here."

"I haven't seen Akabar in over a year," Finder argued. "He returned to Turmish."

"He is near Shadowdale now," Xaran corrected him.

"I see," Finder said.

"Well, nameless one?" Xaran prompted.

Olive stood poised at the door, holding a fistful of the magical light stones in one hand and Finder's dagger in the other. This might be my last chance for a surprise attack, she thought.

She reached up and traced the treble clef carved in the door-frame. The door swung open a foot, and with a banshee shriek, the halfling burst out of the workshop and hurled the light stones down the hallway. The orcs screamed in terror at the brilliant light and covered their eyes with their arms. While they were temporarily blinded, Olive lunged out with Finder's dagger to the right, where she'd heard Xaran's voice coming from, but there was no one there. Olive whirled about and pushed Finder through the workshop doorway.

As she turned around again to close the door, she felt a sharp pain in her shoulder, and blood began oozing into the fabric of her tunic. Olive's eyes widened at the sight of what had just attacked her. There, five feet above the ground, just outside the door, floated Xaran—a hideous ball of flesh with a monstrous maw of fangs, one great central bloodshot eye, and a crown of ten eye stalks waving like serpents. Xaran was a beholder!

The halfling realized with a jolt that when she had tried to attack Xaran with the dagger, she'd lunged just beneath it, ironically in the only place it could not harm her with any of its magical eye rays. When she'd pulled back into the supposed safety of the workshop, she'd stepped into its line of vision, and it had hit her with a look from an eye that caused magical wounds.

Olive slammed the door shut before the monster could turn an even deadlier eye in her direction.

"What are you doing?" Finder shouted, squinting in the brightly lit room .

"What am I doing?" Olive squeaked with astonishment. "I'm saving your life! In case you hadn't noticed, there was a beholder out there!"

"I was in the middle of negotiating a deal with it," Finder said angrily.

"Are you nuts? Beholders are incredibly evil!" Olive shrieked.

"So? They are also honorable . . . in their own fashion."

"They're also vicious," Olive argued. "As soon as you refused to bring Akabar to it, it would have killed you."

"What makes you think I was going to refuse?" Finder asked.

Olive stared up at the bard in horror, but Finder just glared back at her, offering no further explanation.

She thought she'd shut all the monsters out of the workshop. Now she wasn't certain.

❧ 10 ❧

The Hunt

Alias watched with relief as Breck Orcsbane urged his horse down the left-hand fork of the trail they followed in order to scout ahead. The ranger was in a foul mood, and a respite from his company was more than welcome. He scowled constantly at the ground and hardly spoke to her at all, except to complain about Dragonbait. Alias could understand how Breck felt, but silent, uncritical sympathy did not come easily to her. They'd been on the road for three hours now, and at first the ranger's prediction that it would be easy to track Grypht had proven true. They'd begun their search atop Oakwood Knoll and had no trouble finding the creature's path leading down from the knoll. Grypht was large and heavy; his feet sank deep into the wet soil, and his great tail knocked down large swaths of vegetation like a scythe.

Grypht, however, was not a beast, but a creature with intelligence and cunning. He knew enough to travel paths that were rocky whenever possible, where he would leave no prints, or to cut through areas heavily strewn with fallen leaves, where he could use his tail to brush the leaves around to cover his passage. Following Grypht proved to be a challenge to the Harper ranger, despite his keen eye and years of tracking experience. He had put himself under so much pressure to avenge Kyre that Alias didn't like to think what would happen if they lost Grypht's trail.

The ranger would have been happier, Alias realized, tracking alone. Then he could grieve for the half-elf in private. They couldn't risk having him find Akabar and Grypht without the presence of others, though. In the state Breck was in, he'd end up attacking Grypht or Akabar or both and end up dead himself. Since Mourngrym had forced Breck to travel with two relative strangers, the ranger repressed his grief behind a wall of hostility.

As for Breck's complaints about Dragonbait, though, Alias was on the verge of agreeing with the ranger's desire to leave the saurial behind. She'd begun the hunt arguing with Breck in Dragonbait's defense. The ranger didn't want to travel with Dragonbait unless he was mounted, as they were. Breck kept insisting that the creature would slow them down, but Alias had explained that Dragonbait could keep up with a trotting horse for hours. Since then, the saurial paladin had proceeded to make a liar out of her so often that even she was growing annoyed with him. He fell behind again and again for no apparent reason, as if he had no interest in their hunt. Once when the swordswoman had turned around to urge him to keep up, Alias had found him gathering nuts. Several times he seemed to know the path Grypht was taking but would not reveal it until Breck had discovered it for himself.

Alias had first noticed the saurial sniffing the air when they were on Oakwood Knoll. When the party had reached the first stony path, he'd sniffed the air again. Once Breck had disappeared down the path to check the trail to the north, the saurial had taken a few steps down the path to the south and sat down with a sigh. He did the same thing at a second fork, and again at a creek bed. He'd waited a quarter of an hour while Breck rode around searching for the trail beneath a thick carpet of leaves, until it seemed as if the ranger might explode. Then the paladin had casually plodded through the leaves in a direction which Breck, following behind, later found to be correct.

Finally guessing that the saurial's sense of smell might be as sharp as any hunting hound's, Breck had asked Alias to ask Dragonbait to lead the way, but at the next choice of intersections, Dragonbait scratched his head and acted confused. Breck, completely frustrated with the paladin, had resumed the lead.

Alias, familiar with her companion's phony "dumb animal" routine, had glared at the saurial and whispered, "What is wrong with you? Why won't you help him?"

The ranger is beyond my help, Dragonbait had signed.

Alias had ridden off after the ranger in a huff. She didn't know what had gotten into the paladin, but she knew they couldn't afford to alienate Breck completely. Aside from worrying about keeping the ranger from starting a battle with Akabar and Grypht, in the back of Alias's mind was the realization that if they ever did locate Nameless, Breck was one of the bard's judges.

Now, as Breck disappeared down the fork in the road, Alias dismounted to stretch her legs. Dragonbait was nowhere to be seen. The swordswoman walked back down the path to see what he was up to. She spotted him tying a strip of blue cloth to a tree branch just above his head. She crept up behind him until she was a mere three feet away.

"What are you doing?" she asked suddenly.

Dragonbait jumped and whirled around, obviously startled.

"You're marking the trail," she exclaimed in surprise. "Why?"

Mourngrym might come, Dragonbait signed.

"Mourngrym is *not* coming," Alias retorted. She reached up to yank the strip of cloth from the tree and nearly lost her balance when she tripped on a heap of walnuts piled on the trail just below the branch.

"Why are you leaving nuts out on the trail?" she demanded.

An offering to Tymora, the saurial signed.

"Nuts?" Alias cried. "Since when does Lady Luck demand offerings of nuts? Dragonbait, what has gotten into you? Why are you slowing us down?"

Breck's too angry, Dragonbait signed as he had at the tower. *He's not getting any calmer.*

"But you're only making him angrier. And you still haven't told me why you're marking the trail," Alias said. "What are the nuts for, anyway?"

Dragonbait pointed down the trail. Breck had returned. The saurial loped up to the ranger's horse.

Alias growled to herself. Dragonbait was keeping something from her, she was certain of it. She followed her companion back down the trail. "Did you find anything?" she asked Breck as she mounted her horse.

Breck nodded wordlessly and led the way back down the fork of the trail he'd just examined.

Dragonbait slapped at Alias's horse so it trotted down the trail ahead of him. It took the swordswoman a moment to slow her mount and turn to be sure the paladin was following. Dragonbait trotted past her. Alias turned her horse again and followed him. She'd spotted another strip of cloth hanging from a branch to mark the fork they now rode on. It wouldn't do to confront the saurial in front of Breck, but eventually she'd find out what he was up to if she had to shake it out of the paladin.

* * * * *

Akabar watched with fascination as Grypht studied the teleport spell carved into his staff. The carvings didn't look the least bit like any writing Akabar had ever seen. They appeared to be nothing but notches and lines carved at irregular intervals. The Turmish scholar longed to pester the saurial wizard into translating for him, but Grypht's tongues spell had worn off. Besides, they had both agreed that the most important thing was for them to return as soon as possible to Shadowdale, so Akabar remained silent.

In the back of the Turmishman's mind, he was anxious about Zhara. He had a blurry memory of Kyre speaking some spell that included his wife's name. Dragonbait had promised to look after her, though, which assuaged the southern mage's fears considerably. Still, he'd be glad to get back to Zhara.

He'd also be relieved to get out of the forest wilderness all around them. The slender oak saplings that surrounded them were lovely, but there were three especially large maples off to one side whose appearance the mage found disturbing. By their size, Akabar judged them to be hundreds of years old, but he didn't expect they could live much longer. Their trunks were riddled with insect bore holes. Sucker vines covered many of their branches. While some of their leaves were an autumnal gold, most were brown and dry far too early in the season. He hadn't noticed the trees when he first regained consciousness, but now he couldn't get them out of his mind, even when he turned his eyes away from them. As the sun sank lower in the sky and the shadows lengthened and deepened, the sickly trees and even the young oak saplings seemed to close in on the forest clearing where they sat.

Akabar started and gave a shout. The trees *were* closing in on them. The oak saplings surrounded them in a neat ring, twenty feet across, standing so close together that their trunks resembled the bars of a prison. There was no space wide enough to pass between them; the two mages were trapped inside the circle of saplings with the three great maple trees. At Akabar's shout, Grypht looked up from his staff with a look of annoyance that his study had been interrupted. The moment the saurial spotted the maples, he leaped to his feet and roared.

Just then Akabar noticed the features of a face on one of the older maples. He also noticed that the tree's trunk split into two great, bark-covered legs. The maples weren't trees at all, Akabar realized. They were treants, good creatures who protected the forest. All three treants closed in on Grypht. The saurial wizard growled threateningly and held out his hand to cast a spell.

"Wait!" Akabar warned, stepping between the saurial and the treant he was pointing at. "These trees are treants," the Turmishman said. "They won't harm us."

Grypht growled again, shoving Akabar aside. Akabar remembered then that the saurial could no longer understand him. Somehow he had to figure out a way to keep the wizard from injuring the treants. The smell of fresh-mown hay began to fill the meadow as Grypht began sprinkling a tiny white ball with yellow powder.

"No!" Akabar shouted. He rushed toward the saurial wizard and yanked at the sleeve of his robe, jerking his arm to one side, so that the fireball Grypht had summoned exploded off to one side of the treants instead of in their midst. Immediately several of the oak saplings surrounding them crackled into flame.

Suddenly Akabar felt himself being lifted off the ground by the sash around his robe. Akabar strained around and looked up. A huge treant held him in one of its woody hands and glared down at him.

"Please," Akabar said in common, "don't harm the saurial. He's a visitor from another world. He doesn't understand about treants."

The treant cackled wickedly and pointed at Grypht with its free leafy hand. "Kill him!" it ordered the other two treants in a booming voice.

"No!" Akabar shouted, struggling fiercely and beating ineffectively at the wooden hand holding him nearly ten feet off the ground.

Unable to cast a spell before the treants were upon him, Grypht grabbed the arm of the nearest one and swung his feet from the ground like a child swinging from a tree branch. Unable to bear the weight of the giant lizard, the treant's arm broke away from its body with the dull sound of a rotting log when it crumbles beneath a woodsman's axe. Dust rose from the decayed wooden arm as it crashed to the ground.

The injured treant's face formed a scowl, but it gave no indication that it felt any pain.

Akabar's eyes widened in horror. From the hollow depression where the treant's arm had broken away from the trunk, a slimy green tendril shot out and whipped about Grypht's throat. Akabar realized he'd made a terrible mistake. These creatures might once have been treants, but like Kyre, they'd been infested somehow with a rotting parasite that made them servants of the Darkbringer.

The tendril wrapped about Grypht's throat began to constrict, choking the saurial and pulling him closer to the treant's other arm. With both hands, Gryphyt grabbed a section of the tendril between his throat and the treant and gave a sharp, powerful tug. The tendril snapped in two like a piece of rotten twine, but before Grypht could move away to try another spell, a second treant came up behind him and smashed one of its arms down heavily on the saurial's head.

Grypht fell to the ground, stunned, and both treants began kicking at him with their massive wooden legs.

The treant that held Akabar remained motionless. Akabar slid his dagger out of his sleeve and slashed through the sash at his waist. He fell to the ground, landing on his knees, sending needles of pain lancing through them. Quickly he rolled away from the treant, and gritting his teeth against the pain, he staggered to his feet.

Pulling out a piece of red phosphorus from a pocket of his robe, Akabar began to chant in Turmish. The moment before the phosphorus ignited, the mage tossed it into the air and imagined a circle.

A curtain of flame surged up around the treant, trapping it. The wounded treant attacking Grypht was caught in the perimeter of the blazing wall. The creature bellowed, and its dead leaves ignited with a great *whoosh*, though the bark of its skin smoldered and would not burn.

The remaining treant backed away from the fire, and Grypht seized the opportunity to roll away from the monster's feet toward Akabar. The southern mage spat out another spell and rushed forward to distract the treant so the saurial could escape. Instantly six images of Akabar, magical illusions, rushed forward beside him.

The treant wavered with confusion. It reached out to grab the mage, but its wooden hand closed on empty air, and the image before it blinked out of existence. The treant turned to grab another image.

Behind him, Akabar could smell the scent of Grypht's spell-casting. Two flaming bolts shot between Akabar and his images. The fiery magical weaponry pierced the hide of the treant, setting its leaves alight, but its bark burnt little better than that of its companion.

Grypht picked up the Turmish mage by the waist, slung him over his shoulder, and made a run for the wall of saplings that surrounded them. The small trees were no match for nearly a quarter ton of angry saurial. The scaly wizard crashed through the oak saplings as if they were stalks of grass. It was several minutes before he stopped running and set Akabar down on the ground. By the light of the saurial's staff, Akabar could see that the creature was badly injured. His breathing was labored, there was a gash in his armor frill, and his scaly face was lacerated and bruised.

Grypht handed Akabar his staff, and from the sleeves of his robe, he pulled out a strip of parchment, some white powder, and a ten-foot length of silken rope. He twisted the parchment strip once before moistening the ends and fastening them together with a dab of the white powder. Then he slipped one end of the rope through the twisted loop of paper, sprinkled it with the rest of the white powder, and tossed it into the air. The rope caught on something unseen and dangled before the saurial's face, suspended from nowhere. Grypht continued to concentrate on the rope for another minute—extending the length of the spell, Akabar suspected—before motioning for the Turmishman to climb it.

Akabar handed Grypht's staff back to him, spat on his hands, and pulled himself up the rope into the extradimensional space created by the saurial wizard's spell. Grypht tossed him his staff, and then Akabar watched anxiously as the scaly lizard hauled his great bulk up the rope with his muscular arms. Once the wizard had reached the top and collapsed beside him, Akabar pulled the rope up behind them.

The space they found themselves in was white and empty.

The two spell-casters, Grypht's staff, and the rope were the only occupants of the dimension. It was a dull place, but safe—for as long as it lasted. Considering the power Akabar had seen the saurial wizard wield, the Turmishman estimated this dimension spell would last several hours. He turned to ask Grypht what they would do next, but the saurial was unconscious, gasping for air as if he'd been poisoned.

Akabar pulled away the treant vines that remained around the creature's throat, carefully removing the suckers that appeared to be burrowing into the scales and plate protecting Grypht's neck. Almost immediately Grypht began to breathe more easily, though he was still badly injured. One side of his body was scorched from being too close to Akabar's wall of fire. The Turmish mage felt a twinge of guilt at having endangered the wizard, but he'd really had no choice. Mostly, Akabar suspected, Grypht was hurt from the beating he'd taken by the twisted treants.

The only thing to be done now, Akabar realized, was to let the creature rest and heal naturally. He hoped the saurial wizard would awaken before the extradimensional space dissolved, so they could return to Shadowdale without further incident.

* * * * *

Breck scowled across the ravine and cursed under his breath.

"What is it?" Alias asked, pulling her horse up beside the ranger's mount.

"Damn magic trick!" the ranger growled. "The creature's taken a dimensional doorway across. We've got to climb down the ravine and back up and pick up the search for the trail again on the other side."

"Oh," Alias replied softly.

Breck glanced at the sun, which lay low near the horizon. "There's just enough light to make it to the other side before dark."

"It's an awfully steep slope for the horses," Alias ventured.

"There's a trail leading down. We passed it a few minutes back," Breck said, turning his horse and urging the animal south, along the edge of the ravine.

Alias turned her own horse to follow the ranger. Dragonbait was nowhere in sight, but when she and Breck reached the trail leading down into the ravine, they discovered the saurial seated beside it, munching an apple.

Ignoring Dragonbait, the ranger scratched his horse's neck and spoke some encouraging words into its ear. The horse started down the steep trail without the slightest balk. Alias's mount followed the example set by the lead horse. Dragonbait stood up as they passed and followed along behind, tossing his apple core into the brush.

In the ravine, it grew dark before the sun had set, and Dragonbait took the lead. The saurial paladin commanded his magical sword to flame and carried it high, like a torch. The river at the bottom of the ravine was deep and swift, but fortunately the trail led to a rough wooden bridge across the water. They filled their water bottles and continued on. By the time they'd reached the top of the ravine again, the sun had set.

Breck passed the saurial and turned his horse back to the north.

"You're not going to try tracking in the dark, are you?" Alias asked.

"There'll be twilight for at least an hour yet," Breck replied, "and the moon is full tonight." He nudged his horse onward.

Dragonbait stood aside so Alias could follow the ranger. The swordswoman checked often to be sure Dragonbait kept up now that it was growing dark. Occasionally she looked down into the ravine, and on one such occasion, she spotted a light moving across the bridge.

Alias halted her horse and waited until Breck had moved out of earshot. Then she dismounted and grabbed Dragonbait's shirt before he could pass her by.

"Who's following us?" she demanded in an urgent whisper.

The saurial paladin shrugged.

"Who were you marking the trail for?"

Dragonbait looked at her blankly, but Alias wouldn't accept his dumb animal look.

"Dragonbait, I can't believe you're treating me like this. Why don't you trust me?" Alias asked.

Dragonbait stared down at the ground. He looked genuinely ashamed.

"Just tell me," Alias said. "I promise I won't get angry. Who is it? Olive? Nameless? Another saurial?"

Dragonbait signed five letters, spelling a name.

"Zhara!" the swordswoman shouted angrily.

You promised you wouldn't get angry, Dragonbait signed.

"Zhara?" Alias asked more softly. "It can't be Zhara. Mourngrym promised to keep her at the tower."

Dragonbait signed that Zhara was a powerful priestess.

Alias scrunched up her forehead, considering the paladin's words. She hardly knew a thing about the spells gods granted their priests. Healing and removing curses was all she ever considered priests good for. That Zhara could escape a guarded tower had never occurred to her. "Breck is going to be furious when he finds out," she whispered.

He's already furious, Dragonbait signed.

"But not with us," Alias said.

If you don't tell him, Dragonbait signed, *he won't know. And we need her.*

"No, we don't," Alias growled. "You promised Akabar you'd look after her. Suppose she gets hurt chasing after us in the wild. Have you considered that?"

Zhara isn't helpless, Dragonbait signed.

Alias sighed. "If you say so," she said, resigned. She turned back to her horse and remounted.

Just then Breck came back down along the trail, looking for them. "What's keeping you?" he demanded. "I've found the place where the beast crossed over."

"I had to pick a pebble out of my horse's shoe," Alias lied.

"Is the horse all right?" the ranger asked.

Alias nodded. "Let's go," she said, anxious that Breck should not spot the light in the ravine.

Breck turned his mount around. Suddenly he pulled the horse still. "What was that?" he asked.

"What was what?" Alias asked.

"Over there," Breck said, pointing. "A bright light, like a fireball." To Alias's relief, his point indicated, not the ravine where Zhara's light shone, but a spot on the southwest horizon.

Alias scanned the sky for several moments. "I don't see anything," she said.

"Wait awhile," Breck replied.

Alias fidgeted nervously. If they waited too long, Zhara would make her way across the ravine and stumble on them.

Then there would really be an explosion from Breck. "Maybe it was just a shooting star," Alias suggested, "or the campfire of some other adventurer."

Breck shook his head. He sat patiently, watching the dark horizon for another three minutes. Alias signaled hastily to Dragonbait to keep an eye on the rear, then turned back to the ranger.

"There!" Breck said, pointing once again to the same spot.

"It looks like a fire," Alias said, surprised. "A big one."

"It's Grypht," Breck announced.

"How do you know?" Alias asked disbelievingly.

"It's him. I feel it. We'll follow that light."

"But the trail leads north. The light's in the opposite direction," Alias objected.

"Grypht has laid a false trail. If I'm wrong, we can come back to it later, but I know I'm not wrong."

As they spoke, a second burst of light lit the horizon just near the flames in the distance.

"Another fireball," Breck said.

Alias nodded. That's what it looked like to her, too. "You must have sharp eyes to have seen that first fireball," she said. "Or Tymora's luck."

Breck grinned, flattered. "Both," he replied. "Let's go," he said, turning his horse to the southwest and nudging it into a trot.

Alias turned her mount and followed. Dragonbait took a moment to drape a strip of blue cloth over a bush before loping after them.

They spotted no more fireballs bursting in the sky, and the bright fire died down, but there was a residual glow on the horizon that served them as a beacon. They had traveled about four miles when they began to smell the smoke created by the fire. They slowed the horses to a walk. Small brush fires cut across their path. If not for the rain that had fallen in the area during the day, they wouldn't have been able to proceed farther. As it was, there were swollen streams and plenty of sodden foliage to keep the fire from spreading out of control. After crossing a particularly wide stream, Breck stopped his horse and dismounted.

"We'll leave the horses here. They'll be safe by the water," the ranger said, unbridling his mount. He clipped a lead rope onto its halter and tied the rope to a low tree branch. The horse immediately began grazing on the grass growing beneath it.

Alias slid down from her saddle and stretched her legs while Dragonbait took charge of her horse.

Breck nocked an arrow into his bow and began moving cautiously toward the fire.

Alias pulled the bow she'd gotten from Mourngrym from her saddlebag. Dragonbait looked at her in alarm.

"Relax," she whispered. "I'm not going to shoot your friend. I just want to be prepared for whatever else is out there. If that's him hurling fireballs, there's got to be something else out there he's throwing them at."

The three adventurers picked their way through the charred undergrowth until they reached a circle of oak saplings, as close to one another as pickets in a fence. They circled round until they came upon a few saplings that had been broken and flattened to the ground. The ranger leaped into the clearing within the ring. By the light from the smoldering fires and the rising moon, Alias could just make out the silhouettes of three much larger trees lying on the ground.

Breck bent over one of the trees and stroked its charred bark. The swordswoman could have sworn she heard him sob.

"What is it?" Alias asked, stepping up behind the ranger.

"Treants," Breck said, choking back a second sob. "They've been murdered—just like Kyre."

Alias bit her lip. She turned back to see if Dragonbait had anything to say about the fallen treelike creatures. The saurial paladin stood beside the ring of saplings and hissed. Alias smelled the violet scent the lizard used to warn of danger.

"What is it?" Breck asked, turning around to see what upset Alias's companion.

"Dragonbait senses evil," the swordswoman explained.

"Evil was here, all right," Breck said angrily. "It was Grypht. Look there." The ranger pointed to a set of large prints in the mud beside one of the fallen treants. "And there—those must be your friend Akabar's prints," he added, indicating with a nod of his head a set of smaller prints unmistakably made by rope sandals.

Alias felt something brush against her leg. She gave a startled cry and tried to leap aside, but something had hold of her leg, and she fell heavily to the ground. Something curled, serpentlike, about her thigh and up around her waist. Alias's eyes wid-

160 🌸

ened at the sight of the vinelike tendrils wrapping around her. She screamed and struggled to reach the dagger in her boot.

Dragonbait dashed up to one of the treants and hacked through the creature's branchlike arm with his brightly flaming sword.

The tendrils about the swordswoman's body went limp.

Breck dashed up to the saurial paladin, screaming, "What are you doing?"

Dragonbait stepped back and held his flaming sword out to keep Breck from approaching any closer.

"He saved my life," Alias said, wriggling out of the tendrils.

"He's desecrating a dead body," the ranger growled.

Dragonbait signed to Alias.

"Breck," Alias said softly, "I think you'd better take a closer look at these treants. Don't they look peculiar to you?"

"They look dead," Breck answered angrily.

"They look sick," Alias corrected. "They didn't even burn well. They only scorched—like rotted wood."

"They were wet, like the rest of the brush around here," Breck replied stubbornly.

"Look at them!" the swordswoman demanded, grabbing the ranger's shoulders and forcing him to face the treant Dragonbait had just encountered. "They're diseased . . . rotted completely through. Look inside of it," Alias said, pointing at the treant's severed arm. "Have you ever seen a treant with vines growing inside of it like that?"

With the tip of an arrow, Breck poked gingerly at the branch. The vines within looked like maggots infesting a corpse. The ranger turned away from the sight, horror in his eyes.

"Well?" Alias said. "What do you think it is?"

"I . . . don't know," the ranger said slowly. "I've . . . I've never seen anything like it before. Have you?"

"Yes," the swordswoman answered. "They remind me of the tendrils the undead god Moander used to control people, but the first time I saw them, the tendrils were all attached to him."

"Moander's dead," Breck said.

Alias shifted uneasily, realizing that the treants could be a sign that the god was returning to the Realms. Akabar could be right after all, but she still couldn't bring herself to admit it aloud. "Yes . . . Moander's dead." she said.

"Then this rot, these tendrils in the treants must be something Grypht did to them," Breck claimed. "We'll know for certain when we catch him. We'll follow his trail until we're out of the burnt-over region. Then we'll go back and get the horses." The ranger began looking for tracks near the broken saplings.

Alias rubbed her temples. She was tired and hungry and frustrated with the ranger's single-mindedness. "Breck," she called, deciding to try once more to enlighten the ranger. "It could be that Kyre was wrong about Grypht. These treants might have attacked the creature. Of course it would have defended itself as best it could."

Breck spun about angrily. "Is that why it murdered Kyre—to defend itself from her?"

"Something else might have killed Kyre," Alias replied.

"Or someone—like your friend Akabar," Breck suggested.

Alias threw her hands up in the air. For lack of another thought, she addressed the ranger's previous supposition. "Suppose Grypht did kill Kyre in self-defense? Suppose she mistook him for a monster and attacked, and he fired back?"

"Kyre didn't *mistake* Grypht for a monster. He *is* a monster!" Breck declared and stomped off to search for the trail.

Alias looked at Dragonbait and shrugged. After a few moments, the pair of them followed the ranger.

Grypht's trail wasn't hard to follow, even in the moonlight. The creature had been running, oblivious to the fact it left a clear trail behind. Suddenly the trail ended abruptly, however. Beside Grypht's tracks were two sandal prints—Akabar's. Then there was nothing. The creature and the southern mage had vanished into thin air.

"Beshaba's brats!" Breck cursed. "They've whisked themselves away by magic again."

"Let's get back to the horses and make camp," Alias said. "We'll have a look around in the morning."

"They could be anywhere by then," Breck objected.

"They're already gone, ranger," the swordswoman snapped. "And I'm not going anywhere in the dark. Neither are you."

Breck's shoulders slumped. He turned wordlessly and headed back to the stream where they'd tied their horses, with Alias and Dragonbait following him, as usual.

When they'd reached the spot where they'd tied the horses, they found their mounts were missing. No portions of their lead ropes were left attached to the branch at all. The horses hadn't chewed through the ropes; they'd been untied.

"Someone's stolen the horses," Breck said.

Alias glanced at Dragonbait. "Who?" she asked. "We're out in the middle of nowhere."

"I don't know, but I'm going to find out," Breck said, looking over the ground until he found a set of bootprints.

"Here we go again," Alias muttered as they followed the ranger out of the clearing after the horse thief. *This is Zhara's doing, isn't it?* she signed to Dragonbait.

The saurial began examining the ground with exaggerated interest.

Suddenly Breck broke into a run, heading upstream. Alias looked up and gasped. There, not far from the stream, framed in a clearing in the moonlight, was a female figure in robes standing in front of a horse.

"Why doesn't she just throw another light spell so he can see her better?" the swordswoman cracked sarcastically.

Dragonbait sheathed his sword and dashed after Breck.

Apparently unaware that she was being observed and about to be attacked by an angry ranger, the robed figure stood calmly stroking the horse's muzzle and feeding it something from the palm of her hand. Alias was pretty sure it was Zhara—only a priestess was stupid enough to stand out in the open like that.

Alias walked slowly toward the scene. This trouble is Dragonbait's fault, she thought. Let him handle it.

Breck leaped at the woman, knocking her to the ground. The horse neighed and shied backwards. Zhara screamed. Dragonbait pounced on Breck.

Alias pulled an apple out of her knapsack and began munching on it. While the ranger, priestess, and saurial rolled about on the wet grass, Alias grabbed hold of the horse—it was Breck's—and pushed it out of harm's way. Slowly she fed it her apple core as Dragonbait pulled Breck off Zhara.

The priestess made it to her feet and moved away, shielding herself from Alias by standing on the opposite side of Breck's horse. Alias shot a glance at the priestess, but Zhara had already pulled the hood of her cloak back up, hiding her face.

Dragonbait and Breck rolled around in the grass a few more times until the swordswoman asked, "Are you two having fun?"

Dragonbait looked up suddenly. When he caught sight of Zhara, safely out of the fracas, and Alias, watching with a bemused expression, he looked almost sheepish. He went limp and let Breck pin him to the ground.

"I have you now!" the ranger declared.

"Yes, but what are you going to do with him? You can't ride him, and he's too tough to eat," Alias said with a chuckle. "He might make an interesting pair of boots—maybe."

Breck looked at Alias and turned purple with fury at the sight of the swordswoman laughing at him. He released Dragonbait and leaped to his feet. "You!" he shouted, pointing a finger at Alias. "You helped her to escape! No wonder you were so anxious to defend her husband. Did Lord Mourngrym know?"

"Know what?" Alias asked, disdainful of the ranger's confused accusations.

"That she's your sister," Breck snarled.

"What are you talking about?" Alias snapped back. "I haven't any sisters."

"Then who is she?" Breck demanded, yanking the hood of Zhara's cloak off the priestess's head.

The swordswoman squinted in the moonlight at Zhara and saw, for the first time, what Breck had seen when he'd been rolling on the ground with the priestess. There was something familiar about the pointed chin, the high cheekbones, the thin nose, the green eyes, and the red hair. Alias gasped and backed away. Zhara's features were familiar because they were the swordswoman's own features. Except for the dusky hue of her southern skin, Zhara could have been Alias's twin. Alias realized in a flash just what Zhara was.

"No!" Alias shrieked furiously, drawing her sword. "She's not my sister! She's one of the fiend Phalse's spawn!"

❧ 11 ❧

Betrayals

Breck pulled away from Zhara and drew his own sword, but he looked at Alias doubtfully. Then he remembered the sage's words at the tribunal. "Elminster told us Phalse had been destroyed," he said.

"Yes," Alias admitted, "by my own hand. Before that, though, the little monster created her and eleven other of my look-alikes, pawns that he intended to use to destroy his old enemy, Moander." Alias raised the tip of her sword to Zhara's throat. "That's why you're so eager to have Akabar go after Moander, isn't it? Because you're Phalse's creature."

Zhara met Alias's eyes with her own and replied calmly, "And are you still Moander's creature that you are so eager to see the Darkbringer live? Here is your chance to destroy me. You have your weapon in hand. Why not use it and finish me off?"

"You witch!" Alias growled. She threw her sword down and leaped at Zhara.

The two women tumbled to the ground. Dragonbait moved quickly to separate them, but Breck put his hand out to stop the saurial. "One thing you never want to do," he said with a chuckle, "is get between two women in a brawl."

The paladin's eyes narrowed angrily at Breck's patronizing tone and amused grin, but upon consideration, he accepted the wisdom of the ranger's words. He stood by watching Alias and Zhara roll about on the wet ground, thinking how ironic it was that only a few minutes before, the swordswoman had found his own battle with Breck so amusing.

Alias tried to wrap her hands around Zhara's throat, but she drew her hands away hastily, pricked by some shards of metal. Beneath her robe, the priestess wore a studded leather collar around her neck. The swordswoman's eyes widened with a sudden suspicion. She grabbed the front of the priestess's robe and ripped the white fabric from the neck to the waistline. Beneath her robe, Zhara wore a chain shirt cut very low.

"You stole my armor!" Alias screeched. She raised a fist, but before she could slam it into Zhara's face, the priestess whipped a flail out from her sleeve and clubbed the swordswoman on the side of the head.

Alias rolled off Akabar's wife, moaning and clutching her ear and temple with both hands. Zhara stood and backed away from the swordswoman. Dragonbait bent over Alias, who was struggling to her knees.

"Have you finished your little catfight?" Breck asked.

"Catfight?" Zhara repeated, looking puzzled. "What does that mean?"

"When two women fight," Breck explained, "it's called a catfight."

"Why?" Zhara asked.

"Well, because women fight differently from men—more like cats. You know, with your claws," Breck said, grinning.

Zhara's eyes narrowed angrily, and she twirled the end of her flail menacingly. "Come here, ranger, and I will show you how women fight," she growled.

Dragonbait abandoned Alias's side to step between Zhara and Breck. He grabbed the Turmishwoman's weapon arm and shook his head furiously.

"Let me go, Dragonbait!" Zhara demanded. "This arrogant northern barbarian is in need of a lesson," she said, tossing her head in Breck's direction.

Dragonbait threw his hands up in the air. This was like a nightmare, he thought. The only worse thing he could think of would be a fight between himself and Alias.

"Give me back my armor, you thief," Alias said, retrieving her sword and stumbling to her feet. A large bump and a dark bruise were forming on the side of her temple.

"I will return it to you," Zhara snapped. "I never wanted to wear it in the first place. Only a barbarian like yourself would do so without shame."

"You never wanted . . ." Alias looked from Zhara to Dragonbait. "*You* gave her my armor, didn't you?" the swordswoman demanded of the paladin. "And that cloak, and those boots. They're mine, too, aren't they?"

Dragonbait nodded guiltily, signing that he was sorry. He moved toward Alias, reaching out to tend the wound on her head.

Alias drew back sharply from the saurial. "Don't touch me!" she growled.

I'm sorry, Dragonbait signed again. *Forgive me.*

Alias turned her back on the saurial. "Never! Stay away from me. Don't talk to me," she said. "I've nothing to say to you." The swordswoman stalked away from the saurial. At the edge of the clearing, she stopped and leaned against a tree.

Dragonbait could see Alias's shoulder shaking, and he knew she was weeping. He felt sick to his stomach. He sat down on the grass and put his head on his knees.

Suddenly embarrassed, Breck looked for something constructive to do. Bending down to pick up his horse's lead rope, he asked Zhara, "What did you do with Alias's horse?"

"I let it go free," Zhara said.

"You *what?*" Breck snapped.

"I let it go free so that you could not use it to hunt down my Akabar," Zhara explained. "I tried to get this one to run away, too, but it would not."

"Of course it wouldn't. It's my horse, and it's too well trained to do anything stupid like that. Where did you leave Alias's saddle?" Breck asked.

"It's on her horse," Zhara said.

Breck snorted. "Southerners," he muttered. "Don't you know anything about horses?" he asked.

"No," Zhara said simply, not in the least ashamed of her ignorance. "I am a priestess of Tymora, not a stablehand."

"Which way did it go?" Breck asked with annoyance.

"Why should I tell you?" Zhara said with a sniff.

"Because if you don't, the horse you 'let go free' is going to end up with saddle sores and bug bites and infections and probably die because you didn't bother to take off its saddle."

Zhara looked chagrined. "It went that way," she said pointing in the direction of Shadowdale.

"Come on, then," Breck said, pulling Zhara's arm. "You're going to help me find that horse."

Zhara pulled a light stone from her pocket and held it high so the ranger could search the ground for tracks. Fortunately the beast was tired and hungry, and they found it grazing on grass not too far off. Breck called out to it, and it came right up to him. "Silly creature," the ranger chided it as he grabbed its halter and scratched its forehead. "How could you leave us?" He pulled the horse's bedraggled lead rope up from the ground. "She could have caught this in something," Breck said, waving the end of the rope in Zhara's face. "Then she'd have starved to death or died of thirst."

"I am sorry," Zhara said. "I did not know. But I cannot let you kill my Akabar. He is no less innocent than this animal."

"How do you know? You weren't even there when Kyre was killed."

"Akabar is my husband. I know him very well. And Dragonbait says he knows Grypht well, and Grypht is not a monster."

"Kyre wouldn't lie," Breck insisted. "Kyre was my teacher. I knew her well, too."

"Was she your lover?" Zhara asked, with the detachment of a southern scholar.

The ranger flushed. "What kind of question is that?" he said angrily. "That's none of your business."

"Yes, it is," Zhara said. "You loved Kyre. That much is obvious. Lady Shaerl says Kyre was not ugly, but very beautiful. If she would not have you as a lover, perhaps you killed her out of anger or jealousy."

"You're crazy," Breck growled.

"Maybe she was afraid of your temper," Zhara suggested.

"She was not! She thought I was too young!" Breck shouted.

"Oh," Zhara said softly. "How old are you?" she asked the ranger.

"Twenty winters. Tymora! I can't believe I just told you that!" Breck exclaimed.

"That you're twenty years old? Why?" Zhara asked. "Is it some kind of a secret?"

"It's not that," Breck said, rubbing his temples. "Just forget it."

"Twenty is not so young," Zhara said.

Breck sighed with exasperation. "When I was eighteen, I made a fool of myself and pestered her too much about . . . how I felt about her. She thought we should stop working together for a while. She went away—disappeared for over a year. When I heard she'd asked the Harpers to assign me to the same tribunal with her, I thought maybe she finally considered me old enough."

"But she didn't?" Zhara asked.

Breck shrugged. "I don't know. Since she arrived in Shadowdale two days ago, I haven't managed to get more than a few moments alone with her, and she . . ." Breck hesitated.

"She what?" Zhara prompted gently.

"She was different . . . sort of unapproachable." Breck shook himself and looked down at the ground, feeling disloyal to the half-elf's memory. "No," he said, "that's not quite true. I was afraid to approach her . . . afraid of what she'd say. Now it doesn't matter anymore. I just wish she was still alive."

Without another word, Breck began to lead Alias's horse back to the clearing where they'd left Alias and Dragonbait. Zhara followed, lost in thought.

They found Dragonbait starting a cooking fire in the center of the clearing. Alias was grooming Breck's horse at the edge of the clearing with her back to the saurial. She kept her face a tight mask of concentration, trying to hide her turbulent mood.

Breck led Alias's horse over to a tree near Alias and wrapped its lead rope around a branch. His horse's saddle and saddle-bags were spread out over a fallen tree.

"I went in your saddlebags for your brushes," Alias said.

"That's fine," Breck replied. "Hand me my scraper, and I'll start on your horse," he offered, unsaddling Alias's mount. He laid the saddle on the fallen tree beside his own and tossed the sweaty horse blanket on top.

Alias handed a sweat scraper to the ranger.

As Breck began cleaning off Alias's horse he said, "I'm sorry I accused you of helping Zhara escape."

Alias shrugged. "You didn't know how I felt about her."

"You didn't like her even before you knew she was your—um—one of your look-alikes, did you?" Breck asked.

"No, I didn't," Alias said.

"You know, she doesn't seem all that bad. Uh . . . she's loyal to her husband at least," Breck said.

"Hmph!" Alias snorted. "She's just a good actress," the swordswoman replied spitefully.

"Dragonbait seems to like her."

"Dragonbait is a fool," Alias snarled.

Startled by the swordswoman's vehemence, Breck didn't re-ply. Alias finished grooming Breck's horse in silence. Then she pulled her saddlebags off her saddle and walked away to an-other tree at the edge of the clearing. She sat down beneath the tree and began to remove her armor.

When Breck finished grooming Alias's horse, he strolled over to the cooking fire. Dragonbait and Zhara had made up a delicious-looking stew from the rations and some wild herbs the saurial had collected along the trek. The saurial signed something to Zhara.

"Dragonbait wants you to take a bowl to Alias." Zhara explained to the ranger.

"Uh, sure," Breck said. "Does she usually stay angry with you for a long time?" he asked.

Dragonbait signed something for Zhara to translate.

"She's never been angry at him before," Zhara said.

"Great," the ranger muttered. "As if we didn't have enough problems with this hunt." He carried some bread and a bowl of stew for himself and one for the swordswoman over to the edge of the clearing, where Alias sat polishing her sword.

Alias looked up when the ranger approached. "I'm not hungry," she said.

"You've got to eat," Breck insisted squatting down beside her.

"What's the point?" Alias asked.

"The point!" the ranger exclaimed. "The point is that you promised Lord Mourngrym you'd help me bring Akabar and Grypht back to the tower, which you can't do if you fall off your horse from hunger. And if keeping your word to Mourngrym isn't enough, remember, Grypht knows where Nameless is. I thought you wanted to find Nameless."

"I do," Alias said, a spark of hope in her voice once more.

"Then eat your dinner," Breck said.

Alias took the bowl from Breck.

"Mind if I join you?" Breck asked.

"Suit yourself," Alias said. "I'm afraid I'm not very good company just now, though."

"Neither am I, so we should get along just fine," Breck retorted, tearing the hunk of bread in half and tossing her a piece."

Alias grinned ruefully.

"I never did hear what you had to say about Nameless," the ranger said.

"I don't know what I was going to say," Alias admitted. She scooped up a mouthful of stew. When she was finished chewing and swallowing, she asked, "What do you want to know about him?"

"Do you love him?" Breck asked.

"He's my father," Alias answered, as if that explained everything.

"But do you love him?" Breck asked again.

"He made me everything I am," the swordswoman said. "I owe him my life."

Breck took a mouthful of stew.

"I told Morala I loved him," Alias continued. She tried to convince me I shouldn't. You're not going to try to do that, too, are you?"

"I don't know Nameless well enough," Breck said, shaking his head. Privately the ranger wondered what game Morala had been playing. "Were those his songs you were singing last night at The Old Skull?" he asked.

"Mostly," Alias replied.

Breck waited until she'd sopped up the last bit of gravy from her bowl with the remaining bread, then asked, "Would you sing that song about the nymph again—for me?"

Alias looked down at the ground, hiding her look of uncertainty and fear. She wanted Breck to admire Nameless's work. The song about the nymph would sound so natural out here in the forest. She had to risk singing the song, even if its meaning became twisted. "Of course," she said to Breck with an unsteady smile.

Alias set her bowl down and cleared her throat with a sip of water. With a hostile glance toward the sky, she directed an impromptu petition to the gods: I already know about Moander, and I want to help Nameless, so please don't ruin this song.

In the peaceful forest surroundings, Alias began singing, far more softly than she had been able to back in Jhaele's noisy tavern. She began the song with a series of wordless siren calls, then sang the first lyrics: " 'Dappled sunlight dances around a foxglove spike, then transforms into a vision both warm and womanlike.' "

Breck leaned back against a tree and closed his eyes.

Alias's eyes wandered around the moonlit clearing, imagining the sun on the golden-leafed trees and the bright berries and wild flowers. She sang the song through without a hitch. When she was finished, she glanced at Breck to see if he was pleased.

The ranger's cheeks were tear-streaked. He opened his eyes and looked at Alias with a hint of embarrassment. "I'm . . . I'm sorry," he said. "It makes me think of Kyre." He dabbed his eyes hastily with his sleeve. "I'll take first watch. You'd better get some sleep."

Alias nodded wordlessly, and Breck moved away to another spot by the clearing's edge.

All he could think about was Kyre, Alias realized in frustration. He wasn't interested in Nameless. She punched her saddlebag angrily. No one cares about Nameless except me. She wrapped her cloak tightly around herself and laid her head down on the saddlebags. And no one cares about me, except Nameless.

Akabar and his fiend-spawn wife can go chasing after Moander, if they want, and Dragonbait can go with them, for all I care. But once I find Grypht and make him give me the finder's stone, I'm going to search for my father.

* * * * *

Olive bandaged, by herself, the wound the beholder had inflicted upon her. She was still too angry with the bard to accept any help from him. She felt betrayed by his declaration that he intended to deal with Xaran. She had expected him to have too much self-respect to deal with such a creature. After informing him curtly that Flattery had looted the workshop and left behind a death trap for him, she'd stalked off to a corner to steam in silence.

Finder appeared not to notice the halfling's anger. He began feverishly turning his workshop upside down, looking for something, anything, that he could use against the orcs. He'd been unable to get the other door leading out of the workshop to open, so now their only way out lay beyond the orcs. Unfortunately, Finder's search bore precious few results. Flattery had either known or discovered every last hiding place his maker had, for he had taken everything but Finder's musical instruments. Those he had tossed carelessly in a corner and apparently fireballed them. Only one instrument, a brass horn, survived the blast unscathed.

Finder pulled the horn out of the pile of charred yartings, melted flutes, and cracked harps and brushed it off carefully.

"Not completely stingy with your luck today, are you, Tymora?" the bard muttered.

Olive, too curious to remain silent, asked hopefully, "Is that horn magical?"

"Why don't you try it and find out for yourself, Olive?" Finder suggested, handing her the instrument.

Olive needed both hands to hold the heavy brass horn up to her lips. She puffed out her cheeks and blew with all her might, but without results. "My mouth is too small," she said, handing the horn back to the bard.

"Astonishing, considering the amount of noise that manages to come out of it," Finder said, straight-faced. He held the horn up to his own lips and blew a hunting flourish, then a military call to arms. Finally he fastened the horn to his belt, like a weapon.

"Well? Is it magic?" Olive asked again.

Finder nodded.

"What does it do?"

"With the right command words, it will bring down the house," the bard replied, "literally."

"Considering that orc audiences aren't particularly noted for their appreciation of music," Olive said, "that could be useful."

Finder bent back over the pile of destroyed musical instruments. He pulled out a harp. Its wooden frame was broken and charred, and the strings were all snapped and frayed. He slid open a tiny secret compartment in the harp's base. "Did I leave something in— Aha!" the bard exclaimed as something small and glittering dropped into his hand. "Here, Olive. You should wear this," he said and held out an earring.

Without taking it, Olive eyed the piece of jewelry appraisingly. From the wire ear loop hung a platinum pendant set with a brilliant white diamond, which the halfling estimated must weigh more than a carat. The workmanship was obviously elvish and very beautiful. "A little fancy for entertaining orcs, isn't it?" she asked, trying to resist her desire to accept the gift.

Finder sat down beside her. He removed the tiny gold loop earring she already wore and slipped the wire loop of the diamond earring into the pierced hole in her earlobe. He flicked at the diamond pendant to set it swaying. "Olive," he asked suddenly, "do you speak any elvish?"

"Not really," Olive answered, shaking her head. In spite of her anger with Finder, she couldn't help but be delighted by the feel of the tiny pendant bumping against her neck. "Except some numbers and a few words—for trading."

"The elves have a saying: 'May you hear as clear as a diamond.' How's your hearing, Olive?"

Olive looked at Finder with a touch of confusion. Then it dawned on her. "You're speaking elvish!" she exclaimed. "I understood you perfectly! The earring's magic, too!"

Finder nodded. "You should be able to understand most of the languages of the Realms with it," he explained. "Still angry at me?"

"I should be," Olive said haughtily.

"I know. But are you?" he asked.

Olive sighed and shook her head from side to side.

Finder smiled and took a gulp of water from Olive's water flask. "Olive," he began, "is that all Flattery's image said—that he cleaned out the lab, and I should be dead?"

"That was it," Olive lied. "Then he sent the spokes of disintegration around the room and cropped off my hair."

Finder ran a finger along the strip of soft, auburn fuzz that was all that was left of Olive's hair on the crown of her head. "I suppose being short has its advantages," the bard joked feebly.

Olive sniffed. "So does crawling around on your belly, but its not very dignified," she said.

"Olive, will you give it a rest?" the bard growled. "We haven't any choice but to deal with Xaran."

"No, I will not," Olive replied, stamping her foot. Her anger returned instantly. She couldn't allow herself to be bribed by diamonds, magic or not. "You cannot make a deal with a beholder," she told Finder. "Didn't you learn anything after Cassana and Phalse left you to rot in Cassana's dungeon?"

"Olive, we are not exactly negotiating from a position of strength," the bard said, indicating the empty room with a wave of his hand. "We haven't even got a potion of healing for your shoulder."

"You didn't know that before, when you started dealing with Xaran," Olive accused him.

"Immortality is nothing to sneeze at," Finder said angrily.

"Fine!" Olive snapped. "Swallow it whole. I hope you choke on it."

"Oh, for—" Finder broke off and sighed. "By now, immortality is a negotiating point I'll probably have to relinquish. There's nothing here I can offer him, and I have no intention of spending another year building simulacrums for evil monsters."

"So you're going to sell out Akabar just so you can get out of here alive?" Olive asked.

"So *we* can get out of here, Olive," Finder said.

"I'll make my deals with a dagger," the halfling said.

"My, but haven't you gotten proud and brave in the past year?" Finder said sarcastically.

"I had a good teacher," Olive sputtered. "At least, I thought I did."

The side of Finder's face twitched as if he'd been slapped. He grabbed the halfling by her shoulders and pulled her close so their faces were only inches apart. Olive flinched from the pain in her wounded shoulder, but didn't say a word.

"Listen to me, Olive Ruskettle," Finder demanded. "There is no dishonor in surviving. You may manage to kill a few orcs, but they'll get you in the end. They won't kill you right away, though. Oh, no. You're an attractive female, and the fact that you're small won't protect you one bit. They'll find that all the more amusing. You know what sort of monsters they are."

Olive shuddered and the blood drained from her face, but she wouldn't concede. "I won't let you betray Akabar," she said, holding back a sob. "Xaran must have some way to make sure you don't cheat on any deal you make. Suppose he charms you with one of his magic eyes? Then you won't have much of a choice."

"I doubt Xaran's enchantments would have any power over me," Finder said.

"Xaran could put a magic choking collar around you in case you didn't come back, or send a party of orcs to escort us, or use me for a hostage."

"I won't leave here without you, and whatever guarantees Xaran decides to use, we'll find a way around them," Finder assured her. "Besides, Xaran only said he wanted something Akabar had, not that he wanted to kill him. Suppose Akabar wants to sell this thing, whatever it is, to Xaran. Hmm?"

"Akabar is a cloth merchant. What's a beholder going to do with cloth? Hang curtains in the orcs' warren?" Olive asked with sarcasm.

Finder released Olive's shoulders and tugged playfully at the diamond earring. "You are such a stubborn woman," he said. "Trust me. I'm going to get us out of here alive, and I won't let anything happen to Akabar, but I need your help."

Olive looked up into the bard's blue eyes. She felt like a moth drawn to a candle. She was probably always going to end up being drawn into Finder's schemes—at least, until she got burned in one of them, like a moth in a candle flame.

"Here," she said, handing him his dagger. "I found it in the tunnels. You may need it."

Finder's face lit up at the sight of the heirloom weapon. "You really are my little Lady Luck, aren't you?" he said, taking the weapon.

"Maybe that's why you have so little luck," Olive bantered.

"When you have talent like mine," the bard boasted, "a little luck is all you need."

Olive shook her head disapprovingly. "Let's just get this little tea party over with," she muttered.

Finder removed a light stone from the wall and gave it to the halfling to hold. He held his dagger out in his right hand and took up Olive's free hand in his left. "Stay close," he ordered, leading her to the door.

You're so bright, what moth could resist? Olive thought ruefully.

Finder traced the treble clef symbol with his finger. The door opened inward a foot. The orcs in the corridor immediately began to shriek and holler. Finder jerked Olive through the door and whistled three notes. The door slammed shut behind them.

Six especially large orcs with loaded crossbows blocked their way. There must have been at least another twenty sitting in the corridor beyond. The monsters squinted in the light of the stone Olive held up, but they could obviously see well enough to shoot at the human and the halfling.

Undaunted by the numbers of the enemy, Finder took charge immediately. In a fighting stance, with his dagger flashing in the light, he snarled at the assembled orcs.

"Take us to Xaran!" he ordered.

The orcs growled. The largest one snarled at Finder in common, "Throw down your weapons—and that light, too."

Finder stepped close to the orc who had spoken. Ignoring the crossbow bolt pointed at his belly, he snarled back, "You will take us to Xaran as we are, or I will see that Xaran punishes you for your insolence."

The monster cursed in orcish. Olive, wearing the magic ear-ring, understood the words clearly, though she wished she hadn't. The large orc turned his back on Finder and walked down the corridor. Finder followed behind, close enough to smell the stench of the creature's clothing as he pulled Olive be-hind him.

Some of the orcs ran ahead and disappeared through the gap in the corridor wall, dashing down the tunnel beyond to alert the rest of their tribe. Most of the orcs waited for their leader and the prisoner to pass, then they stood up and followed. Ol-ive could see them pointing at her and hear them whispering foul words and feel their eyes on her.

Just before they stepped through the gap in the wall, another especially large orc blocked the leader's path and said in orcish. "Xaran is only interested in the bard. We were promised any treasure he brought out of the magic room. By rights, the little one is ours." The other orcs rumbled approvingly.

The leader of the orcs turned to Finder. "My brother is right. Xaran is interested in only you. Leave the halfling behind," he ordered.

Olive suddenly remembered what it was like to be her old, terrified self again. She clung to Finder's hand but did her best not to whimper.

Finder looked over both the leader orc and his brother with obvious disdain. "She's mine," he said.

"Xaran does not care about the halfling," the leader said. "He will not punish us if we do not bring her."

"But I will," Finder barked in orcish. "Slowly," he added threateningly.

The leader orc snarled, but he turned and led them on. His brother eyed Finder with hostility. Finder returned the look with an even fiercer one, an undisguised hatred that startled the orc into stepping backward.

Finder squeezed through the gap in the wall, pulling Olive af-ter him, and they made their way down the tunnel beyond to the orcs' warren.

* * * * *

Dragonbait started awake at Breck's touch on his shoulder. The ranger looked deeply disturbed. The saurial chirped quizzically.

"It's Alias," the ranger said. "She's walking in her sleep. What should we do? "

Dragonbait felt genuine panic. Alias hadn't walked in her sleep since right after she was "born," when they'd been on the ship en route from Westgate to Suzail after escaping from Cassana's dungeon. Though fully grown, the swordswoman had been like a child then, with all the fears of a child. The horrors of the ceremonies and magic behind her creation had surfaced in her nightmares, only to be blessedly forgotten after her days-long sleep in Suzail, from which she'd awakened as an adult.

Now Alias stood beside the fire, wearing nothing but her tunic. She was very pale, her eyes were closed, and her mouth hung open. She was whimpering slightly.

Dragonbait rose and approached her. He ran a clawed finger up under her right sleeve, along her magical blue brands. The swordswoman quieted instantly and her breathing slowed.

Suddenly the air about the fireside was full of high-pitched clicking and whistling sounds. Dragonbait whirled around, emitting a joyful lemony scent, expecting to see Grypht. There was no one in the clearing but himself, Breck, Alias, and the sleeping Zhara. Dragonbait turned back to Alias, his eyes wide in astonishment.

"What is it?" Breck asked. "What's wrong?"

Dragonbait motioned for Breck to remain silent. The ranger couldn't hear the whistles and clicks coming from Alias's mouth. His ears were as deaf to the sounds as any human ear not augmented by magic. Although Alias made the noises with her extraordinarily gifted voice, even she herself couldn't possibly hear them. Dragonbait heard them, though, for they were not only the sounds a saurial would make, but they were also actual words in saurial.

Although Alias spoke in saurial, what she said seemed to be nothing but babble. "We are ready for the seed. Where is the seed? Find the seed. Bring the seed," she repeated over and over again.

Without the scent glands that saurials would ordinarily employ to convey emotion and emphasis, her speech was as flat as the sign language Dragonbait was forced to use with her. As the paladin listened to the hypnotic rhythm of the words, he realized that, if the swordswoman could only release scents, she would be singing and not merely chanting. Then Alias began a new verse.

"Nameless is found," Alias said in saurial. "Nameless must join us. Nameless will find the seed. Nameless will bring the seed."

Suddenly Alias stopped her saurial chant. She held out her hand, with one forefinger pointed downward, and traced a circle parallel to the ground.

The paladin shuddered.

Alias began to shout in Realms common, "No! No! No!"

She reached out and grabbed Dragonbait's shoulders. Her eyes opened and she blinked in the firelight. Then she started to cry softly.

Dragonbait stroked the brand on her arm again and wrapped his cloak around her. He pushed down on her shoulders until he got her to lie on his blanket beside the fire. He wrapped the blanket around her, too, and Alias closed her eyes again. The saurial stroked her hair until she ceased weeping and lay still and, Dragonbait hoped fervently, slept peacefully.

"Maybe you'd better take second watch instead of her," Breck suggested.

Dragonbait nodded.

"Does she do this often?" the ranger asked.

Dragonbait shook his head in an emphatic negative.

"Never, huh?" Breck asked. "Like she never gets mad at you?"

Dragonbait squinted his eyes angrily at the ranger.

"I'll bet I know why she's sleepwalking," Breck said. "She's upset with you because of Zhara."

Dragonbait looked into the fire.

"You've got to tell her you're sorry for whatever she's angry at you for," Breck said. "We can't be hunting for Kyre's murderer and dealing with weird stuff like sleepwalking at the same time."

The ranger turned and strode away to his own saddlebags, sniffing the air. Curious, he thought, it's too late in the year for violets to be in bloom.

The ranger wasn't familiar enough with Dragonbait to know that was the smell of the saurial's fear.

Dragonbait watched over the campsite with his yellow reptilian eyes, but all he could see was the vision of Alias forming a circle in the air with her forefinger. The motion was not one from the thieves' sign language she had taught him. It was a saurial symbol—the symbol for death.

❧ 12 ❧

The Beholder

The orcs escorting Finder and Olive herded the pair of adventurers through naturally carved tunnels for what seemed to the halfling to be miles. Olive had to jog to keep up with Finder and ahead of the orcs, and she stumbled frequently on the rough, uneven ground. Her wounded shoulder was throbbing, and every jar sent a stabbing pain down her arm and across her back.

Finally they reached a series of passages that looked like circular bores through the rock, as smooth as polished marble. Although these were far easier to move through, to Olive they were more unsettling, since they indicated the work of the beholder's disintegrating eye.

Thinking of the beholder, as Olive could not help but do, and listening to the cadence of the orcs' boots as they trudged behind the prisoners brought to the halfling's mind the adventurer's rhyme:

> One eye to lift and one eye to sleep,
> One to charm man and one for beast.
> One eye to wound and one eye to slow,
> One to bring fear and one to make stone.
> One eye makes dust and one eye brings death,
> But the last eye kills wizards more than all of the rest.

The last eye of a beholder, Olive knew, disrupted magic. Without it, Xaran would be evenly matched with any powerful mage, but with it, not even wizards stood a chance against the the creature. Without the ability to cast spells, a mage was about as useful as a bard with laryngitis. Fortunately there was nothing wrong with Finder's voice, and they were relying on his glib tongue, not his magical abilities, to deal with the beholder. He'd better be at his glibbest, too, Olive thought. Beholders aren't stupid.

Finder stepped in front of the halfling and stopped suddenly, bringing Olive up short and startlinging her out of her reverie. "Pocket the light for a while," Finder whispered.

Olive did as the bard asked. There was a dim glow up ahead. Olive peered around Finder's hip and saw that they had arrived at the main entrance of the orc warren's common cave.

The common cave of an Orcish community was always the largest and most central in the warren, and when another creature, such as a beholder, assumed leadership of an orc tribe, it often made the common cave its own quarters. Despite the cave's great size and desirable location, it was still part of an orc warren, and since orcs lacked any sense of style or gracious living, it looked like a pretty miserable place to live.

Numerous low charcoal fires burned within, but since the ceiling was only seven feet high at most and sloped downward at the edges, the dim red light from the fires didn't penetrate very far, making the cave seem much smaller. Water seeped down from the surface, dripped from the ceiling and walls, and hissed onto the fires' hot coals, sending up clouds of water vapor and noxious gases. The smell of rancid fat dripping from rotting animal carcasses onto the coals masked the odor of the orcs with an even more unpleasant smell. All in all, Olive thought, it was a pretty homey place for a creature from hell.

Orcs swarmed into the common room to get a look at the intruders who demanded an audience with their master. Only the largest and toughest-looking males carried well-maintained weaponry and wore anything resembling armor. Most of the rest had at least an axe. The females wore daggers, and even the young played with sharpened sticks. For every face Olive was able to discern in the dim light, she saw two more pairs of red eyes glowing in the darkness of the passages adjacent to the common room.

Unable to imagine even someone as talented as Finder able to defeat these vicious creatures, Olive commented wryly, "It looks like a tough bunch."

"I've seen worse," Finder replied coolly, but he gave the horn on his belt a pat as if to reassure himself of its presence.

Sure you have, Olive thought silently.

At the center of the cave, the floor rose a few feet. Atop the rise was a pile of moldy, water-stained pillows, mementos from some long-forgotten caravan raid. Xaran was propped on the pillows in the manner of a merchant raj.

The leader of the orcs paused just inside the entrance to the cave. Finder strode past him, with Olive in tow, leaving the leader and the guards to straggle through the phalanx of orcs who parted to make way for the human bard and his tiny companion.

The bard stopped just before the pile of pillows and released the halfling's hand. He bowed low, with his right hand covering his heart and his left hand sweeping outward, as though he were doffing an invisible hat. "Greetings, Xaran. I have come to resume our discussion," the bard said. "Please don't bother to rise."

Disregarding Finder's suggestion, the beholder levitated from its repose and hovered over the cushions, at eye level with the bard. The beholder wobbled as it levitated and its movements were jerky, unlike any beholder Olive had every encountered, as if Xaran was an elderly invalid trying to get out of a sickbed.

Now that she had an opportunity to study Xaran more carefully, she noted that its great central eye and all its smaller eyes were coated with a milky film. The stalks supporting the smaller eyes drooped like thirsty plants. A thin garland of silver moss hung about the stalks, reminding Olive of gray hair and reinforcing the image of Xaran as a sick old man.

"It was wise of you to rejoin us," Xaran commented. The beholder's high-pitched voice grated in Olive's ears and sent a shiver down her spine.

"I hope you found everything in order in your workshop," the beholder added.

"Naturally," Finder said, smiling broadly, eager that Xaran should believe he was here of his own free will, not because he had no other choice. "Of course, there's nothing of interest in there to anyone but myself—just old musical instruments and such."

"Of course," repeated the beholder. Its toothy maw turned up at the corners into a hideous smile.

"Let's get down to business, shall we?" the bard said. "You were offering me immortality. A rare commodity, and certainly worth whatever the market will bear. I presume it did not hinge on remaining in this place." Finder's eyes wandered disdainfully over the orc warren's common room.

"No. If we come to terms that are satisfactory to me," Xaran said, "you will be free to leave. As you pointed out, though, immortality is worth a great deal on the market."

"Suppose I were to forego your offer of immortality for the moment and ask only for safe passage out of here for myself and my companion?" Finder asked.

"It's a package deal," Xaran said sharply. "All or nothing. If you wish to leave here under my protection, you must accept my offer for immortality and pay my price. Of course, if you choose not to accept my offer, you are free to make a deal with my associates."

Finder glanced sideways once at the orc leader and his brother. Both glared at him with undisguised hatred. Even if the bard's workshop had been brimming with gold to ransom his and Olive's lives, the creatures weren't likely to let them go. The adventurers had wounded or killed three members of the tribe, and Finder had challenged the leader's authority.

"I see," Finder said, turning his attention back to Xaran. "And what is the going rate these days for immortality?"

"You'll be pleased to hear that the price has not risen in the past hour. As a matter of fact, because I think a man of your talents was made for immortal life, I'm prepared to make you a special offer."

"Such as?" Finder asked, suddenly more cautious.

"I'm willing to forego the interest my faithful orc followers have in your workshop. As I said before, it is your services that interest me. I wish for you to reveal to me all the secret knowledge of simulacra you have acquired and bring Akabar Bel Akash to me."

"Is Akabar aware of your interest in him?" Finder asked.

"But of course," Xaran replied. "Akabar and I are old friends."

"That's curious," Finder replied. "I remember speaking with Akabar after he'd witnessed the destruction of the beholder head of the fiend Phalse. He told me he'd never seen a beholder before."

Xaran's eye stalks all stood on end, and its central eye squinted angrily. "Phalse!" it exclaimed and spat on the ground with disgust. Finder had struck a nerve by mentioning the fiend. "The servant you created, the one you call Alias, did well to rid the world of that bottle imp." More calmly, the beholder added, "I'm sure what Akabar meant was that he'd never seen such a ridiculous-looking beholder head as Phalse's. Each of Phalse's stalks ended in a mouth, you know, instead of an eye—a thoroughly disgusting-looking creature."

Olive, whose attention had been focused on all the orcs staring at her, was suspicious of something the beholder had said. Xaran's hatred of Phalse wasn't surprising, since Phalse was pretty despicable, and it could just be a coincidence that Xaran should know both Phalse and Akabar. But how had the creature known about Alias? Even if it had heard some of the tales Olive told of Alias's adventures, it couldn't have known that Finder had created Alias. Out of loyalty to Alias, Olive had never revealed the swordswoman's origins. How had Xaran known that, and where had it gained such thorough knowledge of Nameless—the location of his workshop and his all-consuming desire for immortality?

"So. What guarantee do I have that you'll make me immortal once I've done all you ask?" Finder asked.

Wait a minute, Olive thought. For all his faults, Nameless never thought of Alias as a servant. He always referred to her as simply Alias. The only being that ever called Alias "the servant" was . . .

"I will make you immortal before I send you after Akabar Bel Akash," Xaran said.

Moander! Olive remembered.

"Finder!" the halfling whispered urgently.

Finder put a heavy hand on Olive's head as a signal for her to remain quiet. "Then how can you be sure that I'll return with Akabar?" he asked.

"There are ways to ensure your good faith," Xaran said cryptically.

"Finder!" Olive said more loudly, tugging on the bard's sleeve.

"Don't worry," Finder whispered hurriedly to the halfling, then addressed Xaran again. "I'm not leaving without my companion. She is far too useful to me to trust in the care of your . . . troops."

"Believe me, I had nothing so . . . crude in mind. Take this," Xaran said. He unrolled his tongue from his mouth. Resting on the end of his tongue was a green, spine-covered burr about the size and shape of a horse chestnut burr.

Finder reached out and took the bur. It was covered with a sticky substance, and the tips of the spines had tiny hooks on them.

"What is it?" the bard asked.

"Your immortality," Xaran explained.

Olive pinched Finder's thigh. The bard glared down at the halfling.

"Excuse me, Xaran. I have to confer with my companion."

"Is she interested in a similar deal?" Xaran asked, turning several eyestalks in the halfling's direction.

"No thanks," Olive replied. "Life would be dreadfully dull without the constant terror of death hanging over me," she said glibly. "I just wanted to remind Finder of something."

The bard bent over the halfling. "I have everything under control, Olive," he whispered. "Please trust me."

"He called Alias 'the servant,' " Olive hissed back.

"So?"

"That was Moander's name for her, remember?" Olive said softly.

"Olive, you're getting paranoid," Finder said.

"Moander used vines to control Akabar," the halfling reminded him, trying to keep her voice from being overheard. "The vines made him talk and walk and cast spells, all against his will. Kyre had a flower in her hair. Xaran's got moss on its head. What sort of self-respecting beholder wears moss on its head?" the halfling demanded.

Finder scowled for a moment, but when he looked up at Xaran again, he couldn't dismiss Olive's fears.

He tossed the burr onto a pillow beneath Xaran. The sticky substance it left on his fingers he wiped off on his tunic. "I will do your bidding in exchange for our lives, but I cannot accept such a gift from the Darkbringer," he said.

Xaran's eyes, all eleven of them, widened in astonishment. "My, but aren't you perceptive? Yet now that you have guessed the source of the largess offered, you must realize you have no choice. You cannot refuse the gift of the Darkbringer. It would be most hazardous to your well-being. In Moander's name, I must insist that you accept the immortality he offers you."

The beholder barked a few commands in orcish, and Olive heard the sounds of steel blades being drawn from leather and bolts being snapped into crossbows.

"Then let me drive my point home," the bard growled. In one fluid motion, he pulled his grandfather's dagger from his belt and sent it sailing at the beholder.

Olive watched in horror as at least twenty orcs raised their crossbows and daggers and aimed at the bard's back. With a shout, she pulled out the light stone from her pocket and held it up behind Finder. The sudden appearance of brilliant magical light caused the orcs to shriek out in pain. Several fled from the common room.

A green light beam shot out at Finder's dagger from one of Xaran's eyestalks, but the blade split through the beam unscathed and buried itself in Xaran's central eye. White fluid oozed from the puncture.

Finder had already whirled around and pulled his magic horn from his belt. He shouted, "Siege strike," raised the instrument to his lips, and blew into it. With its magic triggered by Finder's words, the horn emitted a terrific blast of sound that knocked most of the remaining orcs to the ground and shook the cavern roof. Already weakened by the seeping water, the roof began to sag like a fortress wall hit by a catapult missile. Great chunks of rock and showers of dirt cascaded from the roof, scattering the remaining orcs. Dust and dirt from the ceiling and charcoal soot and sparks from the fires began to swirl in the air.

Olive looked back at Xaran, expecting the beholder to shoot a death ray at them at any moment, but the old beholder had sunk into the pillows and disappeared like a wounded creature going to ground. She looked back at Finder. The old bard was grinning arrogantly at the chaos all around him as he slipped the horn back in his belt.

The sagging portion of the ceiling crashed just in front of them. With alarm, Olive noticed the ceiling directly over their heads was beginning to sag. The room grew darker as the light stone failed to penetrate the falling rock and dirt and rising dust.

"Which way is out?" Olive screamed.

Finder spun around, then pointed toward a passage leading off the side of the cavern. "That way," he cried, grabbing the halfling by the waist and carrying her away moments before the ceiling over Xaran's pile of pillows collapsed.

As they ran down the passageway, Xaran's voice cried,

"Freeze!"

"Keep going!" Finder ordered, pushing Olive deeper into the dark tunnel. The bard whirled around to face the dark spherical shadow that hovered in the tunnel just behind them. Finder's dagger still protruded from the beholder's central eye socket.

"You cannot refuse the gift of the Darkbringer," the beholder cried. He spat the green, sticky burr at the bard and laughed maniacally.

Finder fell backward, brushing frantically at his tunic. He caught the burr in one hand, but he couldn't pull the sticky thing away from his clothing.

Suddenly the burr opened with the crack of a small explosion. A cloud of moldy dust wafted into the bard's face, and he choked and sneezed and spat, trying to keep from inhaling whatever it was.

"Finder!" Olive shouted as she turned and lunged forward to help. She grabbed the bard's belt to pull him away from the beholder.

"Your turn," Xaran sang out gleefully, floating toward Olive. "All must serve the Darkbringer!"

Olive snatched the horn from Finder's belt, intent on throwing it at the beholder, but some instinct prompted her to raise it to her lips instead. She shouted the command words she'd heard Finder use, "Siege strike," and blew into the mouthpiece with all her might.

No sound issued forth from the instrument. Xaran's lips puckered to spit a second seed at Olive. Frantic with terror, Olive blew again into the horn, and a feeble blat sounded in the beholder's face. The noise was nothing compared to the blast Finder had blown, but combined with the magic of the horn, it was more than enough to blow Xaran backward like a soap bubble caught in the wind.

"I did it! I did it!" Olive shouted. In her excitement, she was oblivious to the sagging ceiling over her head.

Finder scrambled to his feet, grabbed up the halfling, and dashed down the tunnel a split second before the ceiling gave way. Farther down the passage, he set Olive down and took his horn back from her. "You could have brought the roof down on yourself and been killed," the bard chided.

"That would've been better than being made immortal the

Darkbringer way," Olive retorted. "At least I've sealed the tunnel between us and Xaran. Are you all right? What happened when that thing exploded?" she asked.

"Nothing," Finder said with a shrug. "Either my clothes protected me, or it was a dud. Maybe it was meant to be swallowed for it to work."

"You're sure you're feeling all right?" Olive asked.

"Better than you, I'll bet. How's your shoulder?"

"Lousy. Um, Finder?" Olive said, looking down the corridor with her brow knit in concern.

"Yes, Olive?"

"This tunnel is a dead end."

"It can't be," Finder said spinning around. He walked down the passageway until he could inspect the end with his hands as well as his eyes. He glared at the rock wall before them. There was no way out of the passage. They were sealed in a cul-de-sac.

"This is impossible. I'm sure I heard the wind whistling in this passageway. It has to lead to the outside," the bard growled angrily. He stood very still for a moment. "Listen," he told Olive. "Don't you hear it?"

Olive stood still and listened. Sure enough, there was a whistling noise in the cul-de-sac, and a stream of cold air, too. The halfling held her light stone up high. The passageway ceiling was some twenty feet overhead. The cave must once have been full of water, for breaking through the ceiling was an old well shaft. Even with the light stone, it was impossible to judge how much higher up the well went.

"It would be a good way out," Olive said. "If we were birds."

* * * * *

Alias awoke in the dawn twilight before sunrise. She hadn't slept well. She had had nightmares about the time Moander had captured her, and all through the dreams, she'd had the feeling that Nameless was in danger, too, though she couldn't say what in the dream made her think so. The sooner she found Grypht and made him tell her what he'd done with Nameless, the better she would feel.

The swordswoman threw off Dragonbait's blanket and cloak and stomped off into the forest. When she returned, she went to her own blanket and cloak at the edge of the clearing and began rolling them into her saddlebags. Dragonbait had left her enchanted chain mail on her saddle, and she slipped into it with righteous indignation. She pulled on a clean tunic and clean socks and her pants and boots. Then she went over to the fire and poured herself a cup of tea from the kettle Dragonbait must have prepared earlier.

Dragonbait signed something to her, but Alias turned away to stand by the fire with her back to him. Breck rose and joined her a few minutes later. His face was scraggly with a day's growth of beard, but he was fully dressed and armed. He gave the swordswoman an odd look as he poured himself some tea. "How are you feeling?" he asked.

"Just fine," Alias said. "Why didn't you wake me to take second watch?" she asked.

"Dragonbait offered to take it," Breck said with a shrug. Hastily he added, "I thought we'd break camp at sunrise and start searching in a circular pattern from the place where we lost Grypht's trail. We may as well keep Zhara with us."

Alias nodded. She didn't want to lose any time finding Grypht now. She'd resigned herself to the idea of remaining in Zhara's and Dragonbait's company until she could discover Nameless's whereabouts.

"In the meantime, I want to take another look at those treants," the ranger said. He gulped down his tea. "I'll be back by sunrise," he promised, and he trudged out of camp.

Alias sipped her tea slowly. When she finished, she strapped on her sword. Then she nudged the sleeping Zhara with the toe of her boot.

The priestess awoke with a tiny gasp. She sat up, immediately alert. "What's wrong?" she said.

Alias snorted. "I want to talk to you," she said.

*　*　*　*　*

Akabar shook Grypht awake. The beast growled at him.

"It's dawn," the Turmishman said. "We should be going before this place collapses."

Grypht didn't understand a word the mage had said, but the tone was clear. Akabar was impatient to be on the road. The saurial wizard looked around them. He'd forgotten they were in the extradimensional space he had created. They'd have to leave soon before it collapsed and they fell to the ground. Grypht already hurt all over his body, and he was anxious to avoid acquiring any extra bruises.

Akabar lowered the rope out of the space and climbed down to the ground. Grypht tossed down his staff and climbed down after it. He made a soft bellowing sound as he climbed.

Akabar pointed to the ground. "Look there. We've been followed," he said, indicating two sets of bootprints and another set of three-toed prints. "You know, these almost look like Dragonbait's prints," the Turmishman said.

Grypht sniffed the air. His head perked up and his eyes grew bright with surprise. Akabar could smell the lemony scent of the saurial.

"Shall we follow?" Akabar asked.

Grypht was already tracking Champion with his nose.

*   *   *   *   *

Zhara stood face-to-face with Alias. From beside the fire, Dragonbait watched both women nervously. If Alias wouldn't pay attention to his signing, Zhara was his only hope of reconciling with the swordswoman. Now he prayed the priestess could calm Alias's anger enough for her to give him a chance to apologize.

"Assuming you're right and Moander is returning—which I still refuse to believe—I want to know why Akabar must be the one to destroy Moander," Alias demanded. "Why couldn't the gods have picked some powerful wizard—like Elminster or Khelben of Waterdeep or King Azoun's flunky, Vangerdahast."

"I do not know," Zhara answered calmly. "I presume because Akabar has fought Moander once already."

"I think it's because Akabar is the one you've got wrapped around your finger," Alias retorted. "If you could have wormed your way into a more powerful mage's heart, you'd have chosen him to fight Moander. If you really loved Akabar, you'd keep him as far away as possible from Moander. Don't you know what Moander did to Akabar before? How it used him?"

"I know," Zhara whispered. "But if Akabar does not destroy Moander, then Moander will destroy him."

"What do you mean?" Alias snapped.

"Moander wants revenge on Akabar. Tymora warned me that the Darkbringer's minions are searching everywhere for my husband. Our family decided that Akabar should flee to the north. My co-wives sent me with him so he couldn't be scried upon. I possess the same misdirection shield as you do," Zhara explained.

"Then you're safe. There's no need to go looking for Moander," Alias argued.

"We cannot stay in hiding all our lives," Zhara retorted. In a softer voice, she added, "I know that you have good reason to be afraid of Moander, but you cannot run from your fears."

"Can't I? You just watch me," Alias said. "As soon as we find Grypht, and I get the finder's stone, I'm leaving. I was stupid enough to get drawn in by Moander's siren call once, but I'm not going to let it capture me again. I'm going to go find Nameless and stay with him as far away from Moander as I can get."

"Akabar needs your help. Don't you care about him anymore?"

"Why should I?" Alias growled. "He obviously doesn't care about me."

"Don't be ridiculous. He cares about you very much," Zhara persisted.

"If Akabar cared about me, he wouldn't have married you, would he?" Alias snapped.

"He asked you to come to Turmish with him, and you turned him down. What did you expect him to do, follow you around the Realms? Please don't abandon him when he needs your help just because you're jealous of me."

Alias stepped up to Zhara and waved her forefinger in the priestess's face. "For your information, this has absolutely nothing to do with being jealous of you. You're just a copy of me—one of Phalse's second-rate copies. Akabar told me he was my friend, that he thought of me as a human, and then he turned around and married you, as if my body was a thing he could have for the right price." Alias's voice cracked with anger and pain.

"I am not a thing," Zhara snapped. "I am nothing like you. I am a person, too—"

"Did you know," Alias interrupted, "that when we found you in the Citadel of Exile and Akabar saw how upset I was, he offered to destroy you for me?"

"Yes," Zhara replied quietly, nodding her head. "He told me all about it."

"And you married him anyway? Are you crazy?" Alias cried. "Of course you are," she said bitterly. "After all, Phalse made you."

"Of all our sisters that I have met, you are the only one to treat me this way. The others were pleased to have a family."

"Sisters! You mean the other eleven monsters are walking around?"

Zhara gritted her teeth to hold back her anger. She took a deep breath and spoke in measured, even tones. "I have met three others. One is a sage in Candlekeep, one a mage in Immersea, one a warrior like yourself from the eastern lands. I know of two others. One was a thief who was murdered this past spring. The other is a lady of some power in Waterdeep."

"Did Akabar marry any of these others, too?" Alias asked. "I'm surprised a shrewd merchant like him didn't think of it when we discovered you in the Citadel of Exile. He could have picked you up cheaper by the dozen and sold you off for a profit."

Zhara's face went livid with rage. "You witch! How dare you!" she cried and backhanded Alias solidly across the face.

The swordswoman stumbled back several feet. Then she leaped forward onto Zhara. "Let's finish what we started yesterday, shall we?" she growled as they both fell to the ground.

Zhara fought back with fury, but she had no weapons or armor to protect her now. She stubbed her toes kicking at the swordswoman and bruised her knuckles on Alias's skull.

Alias punched at Zhara's stomach, and Zhara curled up, whimpering like a dog. "Had enough?" Alias snarled, sitting up over the priestess.

Zhara slammed her elbow into Alias's kidney. Alias raised her fist over the priestess's head, but something overhead grabbed her wrist and lifted her off the ground by her arm. She twisted her neck around to see what was holding her.

A beast over ten feet tall, covered in scales and armor plates of bone, dangled the swordswoman in front of his face, studying her with some interest. In his other hand, he held out a lump of clay fashioned into a miniature four-story tower.

Alias looked around for Dragonbait. The saurial paladin stood at the edge of the forest, looking down at the ground.

Akabar stood beside him with an astonished look on his face.

"Are you through beating my wife?" Akabar asked the swordswoman angrily.

"She started it," Alias growled. "You must be Grypht," she said to the creature holding her. "Put me down."

Akabar stepped into the clearing and helped Zhara to her feet.

"How could you do such a thing?" the Turmish mage asked his wife. "Have you forgotten the promise you made after you broke Kasim's arm? You swore you would not hit another woman," he said angrily.

Zhara spat in Alias's direction. "That witch makes Kasim seem like an angel. Alias is no different from her mother, Cassana. I do not care one bit if I hurt her."

Akabar looked up at Alias. "What is going on here?" he asked, motioning for Grypht to set the swordswoman down.

Grypht lowered Alias until her feet touched the ground. The saurial wizard did not, however, release her wrist. The scent of fresh-mown hay rose from his body, and the tower in his hand glowed red hot, then shattered. Startled, Alias tried to pull away from the beast, but it wouldn't release her.

Alias and Zhara both glared at each other but did not speak.

"How could you hit my wife, your own sister?" Akabar asked Alias.

Alias glared at the mage. "She seemed like a good substitute in your absence, Turmite," Alias replied.

"I beg your pardon?" Akabar said coolly, offended by the vulgar term.

"You heard me," Alias shouted. "You married this fiend spawn. Why didn't you just accept Cassana when she offered herself to you? Was Zhara better because she was younger, or because you could have her behind my back?"

The blood rushed from Akabar's face, shocked as he was by Alias's words.

In saurial, Grypht asked Dragonbait. "Who is Cassana?"

"A dead sorceress," the paladin answered in saurial. "Please, Grypht, try to convince them to turn their energies to the dangers we face."

Grypht nodded. "Alias," the beast began.

Alias turned suddenly and stared at the huge saurial in astonishment. "You can talk!" she exclaimed.

Grypht snorted with amusement. "Since I was two years old," he said.

"I mean, you can talk in common, not just in saurial," Alias explained.

"I know what you meant," Grypht said. "I cast a tongues spell. It will not last for long, so I need your undivided attention, child. You must let go of your anger for now. We face a great danger, and you must behave now like an adult and set your differences with these people aside, for they are your allies."

"I don't need any allies," Alias snapped. "All I need to know is what you did with Nameless. Where is he?" she demanded. "And Olive, too?"

"The bard and the halfling must have fled to escape Kyre after she imprisoned me in a soul trap. I do not know where they went. We have more important things to concern ourselves with at the moment."

"Kyre imprisoned you in a soul trap?" Alias asked incredulously. "Why didn't she tell anyone?"

"Because she was a minion of Moander, preparing the way for the Darkbringer's return to your world," Grypht said.

"You're all crazy!" Alias declared. "Moander is dead. Dead!"

"You merely destroyed the body of Moander in this world, but Moander's power and spirit live on in the Abyss, and the Darkbringer's slaves in this world are building it a new body, a new abomination for it to possess. The Darkbringer will return once the body is finished."

"Moander hasn't got any followers left in the Realms to build him a body," Alias protested.

"That," Grypht explained, "is why Moander enslaved my tribe and brought them to the Realms—"

Grypht gurgled suddenly, released Alias, and clutched at his throat. There was an arrow lodged in his neck. The great creature teetered once, then fell over backward and landed on the forest floor with a crash.

♥ 13 ♥

The Soul Song

Dragonbait rushed to Grypht's side as Alias whirled around. Breck stood at the edge of the clearing, a second arrow already notched in his bow. He must have rediscovered Akabar and Grypht's trail and tracked them right back to the camp, the swordswoman realized.

Dragonbait knelt beside the saurial wizard, cursing himself for having forgotten the ranger's bloodlust.

Breck cried out, "Don't touch him!"

Dragonbait ignored the ranger's order and laid his hands on the larger saurial's chest. He began to pray for the power to heal.

"Breck, you idiot!" Alias called out. "What do you think you're doing?"

Breck approached them. "I thought I was saving your life," he said. "That creature could have killed you in an instant. What does Dragonbait think he's doing?"

"Healing him," Alias explained.

"No!" Breck shouted, and shoved the saurial paladin away from Grypht. "Are you crazy? That's the monster that killed Kyre!"

"No, he isn't," Alias said. "Grypht is a saurial like Dragonbait. He's a friend of Dragonbait's. He couldn't have killed Kyre."

"Well, actually," Akabar said, "he did kill her."

"See? I told you so!" Breck said, waving his finger in Alias's face.

Alias shot Akabar a look of frustration. Even if the Turmishman didn't want to lie, he could at least have had sense enough to keep his mouth shut.

"He had no choice, though," Akabar explained. "Kyre was a minion of Moander. She would have enslaved both of us to the Darkbringer if Grypht hadn't destroyed her."

"How dare you speak such lies?" Breck growled at Akabar.

"Kyre was a Master Harper! How dare you slander her like that? And with such a feeble story. Moander is dead." The ranger turned his bow on the Turmishman. "You're lying about Kyre. Admit that you're lying!" he demanded.

Alias pushed Breck's bow aside. Despite her anger with Akabar and Zhara and Dragonbait, she couldn't let Breck shoot them full of arrows. "Lord Mourngrym said we were to capture Grypht, if we could, and bring Akabar back alive," she reminded him sharply. "If we don't do something for Grypht soon, he's going to die, and if you don't stop waving that bow at Akabar, your fingers are going to slip and we won't be able to bring him back alive either."

"All right," Breck said, "you can heal Grypht, but I want him tied up first."

"With what?" Alias asked. "Breck, he's too big to tie up. He's not going to run off anyway."

Dragonbait signed something to Alias.

"Dragonbait says he guarantees Grypht's good behavior," Alias explained to the ranger.

"He's going to guarantee the good behavior of a murderer?" Breck asked sarcastically.

"It was self-defense," Akabar insisted.

"Kyre wouldn't hurt anyone." Breck retorted.

"She was possessed by Moander," Akabar explained. "It's true Moander was dead, but the evil god's spirit is trying to return to the Realms. It can possess good creatures as well as evil."

"Like the treants," Alias pointed out. She shifted her position very subtly, blocking the ranger's view of Grypht as Zhara bent over the saurial wizard .

"You saw the treants, then?" Akabar asked. "They were controlled by Moander the same way Kyre was," the mage explained, motioning with his hands to keep Breck's eyes away from his wife. "She might never have joined Moander willingly, but she was possessed by a vine of some sort, the same thing that possessed the treants. We had no choice but to destroy them. They tried to kidnap me and nearly killed Grypht. Why do you think a single arrow brought him down so easily? He received so many injuries from them that he passed out in our hiding place and slept for hours."

Akabar put a hand on Breck's shoulder. "I am sorry for the loss of your fellow Harper," he said to the ranger. "She seemed to me a beautiful and clever woman, traits that Moander could not have made her mimic were they not already her own. I can understand your anguish. I share it with you."

Breck took a deep breath and let it out slowly. Replacing his arrow in his quiver and shouldering his bow, the ranger nodded respectfully at Akabar. "Thank you," he said. "However, you must realize I cannot accept your story without proof. There was nothing left of Kyre's body. You will have to come back to Shadowdale, so Morala and Lord Mourngrym can judge whether you are telling the truth or not."

Behind the ranger, Zhara finished her prayers to cure Grypht's wounds.

Akabar looked up at the trees hesitantly, reluctant to agree with the ranger but equally reluctant to refuse him. He looked anxiously at Grypht, who was rising slowly to his feet.

"He hasn't time to return to Shadowdale," Grypht said in Realms common.

Breck whirled around and discovered the saurial on his feet. The ranger reached for his sword, but Grypht caught his wrists. As burly as he was, the ranger was no match for the five-hundred-pound saurial.

"You've drawn my blood twice in as many days," the wizard said to Breck. "Frankly, I'm getting a little tired of it. Now you will listen to me without attacking me."

Breck's body went limp and he glared at Grypht. "I'm listening, monster."

"Good," Grypht said, but he didn't release the ranger. "In our world," the wizard explained, "there are still fools who worship the Darkbringer and give his minions power to walk among us. Kyre came to our world as a visitor to study our music, and we welcomed her, but while she was among us, our tribe was attacked by minions of Moander. Kyre helped defend our tribe most heroically, but she was captured by the enemy. The Darkbringer made her one of its minions by possessing her body with its vines. Since she is native to this world, she can walk among your people without raising suspicion, so Moander sent her back here to prepare things for his return. In the meantime, my tribe has fought against the attacks of other minions of Moander for months now, until all but I and my apprentices and the Champion, the one you call Dragonbait, have been caught and enslaved. Moander has marched my tribe forcibly through the plane of Tarterus and into this world. The Darkbringer is using them to create a new body to use in the Realms. I came to your world seeking Champion's help.

"Unfortunately I arrived in Kyre's presence, and she used your ignorance to her own purposes and convinced you to attack me. When she'd cornered me in Nameless's room, she imprisoned me in a soul trap. Akabar freed me, and I destroyed her before she could enslave us both. I would not have destroyed her if there was any hope she would live once Moander had dispossessed her, but there wasn't. Moander's possession had eaten away the inside of her body."

"You kidnapped Elminster and Nameless, and you expect me to believe what you're saying?" Breck said, tossing his head back haughtily.

"I didn't kidnap Elminster or Nameless," Grypht replied. "I used a transference spell on Elminster—"

"That agrees with what Lhaeo said must have happened," Alias interspersed. "That strange place where Morala saw Elminster in her scrying bowl must be Grypht and Dragonbait's home world."

"Then why hasn't Elminster returned home?" Breck demanded.

"I can only assume that somehow the Darkbringer has interfered with his returning," Grypht answered.

"What did you do with Nameless?" Breck asked.

"Nothing," Grypht replied. "As I already told Alias, the bard and Olive must have fled to escape from Kyre after she trapped me in her soul gem. I was tracking Olive with the bard's magic stone, but I turned back when Akabar told me Champion was in Shadowdale."

Unable to refute the wizard's story, the ranger became less adamant, but he remained cautious. "I still need more proof," he said. "Where's the finder's stone now?"

Grypht released the ranger and pulled from his robe the prize he had looted from Kyre's body.

"All right," Breck said. "Think of someone in your tribe whom Moander has enslaved and sent to the Realms," he ordered the wizard.

Grypht held the stone and concentrated on a saurial he suspected would still be alive, despite the deprivations Moander put its slaves through. The finder's stone sent a beam northwest by westward, toward the peaks of the Desertsmouth Mountains.

"Give Alias the stone," Breck ordered.

Grypht tossed the stone to the swordswoman.

"Think about Nameless," the ranger told Alias.

Alias did as the ranger asked. The first beam of light faded and a second one shot out to the southwest. Alias felt a sense of relief. Wherever the bard was, he was far from Moander's saurial slaves.

Breck wore a thoughtful expression on his face.

"Nameless used the stone to cast a tongues spell so he could speak with Grypht," Akabar explained. "I tried to tap into the stone's magic last night, but it wouldn't work for me except as a compass."

"I'll bet it would work for Alias," Breck said.

"Me? I'm not a mage," the swordswoman said. "What do I know about magic stones?"

"You're Nameless's heir apparent, so to speak," Breck said. "Try the stone for something other than detecting someone," he suggested.

Alias peered into the depths of the stone, remembering how cryptic Elminster had been on the night last year when he'd given it to her. He must have thought she could use it, too. Back then, when she hadn't even known about Nameless, the magic object had seemed to her to be just another light stone. Now that she knew it had belonged to the bard, however, a whole new set of memories came to her—memories that Nameless must have implanted in her before she was "born"—memories of how to use the stone.

"Nameless triggered it with—" Grypht began.

"Music," Alias interrupted.

Grypht nodded. "The bard cast a tongues spell with it. Since my own tongues spell will wear off shortly, it would be helpful if you could speak saurial. The bard sang eight notes. I'll try to hum them—"

Alias waved to Grypht to be silent and closed her eyes. "I know what to do," she said. It was almost as if she could hear Nameless instructing her: "To cast a tongues spell, sing an A-minor scale. . . ."

Alias sang the scale, at the same time concentrating on the strange saurial tongue. The stone glowed yellow in her hand;

then the glow traveled up her arms and surrounded her whole body. Alias was suddenly aware of a myriad of scents wafting from both Grypht and Dragonbait. She could not only smell the scents, but also taste them as well. Then, unexpectedly, the air filled with noises, too—high-pitched whistles and clicks that complemented the scents.

"It seems to have worked. Tell me it worked," Grypht said to Alias in saurial. He gave off a scent like chicken soup, which the swordswoman realized indicated impatience.

"But I don't just smell you," Alias said in saurial. "I hear you!"

"Smells merely convey emotions, emphasis, intonation—" Grypht began to explain.

"But the words are clicks and whistles!" Alias completed the thought for him. "Why couldn't I hear them before?" she asked with puzzlement.

"Your ears normally don't work as well as ours," Grypht said with a shrug.

Dragonbait reached up and tapped Grypht's elbow. "High One," the paladin addressed the wizard, and Alias realized that the name "Grypht" was the closest human approximation to the saurial words for "High One," though whether it was the wizard's name or title she could not tell.

"I would like to speak with my sister," Dragonbait said, issuing a scent like basil, which Alias realized indicated he desired privacy.

"Champion, there simply isn't time," Grypht replied. "We have much to discuss before the spell Alias cast wears off."

"The tongues spell cast from the stone is permanent," Alias said.

Grypht looked at the swordswoman in disbelief. "You must be mistaken. You do not understand magic. It takes a tremendous amount of power to make a spell permanent," the wizard explained.

Alias shrugged. "You're right. I don't understand magic, but I know this spell is permanent."

Grypht still looked doubtful. He nodded to Dragonbait. "Have your talk," he said, "but speak quickly." The saurial wizard turned away and walked off, taking Akabar and Zhara and Breck with him.

Alias was left alone with Dragonbait. The swordswoman looked down at the ground and shifted her weight nervously onto one leg. She could no longer shut out the paladin's words now by turning her back on his signing fingers, and the memory of how she had done so filled her with embarrassment.

"Sister," Dragonbait said, "will you accept my apology now, if I offer it in my own language?"

Alias could smell the saurial's sadness and tenderness. She could smell and taste something minty, too, an emotion she'd never sensed in Dragonbait. It was remorse. He was really sorry, and there was no way she could deny it.

Yesterday, Alias thought, I told Morala that I would love Finder no matter what secret he told me, yet I would have left Dragonbait without even giving him a chance to explain. How could I be so cruel and unforgiving? The swordswoman put her hands on the paladin's chest and started to weep.

"You are right to complain that I treat you like a child," Dragonbait said, stroking the brand on her right arm. "I am overprotective and domineering. I was afraid you'd be angry, so I said nothing about Zhara, though I could smell that she was your sister immediately. Then I made matters worse by bringing Zhara along without asking you, because I did not want to argue with you. I just did what I thought should be done. I took your property and gave it to her without your permission. I am no better than a thief."

"Much worse," Alias said, looking up at the paladin. "A good thief wouldn't get caught."

Dragonbait looked startled, then caught the scent of mischief in Alias's scent and realized she was teasing him. He smiled and brushed the tears from her face.

"I'm sorry about fighting with Zhara," she said.

"As I said before, if you offend Zhara, it is Zhara you must apologize to," the paladin reminded her.

"Right," Alias said. "I still don't trust her, though."

"Alias," the saurial said with an earthy scent of frustration, "she is your sister."

"That's why I don't trust her," Alias said. "Dragonbait, the spell Moander's minions cast on me last year made me unleash Moander on the Realms without even realizing what I was doing. Phalse put a quest spell on me to hunt down Moander in the Abyss. It nearly tore me apart resisting it. I managed to break the spell only by killing Phalse. Zhara may think she's working against Moander, but she could be working for

Phalse."

"Destroying Moander would not be an evil thing merely because some other evil being wishes it," the paladin argued. "Besides, there is more at stake here, or had you forgotten what Grypht just said. The Darkbringer has enslaved my people. I must accompany Grypht and challenge Moander. Akabar and I destroyed the Darkbringer once. It is my hope we can do so again."

"But you had Mist with you!" Alias declared, referring to the ancient red dragon who had helped Dragonbait and Akabar battle the Darkbringer.

"And now we have Grypht," Dragonbait countered. "His apprentices often call him the old lair beast," the paladin added with a smile. "That's what we call Mist's kind on our world."

He could smell Alias's fear and anxiety, and he understood why she was terrified of the evil god. Of all the masters who had tried to enslave her, Moander was the only one whose command she'd been unable to resist, the only one who had captured her unaided, the only one whose defeat she had not been a part of.

"Maybe you should find Nameless and stay behind with him," Dragonbait suggested.

Alias lowered her head, ashamed of her cowardice, struggling to fight it. "No . . . I want to help you," she said, but she began shivering in the warm sunlight, and her eyes began to glaze over.

Dragonbait grabbed the swordswoman's shoulders, alarmed by her expression, afraid she might faint, but instead she seemed to fall into a trance and started repeating, over and over, the same words she had spoken last evening. "We are ready for the seed. Where is the seed? Find the seed. Bring the seed." This time, though, her words were accompanied by a myriad of scents that rose from her body, communicating a plethora of conflicting emotions—excitement and fear, joy and anguish, impatience and dread, determination and resignation, pride and remorse. Dragonbait realized at once that it had all the earmarks of a true saurial song.

"High One," Dragonbait shouted, "come quickly!"

Grypht came running up to the paladin. "What is it?" he asked.

"Listen to her song," Dragonbait insisted.

Grypht stared at Alias and furrowed his brow, confused by her trance and the words she spoke. "What seed?" he asked. "What is she singing about?"

"Shh. There's another verse," Dragonbait said.

"Nameless is found," Alias said in Saurial. "Nameless must join us. Nameless will find the seed. Nameless will bring the seed."

"He will, will he?" Grypht muttered.

The scents rising from the swordswoman's body sent an eerie shiver down Dragonbait's spine, frightening him far more than the earlier songs of Nameless that Alias had twisted.

Suddenly Alias stopped her saurial chant. Then, just as she had done the night before, she held out her hand, with her forefinger pointing downward, and traced a circle parallel to the ground.

"The saurial sign of death," Grypht whispered.

Alias screamed and began to shout in Realms common, "No! No! No!"

When Alias screamed, Breck Orcsbane, who had been seated by the fire toasting bread with Akabar and Zhara, leaped to his feet immediately. He ran through the clearing to the swordswoman's side, his sword drawn and pointed at Grypht's midsection. "What's going on here?" he demanded. "Alias, are you all right? What have you done to her?" he shouted at Grypht.

Akabar and Zhara came up behind the ranger, equally concerned for the swordswoman, though less inclined to blame Grypht. Akabar stepped between the wizard and Breck's sword.

Alias snapped out of her trance. She gasped and looked around in confusion.

"Alias? What is it?" Akabar asked. "What's wrong?"

"I just had a . . . a bad dream," she said. "It was something about Nameless." She paused, concentrating hard, but whatever it was, she couldn't remember now.

"First you walk in your sleep, now you dream when you're wide awake," Breck growled. "What manner of curse are you under?"

"I do *not* walk in my sleep," Alias snapped.

"You did last night. Ask Dragonbait if you don't believe me," Breck replied.

Alias looked at Dragonbait, and the paladin nodded.

"It sounded as if you were singing a saurial soul song," Grypht said. "But how can that be?" the wizard asked Dragonbait. "She's not a saurial."

"What's a soul song?" Alias asked in saurial.

"Her soul and spirit are bound by magic to my own, High One," Dragonbait explained to Grypht.

"But you haven't received the gift of soul singing," Grypht said, still confused.

"My mother had the gift, High One," Dragonbait reminded the wizard.

"That's right . . . so she did." Grypht nodded, remembering.

"Would someone please tell me what a soul song is?" Alias asked again.

Grypht clapped his hands once and bounced on his heels. "This is marvelous—even better than the magic stone. If she sings what our people know, she will be our eyes and ears in the enemy's camp."

"What are they talking about?" Breck asked Alias. Although he was unable to follow any of the conversation in saurial, the ranger recognized Grypht's excitement.

Alias waved Breck silent and shouted in saurial, "What is a soul song?"

"A song of our people that reflects our tribe's state of being," Grypht explained calmly. "When a singer of a soul song sings, her mind opens up to what is within the souls of her tribe, and she sings their song. Sometimes when she sleeps, she often dreams their dreams and wakes singing their song. The song will change as the tribe's condition changes. It may be a song of joy or contentment, which we accept with pleasure, or it may be a song of grief, which we learn to bear. When it is a song of evil, though, we must act—fight the evil, whether it comes from without or within, until the song grows good again. Because our tribe is controlled by Moander, the tribe knows much anguish, but it also knows of the Darkbringer's plans. You probably have just been singing of those plans. I hope you can do it again. Something opened your mind to the souls of our tribe and you began to sing. What was it? What were you thinking about before you went into the trance?"

Alias's brow furrowed. "I . . . I don't remember."

"Your fear of Moander," Dragonbait said.

Alias lowered her eyes, embarrassed, then it occurred to her that this soul-singing trance could explain her other problem.

"That must be why I've been singing Nameless's songs differently. I've been turning them into soul songs."

"It is very likely," Dragonbait agreed.

"Dragonbait, if you knew what was happening, why didn't you try to tell me what was wrong?" Alias asked the paladin.

"I only started to suspect last night," Dragonbait said, "when you sang in saurial. At least, you tried to sing, but your words had no feeling, since you hadn't the power to produce scents. Just now when you sang, it was much more obvious that it was a soul song."

"Would someone please explain what is going on?" Breck demanded, frustrated beyond endurance at not being able to understand the swordswoman's conversation with the saurials.

Alias explained everything that Grypht and Dragonbait had just told her. "So," she said in conclusion, staring pointedly at Akabar and Zhara, "I was right after all. I knew I wasn't singing the songs wrong because of the gods."

"Actually," Dragonbait said, "our people believe that soul singing is a gift of the gods."

Alias didn't bother to translate the paladin's correction. "You said I sang about Moander's plans. What did I sing? I have no recollection of it whatsoever."

Grypht quoted the lyrics of the first verse of Alias's soul song. " 'We are ready for the seed. Where is the seed? Find the seed. Bring the seed.' "

"What seed?" Alias asked.

"We don't know," Grypht said. "Obviously it is something Moander wants very badly, and he thinks Nameless will bring it to him. The second verse of your song went, 'Nameless is found. Nameless must join us. Nameless will find the seed. Nameless will bring the seed.' "

"And then you screamed," Dragonbait interjected.

"Yes!" Alias exclaimed, suddenly remembering what had made her scream out in fear. "Nameless is in terrible danger! We must find him before it's too late! Moander is trying to turn him into one of its minions!"

*　*　*　*　*

Olive shifted in her sleep from one uncomfortable position to another. Somewhere far overhead, birds started to chirp loudly. Olive came half awake, but from the back of her mind came a reminder that she didn't want to be awake, so she kept her eyes closed and ignored the birds. A beam of sunlight struck her face. Olive drew her hood up over her eyes. Then her stomach rumbled.

"Damn!" the halfling grumbled. She glared up angrily at the well shaft overhead, which taunted her with its inaccessibility. If only it had been nearer a wall, they could escape. She was experienced at climbing walls. Unfortunately, she couldn't hang from ceilings, and the well came out in the center of the ceiling. She sat up and rubbed the sleep out of her eyes.

"Stupid well!" she muttered, rummaging through her knapsack. There wasn't any fruit left. She and Finder had finished it off last night. Buried in the bottom of the knapsack, she found three stale sweet rolls. She left two for the bard and took one for herself, nibbling at it slowly as she studied the excavation Finder had begun last night.

The bard had climbed to the top of the passageway wall, where he had dug into the dirt and pounded at the stone with Olive's broken shovel until he'd created a second shaft in the ceiling. It was all of four feet deep. He'd finally slipped down from the wall, frustrated and exhausted. In the morning light, Olive judged the old well shaft to be at least fifty feet deep. She estimated it would take about a week for one man and a halfling to dig that far straight up. Finder was trying to angle his shaft toward the well shaft, hoping to connect with it so they could climb out the rest of the way through the well. Since the well shaft was only twenty feet from Finder's shaft, digging to it should only take days . . . days without water or food.

Olive crept over to the corner where Finder lay sleeping. He slept like the dead, heavy and still. Asleep, the power of his voice and the animation of his face were not apparent, and he looked far older. Once he'd been lord of the ruined manor house somewhere above them, commanding the respect of his peers and the worship of his apprentices. Now he was curled up like a corpse, buried alive by his own magical horn.

Olive studied his face and hands carefully. There were no signs of vegetation growing out of his ears or his wrists. There was no hint of green in his skin. Maybe Finder had been right and his clothing had protected him from whatever had burst out of the burr.

Something clattered in the passage behind Olive. The halfling swung around with her dagger drawn. Pebbles were rolling from the top of the fresh wall of dirt created when Olive had collapsed the ceiling. Something was shifting inside the pile.

Olive knelt beside the bard and shook his shoulder frantically. "Finder!" she whined.

Finder groaned and looked up groggily at the halfling. "Go 'way," he growled.

"Finder, something's trying to get in by digging through the cave-in!" Olive whispered urgently.

The bard sat up and reached for Olive's sword, which he'd been using as a dagger.

A large rock tumbled down the pile, and a muck-encrusted vine as thick as Olive's arm slithered out from where the rock had been. It rose up like an angry snake, and they could see that there was a mouth at its tip—a lipless maw full of rows of sharp fangs. Olive had seen just such a growth before on Moander's body in the Realms.

"Nameless," the mouth called out. It spoke in the same grating, high-pitched voice as Xaran.

Finder rose to his feet and approached the vine carefully. "Is that you, Xaran?" he asked, halting a few feet from the mouth.

The vine twisted so that the mouth faced the bard. "You will do Moander's bidding whether you choose to or not. It is only a matter of time," the vine mouth said.

"You are mistaken," Finder said heatedly. "Moander tried to pervert my singer. I will never deal with the Darkbringer."

"In time, you will return even your precious singer to Moander," the vine mouth said.

"You can go to hell!" Finder snarled. He slashed out with Olive's sword and sliced the mouth off the end of the vine. The vine whipped around his sword arm. Finder tried to pull it loose with his other hand, but twinelike tendrils flared out from the vine and lashed his hands together at the wrists.

Olive leaped forward, slashing with her dagger, and hacked through the vine near where it came out of the pile of rubble. What was left of the vine retreated back into the debris. The tendrils wrapped around Finder's arms went limp, but Olive had to help the bard free himself from them.

"Well, that was heartening," Finder said glibly.

"What was heartening?" Olive asked incredulously. "That

Xaran is still alive waiting to grab you and turn you into a vegetable?"

"No," Finder said. "what was heartening was that Xaran used a tendril to slither in here, instead of simply disintegrating this pile of rubble. It must have injured its disintegrating eye."

"Great. Since you stabbed its central eye, now it has only nine more to use on us," Olive said.

"Eight. The eye that charms beasts will be useless against us," Finder reminded the halfling. "And I imagine both of us have the will to resist the eye that causes sleep."

"Oh . . . now I feel better," Olive said sarcastically. "There are only seven ways left for it to kill or capture me."

"Xaran doesn't have any hands to dig himself out, but we do," Finder said.

"But Xaran can put out another tendril and strangle us in our sleep," Olive protested.

"We'll just have to keep watch."

Olive heard a shout, as if from far away. She silenced the bard with a wave of her hand and listened hard. In a few seconds, there was another shout.

"Orcs!" the halfling said in panic. "There are still orcs alive out there! They'll dig Xaran out, then come in after us! Then what?"

"A good question," the bard muttered. "A good question indeed."

*　*　*　*　*

The Mouth of Moander peered into her scrying pool at the Nameless Bard and his halfling companion. It was only a matter of time before they were recaptured, but Moander didn't allow her to take her eyes off them. Last night, the high priestess had felt a rare moment of pleasure and hope when the bard's dagger had survived Xaran's disintegration ray and destroyed the beholder's central eye, and she had dared to gloat over her master's setback when the bard had felled the orcs and ruined their warren with his magical horn. Now the evil god kept the priestess's eyes fixed on the bard, savoring her fresh despair.

Coral wished fervently that she was standing at the top of the well with a rope to help the bard escape. Since the priestess had been unable to scry Akabar this morning, presumably because he'd rejoined the protected Alias, Moander was now relying on Nameless to locate the Turmishman. Without Nameless's help, the search for Akabar could go on far too long, increasing the risk that someone would find the hiding place of the god's new body, perhaps even someone with power enough to destroy the body and free the possessed saurials.

Moander forced Coral to speak the very words it used to taunt her. "Even if the bard could fly out of that trap, he cannot escape the Darkbringer now. The seeds of possession grow in him," the god declared through Coral's mouth.

"No!" Coral insisted. "Xaran's spores exploded hours ago, and the bard still shows no signs of possession. He has resisted your evil seeds."

"No, he hasn't," Moander forced Coral to say. "The seeds are simply taking longer to grow within him because he is human and such a large man."

"You lie!" Coral shouted in anger. "You lie to torture me!"

"Do I? We shall see," Moander said via the priestess's voice, and the Darkbringer made Coral laugh the high-pitched cackle of the insane.

❧ 14 ❧

The Rescue

Alias held the finder's stone at arm's length and thought of Nameless again. Once more the stone sent out a beacon of light to the southwest.

"You know these lands," Akabar said to Breck Orcsbane. "What places where the bard might be fall along the beacon's path?"

Breck whistled softly. "He could be practically anywhere—Spiderhaunt Woods, Shadow Gap, Gnoll Pass, Cormyr. They all lie in that direction," the ranger replied. "If you or Grypht could teleport us to another place, we could use the stone to triangulate and get a better fix."

Akabar shook his head. "I do not yet possess the power for such a spell, and Grypht is not familiar enough with this world to teleport us anywhere but Shadowdale. That is not far enough off the beam's path to triangulate accurately."

Alias rocked nervously on the balls of her feet. She had to find a way to reach Nameless quickly. Now that the swordswoman was finally conscious of her soul song link with the saurials whom Moander had enslaved, she could no longer deny that Moander was indeed returning to the Realms. She knew, too, with absolute certainty, that Nameless was in grave danger from Moander and that all the evil god's attention was focused on the bard. There just wasn't time to trek across country following the stone's light beam. She peered anxiously into the stone. The longer she looked at it, the more she remembered of its powers. It held all sorts of spells for Nameless, including spells to teleport him to safe places if he ever found himself threatened.

Alias looked up from the finder's stone with a hopeful look on her face. "There's a teleport spell in the finder's stone that can transport us to the Spiderhaunt Woods," she said. "I'm going to use it."

"Alias, we can't just teleport all around the Realms," Akabar said. "We have to think this through."

"There isn't time!" Alias said. "I"m going."

"Can it transport all of us?" Breck asked.

Alias nodded. "I think so," she said. "The stone is very powerful. All we need to do is hold hands," she said, reaching for Dragonbait with her left hand.

Dragonbait translated the plan to Grypht and reached for the wizard's hand. Grypht took Akabar's hand, Akabar grasped Zhara's hand, and Zhara held Breck's.

Alias held the finder's stone out in her right hand and sang out a clear musical note. Immediately a yellow glow surrounded her body. The glow slid from her arm to Dragonbait and then across the chain of Grypht, Akabar, Zhara and Breck. Within moments, the light grew so bright that Alias could see nothing but yellow. Then the light faded. She and her companions stood on a grassy hillside meadow.

Alias swayed dizzily and looked down at the finder's stone with a sense of awe. She'd never thought much about the genius it must have taken to build her own body, but now that she'd actually cast such powerful magic with one of Nameless's other creations she was far more impressed with the bard's skills than she'd ever been before.

Grypht recovered first from the disorienting effects of teleporting and looked around with interest. He nudged the swordswoman and pointed behind her. Atop the hill stood the remains of a crumbling stone manor. Grypht approached the ruins and walked up the front steps and through the doorless doorway. Alias raced alongside him, holding out the finder's stone and thinking of Nameless. A light shot out toward the back of the manor house. She followed it until she reached a doorway to a dark staircase that led downward.

The other adventurers hurried to catch up to her. Breck gave a low whistle. "Nameless is really here," he said with astonishment. "Talk about luck."

Grypht emitted the scent of warm tar, elated over their prospects for success. "We may actually reach him before Moander does."

Alias had already started down the stairs with Dragonbait at her side. Akabar and Zhara followed. Grypht and Breck brought up the rear.

They hadn't descended more than twenty steps when their way was blocked by a caved-in section of the ceiling. The finder's stone pinpointed a tunnel, big enough for everyone but Grypht to crawl through, dug through the rubble. Once Dragonbait made it through to the other side, he whistled back the distance to Grypht, and the wizard summoned a dimensional door to carry him past the cave-in. Grypht's head brushed the passageway ceiling, but he motioned them onward, unconcerned.

Both Grypht's staff and the finder's stone lit the darkness around them, glowing like torches, but the finder's stone also sent out a bright beacon of light to indicate Nameless's direction. The beacon led them to two more cave-ins. Each time Grypht circumvented crawling through them with dimensional doors, so that the huge lizard was the only one of them not covered with dirt when they reached the locked iron grate.

"Olive would be useful right about now," Alias said to Akabar as she shook the door to test its strength.

Grypht motioned for everyone to back away from the grate. Lifting his robe like a grand lady crossing a puddle, the saurial wizard kicked one of his huge legs at the lock. The door flew open with a crash.

"Now, that's a trick I've never seen Elminster do," Breck said with a chuckle as he followed the others through the open grate.

The finder's stone's beam suddenly shifted direction, shining down a gap in the passageway's lined stone walls. Beyond the gap lay a natural tunnel.

Dragonbait sniffed the air and hesitated.

"What is it?" Alias asked.

"Orcs," the paladin said in saurial.

Alias whispered back to Akabar, Zhara, and Breck, "Dragonbait smells—"

"Orcs," Breck finished the swordswoman's sentence.

"How did you know?" Alias asked, surprised.

"I've smelled them many times before," the ranger answered. "How do you think I got the name Orcsbane?" Breck moved to the front of the party and drew his sword. Anticipation gleamed in his eyes.

Alias held the ranger back. "Let Dragonbait look with his shen sight first," she said.

"His what?" Breck asked.

"His shen sight," Alias explained. "He can detect evil like a paladin in the Realms can, only he can detect more detail about what sort of evil."

Dragonbait summoned his shen sight and concentrated on the passageway ahead of them. "There's something else up there," Dragonbait said to Alias after several moments. "Something even more evil than orcs."

The swordswoman translated the paladin's words for the others.

"There must be some other kind of creature leading them," Breck said, stepping into the cleft. "Probably ogres." He hurried down the passage.

"It is not ogres," Dragonbait said in Saurial. "It is something much, much worse."

Alias eyed the ranger's hastily disappearing form. "Then we'd better hurry before whatever it is gets to Nameless," she said, following the ranger. Akabar and Zhara hurried after her, leaving the two saurials behind momentarily.

"What is it, Champion?" Grypht asked the smaller saurial as he moved up beside him.

"I think—" Dragonbait hesitated.

Grypht stood patiently while the paladin reached out with his shen sight to try to determine what sort of evil he sensed. "It's too far off to see clearly, but it's so powerful and dark that I think it must be a minion of Moander's," the saurial said.

"Not surprising," the wizard said. "Let us hope it is not the bard whom you see."

Dragonbait nodded in agreement. He didn't even want to think about how terrible it would be to try to convince Alias they couldn't trust Nameless, that they may even have to destroy him.

The paladin stepped into the cleft between the rocks. The wizard squeezed in behind him, and together they hurried after the others.

The stench of the orc warren soon grew strong enough for even Alias, Akabar, and Zhara to detect. They proceeded with more caution. Even Breck, who could have followed his nose directly to their lair, remained close to the light of the Finder's stone.

"They hate sunlight," the ranger offered, "and they can sometimes be frightened off with a very bright magical light."

"Like a light stone?" Zhara said, pulling one from the robe of her pocket. The damp walls around them glittered in the bright light.

"Yes," Breck nodded. "Keep it hidden for now, though, and spring it on them suddenly. The surprise will add to their fear."

Zhara pocketed the light stone.

The party finally reached the entryway to a cave that reeked of burnt flesh and smoke. Tiny pricks of red light indicated coals still burning in the dark room ahead. Alias held up the finder's stone to see into the room.

It looked as if the center of the ceiling had crashed into the room, and it appeared to have happened very recently. Several dead orcs lay about the floor under piles of rock. Others lay on the ground, felled by some mysterious magic that left no mark. Dead animals lay smoldering over dying charcoal fires.

"If this is the work of the Nameless Bard," Breck said, "I'm impressed."

Alias said nothing. She had done her share of killing, but it was impossible not to notice how young some of the dead orcs were. If causing such destruction was the only way to save his life, she could understand. What she couldn't understand was how Nameless could have been so foolish as to come this close to an orc warren to begin with.

Breck leaned over and yanked a leather thong off the neck of a dead orc. He held it out for Alias to examine. On the end was an ear—an elven ear. "This is the orc tribe of the Torn Ear," the ranger said. "They've been preying on small caravans in the dales for twenty years now. The Dalesmen have tried sending out caravans full of adventurers disguised as merchants, but the Torn Ear always seem to know if a caravan is authentic. Once they've cut off their victims' ears, they loot only the most precious treasures, leaving the rest with the corpses for the crows to pick over. They're expert at covering their trail, too. No one has ever been able to track them to their lair. This season they've attacked nearly three times as many caravans as in any other year. Lord Mourngrym has sent out two parties to search for their warren. Neither group came back."

The ranger laid the thong with the elven ear back down on the chest of the fallen orc. "Well, let's find your Nameless Bard. I'd like to meet him," Breck said.

The beacon light from the finder's stone led them around the collapsed ceiling. They had to stoop now to pass through the edges of the room where the ceiling remained intact. Grypht remained behind, waiting for Dragonbait to return with a report of how far it was to an area that was open enough for the larger saurial to move through comfortably.

They came to another tunnel about fifteen feet wide, leading away from the main room of the orc warren. The voices of orcs drifted down the tunnel to their ears. Knowing danger lay in that direction made no difference. The finder's stone indicated that Nameless was in the same direction, so they couldn't avoid it.

The tunnel's ceiling was higher here, so Dragonbait returned to tell Grypht. Breck paced impatiently until Dragonbait reappeared. "Well, where's that lumbering wizard friend of yours?" he asked the paladin in a whisper.

A giant finger tapped Breck on the head. Grypht had stepped through his dimension door directly behind the ranger and crept up on him in the darkness.

"Uh . . . let's go," Breck said sheepishly.

Grypht held the ranger back by the collar of his leather armor and addressed Alias for a moment.

Alias rolled her eyes with annoyance, but she translated the wizard's words faithfully. "Grypht says we should wait for Zhara to grant us Tymora's blessing."

Breck and the others stood by while Zhara pulled out a vial of holy water and began chanting for the goddess of luck to grant them her favors. As the priestess poured the water on the ground, Alias sighed. The swordswoman had seen priests heal people and cure curses, but when it came to bestowing blessings on people, there was no visible proof to convince her it actually did any good. Still, as Dragonbait constantly reminded her, it wouldn't hurt her to give the priestess's blessing the benefit of the doubt.

Grypht turned to Alias again. This time the swordswoman agreed wholeheartedly with the saurial wizard's suggestion.

"Stay behind Grypht," Alias told Zhara, repeating the saurial wizard's message.

The priestess glared at Alias. "I will not! I will fight at my husband's side. I do not need additional protection. I am wearing your old plate mail beneath my robe," she argued.

"You swing a mean flail," Alias said, "but we'll need your skill as a healer again before the battle is over. Besides, Grypht is vulnerable when he's casting spells. He needs someone to cover his back. That's you."

Akabar addressed a few words to Zhara in Turmish. Zhara sighed and nodded.

Breck and Alias took the lead, creeping up the passage, and Dragonbait and Akabar followed closely behind. Grypht hung back some distance, saving his magic to deal with whatever sort of evil minion of Moander ruled this place. He kept Zhara behind him, hoping to hide and shield her from anything that might rush toward them.

A hundred feet up the passage, Alias and Breck halted. Another thirty feet ahead of them were a dozen large orcs clearing away a pile of rubble. It appeared that the ceiling had collapsed in the tunnel just as it had in the main room. As they watched, a set of orc legs disappeared down a hole in the rubble, and another orc prepared to follow.

"Greater evil lies beyond the wall," Dragonbait said softly to Alias.

"So does Nameless," Alias replied in saurial, pointing out how the beacon emanating from the finder's stone was striking the pile of rubble.

Breck, who couldn't hear their conversation, asked, "What are we waiting for? Torn Ear!" he shouted loudly. "Prepare to die!"

The dozen orcs at the cave-in whirled around with drawn battle-axes or loaded crossbows. Breck leaped forward with his sword in one hand and his dagger in the other. He beheaded one orc with a single swing of his sword and sent another one stumbling backward to avoid being jabbed by the ranger's flashing dagger.

Two crossbow bolts whizzed past Breck's head, missing him narrowly, but a third buried itself in his chest. Three orcs with axes surrounded the ranger and began hacking at him. Alias sliced down one orc who had foolishly turned his own back on her to position himself at the ranger's back. Then she and Dragonbait took position on either side of Breck. Having reestablished a defensive line, the swordswoman and the paladin were careful to hold the line across the width of the corridor so that no orcs could break through and engage Akabar as he cast his spells.

From behind her, Alias could hear the southern mage raise his voice in a Turmish chant. In a moment, two pairs of magic missiles whizzed past her shoulders, burying themselves in the chests of two orcs armed with crossbows. The orcs' crossbows fired wildly, hitting the ceiling, and the orcs fell to the ground, dead.

Another orc positioned himself in front of Alias. He leered at her and aimed his battle-axe over the part of her sternum that her chain mail did not protect. The field of enchantment surrounding her armored shirt deflected the axe's edge before it could cleave her chest open. Taken off guard by the way his blade had skittered across the woman's chest, the orc lost his balance and fell toward Alias. With a backhanded swing, the swordswoman skewered the orc's midsection. She lost a few moments pulling her weapon free, but she had it readied before another orc, intent on destroying the female fighter, stepped over his dead compatriot.

Dragonbait called out in saurial, "Toast!" and his sword began glowing, then burst into flame. The two orcs before him cried out in fear. One dropped his axe and fell back, but the other held his position, only to lose an arm and have his clothing set alight by the paladin's weapon.

Breck was hit by two more crossbow bolts, one in his shoulder and another in his leg. Since he was the biggest member of the party, and the only human male fighter, the orcs no doubt perceived him as the greatest threat, but the Torn Ear's attempts to fell him first came to naught. He ignored the pain from his injuries and separated another orc head from its neck.

Back behind Grypht, Zhara watched all the bloodshed with horror. This was the first battle she'd ever witnessed, and she realized now that she really didn't want to see a second. Even so, it took all her willpower to turn her eyes from the gory scene and fix her sight on the dark tunnel behind her. It was fortunate she did, for she turned in time to spy four pairs of red eyes glittering in the dark—orcs creeping up on her and Grypht.

The priestess drew the light stone out of her pocket and held it up with a shout. The orcs fell back in fear just as Breck had said they would. Zhara shuddered and moved closer to Grypht. The saurial wizard scooped up a stone from the floor of the passage and heaved it at the retreating orcs. It caught one of them in the head, and he collapsed to the ground, still and silent. Noting the size of the beast that had just felled their companion, the other three orcs turned and fled.

Meanwhile, the battle farther down the tunnel was in full swing. The second orc to close on Alias swung at the swordswoman's head with his axe. Alias ducked his first blow and parried the second with her blade. A crossbow bolt grazed Alias's head, and the orc with the axe hit her shield arm. She lost her grip on the finder's stone, and the crystal bounced behind the orcs. Alias retreated a step, and before the orc could follow, she lunged back at him, stabbing right through his leather armor, between his ribs and into his heart.

While Breck and Dragonbait engaged the remaining orcs, Alias crawled over the corpses after the precious finder's stone. Just as she reached for it, a heavy green vine batted her hand away. At the end of the vine was a fanged mouth, which swallowed half the stone and pulled it away. Alias looked up and gasped.

Hovering overhead was a creature out of nightmares—a huge beholder from whose three broken eyestalks and empty central eye socket grew slimy vines, as mobile as arms, with mouths growing from the ends. A second vine shot out at Alias and started to whip about her throat, but the swordswoman slashed it from the beholder's body with her sword.

The beholder turned ever so slightly, focusing one of its deadly eyes on Alias. "Servant," the beholder whispered. "Come!"

Alias felt a sudden warmth for the beholder, as if it, not Dragonbait or Finder or Akabar, could offer her all the friendship she would ever need. The finder's stone flared brightly in the beholder's vine mouth, and the beholder was forced to close its eye of charm, breaking its spell before Alias was completely besotted.

Akabar, who had just fired a pair of magic missiles at an orc retreating into the hole in the rubble, had already noted the vine-ridden beholder as it pushed an orc from its path and emerged from the hole. The southern mage hurried back to where Grypht stood with Zhara, watching the orcs who had tried to sneak up on them retreat. Akabar tugged on the saurial wizard's sleeve and pointed at the beholder.

Grypht hissed at the sight of the monster, then grinned with satisfaction at the sight of the beholder's central eye socket, empty but for the dagger hilt sticking out of it. This is one eye tyrant who will learn to respect the power of a wizard, Grypht thought. The great saurial moved closer to the battle line, pulling a clear cone-shaped crystal from his robe pocket. When he could aim his spell safely without hitting Breck or Dragonbait, the wizard spoke the word "Deathfrost" in saurial and triggered the spell.

Blinded by the finder's stone light, the beholder failed to see Grypht's enchantment heading toward it. A blast of frigid air hit the beholder dead on, freezing the vines so they snapped off from the beholder's body like icicles. The finder's stone fell to the ground, still encased in the beholder's vine mouth. The stone glowed more softly once again, but the beholder had had enough. It retreated into the hole in the rubble and disappeared from view.

Alias cut the vine mouth away from Nameless's glowing yellow crystal and took it up in her hand. She thought of Nameless, and the stone still indicated he was beyond the pile of rubble. Alias climbed up to the hole the beholder had escaped through and followed.

Grypht watched with horror as Dragonbait's soul sister chased after the beholder without a thought for what lay in wait on the other side. She's just like Dragonbait—headstrong and foolhardy, the saurial wizard thought. Dragonbait and Breck were still busy battling the remaining orcs, bigger orcs than the others and better fighters, probably a chieftain and his three bodyguards.

There's no getting around it, Grypht thought. He had to follow Alias. Shoving Zhara toward Akabar, the great saurial moved toward the battle, drawing a bit of gauzy fabric from his pocket.

Grypht tapped his foot impatiently as he surveyed the ground for the remaining component that he needed to fuel his spell. Spying an orc that Dragonbait had felled with his flaming sword, the wizard snatched up a bit of the dead creature's flaming clothing. He blew on the flame until a mere wisp of smoke rose from the clothing. Grypht held the gauze in the smoke as he uttered in saurial, "Wraithform."

Akabar and Zhara watched as the saurial wizard's body faded into insubstantiality. Like a wisp of smoke drawn by a funnel of air, the saurial's ethereal body drifted into the hole in the rubble after Alias and the beholder.

* * * * *

On the other side of the rubble, the passage was flooded with sunshine pouring in from the well shaft overhead. Alias blinked in the bright light. Before she was able to see clearly or stand to defend herself with her weapon, she was grabbed by several pairs of strong, hairy orc hands. Thinking rapidly, she dropped the finder's stone, and it fell back into the hole, unnoticed. The orcs pulled her away from the pile of rubble, laid her on the floor, and held her pinned down by her legs and arms.

A grating, high-pitched voice shouted, "I have your singer, nameless one. She will be a servant of Moander's yet, but you can still share her. If you don't show yourself immediately, however, I'll have these orcs slice out her tongue. Moander doesn't need her voice—only her skill as an assassin."

One of the orcs kicked Alias in the ribs, and she cried out in spite of herself.

Hiding with Olive in the ceiling hole he'd dug out the night before, Finder stiffened.

Olive bit her lip. Could it really be Alias? she wondered. How in the Nine Hells had she gotten here? Why in Tymora's name had she allowed herself to be captured? That girl is nothing but trouble, the halfling thought with annoyance. Now Finder would give away their hiding place, and they'd end up compost for Moander's vines.

However, Finder said nothing immediately. Instead, he drew the horn of blasting from his belt and let it fall from the hole to the ground. Xaran and the other orcs spun around at the clattering of the brass instrument on the rocks. One of the orcs released his grip on Alias and rushed forward to grab the horn. The moment the creature came into view, Finder dropped down from the hole, using the orc's body to break his fall. The orc fell to the ground, and Finder slit the creature's throat with Olive's sword.

The other orcs howled, ready to avenge their comrade, but

Xaran shouted, "Don't let go of the woman!" and the orcs obeyed. Thus Finder was given the opportunity to rise to his feet.

"No more false moves, nameless one," the beholder said. "Remember, you still have your singer's tongue to consider. Drop your weapon."

Finder dropped Olive's sword and stood motionless. He could see now that the orcs did indeed have Alias pinned to the floor. "Are you all right?" he asked the swordswoman.

"I'm just fine," Alias growled through clenched teeth. "How in the Nine Hells do you manage to get us into messes like this?" she asked.

"Silence!" Xaran shouted, hovering nearer to the bard. Three of his eyes had been crushed in the cave-in, but tendrils tipped with fanged maws slithered from the damaged eye stalks. The mouths waved in Finder's face, hissing like snakes. "How you resisted the seeds of possession I will never know," the beholder said to Finder, "but you will not resist them a second time. If it weren't for the master's interest in you, bard, you'd be a dead man. Still, there is no reason you should not suffer as I have suffered."

The bard gasped as Xaran focused his wound-giving eye on the bard's right hand. Instantly an ugly gash appeared across the back of the bard's hand and thumb, cutting through the flesh and muscles down to the bones. Blood oozed from the veins and dripped to the floor. The pain in his hand traveled up his arm like a fire through dry undergrowth, but Finder gritted his teeth and said nothing. He wrapped his hand in the hem of his cloak.

"You endure pain easily," Xaran said. "How else can I make you suffer, bard? Hmm? Shall we see if your singer is as brave as you are?" The beholder turned slightly and focused its wounding eye on Alias. A long gash quickly spread along her sternum, and blood dripped into her chain mail shirt. She drew in a sharp breath, but she made no other noise.

"Leave her be, you fiend!" Finder shouted. "I'll . . . I'll do what you want."

"That's better. Now tell the halfling to come down," the beholder ordered.

"It won't do any good," Finder said. "She has a mind of her own. She won't obey me."

That's for sure, Olive thought vehemently.

"Then I'll have to go up and get her," the beholder said. "She can have a taste of pain as well."

Olive tightened her grip on her dagger. The moment she saw Xaran hovering beneath the hole, she leaped down on top of the monster. She grabbed hold of an eyestalk and used it as a handle so she could remain perched on the beholder's head. Xaran sank the mouths at the end of its tendrils into the arm Olive was using to hold onto its eyestalk.

The halfling screamed and slashed through one of the tendrils where it emerged from the eye stalk. The mouth at the end of the severed tendril released its grip on her flesh and dropped to the floor. Olive stabbed the eye at the end of the eyestalk she was using to hold onto the beholder.

Xaran shrieked with its own mouth and the two tendril mouths biting the halfling.

Alarmed by the noise made by the beholder, one of the orcs released Alias's legs and aimed a crossbow at the halfling.

With her one free leg, Alias kicked savagely at the orc's face and sent him sprawling backward. Using her other leg to gain leverage, the swordswoman pushed herself into a backward somersault and twisted her arms free from the grips of the other two orcs.

Finder grabbed Olive's sword from the ground and ran to help Alias. He slammed into one of the orcs and stabbed at it furiously while the swordswoman fought with the other two.

Loaded down with the extra weight of the halfling, the beholder began sinking toward the ground. It retracted its tendril mouths from Olive's arm and focused its eye of levitation on her. Olive felt herself slowly begin to float upward, but she kept her grip on Xaran's eye stalk. "I'm not going anywhere without you, Xaran!" she snarled.

"Release me or I will use my death ray," the beholder threatened her.

"I'm betting it was crushed in the cave-in," Olive said, "or you would have used it by now."

"There is something I have yet to use on you, halfling," Xaran whined. The beholder's tongue rolled out of its mouth and flipped a chestnut seed burr at the halfling. The burr stuck to Olive's cloak.

Olive gave a shriek, dropped her dagger, and released the beholder's eye stalk as she frantically groped at the strings of her cloak. Xaran turned its eye of levitation on the halfling and levitated her rapidly away from itself until she slammed against the ceiling.

Olive flung her cloak down on top of beholder's head, covering all the creature's eye stalks, including the one that held the levitation eye. The halfling screamed as she began falling, but to her amazement, something appeared suddenly and caught her before she hit the ground.

The halfling stared up into the blue eyes and green snout of Dragonbait's saurial friend. "Grypht!" Olive cried. "It's good to see you!"

Between the two of them, Alias and Finder quickly dispatched the three orcs who had been holding Alias. Alias reached down to retrieve her sword from the orc that had taken it from her, then turned her attention to the beholder.

"Let Grypht handle it," Finder said, holding her back by her cloak. "It's good to see you," he said with a grin. "How have you been?"

Alias looked at the bard in astonishment at his nonchalance. "How have I been! I've been worried sick about you! What are you doing in this awful place?" she demanded, surveying the surroundings.

While Finder paused to consider his words before answering the angry swordswoman, Grypht bent over to set the halfling down gently and pat her on the head. Then the saurial wizard stood back up straight and turned his attention to Moander's minion. Olive could smell the scent of fresh-mown hay, and Alias and Finder could hear him as he called out in saurial, "Firefingers!"

A fan of flame burst out of Grypht's fingertips and ignited Olive's cloak, which still hung over the beholder.

Xaran shrieked and rolled over, so that Olive's burning cloak fell to the floor, but the beholder was already charred horribly and sinking downward.

Olive ran forward and snatched up her dagger. She pounced on Xaran as the creature reached the ground and stabbed the beholder with her dagger, twisting her weapon viciously before yanking it out.

The beholder lay still on the ground.

Just then Breck came crawling through the hole in the rubble, screaming a battle cry as he ran down the pile of rubble with his sword drawn. He stopped short just in front of the dead beholder and stared wordlessly at the slimy tendrils oozing out of the creature's wounded eye.

A moment later, Dragonbait, Akabar, and Zhara came crawling through the rubble to join the others in the cul-de-sac.

"You missed all the excitement," Olive said cheerfully. "I just finished off the beholder."

❦ 15 ❦

The Reunion

While Akabar was convincing Breck to hold still so that Zhara could use her clerical powers to heal his injuries, Dragonbait hurried to Alias's side. Through the soul link he shared with her, he could sense the pain the swordswoman felt from the wound Xaran had given her. The paladin laid his hands on Alias's shoulders and began a prayer.

Although Dragonbait had once explained to Alias that he prayed when he healed, she had never actually heard the words of his prayer before. A sense of embarrassment came over her as she listened to the paladin's pious request to his gods for the power to relieve her pain. Dragonbait, she realized, was as devout as all the clergy members she had joked about for as long as she had known him.

When the wound on Alias's chest had ceased bleeding and the skin had knit together, Dragonbait ran a teasing finger down the brand on her arm so that it tingled pleasantly, as if to remind her that he still cared for her even if she was an impious barbarian.

"The beholder injured Nameless's hand, too," Alias reminded him.

Dragonbait turned wordlessly and, taking the bard's hand in his own, repeated his prayer. The gash in Finder's hand stopped bleeding and closed, though the bard was left with a long scar.

As Olive watched Dragonbait heal Alias and Finder, she caught sight of a familiar yellow gem tucked in the paladin's belt. "Finder! Dragonbait's found your stone!" the halfling cried.

Dragonbait pulled out the gleaming magical stone. "I found it in the passage through the rubble," he said in saurial, handing the stone to the swordswoman.

"I dropped it when the orcs grabbed me," Alias recalled, taking the stone. She glanced at Olive, then looked at the bard with surprise. "What did Olive just call you?" she asked.

"Finder," the bard replied. "That's my name, Alias. Finder Wyvernspur. The Harpers didn't quite succeed in wiping it out completely. Olive discovered what it was."

"Leave it to Olive to uncover the Harpers' best-kept secrets," Alias muttered. Suddenly she laughed. "Finder, as in the finder's stone? All this time we've been using your name and never knew it." She held the magic stone out to the bard and said, "I believe this is yours. We used it to find you."

Finder smiled with delight. "That's the second time in as many days that a pretty woman has returned my property to me," he said, taking the stone.

The bard's compliment wasn't lost on either Olive or Alias. Olive shook her head at Finder's unrelenting flattery as she bent over to retrieve the bard's magical horn. Alias, though, hadn't seen the bard for over a year, and she was overcome with emotion. Her joy at finding him safe and all her yearning to be with him and please him came rushing to the surface. She threw her arms around Finder's neck and hugged him.

"I've missed you so," the swordswoman whispered. "I tried to see you back in Shadowdale, but the Harpers wouldn't let me visit you. I was so worried when you disappeared."

For a moment, Finder felt uncomfortable in Alias's embrace; she had never been quite so demonstrative toward him before. Then he noticed Dragonbait watching him curiously. The paladin was looking, Finder suspected, for some proof that the bard loved Alias as a daughter, not merely as his singing simulacrum.

Almost defiantly, Finder embraced Alias in return and discovered to his surprise that, beyond the fierce pride he felt as her creator, he did indeed harbor some tender feelings for her. "I missed you, too," he admitted softly.

Akabar watched the bard and swordswoman's reunion with satisfaction. He liked Dragonbait, but the mage felt Alias needed more contact with humans. He felt even greater pleasure noting how thoughtfully Breck watched Finder and Alias. *I hope the Harper will show some mercy and take the father's and daughter's affection for one another into account in his final judgment upon the bard,* Akabar thought.

Olive, who was trying to remain casual about the fuss Finder was making over Alias, kept her eyes on the Turmish woman who was healing the Harper ranger. Despite the dark shade of the woman's skin and the different texture of her hair, the halfling quickly recognized that the priestess was another one of Alias's "sisters." Finder, the halfling noted, hadn't even noticed the woman yet. He only had eyes for his eldest "daughter," the one who sang.

When the priestess finished healing the ranger, she began speaking softly to Akabar in Turmish. With the magic earring Finder had given her, Olive eavesdropped on the couple's conversation.

Zhara tugged on her husband's sleeve. "Our reunion has not yet been so sweet as theirs," she whispered in Turmish. "Are you still angry with me for fighting with Alias?"

Akabar looked down at his wife and sighed. She, too, he realized, needed human contact. She'd had her share of terror since yesterday, and although she was very much like Alias, she wasn't used to the horrors and rigors of adventuring. The mage slipped his arms around his wife's shoulders and kissed her tenderly on the lips. "There is nothing left of my anger but smoke," he whispered back.

Zhara squeezed him around the waist, laid her head on his chest, and sighed deeply.

Akabar stroked Zhara's thick auburn hair. Unbidden, a vision of Kyre came to his mind. He couldn't keep from picturing the half-elf's long, silky black hair.

Zhara sensed his unease. "What's wrong?" she asked, gazing up at him, concerned.

"Nothing," Akabar replied, shaking his head. There was no sense worrying Zhara about his feelings for a dead woman. He held Zhara even tighter, but the vision of the half-elf remained.

Olive grew uncomfortable watching Akabar embrace his wife, so she turned her attention to the remains of Xaran's body. Someone had once told her that alchemists would buy beholder eyes for potions, but she doubted she could get much for Xaran's eyes. Even before they'd been crushed by the cavein, stabbed at by herself, and frozen and then burnt by Grypht, they hadn't exactly been fresh-looking.

There was something worth retrieving from the beholder, though. Finder's dagger was still lodged in Xaran's central eye. Olive began to roll the beholder over so she could reach the dagger.

Grypht caught Dragonbait's eye and cocked his head. The paladin moved away from the others to join his fellow saurial.

"Well, Champion, what does your shen sight tell you about the bard?" Grypht asked quietly.

"The Darkbringer does not possess him," Dragonbait replied, but there was not much relief or pleasure in his voice.

"So he does not burn with the fires of evil," Grypht said with a shrug. "But you have not told me what your shen sight does reveal about him," the wizard said.

"He is much the same as before, High One," Dragonbait said. "A mountain of pride, wrapped in gray fog."

"Neutral . . . neither good nor evil," Grypht noted. "A man who walks the wall. He does not lack the strength to abide by convictions. Why doesn't he have any?" the wizard growled.

"Perhaps," Dragonbait suggested, "convictions are not as interesting to him as he is to himself."

"Do you want your dagger, Finder?" Olive called out.

The bard looked in Olive's direction. "Of course I do, little Lady Luck," he said, winking at the thief.

Olive sniffed in mock disdain at the flattering nickname and turned away so no one could see her blushing. Leaning over Xaran's corpse, she pulled Finder's dagger from the beholder's central eye.

As Olive's leg brushed against the remains of her cloak, Grypht could see that the burr that Xaran had spit at the halfling still lay in the folds of the charred fabric. Alarmed, the wizard noticed that the magic seed pod had begun to swell. He rushed to Olive's side and lifted her from the ground by her arm, snatching her away from the seed.

"Hey!" she shouted. "Put me down!" she demanded. "You're hurting my arm!"

An explosive crack came from Olive's cloak as the burr split open, releasing a cloud of blue-black dust.

With his free hand, Grypht grabbed Akabar's robe and pulled the merchant-mage and his wife farther away from the cloud. "Use the stone!" the wizard ordered. "Get us out of here! Now!"

Finder held up his magic stone with his good hand and took up Alias's right hand with his injured one. "Dragonbait, get over here," the bard shouted.

The paladin leaped to Alias's side and grabbed her left hand.

As if it had a mind of its own, the black cloud drifted toward the halfling, tucked under the wizard's arm.

Dragonbait grabbed Zhara, and Zhara held onto Akabar. Grypht reached out for Akabar. Finder sang a note, and the party glowed a vivid yellow, then vanished.

The cloud of black dust swirled once around the spot where they'd stood, then sank to the floor, unable to sustain itself without a host.

When the light from the finder's stone's teleportation spell died out, the adventurers found themselves once again on the hillside outside the crumbling stone manor.

"We should be safe here for a while, at least," Finder said. To Olive, he added, "You should be more careful, little Lady Luck."

"Me?" the halfling said increduously, thinking of all the risks Finder had taken in the past day alone.

Grypht set Olive down, and the halfling sank into the grass, exhausted by the teleportation and groaning from the pain in her injured shoulder.

Grypht waved a finger at the halfling, and the scent of honeysuckle rose from his body.

"Grypht says you should be more careful, too, Olive," Alias translated for the halfling. "You nearly became Moander's smallest minion."

Confused, Olive looked at Finder. "How come I didn't understand what he said?" she asked the bard, tapping meaningfully on the magical diamond earring he'd given her.

"The earring will only work for languages that are spoken in the Realms," the bard explained. Suddenly he turned to Alias. "How did *you* understand what Grypht said?" he asked.

"I cast the tongues spell from the finder's stone—your stone," Alias said.

"That's impossible," Finder said. "I enchanted the stone so that only a Wyvernspur can cast—" The bard halted in midsentence, and his brow furrowed. "Then Olive was right," he said. "In the eyes of the gods, you are my daughter."

"It's true, then, that the tongues spell cast from your stone is permanent?" Grypht interrupted. "You can still understand me?"

Finder nodded.

"But permanency requires tremendous power," Grypht said.

"Where does it come from?"

"From the stone," Finder explained in saurial. "It was a simple artifact before I inserted a shard of para-elemental ice into it, making it a device which could store music, lore and magic "

"You tampered with an artifact?" Grypht asked, looking at the bard as if he were insane.

"Why not?" Finder asked Grypht. "It worked." Turning away from the saurial wizard, the bard glanced at the other adventurers. "This is quite a party you've assembled to rescue me," he commended Alias.

Zhara sniffed in annoyance. "You flatter yourself, bard," the priestess said. "We are here because we wanted to make sure you did not do Moander's bidding."

Finder looked at Zhara in surprise, finally taking notice of her resemblance to Alias. "You're one of the copies of Alias that Phalse made, aren't you?" the bard asked Zhara.

"Nameless—um, Finder," Alias said, "this is Zhara, priestess of Tymora and Akabar's wife," she added. Although she managed to keep her voice even when she said it, she couldn't keep herself from glowering at the merchant-mage.

Finder turned his most charming smile on the priestess and bowed low. "I am pleased to meet you, my lady," he said.

"Why should you be pleased?" Zhara asked coolly. "I don't sing."

"What? Not even the prayer to the stars?" the bard asked with mock surprise, his eyes twinkling with mischief. "I thought all of Lady Luck's priests sang that prayer each night."

Zhara looked flustered. She hadn't expected this self-serving man to have any knowledge of religion, let alone to know intimate details about prayers to her goddess. "Well, yes . . . I sing that," she admitted.

"And I'll wager you sing it beautifully, too," Finder replied, then he turned his smile on Breck Orcsbane. Although he hadn't met the man, he had already guessed who Breck was from the Harpers pin that the ranger wore on his cloak. "And you, Harper?" Finder asked. "Is your only concern that I do not do the Darkbringer's bidding? Or have you come to whisk me back to prison?"

"I must hear your story first, sir," Breck Orcsbane said, "to discover whether it confirms or denies what Akabar and Grypht have told me. Please tell me all that has happened to you since yesterday," the ranger requested.

"All that has happened to me since yesterday will make a rather long tale," the bard said. "I hope you don't mind if I sit down before I begin."

"Of course not," Breck replied politely.

Finder settled down in the grass. Olive handed him his dagger and horn, and she and Alias sat on either side of him like doting daughters. The others, save for Grypht, sat before him like children listening to a bedtime tale.

Grypht stood off from the others, watching with considerable interest as Finder recounted the events of the past day in true bardic tradition. The wizard could hear, but not understand, Finder, so he was acutely aware of the power the human held over his audience. The other six adventurers listened with fascination to the bard's story, enthralled by the sound of his voice.

It was a rare gift, this ability to entertain others, and it attracted people to it, as did anything rare. It was also a very minor enchantment, Grypht realized, but one so subtle as to prove nearly irresistible. Not even Breck Orcsbane proved immune to it. When he first began listening to Finder, the ranger's face had been an impartial mask, but soon Breck too, was swayed by the bard's words, and he looked at the older man with obvious admiration and respect. At least now, Grypht thought, the ranger will finally accept the truth about Kyre.

Olive listened with delight to how heroically Finder portrayed her role in their first escape from the orcs and her subsequent return to the workshop. When she caught sight of the blank look on Grypht's face and realized he couldn't understand the bard, she rose quietly and slipped over to where the saurial wizard stood. She slipped her diamond earring off and held it out to him, signing for him to try it. With some amusement, Grypht accepted the tiny piece of jewelry and slipped it on a horn beside one of his ear slits.

"I know you can cast magic to understand what we're saying," she whispered, "but my earring won't wear out like your spells. You can borrow it for a while."

Wearing the earring, Grypht was able to understand the halfling perfectly, though it didn't give him the power to reply, so he merely nodded his thanks to Olive. As he watched the halfling return to the bard's side, he wondered if she realized that by offering him the loan of her magical jewelry, she was paving the way for him to fall under the bard's spell along with the others.

Finder finished his tale with a description of the final battle with Xaran in which they had all been involved. Only Olive recognized the omissions in the bard's story. He hadn't mentioned the plan he'd made in the Tower of Ashaba to escape with his magical stone in the event the Harpers judged against him, nor his plan to elude their judgment once he'd fled from Kyre. And, of course, he had not revealed that he knew who had looted his workshop. Loyally, Olive said nothing to correct the bard. It could be disastrous, she realized, if the Harpers found out about Flattery.

"So, Harper," Finder said to Breck. "What's your verdict? Are you hauling me back to Shadowdale in chains?"

"Considering the emergency, I have more important things to do than to escort prisoners around, sir," Breck said to the bard. Briefly the ranger and the merchant-mage updated Finder on Elminster's disappearance, Kyre's death, Grypht's flight from the tower with Akabar, Morala's scrying visions, and the hunt for Grypht.

"According to Grypht," Breck explained to Finder, "Moander turned most of his people into its minions and forced them from his world, through Tarterus, to the Realms. These minions are now building the god a new body."

"How do you know all this?" Finder asked Grypht.

"I've been scrying on my people and watching their suffering for many months now," Grypht explained.

"We have to find this new body and destroy it before Moander's minions complete it," Breck said. He slipped off his pack, and from it he pulled out a large parchment map and a thin stick of writing lead. He spread the map out on the grass in front of him.

"Nice map," Alias said, impressed with the detailed attention to geography and scale. "Where'd you get it?"

"I made it," Breck said with a shrug, though from his smile, it was obvious he was proud of his handiwork. "This is the clearing near Shadowdale where we met with Zhara and Grypht and Akabar," the ranger explained, setting his stick of lead down on the map. "This is the direction the finder's stone indicated when Grypht thought of a saurial whom Moander has possessed and brought to the Realms," he said, drawing a line northwest by west on the map. "Was the saurial you thought of helping to build this body for Moander?" Breck asked Grypht.

The wizard nodded.

"So Moander's new body must be somewhere along this line," Breck said, tracing with his finger the line he'd drawn. He pointed to the region of the map representing the dales. "I can't believe they could have been building a god's body for three months anywhere in the dales without having been detected by Elminster," he said. "The mountains would be a much more likely hiding place." Breck slid his fingers across the individual peaks of the Desertsmouth Mountains. "They might be as far off as Anauroch, but there's nothing in the desert for them to use to build Moander's new body. There's not enough to eat or drink there for a large party of adventurers, let alone a whole tribe."

"Are you certain you've drawn your line accurately?" Finder asked. "You could be off by miles."

Breck shook his head. "You bards have a boast that you never lose count of the measure. Well, we rangers have a boast of our own. We never get lost. I stood beside Grypht and watched the beam from the finder's stone very carefully. It ran just between these two peaks—Mount Andria and Mount Dix."

"Then Moander's minions must be building his new body approximately here," Finder said. "The Lost Vale." He pointed to a spot on the line just to the south of a peak labeled "Mount Hans."

"The Lost Vale is nothing but a myth," Breck said. "Adventurers have been searching for it for centuries without finding a thing."

"How quickly old Harper secrets are forgotten," Finder said, chuckling. "You can't *search* for the Lost Vale," he explained. "Someone must take you to it magically. It makes perfect sense that Moander would choose the Lost Vale. It's magically hidden and warmed, and there's a gate to Tarterus nearby. Isn't that how Moander got your people from Tarterus to the Realms?" Finder asked Grypht. "Through a gate?"

Grypht nodded.

"We can triangulate with the stone to be sure, but my money is on the Lost Vale. Care to make a bet, ranger? My hundred gold to your one says I'm right."

"How could I resist?" Breck replied, gathering up his map.

"We'll have a better view from the top of the hill," Finder said, rising to his feet.

The other adventurers stood, except for the halfling. "I'll just wait here until you get back," Olive said, lying back in the grass.

Grypht looked thoughtfully at the halfling, then pulled out a small vial and handed it to Dragonbait. "Stay here with Olive," he ordered the paladin. "See if this salve will help her injury any."

As the others followed the bard up the hillside Dragonbait knelt beside Olive. The paladin hadn't realized the halfling was injured. It was so unlike her to suffer in silence. Now, though, he could see what Grypht must have noticed earlier, the blood-stain on the shoulder of her tunic.

What happened to your shoulder? he signed.

"Xaran took a shot at me last night with its wounding eye," Olive said. The halfling sat up suddenly, staring at the paladin in surprise. "You're using a hand cant!" she squeaked. "How did you learn it? No one's supposed to teach it to outsiders."

Dragonbait pointed toward Alias's retreating figure.

Olive rolled her eyes up to the ceiling. "That girl is nothing but trouble!" she exclaimed. "Just what the Realms needs—a paladin who understands the thieves' hand cant! Lord of Shadows, is nothing sacred anymore?"

Dragonbait chuckled at the halfling's rhetorical question. *Grypht recommended we try this salve on your wound*, he signed.

"I'm not hurt that bad," Olive said, but when she tried to shrug, the pain made her grimace in spite of herself.

Let me see the wound, the paladin insisted.

Olive sighed and loosened the drawstring at the neck of her tunic and let the garment slip down her shoulder, revealing a blood-caked bandage.

Gingerly the paladin lifted the bandage from the wound. A honeysuckle scent of concern issued from the saurial's neck glands. The halfling's shoulder was in worse shape than Finder's hand had been, yet she hadn't said a word when he'd used all of his healing energies on Alias and Finder. Dragonbait poured Grypht's salve onto the wound.

The sticky salve wasn't a magical healing potion, but as Dragonbait pulled a spare shirt from his knapsack and fashioned it into a fresh bandage, Olive could feel the pain in her shoulder easing.

When the paladin finished tending her injury, Olive stood up, saying, "Let's join the others, shall we?"

As Dragonbait walked up the hill beside the halfling, he signed, *Are you coming with us to fight Moander again?*

"I'm going with Finder," Olive said. "Whatever he decides to do, I'll do."

Dragonbait's brow furrowed slightly. He remembered Alias commenting once that Nameless was a good influence on Olive. The paladin wasn't so sure that was exactly accurate. He suspected it was the bard's reputation, more than the man himself, that influenced Olive. Like Alias, the halfling probably perceived the bard as a good man. Both women thought his brilliance made up for his vanity. Finder's special attention to them made him seem to them less selfish and reckless than he really was. The paladin doubted he'd ever convince either woman of Finder's true nature.

Then Olive surprised him by whispering, "Someone has to keep an eye on him in case he tries to do something especially stupid."

I thought you liked him, Dragonbait signed.

"I love him," Olive snapped, "but I'm not an idiot, you know."

I know now, the saurial signed in reply.

* * * * *

In the ruins of the manor house atop the hill, Finder handed Grypht his magical stone. "Think of the same saurial you thought of before," he instructed the wizard.

As the others watched, a beacon of light sprang out from the finder's stone, heading northwest.

"We're right here," Finder said, pointing out on Breck's map the position of his keep, "and the beam cuts to the right of that mountain—the one that looks like it's been sliced in half."

Breck nodded. "That's Wizards' Folly. It used to be a whole mountain thirty years ago, before two wizards decided to use it for a battlefield." The ranger drew a second line on his map. The two lines intersected at precisely the spot Finder had claimed to be the Lost Vale. "It seems you've won your wager," Breck said.

Olive and Dragonbait rejoined the others just as the ranger pulled a gold coin from a pouch on his belt and tossed it to the bard.

Finder twirled the gold piece around his fingers and seemed to make it disappear into thin air. Only Olive caught sight of the glimmering coin as it slid down the sleeve of the bard's shirt.

"So, can your magical stone take us to the Lost Vale?" Breck asked Finder.

"To the Singing Cave at the northern edge of the vale," the bard replied. "From the cave's mouth, you can see the whole vale."

"First we should find out about the seed," Grypht said. "You didn't say in your tale, but are you sure the beholder didn't mention a seed to you?" the wizard asked Finder.

"I'm sure," Finder replied. "What is this seed?"

"Let me explain," Alias said, shooting a warning glance at the others. She didn't want Finder to know that she'd changed any of his songs. It would only anger him, so she decided to leave that part out of her explanation. "Because my soul is linked to Dragonbait's, it seems I have a strange ability," the swordswoman explained carefully. "It makes me go into a trance and sing about things related to Dragonbait's people. Since the saurials are minions of Moander, they know about this seed, and somehow I sang a song about it."

"Sing the song for me now," Finder ordered.

Alias repeated both verses of the saurial soul song for the bard. Now that she was sure that Finder was safe from Moander, she was better able to concentrate on the first verse. She felt as if some stranger had whispered Moander's secrets to her in her dreams, and she only had to remember the dream and how it had made her feel to understand it. With a jolt of alarm, she realized that she knew the purpose of the seed as clearly as she had known that Moander had meant to possess Finder. "The minions have already completed Moander's new body!" she declared. "That's why they need the seed."

"What?" Grypht and Akabar asked in unison.

"The seed in the song is a seed of possession," Alias explained.

"Like the one Xaran used to try to possess Finder?" Olive asked.

Alias shook her head. "Not exactly," she said. "When Moander was in the Realms last year, it stored most of the power it acquired in the Realms in this seed, so this seed is much more powerful. Larger, too, I think." Alias looked confused for a moment. "The saurials have never seen the seed, so I can't picture it. Moander needs the seed, though, to possess its new body. Without it, the god can't return to the Realms."

"Good," Breck said. "Then all we have to do is find the seed and destroy it."

"If Moander can't find it," Akabar asked, "how are we supposed to discover it?"

"Use the finder's stone," Breck said excitedly.

Finder shook his head and explained. "It won't work if you haven't got a clear picture of what you're trying to locate."

"We can try," the ranger insisted.

Finder handed Alias the magical stone, and Alias concentrated hard on the song. She seemed to sense excitement and impatience emanating from Moander. Although the finder's stone glowed in her hands, it sent out no beam of light.

"Hey!" Olive said excitedly. "Maybe the finder's stone is the seed! Maybe it's glowing to point to itself!"

"Try to keep your imagination under control, little Lady Luck," Finder chided. "That's impossible. Moander has never been anywhere near the stone."

"Not so," Akabar said. "Alias had the stone with her last year when she freed Moander from its prison in Yulash, and Dragonbait used it to follow the god through the gate it created to go to Westgate. Although Moander never actually touched it, the god did get quite close to the stone."

Finder took exception. "Xaran never said anything about the stone, and I'd know if anyone had tampered with it."

"But would you tell us if you did know?" Akabar asked suspiciously. "How do we know for sure that you haven't been possessed by Moander?"

"How do we know *you* haven't been?" Finder growled back.

Anxious to restore unity, Grypht said, "Dragonbait sensed no evil in Finder."

Alias translated the wizard's statement, and Dragonbait confirmed the swordswoman's words with a nod.

"But there is something wrong with Akabar," Olive said, remembering the conversation she'd eavesdropped on. "At least Zhara thought so."

"What is it, priestess?" Breck demanded.

Zhara looked down at the ground, unable to deny what the halfling said but unwilling to speak out against her husband.

"I have not been possessed but merely enchanted," Akabar said with a sigh. "It is the sort of enchantment women can always sense. Kyre fed me a philter of love so I would follow her to Moander."

Alias noted the pained look on Breck's face. He'd suffered enough grief from Kyre's death already. The news that the half-elf had used magic to seduce another man came as just one more slap in the ranger's face.

"Grypht can dispel the enchantment," Finder said. "Then Moander won't be able to use your love for her against us."

"Breck loved Kyre, too," Akabar pointed out. "Will you try to disenchant him? Kyre was a beautiful, talented woman. Why shouldn't both of us remember her with feelings of love. Do not waste your spell, wizard," the mage said to Grypht. "How I felt about Kyre does not matter now that she is dead."

"He's right," Breck said.

Only Alias noted the look of pain on Zhara's face. It's so like Akabar, the swordswoman thought, to think it doesn't matter that he loves another woman. He expects Zhara to share his affections with his other wives and any other woman he desires. If it hadn't been for her friendships with Dragonbait and Finder and Olive, Alias realized, she, too, might have accepted Akabar's shared affections. A wave of sympathy for the priestess swept over her, and a feeling of guilt niggled at her conscience, remembering how she had actually hoped Akabar would fall in love with Kyre and become disenchanted with Zhara.

The other members of the party had already accepted Breck's judgment about Akabar's decision and had returned to arguing about the finder's stone.

"According to your story, Kyre grabbed the stone just before you used it to teleport yourself to this place yesterday," Grypht reminded Finder. "This morning the beholder grabbed for it when Alias dropped it. These events suggest that Moander's minions have some interest in the stone."

"Maybe they just wanted to use it to find their seed," Finder argued.

"That's possible," Grypht said, "but it doesn't disprove the theory that the stone is the seed."

Finder scowled. "Moander traveled on land from Yulash deep into the Elven Woods. The god could have left its power anywhere. The seed could be practically anything."

Olive cursed herself for making the suggestion about the stone. The bard cherished the stone, and if the others insisted on destroying it, Finder would be furious. She wracked her brain for some way to convince the others that the idea was wrong. Fortunately Alias succeeded where the halfling could not.

"Moander would never have chosen the finder's stone to hold the seed," the swordswoman said. "The seed's casing has to break open for the seedling of possession to sprout, but breaking open the finder's stone would release the para-elemental ice at the center of the stone, and the seedling would die in the cold."

"Yes," Grypht agreed. "That's true."

Olive breathed a sigh of relief as Alias returned Finder's stone to him. The bard studied the gem thoughtfully.

"Well, if we can't find the seed," Breck said, "we're back to the first plan. We've got to destroy Moander's new body before the minions manage to find the seed and resurrect the god. Are you ready to take us to this Singing Cave?" he asked Finder.

"Just as soon as I take Alias somewhere safe," the bard said.

"What?" Alias exclaimed.

"Moander tried to use you once. It will try again," Finder said. "I don't want you anywhere near it."

"Finder, why did you bother to make me a swordswoman if it wasn't to fight?" Alias snapped.

"So you could defend yourself if you were in trouble," Finder said. "I didn't expect you to go looking for fights. And I most certainly never dreamed you'd run around trying to destroy evil gods."

"Be reasonable, bard," Breck said. "This is no time to be overly paternal. Alias is a good fighter. We need her."

Grypht added, "Her presence can protect us from the scrying of Moander's minions."

"So can Zhara's," Finder countered.

"But Alias might sing another soul song that could help us defeat the Darkbringer," Grypht persisted.

Finder glared at the wizard. "I won't have you using her to sing soul songs."

"Only you can use her to sing your songs, is that it, Finder?" Akabar asked.

"Stop it, all of you!" Alias shouted. "No one uses me! I choose to do things or not on my own." She turned to Finder and addressed him with her hands on her hips. "Dragonbait is my brother. His tribe is my tribe. You would do well to remember that, Father. I'm going to help the saurials, and you are not going to stop me. Grypht has scried the vale; he can teleport me there if you won't."

"An hour ago the thought of Moander filled you with terror," Dragonbait reminded her.

"It doesn't matter," Alias said stubbornly. "I'm not staying behind."

"Fine," Finder said coldly.

Alias looked as if the bard had slapped her in the face.

Olive knew exactly what the swordswoman was feeling and thinking. Alias was on the verge of considering some compromise, just as the halfling had found herself doing so often with Finder. I can't let that happen, Olive decided. She hurried to Finder's side and pushed the bard's hand into Alias's, saying, "Now that that's settled, let's get going."

Finder shot an annoyed look at Olive, but to his own surprise, he realized he'd grown too superstitious about the halfling's instinctive actions to defy them. He tightened his grip on Alias's hand and stole a glance at her.

Alias smiled at him shyly.

"I just don't want you to be hurt," he said.

"I know," Alias answered.

The others hastily formed a chain with their hands. Finder sang a series of notes, and the stone's glow of teleportation surrounded all of them.

* * * * *

The Mouth of Moander looked up suddenly from Moander's new body. With Moander controlling her, she shouted, "Gather the fliers. Cast a spell of invisibility on them. They must patrol the vale."

Several lesser minions hurried to obey the god's high priestess. They began to climb down from the immense mount of vegetation that Moander would soon inhabit.

Coral felt her heart sink. When her scrying on Xaran and the Nameless Bard had failed, she had been certain the swordswoman Alias had rescued the bard.

No, my priestess, Moander whispered in her head. *I can sense the power of the seed. The bard has brought it to the vale. I told you he was possessed.*

"Then why hasn't he brought the seed directly to you?" Coral asked defiantly. "Why do you need the fliers to search for him?"

Moander ignored her goading. *No doubt the bard will have my servant Alias with him,* the god informed Coral. *And where Alias is, the paladin will be, too. They must be reeled in carefully. You will have that honor, Coral. Champion will be pleased to see you again . . . at first.*

Coral looked down at the ground, far below the top of the god's new body. *If I can make it close enough to the edge to jump,* she thought, *I could end this torment.*

Curiously, Moander didn't seem to notice her thought or take control of her limbs. Whispering her former goddess's name, Coral dashed to the edge of the vast pile of greenery and flung herself away from it. She began to drift down as gently as a feather. On the ground beneath her, she could see a possessed magic-user staring up at her. Moander had used the mage's body to cast a feather fall spell on her. She had gained nothing by her suicide attempt.

But I have learned much, Moander's voice came to her. *Now I know just how far you will go. I must keep you on a tighter leash, mustn't I? It is hopeless to defy me. You, and you alone, will be the one to sacrifice Champion, and no other—just as soon as you have planted the seed to resurrect me in the Realms.*

Coral's tears splashed to the ground like rain. Some time later she landed beside them. Under Moander's control, she rose to her feet and strode off to make preparations to capture Dragonbait and Alias.

❧ 16 ❧

The Lost Vale

Finder's stone teleported the eight adventurers into the Singing Cave at the edge of the Lost Vale. They stood about twenty feet from the cave's mouth. Sunlight poured in on the green carpet of moss and ferns just inside the cave's entrance. Condensation sparkled on the stone walls. Little red and yellow skinks skittered over the floor, walls, and ceiling, and orange swallows shot in and out of the cave carrying insects for their young, which twittered in nests in nooks and crannies at the back of the cave.

Olive pulled her hands away from Alias and Dragonbait. For the first time, the teleportation hadn't exhausted her. I must be getting used to it, she thought as she walked to the mouth of the cave, which faced a steep mountainslope to the south. Olive stared down the mountainside and her eyes widened. "What a mess!" she muttered.

The others came up beside the halfling to look out. Far below them, a vale nearly five miles wide stretched from the mountains to the east down into the foothills bordering on the Anauroch Desert to the west. The steeper slopes of the vale were covered with meadows, which sparkled with wild flowers, and woods carpeted with ferns and teeming with a great variety of trees. Many of the trees were laden with fruit and flowering vines. Crystal blue streams ran from the mountains through the meadows and woods.

The greenery on the gentler slopes and in the lowlands, though, had been devastated. Nearly a quarter of the vale's plants had been hacked to the ground and uprooted. Some larger trees still lay dying where they'd been cut down, but most of the vegetation had been hauled off, leaving the reddish brown earth bare. As the streams flowed lower into the vale, they, too, took on the color of the earth.

Breck Orcsbane whistled softly. "I've seen a flight of dragons cause less damage," he said. The ranger pointed to a great green butte nearly a thousand feet in diameter that rose several hundred feet straight up from the bottom of the vale. "Those specks moving around that hill must be the possessed saurials," the ranger speculated. "With all that activity around one spot, I'll bet Moander's new body is hidden in a cave somewhere in that hill."

Alias, Dragonbait, Akabar, and Olive exchanged nervous glances with one another.

"Who wants to tell him?" Olive asked.

Akabar put one hand on the ranger's shoulder. "That hill," the mage said slowly, "*is* Moander's new body."

"What?" the ranger exclaimed.

"Moander's minions must have created the hill from all the plants and trees they've cut down in the vale," Alias said. "Moander grows on decaying things. When I first released the god from its prison in Yulash last year, it plunged into a refuse pit and soaked it up, ate some soldiers' corpses, and then headed for the elven wood to tear up a few hundred acres of trees."

"This body is a bit smaller than Moander was in the Elven Woods," Olive noted.

"You can't be serious!" Breck said.

"I have scried on my people for months as they built this new body, but I had no idea it was so huge," Grypht said. "I never attempted to view it all at once. I never imagined the scale they've built it to." From the hamlike smell the wizard emitted, Alias could tell that Grypht was extremely worried.

"Grypht didn't realize it was so large, either," Alias explained to the adventurers who couldn't understand saurial.

"If Moander's last body was bigger than this one, how did you ever destroy it?" Breck asked incredulously.

"We burned it . . . with the help of a red dragon," Akabar said.

Grypht shook his head unhappily. "That must be why the minions have been casting special enchantments on this new body to protect it from fire," he said.

"Grypht says this one's protected from fire," Alias translated. From the surprised look on Akabar's face, she could see the mage hadn't counted on this possibility.

"Well, what are we supposed to do with it, then?" Breck asked. Fear and frustration had begun to creep into his voice.

"Grypht could disintegrate it," Olive suggested.

"Perhaps," the wizard mumbled. "Given a thousand years."

"It's simply too big," Akabar replied. "It would take hundreds of wizards working years and years."

"Then gate it into another dimension," the halfling said.

"It would take the power of a god to create a gate large enough," Akabar said.

"As long as the seed isn't brought to it, the body isn't important. Right?" Zhara declared. "Without its minions, Moander is helpless. Somehow we must free the saurials from the Darkbringer's possession."

"Is that possible?" Alias asked.

"There are ways to free those who haven't been possessed too long," Grypht replied. "Those who were possessed first, at the same time Kyre was, harbor too many tendrils of possession. Even if we succeeded in destroying all the tendrils in their bodies, so much of their flesh is rotted away that they would die anyway. But those are blessedly few. Most of our people could be saved by a cure disease spell. That will destroy the tendrils that possess them. If we cannot get near them easily, we can cast cold spells on them instead. That will also destroy the tendrils."

After Finder had translated Grypht's words into Realms common, Akabar said, "But cold spells could kill the saurials."

"No," Dragonbait said. "We saurials don't react to cold the same way you humans do." The paladin turned to Alias. "Remember what happened to me last winter in Shadowdale when I was watching you skate on the duck pond?"

"You fell asleep, and we couldn't get you to wake up until we brought you back inside the inn," Alias recalled.

The paladin nodded. "Cold doesn't harm saurials the way it harms you humans—damaging your flesh and hurting your lungs, pulling so much heat from your bodies that you could die. Instead, our scales protect the flesh. We fall into a torpor so we breathe less cold air, and we stop moving, which conserves heat. The larger we are, the less prone we are to the effect, but we can't control it. Even the High One," Dragonbait said, nodding in Grypht's direction, "would fall into the cold sleep if he stayed outdoors in Shadowdale in winter for more than an hour or so."

Alias translated all this for Akabar.

"Well, maybe we'll get lucky and the vale will have an early frost," Olive said.

Finder shook his head. "Part of the vale's magic keeps it especially warm in the winter," he said.

"There are over a hundred of my people down there," Gryph said. "We will need the help of warriors to capture them without harming them and priests who can cast spells to cure diseases and mages who know magical cold spells."

Alias translated Gryph's words.

"If Finder can teleport me back to Shadowdale," Breck said, "I'll muster a force of fighters and spellcasters."

"I can take you to Elminster's tower," Finder said, "but I can't wait for you. If Morala discovers I've returned, she may insist be returned to prison. I refuse to risk leaving my daughter to face Moander without me."

Breck nodded in agreement. Finder was right—Morala could be aggravatingly stubborn. She might refuse to recognize their need for Finder's help.

"If you can't find mages to teleport you back here to this place by tomorrow noon," Finder said, "I'll return for your forces then."

"He should take Zhara with him," Akabar said. "If she is with him in Shadowdale, Moander won't be able to detect them as they raise the forces we need to combat its minions."

Zhara frowned. "I don't want to be parted from you, husband," she said.

"It's only for a day," Akabar replied.

For a moment, Zhara looked as if she might argue further but instead she said to Alias, "You will look out for my Akabar?"

"He'll be fine," Alias said, surprised that Zhara would entrust the mage to her care.

"That is not what I asked," the priestess said.

The swordswoman stole a glance at Akabar; he looked embarrassed by Zhara's request.

Zhara stepped closer to Alias and whispered to her, "Please It is not true, what you said, that he does not care for you. He once destroyed Moander to save you. I know you care for him as well."

Alias sighed. She didn't approve of the way Akabar shared his love with so many women, and she couldn't believe his marriage to Zhara had nothing to do with Zhara's resemblance to herself, but she couldn't deny the priestess's words. Akabar had risked his life to save her because they were friends, and she still cared deeply for him.

"Yes . . . I'll look out for him," she promised. She could see Dragonbait looking at her expectantly. He didn't need to speak or even sign for her to know what was on his mind.

"I'm sorry I hit you and for the things I said," the swordswoman apologized to Zhara. "I guess you aren't so bad, as priestesses go."

A smile flickered across Zhara's face. "And you aren't so bad for a northern barbarian who smells of wet wool," she said.

Alias laughed. She held out her arms wrists upward.

Zhara laid her own arms over Alias's, and they both clasped their hands over the other's forearm in an adventurer's embrace. The magical brand on Alias's arm tingled, just as it did when Dragonbait touched it, and Alias realized Zhara must feel the same sensation from the brand Phalse had put on her.

"Till next season, sister," Alias whispered.

"Tymora's luck be yours," Zhara replied.

Akabar moved to his wife's side, and Alias stepped back. She looked away as Akabar embraced Zhara and kissed her.

"If Breck and Zhara are to return here by tomorrow, they have to leave before then," Finder noted wryly.

Akabar nodded and stepped away from his wife. Zhara took Finder's and Breck's hands and the bard sang out a note.

Less than a minute after the three disappeared, Finder reappeared alone. "Lhaeo said Elminster hasn't returned yet," the bard reported.

"Morala said the sage was all right when she scried for him. Could Moander really prevent him from returning home?" Alias asked.

"The Darkbringer's power is very great in our world," Grypht said, "but it couldn't prevent me from leaving."

"Perhaps it could have stopped you but chose not to," Alias suggested. "Then when Elminster arrived on your world, Moander decided it couldn't chance allowing the sage to return and interfere with its plans. It knows we could use Elminster's help."

"We could use some food, too," Olive piped up.

"She's right," Dragonbait said. "There's not much left in our supplies. I'll see what I can scavenge."

"Not alone," Alias insisted. "Take Olive with you."

Dragonbait nodded and signed for Olive to follow. The paladin and the halfling slipped out of the cave and down the mountainside.

From the pocket of his robe, Grypht pulled out a long thin silver box and slid open the top. Inside was a wand made of bone. "This is a wand of frost. It's seen a lot of use these past few months, so there isn't much power left in it, but I want Akabar to use it to cast cones of cold against Moander's minions. I can cast such spells without the wand."

Alias translated the wizard's words for Akabar. Akabar bowed and accepted the wand. "What about your stone?" the Turmishman asked Finder. "You could release the shard of para-elemental ice. That would blanket a large area in deep cold."

"*If* I released it," Finder said. "But I won't release it. That would destroy the stone.

"But you would be freeing the saurials and preventing Moander's return," Akabar argued.

"I spent a decade searching for that stone, and another decade improving it at the risk of my own life," Finder replied coolly. "The stone holds more powerful magic than most mages learn in a lifetime, and it can recall any one of my songs on command."

"So can Alias," Akabar snapped, "but you are ready to risk her life!"

"No, I am not," Finder growled. "I asked her to stay behind, but she wouldn't. She chose to risk her own life. If she dies, the stone will be the only record left of my music."

"She is acting in a selfless manner to save her friend's tribe," Akabar said, his voice rising in pitch and volume. "How can you be so greedy as to save a stupid piece of magic instead of her life?"

"Akabar!" Alias said sharply. "Calm down, and leave me out of your arguments. Finder's right. I chose to do this myself. As for the stone, it's Finder's stone. He may use it or not as he pleases."

Grypht tugged on Akabar's sleeve.

"Grypht says you should cast a spell so you can understand him. He wants to show you how to use the wand," Alias translated for the wizard.

Akabar shot Finder an angry look, but he allowed Grypht to lead him away from the bard. The two magic-users settled down near the cave entrance. Akabar pulled out his magic book to study the comprehend languages spell.

Alias sighed. "There's nothing for us to do now but wait, is there?" she asked Finder.

"We could sing," the bard suggested, "to pass the time."

* * * * *

"I smell roses," Olive said as she inspected a small golden apple and tossed it into her knapsack. Dragonbait was digging in the dirt nearby while she collected windfalls beneath a gnarled old apple tree. Dragonbait had discovered the tree by following his nose to the vinegary scent of the fruit rotting on the ground. "It's a little late in the year for roses. Guess it's that magical warmth of the vale."

Olive hefted her knapsack with a groan. It was loaded. Dragonbait helped her slip it on over her shoulders. Then he shoved in a bunch of wild carrots and onions he'd dug up.

"Aren't you going to carry anything?" Olive asked with a huff.

I'm going to hunt, the paladin signed. *Go back to the cave.*

"Alias wouldn't want me to leave you alone," the halfling protested.

I'll be fine, Dragonbait signed.

Olive stood with her feet apart and her hands on her hips, scowling with stubborn disapproval.

Wouldn't you like duck? Or wild pig? the paladin asked.

"You're doing just what Finder does," Olive said. "He gets around my better judgment with bribes. The last time I let him have his way, we got captured by orcs. I can't believe I'm getting the same thing from you, too, of all people."

Dragonbait hung his head sheepishly. *Sorry*, he signed.

"Apology accepted," Olive said. "Now let's go. We can do without meat for once."

Dragonbait shook his head. *I'm going to scout out the vale*, he signed.

"What? Are you crazy?" Olive gasped. "It's too dangerous!"

I have to do it, the paladin signed.

Olive sighed. "Fine. Go right ahead." She waved a finger up at the saurial's chest. "If you don't come back, though, I'm never going to speak to you again."

I'll be back, the saurial's hands promised. *Tell Alias not to worry.*

"I'll tell her, but it won't do any good," Olive said. She turned around and stormed back up the mountain road to the Singing Cave.

Dragonbait watched her disappear around a bend, all the while sniffing the rose scent that came from the brush deeper into the vale. Olive had forgotten how similar the smell of saurial grief was to the flower's perfume. Of course, not even the halfling's sharp ears could discern the sound of a saurial weeping.

The paladin walked into the brush about fifty feet toward the scent and the sound. When he spotted the source of the grief, he froze. Twenty feet away from him stood another saurial, a female, very similar in size and shape to the paladin but with scales of pearly white. She wore a tattered black smock, and a circlet of wilted clover hung from her head fin. Otherwise she was unadorned and unarmed. She was picking apples off another apple tree and dropping them in a sack. Her work, however, did not interfere with her weeping.

The lemony scent of joy rose uncontrollably from Dragonbait's body. He whispered in saurial, "Coral."

The white saurial turned to face him. Her eyes widened in surprise, and the violet scent of fear wafted from her skin. "Champion!" she gasped. "Stay back!"

Dragonbait moved closer. "Coral, it's all right. I won't hurt you."

"You fool," Coral said. "What makes you think I won't hurt you? I'm tainted. I'm under the Darkbringer's power."

"I can cure you," the paladin said. He moved closer to Coral.

"Yes," Coral said, "I remember. You can cure diseases with your touch." A waft of lemon scent rose from her body as her hopes rose with it.

"You'd never hurt me," Dragonbait said, hurrying to her side. "I know you could never hurt me." A honeysuckle scent of tenderness mingled with the smell of woodsmoke as he began a prayer for power to destroy the tendril disease that controlled Coral. His hands glowed blue as he laid them on the white saurial's shoulders. He felt the power flow from his soul into her body.

Coral gasped and stumbled against him.

"You did it!" she exclaimed. "You destroyed Moander's tendrils of possession! I'm free again!" She leaned heavily on him though, as if she'd been injured.

"Are you all right?" he asked.

"I feel weak," she replied.

"Lean on me."

Coral threw her arms around the paladin's neck and clung to him. Dragonbait wrapped his arms around her waist and pulled her close.

"I'm so sorry for all the things I did, for all the things I said. For leaving you," the paladin whispered, emitting a minty smell of remorse.

"It's all right now," Coral answered. From her throat came the scent of cinnamon.

Dragonbait ran the tip of his muzzle along Coral's neck glands, breathing in the reassuring scent of her love. "I insulted your goddess and your friends and tried to bully you into leaving them. I damned you and left you. How can you forgive me for all of that?" he wondered aloud.

Coral looked up at him. "You said you were sorry, and I know you meant it," she answered. She stroked his throat with her fingers, and the scent of cinnamon wafted from him so strongly that it masked even the smell of the rotting apples on the ground about them.

He wanted to hold her longer, but Coral pushed him away. "You can't stay here," she said. "It's not safe."

"We have a hiding place," Dragonbait said. "I'll take you there. We'll surprise the High One."

"The High One!" Coral gasped. "Grypht is here? Where is he?"

"I'll take you there. Come." Dragonbait tugged on Coral's arm.

"I . . . I can't," the white saurial said, holding her ground.

"You must," Dragonbait said. "Now that I've cured you, you can't fall under the Darkbringer's power again."

"I must go back, or the overlords will look for me in my hut, and they will find the egg."

"What egg?" Dragonbait asked in surprise.

"My sister Lily's egg. She died last week. Her mate was an overlord. I'm the only one left to hide the egg. The young can't work, so the overlords don't let us hatch our eggs. They break them into the pile to become one with the Darkbringer."

The scent of baking bread rose from the paladin and his body shook, so great was his fury.

"Champion, wait here. I will get the egg and return," Coral said.

Dragonbait shook his head. "I'll go with you."

"One minute," Coral said. "If you are to pass unnoticed before the overlords, you'll need to look as if some plant possesses you." The priestess pulled a twig of ivy from the ground, fashioned it into a wreath, and laid it over the paladin's head fin.

"Is there anything else I need to know to pass for one of the possessed?" the paladin asked.

"Hide your weapon in here," Coral said, holding out her sack.

Dragonbait unfastened his sword and scabbard from his belt and slid them inside, amongst the apples.

Coral embraced him again. "I'm so glad you have come back to us," she said.

Dragonbait ran his palm along the ridge of her head fin. "So am I," he replied. "We have to hurry, though. The High One and my other friends will become worried if I'm away too long."

Coral nodded. She released the paladin and motioned for him to follow her. She led him to a path that twisted down into the vale.

As Dragonbait followed Coral into the clearing at the bottom of the vale, he was reminded of the last verse of the song Alias had sung back at the inn in Shadowdale:

We hack the vines, we cut the trees,
We trample the roots and burn the seeds.
When the rain comes down, the soil floods away,
Leaving barren rock and heavy clay.
We wear chains of green, till our bodies rot,
The corpses keep moving, their minds without thought.
Soon the darkness will devour the Realms,
Death is the power that overwhelms.

The lyrics described exactly the conditions Dragonbait witnessed. A few members of the tribe, mages and clerics like Coral, wore only a token vine or flower about their heads. Most of the tribe members, though, those who were incapable of casting spells, wore vast tangles of slimy green vines about their legs or waists or throats. The vines grew out of holes in their backs. Dragonbait struggled to keep his face an impassive mask.

He sneaked a quick glance at the huge pile of rotting vegetation that the possessed intended to turn into Moander's new body. Mages and clerics stood around the mountain of greenery chanting spells at it, while others moved back and forth between it and the forest, building it larger and higher with trees and brush.

Set in rings around the pile were several tiny huts made of pine boughs.

"Here," Coral whispered, stopping at the entrance to one of the huts in the innermost ring. "The egg is buried under my blanket. I'll keep watch at the door."

Dragonbait slipped past the door curtain. The structure was so small he had to duck his head to keep from brushing the roof, and the blanket spread out against the opposite wall was only a pace away. There were no windows in the hut, so the only light was heavily filtered through the needles of pine in the roof and walls. Dragonbait pulled aside the blanket. He tried to use his warmth vision to detect exactly where the egg was buried, but he could see nothing warm in the ground. He began clawing quickly at the dirt, afraid that the egg might have gotten too cold buried in so dark a place.

Outside the hut, he heard Coral chanting a prayer. The woodsmoke scent of devotion drifted though the pine boughs. No doubt she was casting something to protect herself, perhaps even to make her less noticeable to the enemy all around them. Coral was a priestess of the goddess of luck. She would be a powerful addition to the attack the High One planned. He had to get her back to the Singing Cave. He began to dig with even more energy.

After several minutes, when he'd dug up nearly half the floor of the hut and still found nothing, Dragonbait finally realized there was no egg. Moander's higher minions, the overlords, must have found it while Coral was out picking apples. The paladin swallowed hard, knowing the pain the priestess would suffer when he told her.

He began to slip past the curtain over the door, but as

he did, a powerful electrical tingling ran down his shoulder, and he leaped back into the hut. Someone outside yanked the curtain aside. Dragonbait peered out. Several saurial mages and clerics stood outside the door, staring at him. The paladin looked around anxiously for Coral. Have they discovered her, or has she escaped? he wondered.

Then Coral stepped in front of the doorway, and his heart sank. The priestess wore a clean white robe. Painted in red in the center of the robe was an eye, surrounded by a mouth of fangs—the symbol of Moander's high priest.

"Well, Champion," Coral said, "you wanted me to give up my goddess for another. What do you think of my choice?"

Dragonbait was too shocked to reply. He could only manage to mumble, "But I cured you!"

Coral laughed. "You fool! Your feeble power can have no influence on the Mouth of Moander. The root of the Darkbringer was planted in me months ago. It grows strong in every limb, down my tail, and even in my brain. You are getting careless, paladin. There was a time when you never met anyone—friend or stranger—without using your shen sight. You were always keeping watch over our souls, judging us constantly. Yet how eagerly you came to me today, even after I warned you. I knew you'd never believe my warning."

"I loved you," Dragonbait said. "Coral, I'm sorry this happened to you."

The priestess scowled. "You should be, paladin, for now I am your doom. While you were busy digging for Lily's egg— which, by the way, went into the pile with my sister's corpse—I traced a glyph of warding around this hut. You cannot escape. Moander's root could never grow in anything as pure as you, but you will serve Moander in another way. Where you are, the servant can't be far off. She will come to rescue you, and we will capture her. Then we will sacrifice you to bind the servant's will to Moander's."

"You can't bind Alias to Moander as long as Moander isn't in the Realms," Dragonbait protested.

"Moander will take possession of its new body before the moon sets tonight," Coral announced.

Dragonbait shivered. The minions must have recovered the seed somehow. He couldn't believe how badly things were going, nor could he believe he'd been fooled so easily. "I don't understand. Coral, you were so different on the mountain. Why were you weeping?"

Coral sneered. "To attract your attention, of course," she replied. "One of our fliers spotted you from the air. I teleported to a spot nearby and feigned tears until you came to me. You were incredibly easy to fool!"

"I smelled your grief, your hope, your love. What I smelled was true," Dragonbait said.

"You have deceived yourself. I felt none of those things," Coral snapped. "The only truth I told was that I was glad you had returned to us. Now I can slay you in the name of the Darkbringer. Yours will be the first blood Moander tastes in its new body."

❧ 17 ❧

Finder's Secret

As Olive approached the cave, she could hear Alias singing. Though she couldn't quite make out the swordswoman's words, the halfling recognized the melody. Alias was singing "The Tears of Selune," one of Finder's most haunting love songs. Something didn't sound quite right, however. Olive halted to listen more carefully. It took her a moment to realize what was wrong—Alias was singing the song in the wrong key.

Olive heard a shout, and the singing stopped suddenly in the middle of a verse. She could imagine what had happened. Finder had ordered Alias to stop. Why the swordswoman had sung the song in the wrong key, Olive couldn't imagine. Alias knew how Finder hated anyone altering his tunes, and it wasn't like her to goad the bard. Olive crept to the mouth of the cave and peered in.

Alias sat on the floor of the cave, her head hanging like an embarrassed child. Finder sat nearby, glowering at the woman. Akabar and Grypht sat opposite the bard and swordswoman. Both spell-casters stared at Alias anxiously .

Olive could hear Alias whispering, "I'm sorry."

"Don't be a fool, Finder," Akabar said. "She was just expressing what the saurials are feeling by turning your song into a soul song."

"Why didn't you tell me you were changing my songs to sing these saurial things?" Finder demanded of Alias.

"I thought it might upset you," Alias said softly.

"If you'd let her finish," Akabar said, "we might learn something."

"She was singing gibberish," Finder protested.

Grypht must have begun speaking to the bard in saurial, for Finder turned his attention to the wizard for a moment. The bard answered Grypht in Realms common. "We've learned enough about Moander. We don't need to hear any more."

Finder turned and snapped at Alias, "How dare you change my songs?"

"I can't help it," Alias whispered. "It just happens."

"Nothing just happens," Finder said. "If I meant as much to you as the saurials do, you'd be able to control it. If you can't control it, don't bother to sing my songs anymore."

The swordswoman blanched, and Olive could detect the smell of violets in the cave. Alias was frightened and was communicating her fear through the saurial scent.

Grypht and Finder glared at each other, and now Olive could also smell baking bread, the scent of anger. Meanwhile, Akabar leaned toward Alias and tried to encourage her to ignore Finder and resume her singing.

After listening to Grypht for a short time, Finder had had enough. As the bard rose to his feet and turned away from the others, his blue eyes flashed red in the sunlight streaming into the cave. "Go ahead and sing their songs if you want," he said coldly to Alias. "It makes no difference to me what you do."

Alias swallowed, licked her lips, and took a deep breath. It was obvious she wanted to sing, but from the way the swordswoman trembled, Olive could see that she was too frightened to rise to her father's challenge.

"Careful, bard," Akabar taunted Finder. "She might just improve on your song. Then what would you do? Go ahead and sing, Alias."

Akabar's goading of the bard wasn't helping to encourage Alias any. Akabar didn't understand how desperately she wanted to please Finder. Olive understood it all too well.

Alias began rocking back and forth, clutching her knees to her chest and whimpering softly with a glazed look in her eyes. Grypht and Akabar hovered over her, trying unsuccessfully to comfort her. Finder stood stubbornly with his back to his daughter.

Olive entered the cave and padded over to the bard's side. "Finder, think about what you're saying for once," the halfling said softly. "Look what you've done to her," she insisted, pointing toward the swordswoman. "Have you forgotten? She's not even two years old. She needs your love even when you don't agree with her. You can't just slap her and make her do everything your way like you do with everyone else."

"I didn't touch her," Finder said, offended.

"You don't have to touch her. You're a master at using words as weapons," Olive accused him. "Whether you injure her body or her heart, you'll be making the same mistake you made with Flattery."

The bard looked down at Olive with confusion—and fear. "What are you talking about?" he whispered.

"You know what I mean," Olive said impatiently. "The way you bullied him."

"How do you know about that?" the bard demanded.

"He left a long message in your workshop," Olive said.

"So why didn't you say anything?" the bard asked coldly. "Did you intend to sneak back to Elminster and tell him?"

Olive brushed angrily at the tears beginning to form in her eyes, but she held her head up proudly "The message was two centuries old, Finder," she said. "I didn't think it mattered anymore. I thought you'd changed."

Finder stepped back as though he'd been slapped.

Olive turned her attention to the swordswoman. "Come on, Alias," she said, patting the swordswoman's shoulder. "Sing for us. It doesn't matter if you change the song. Finder will understand. Won't you, Finder?" the halfling asked with feigned sweetness.

Finder shot an angry look at Olive, but the glare she gave him in return shocked him into submission. "Yes," he answered softly.

Olive signed sharply for the bard to sit down near Alias. He obeyed with a defiant look, but when Olive put his hand on Alias's and he felt the swordswoman's trembling, his expression changed to one of alarm. Not even a trapped bird trembled as fiercely as the woman before him did now. The bard saw, too, how pale she'd become—as white as the moment before she'd drawn her first breath. Her eyes stared blindly at him.

"I didn't do this to her," he said, refusing to admit his words could have so much power over anyone.

"Yes, you did," Olive hissed. "Now fix it."

"How?" the bard challenged.

"How do you think?" Olive whispered with frustration. "Apologize, you idiot."

Finder bristled at the insult, but the blind look in Alias's eyes softened his anger. "Alias . . . I'm sorry," he whispered, squeezing her hand gently, "I didn't . . . think about what I was saying. I want you you to sing. It doesn't matter about the soul songs."

Alias tilted her head and seemed to see the bard for the first time. She looked uncertain.

"Really. It's all right," Olive said encouragingly.

Alias looked at the halfling, confused. "Will you sing with me?" she asked Olive.

Olive started with surprise. Alias had taught her some of Finder's songs, but they had never sung together. Olive had always been too jealous of the swordswoman's voice to dare try to blend her own in with it.

"Please," Alias whispered.

Olive was suddenly reminded of Jade, the copy of Alias who had been a thief. Olive had loved Jade, but Flattery had killed the thief. If I wasn't jealous of Alias, would I love her, too? the halfling wondered. "Sure, I'll sing with you," she said. She sat down beside the swordswoman. "What should we sing?" she asked.

Alias seemed at a loss to suggest any songs, so Olive chose one Finder hadn't written, a lighthearted one. The song seemed to improve Alias's mood. When they had finished, Olive suggested a tune of Finder's, "The Hero of the Watch," a seemingly innocuous song about a cat that saved a regiment of soldiers from an attacking horde of goblins. The swordswoman shivered slightly but nodded in agreement.

The voices of the two women blended nicely, but Olive felt as if she were the carrying Finder's song alone. Alias was concentrating too hard on keeping control of the song instead of letting the music flow naturally. She kept her eyes fixed on the ground or Olive instead of directing them at her audience. She didn't change the lyrics or tune or key, but without her spirit behind them, the songs were like ghosts.

Sensing that the song wasn't going well, the swordswoman protested with a childlike cry, "I . . . I can't do it," and stopped singing in the middle of the last verse.

"Alias, just relax," Olive said. "Don't worry about changing the song. Finder said it was all right."

Alias looked toward the bard. Finder nodded, but something in his look made Alias flinch as if the bard had struck her.

"That's what he said," Alias answered, "but Finder won't love me if I change his songs." .

The bard rubbed at his temples, confused at how stubbornly Alias clung to her desire to please him. Flattery, on the other hand, had grown to hate him readily. "Alias, love is something people are supposed to give freely. It's not a commodity to be earned or forfeited," he said.

"Yes," Alias said. "That's what you taught me, but it's not what you believe . . . is it?"

"Of course it's what I believe," Finder protested. "It's what most of my songs are about."

"You hold it up as an ideal," Alias said, "but you don't act that way yourself."

Olive nodded, knowing Alias was right. Finder withheld his love when he was displeased and dispensed it lavishly only when Alias was behaving as he thought she should.

"Alias, I'm not perfect," Finder said. "I became angry and said some stupid things. It doesn't mean I won't love you if you change my songs."

"You say that, but it's not true," Alias insisted.

Finder sighed in frustration. "It is true. How can I prove it to you if you won't sing?"

Alias's eyes lit up suddenly. "Prove you believe it," she said. "Take the risk yourself."

"What?" Finder asked.

"You know I love you. Prove to me you're sure I love you no matter what you do . . . or did," Alias demanded.

"What are you talking about?" Finder asked. He looked frightened.

"Morala said there was something you didn't tell the Harpers about the first singer you tried to create . . . something Maryje knew, something you were ashamed of," Alias said. "Tell me what it was."

Finder shuddered and shook his head. "I . . . I can't," he said.

"We need to hear Alias sing her soul song," Akabar said. "It may make all the difference in whether or not we can defeat Moander. Does your pride mean more than that, bard?"

Olive shot Akabar an angry look. The mage's life was so virtuous, he couldn't understand the shame the bard felt. Olive patted Finder's hand. "Tell her, Finder," the halfling said. "She's not going to love you any less for admitting your mistakes. I didn't."

Finder smiled sadly at the halfling, wondering if she was speaking as an agent for the goddess of luck or the god of justice. He looked back at Alias. Would his confession bind her closer to him or drive her away? Cast the dice, he thought, and pray for better luck than you deserve. "Very well," he said.

In an impassive, distant tone, Finder began his tale. "I lied when I told the Harpers that I failed in my first attempt at making a singer like you. I created a man identical to me, with my thoughts and memories. My apprentice Kirkson named the man Flattery to tease me about my ego. The singer accepted the name and would take no other."

Finder looked down at the floor for a moment, then raised his head back up and looked directly into Alias's eyes as he made his confession. "I wasn't the good parent to Flattery that Dragonbait was to you when you were created. When Flattery came to life, I demanded immediately that he sing for me, much the same way I ordered the finder's stone to perform a task for me. Flattery attempted a tune. His voice was weak and immature. He was only a child, but I didn't understand that. After my success with the finder's stone, I expected instant success with Flattery. I grew frustrated when, after a mere three days of drilling, Flattery didn't produce the quality of music it had taken me over a hundred years to achieve. In a rage, I struck him."

"After that, Flattery wouldn't attempt to sing again. He even refused to speak. I apologized, I begged, I shouted, I . . . beat him. Every day I went through the same cycle of contrition and violence, but he said nothing. Kirkson tried to convince me that what I was doing was wrong, but I wouldn't listen. My other apprentice, Maryje, was too loyal to speak out in any sort of protest, but I could see she was terrified over what I was doing. That didn't matter to me either. I refused to quit. On the thirteenth day of his life, Flattery escaped from his cage and stole a disintegration ring from my desk. He aimed it at me, but Kirkson threw himself in front of the ray and saved my life, forfeiting his own. Flattery slashed Maryje's throat and fled from the workshop.

"I teleported Maryje to Shadowdale to be healed, then rushed back to the workshop to hide the evidence of Flattery's existence. I knew what I had done to him was evil, but I was too ashamed to admit I'd done it. I concocted a story about the para-elemental ice exploding and asked Maryje to back up my lie. Maryje couldn't lie, but she couldn't betray me either. She simply stopped talking altogether. Her wound was healed, but she wouldn't speak, or sing, ever again.

"Imagine my surprise when the Harpers condemned me for recklessly endangering my apprentices. A lifetime of exile and my songs wiped out forever. What, I've often wondered, would they have done if they'd learned the full extent of my crimes?"

"What happened to Flattery?" Alias asked.

"He's dead. Olive can tell you more about that than I," the bard replied. He stroked Alias's hair with his hand. "So tell me, my daughter," he asked, "can you still love me knowing how evil I've been?"

"Flattery, Kirkson, and Maryje are the people you have wronged," Alias said. "Since they are dead, you can never make peace with them. You must try to make it with yourself. As for me, I'll always love you." She embraced the bard and kissed him on the cheek.

"And I you," Finder replied. "Now will you sing?" he asked softly.

Alias nodded.

"Try 'The Tears of Selune' again," Akabar said. "It made you think of something that started you soul singing before."

"You know," the halfling said, "an old priestess of Selune told me something interesting about that song. Selune is the goddess of the moon," Olive explained for Grypht's benefit. "Anyway, this priestess said that the Shards—those are Selune's most powerful minions," she explained for Grypht again. "The Shards sing the song for Selune, but they sing it as a duet."

"It should be sung as a solo," Finder said automatically.

"I know," Olive said, "but a modest halfling like me—"

Akabar guffawed at Olive's description of herself.

"—like me," Olive continued, "didn't have the nerve to correct so venerable a priestess. Perhaps, Master Wyvernspur, the next time you run into the goddess Selune, you should tell her to keep her minions under control. In the meantime, why don't you try singing it with Alias, just this once?"

"Just this once," Finder agreed with a chuckle. He took Alias's hand and they began the song.

The first two verses went without a hitch, but as they began the third, Alias's voice began to trail off, although her mouth still moved. Finder stopped singing and stared at the swordswoman. From the way Alias rocked back and forth and stared unblinkingly at the cave wall, Olive and Akabar could tell the swordswoman had gone into a soul-song trance. Finder and Grypht were listening to her intently. The cave became awash in the scents of violets and roses, and Olive realized that Alias was singing in saurial—singing with terror and despair.

The swordswoman began to shout in Realms common, "Release me! Release me! Release me!" Then she gasped and swayed and snapped out of her trance. "Dragonbait!" she cried out. "They've captured Dragonbait!"

Finder looked quickly at Olive. "Where is Dragonbait?" he demanded.

"He said he wanted to scout the vale," the halfling replied, cursing herself for leaving the paladin alone.

Grypht put a hand on Alias's shoulder. Olive supposed he'd said something, for Alias calmed slightly.

"The soul song was mostly Dragonbait's song," the swordswoman explained. "He followed Coral into the saurial camp."

"Who is Coral?" Akabar asked.

Alias looked at Grypht. "Coral was Dragonbait's lover, wasn't she?" she asked the wizard, though she was already certain of it from the soul link she'd just experienced.

Grypht nodded. "Once she was. She was also a priestess of the goddess of luck before Moander captured her. She's the Mouth of Moander now, the most powerful minion the god has in the Realms."

"The last part of the song came from her, not Dragonbait," Alias said. "Moander is keeping such a tight hold on her mind that her thoughts are hard to understand, but I know she doesn't want to live. She's begging for her goddess to release her from life before—" Alias gasped again. "Before Moander makes her kill Dragonbait! Moander plans for her to sacrifice Dragonbait to enslave my will! We have to free Dragonbait before it's too late!" Alias cried, rising suddenly to her feet.

"They can't sacrifice the paladin before Moander is resurrected," Finder said, standing and grabbing hold of Alias's arms before she rushed off and did something foolish. "And they can't perform the sacrifice without you. Stay put, and when Breck gets back from Shadowdale, we'll rescue Dragonbait."

"There isn't time to wait for Breck to get back!" Alias insisted. "They have the seed! They're going to resurrect Moander tonight! We have to stop them now!"

Akabar turned pale, and Grypht muttered an oath under his breath.

"How did they find the seed?" Olive asked. "Only this morning they expected Finder to go look for it."

"I don't know," Alias said, "but Coral told Dragonbait that Moander will be resurrected tonight. If we hurry, we have a chance of reaching Dragonbait before then. Coral's keeping Dragonbait in a hut warded with a glyph."

"Alias, there are only five of us against over a hundred saurial minions," Finder protested. "A lot of those minions are spell-casters. Even with Grypht's and Akabar's magic and the spells I have in the finder's stone, we don't stand a chance."

"We would if you used the piece of para-elemental ice in the finder's stone as Akabar suggested," Alias said. Her voice rose excitedly. "It could put most of the saurials into a torpor, and Grypht and Akabar could handle anyone it misses. Then we could just walk in and get Dragonbait. We could find the seed, too, and destroy it. It would be centuries before Moander could get back the energy to return to the Realms."

"Alias, I'm sorry about Dragonbait," Finder replied softly, "but it's not my fault he was captured. You've got to keep away from Moander so the god can't enslave you again."

Alias looked at Finder with astonishment. "What are you saying?" she asked suspiciously.

"I'm not going to destroy the finder's stone," Finder answered calmly. "Maybe the reinforcements Breck brings can manage to rescue Dragonbait."

"If we wait too long and give the minions a chance to resurrect Moander," Alias protested, "the god will suck Dragonbait into his body and we'll never be able to rescue him. We have to use that ice, Finder."

"No," Finder said determinedly.

"Finder, we're talking about Dragonbait!" Alias shouted. "How can you turn your back on him after all he's done for you?"

"Alias, try to understand. There's nothing like this stone anywhere in the Realms. I made it. If you destroy it, I can't make another."

"Give me that stone!" Alias demanded, lunging for Finder.

The bard just barely managed to sidestep the swordswoman, and Alias fell into the ferns on the cave floor.

Akabar reached out to grab the bard, but Finder had drawn his dagger and thrust it out in front of him. The mage retreated hastily. "I curse your stone!" the Turmishman said hotly. "May it bring you no joy. May it be your death."

Olive shuddered. A curse was bad luck.

"Olive, over here!" the bard barked, pulling out the stone.

Olive shook her head. "I'm staying here, Finder," she said.

For a brief moment, the bard looked shocked and hurt. Then he snapped, "Fine. Have it your way." He sang out an E-flat and vanished in a yellow light.

*　*　*　*　*

Alias stood in the mouth of the cave watching the sun sink into the desert beyond the vale. Although there was no sign of movement from Moander's new body, she kept imagining Dragonbait being swallowed by it, lying trapped inside the god's body. In her mind, she pictured the cage Moander had used to imprison her last year, when the god had tortured her with its lies and tried to seduce her into its service with the promise of freedom. She didn't regret trying to take Finder's stone from the bard, and she was still furious with him for his selfishness, but she wished he'd come back. They could use him, with or without the stone.

Olive sat beside the swordswoman, idly throwing rocks at trees. She was regretting staying behind. It was a grand gesture, but if she'd gone along with the bard, she might have been able to talk some sense into him. Now he was no doubt feeling self-righteous and getting himself into some other trouble. She missed him already, and she was afraid she'd never see him again.

Akabar and Grypht were in the back of the cave. Grypht was rehearsing Akabar in the use of the saurial command word that triggered the wand of frost he'd given the mage.

The four of them had worked out a strategy to sneak into the vale, free Dragonbait, and hit as many saurials as possible with the cold magic they had at their disposal. Grypht would hide their forms and scents with magic. In order to disguise the warmth of their bodies from those saurials who could detect heat, Akabar had suggested that they go at sunset when the day's heat rising from the ground would mask their own warmth. They could have left ten minutes ago, but Alias had wanted to wait a few more minutes in case Finder changed his mind.

Finder had been gone for an hour. If he didn't return in the next few minutes, they'd have to leave without him.

"He's not coming back, Olive," Alias said.

Olive sighed and tossed another rock at a tree twenty feet off, hitting it dead center. "Not in time, anyway," the halfling said.

"I can't believe he wouldn't help us," Alias said. "Why won't he give up that stupid stone?"

Olive shrugged. She'd been trying to understand that herself. "Before you came along," she said, "the stone was Finder's crowning achievement. He can't really take all the credit for you, though, like he can for the stone. The stone is a little like his life. He can never make another one. It's one thing to say his songs and his daughter make him immortal, but in the end, his songs will change, and you aren't him. He's never going to get another chance to live."

Akabar joined the two women. "Grypht says we've got to leave in a few minutes," he said.

Alias nodded.

The Turmishman put his hand on Alias's shoulder. "Don't feel bad about Finder. He's not worth your grief," he said. "He's a selfish, arrogant man. He hasn't returned because he's too cowardly to join us."

"Akabar," Olive snapped angrily, "we're about to go into the camp of an enemy god. We may get possessed or killed. Aren't you afraid at all?"

Akabar looked down at Olive with a faint smile. "You forget that I was possessed by Moander before," he reminded the halfling. "It's not an experience I'd care to repeat. But I must do all I can to fight Moander. I defeated the Darkbringer once. I must believe I will defeat it again."

"The last time we fought against Moander, we had a red dragon fighting alongside us. This time you might die," Olive pointed out.

"Then I'll die for a good cause," Akabar said.

"My mother used to say life is wasted on the young, that the young always believe they'll never die. You're not very old. Maybe you don't believe you'll ever die," the halfling suggested, "and that's why you're not afraid."

"I didn't say I wasn't afraid. All men are afraid. I'm prepared to die because my life has been full. I have lived with three beautiful wives and will leave behind four beautiful children. That was Finder's mistake. He was too interested in himself. He should have had a family."

"He has a family. He has Alias and me," Olive said. "Some people aren't as easily satisfied as you are. They want more out of life than to have children and die for a good cause."

"To get something more out of life, a man must live for others," Akabar replied. "No monument, no empire, no song or tale left to posterity will satisfy the soul the way bringing joy to another person will. Finder Wyvernspur will not learn this, so he could live another three and a half centuries and still not be satisfied, still be unprepared for death. Death will come, though, whether a man is prepared or not."

Grypht came up behind Akabar. "It's time to go," he said.

With the setting of the sun, the wind began to whistle into the cave.

* * * * *

Finder sat in the ruins of his old mansion, staring at the sun setting over the Desertsmouth Mountains and the moon rising over the Elven Wood. Beside him, courtesy of the finder's stone, sat an illusion of himself singing "The Tears of Selune" the way it was meant to be sung, the way he'd written it three centuries ago.

The first part of Akabar's curse seemed to be working. Finder had been listening to the song for hours without pleasure.

The bard ordered the stone to halt. He looked at his image seated beside him—a young image with a charming smile, more sure of itself than the master beside it. The image was one of a man who'd thought he'd discovered the secret of cheating death. He'd deceived himself into thinking his music would be immortality enough. Now Finder realized that it wasn't. He wanted to live forever. "Damn!" he muttered.

"Sleep," he ordered the stone. Instantly the image beside him vanished.

Finder's mind began to wander. Unable to resolve the problem of death, he began to plan ways to improve the finder's stone. He should record Alias singing into the stone. He should record her singing some songs with Olive, too. Their voices blended well together.

Finder looked at the stone. It wouldn't be the same, though, he thought. The recording wouldn't be Alias and Olive. He couldn't teach the stone to compliment him when he was especially clever, or worry about him or tease or chide him the way Alias and Olive did. He couldn't get the stone to love him.

He wanted to be with Alias and Olive, he realized. Before he could change his mind, he sang to the stone to return him to the Singing Cave. The yellow light appeared, blocking out his vision of the ruined keep. When it faded again, he stood inside the Singing Cave.

The cave was empty. The wind whistled through it like an eerie voice. The four of them couldn't have gone alone to rescue Dragonbait, he thought. It would be suicide, yet he realized that was exactly what they'd done.

Finder stroked his beard, trying to decide the best way to help without risking the finder's stone. Some sort of diversion, perhaps, he thought.

As he brought his hand down from his chin, he noticed that his fingers were stained green, as if he'd been rubbing a leaf. He scratched at his beard with both hands. A moment later, he looked down at his fingernails with disgust. He'd scratched away great gobs of moss and lichen from his face.

Then he felt something sticky moving in his ear. Shuddering at the thought of earwigs and other gruesome bugs, the bard brushed at his ear. His fingers caught on something fragile and soft, but when he pulled on it, a stabbing pain shot across his temple.

He held up the finder's stone to look at his reflection. A small orchid hung beside his ear, its tendrils wrapped around his earring and other tendrils were sliding into his ear.

"No!" Finder gasped. He slipped his earring off and yanked harder at the orchid, ignoring the stabbing pain in his head. The flower snapped off in his fingers, and he threw it to the ground and crushed it under the heel of his boot.

He felt something trickle back down his ear canal, then tickle his ear again. Finder looked again at his reflection in the stone. Another orchid squeezed its way out of his ear and began to wrap its tendrils about his hair.

Breathing hard with fear, Finder reached up to pinch the second orchid away between his fingernails, but at that moment, a pain gnawed at his stomach. He doubled over with a howl. Something was inside him, growing and eating his insides.

The pain in his stomach subsided. With a sense of horror mixed with irony, the bard realized what had happened. The black spores that had burst from the burr that Xaran had thrown at him had indeed penetrated into his body. They must have been partially destroyed and greatly slowed down by the potions that had been in his blood. It had taken them a full day to grow. He'd been possessed by Moander all that time without even knowing it.

❧ 18 ❧

The Seed

Olive clung to the little bit of wild grapevine Akabar ha[.]
handed her to keep the group together. With the circle of invis[.]
ibility that hid the group, they needed some way to keep to[.]
gether, and it had been Akabar who had suggested that each o[.]
them keep hold of the vine.

As the adventurers approached the camp, walking along th[.]
trails of devastation, they were surrounded on all sides by th[.]
possessed saurial workers, who wore ragged shifts with vin[.]
tendrils poking through holes out of their backs, which
wrapped around the saurials' legs or waists or throats. Oliv[.]
didn't care to look too closely at the vines or the holes from
which they issued.

The workers all looked exhausted and numb. They stumble[.]
frequently; their eyes were listless; no saurial emotional scent
rose from their bodies. Even if magic and the ground's hea[.]
hadn't masked the adventurers' presence, Olive doubte[.]
they'd be noticed by these enslaved creatures.

The halfling counted three different kinds of saurials. A fev[.]
were as small as halflings and had long slender necks an[.]
snouts and leathery wings hanging beneath their forearms[.]
These flew into the clearing laden with nets of captured bird[.]
and fish and eggs and small forest creatures. Another larg[.]
group of the saurials were approximately the size and shape o[.]
Dragonbait. They carried underbrush and small saplings o[.]
buckets of water. A third group, the largest in number, wer[.]
bigger than Dragonbait, a little taller than Akabar, but muc[.]
more powerfully built, with sharp diamond-shaped blade[.]
running from their skulls and down their backs to the ends o[.]
their spiked tails. These creatures dragged great trees towar[.]
the pile. None of the saurials appeared to be as big as Grypht[.]

The adventurers stopped at the edge of the clearing. The[.]
watched as each saurial scrambled to the top of the pile an[.]

added his or her burden to the growing mountain. Saurial spell-casters in white robes stood waiting at the top of the pile to take the nets brought by the flying saurial workers and butcher the captured wildlife over the pile, tossing the corpses in with the fresh trees and splashing water over it all, chanting spells all the while.

As the sun sank beneath the horizon, the saurial workers climbing down from the pile headed to the huts that surrounded the pile. Each saurial slid into a separate hut and did not come out again. Some time later, by the light of the moon, the spell-casters climbed down from the pile and slipped into the huts nearest the pile.

"When exactly are they going to resurrect Moander?" Akabar whispered.

"I'm not certain," Alias answered. "Before moonset. They must be resting before the ceremony. Remember," she whispered to Olive, "it's the inner ring of huts. Dragonbait's hut has a rainbow-striped curtain on the door and Coral's has a golden one with the high priest of Moander's symbol—"

"—an eye in a fanged mouth. I know," Olive said.

Aside from knowing what huts to look for, Alias's soul song rapport with Dragonbait and Coral had warned the swordswoman that Coral had set an alarm to sound if Grypht, Akabar, or she entered the camp. The priestess either hadn't known about the halfling or hadn't considered her a threat and had neglected to mention Olive in her spell, so Olive was to be their advance scout.

As the halfling slid away, the saurial and the two humans became visible again. They crouched down in the shadows of the trees that hadn't yet been sacrificed to the god Moander's new body.

Olive crept through the camp, threading her way among the huts of the possessed saurials. She set up trip wires in front of the entrances to the huts of the spell-casters in the inner circle, bypassing only the gold-curtained hut of the Mouth of Moander and the rainbow-curtained one that imprisoned Dragonbait. When she finished, she moved to the rainbow-curtained hut and whistled the first four notes of "The Tears of Selune."

The curtain drew back immediately. Dragonbait stood in the doorway, looking out warily.

"It's me, Olive," the halfling whispered. She pulled a light stone out of her pocket, keeping its light carefully covered with a rag, since her circle of invisibility could not hide a light. She pushed the stone down in the dirt and covered all but a small portion of it, so that a narrow beam of light shone up into the darkening sky. The light stone had been Akabar's idea; it was to serve as a beacon for Grypht so the wizard could locate Dragonbait's hut. When Grypht dispelled the light, it would signal the others that they should begin their assigned tasks.

"In a hundred breaths, Grypht's going to cast a dispel magic spell," Olive whispered. "It will knock out this light and the ward around you. That's sure to set off all sorts of alarms, so the plan is for you to run straight toward the trees to meet the others. Alias says if you don't come straightaway, if you stop for any heroic deeds, she's going to make herself a new armor shirt out of your scaly hide. Got all that?"

Dragonbait nodded soundlessly.

Olive slipped away from Dragonbait's hut and returned to the golden-curtained hut of the Mouth of Moander. It was eight huts away from Dragonbait's, but if Coral stood in the hut's doorway, she had a clear view of Dragonbait's hut—undoubtedly so she could direct a spell at the hut should Alias or any of the others try to sneak into the camp to rescue the paladin.

Grypht had warned the halfling that Coral was powerful enough that she might detect Olive despite her invisibility, so Olive wasn't taking any chances. She wasn't going to attempt to sneak into Coral's hut. Instead, she crept up to the back of it and pressed her eye against a gap in the pine boughs.

Mingled with the scent of the pine boughs was the scent of roses. Moander's high priestess wasn't too exhausted to emit emotional scents, Olive noted, though it surprised the halfling that the scent was one of grief. Once her vision had adjusted to the hut's interior darkness, Olive could see a white saurial curled up on her side on a blanket in the center of the hut, facing the back of the building. Olive could see her face. The saurial's eyes were closed, but little snarling sounds came from her mouth, and her nostrils flared from her heavy breathing. Dragonbait's sword and scabbard lay on another blanket beside her. The tip of her tail lay across the sword's hilt.

Olive gritted her teeth in frustration, repressing an urge to growl. Rotten luck, she thought. Roll over, Coral. You don't want to sleep all night with a stupid sword.

Just then something glowed momentarily at the front of the hut, shining through the golden curtain and lighting up the interior. Coral rose quickly, pushed aside the curtain, and stepped outside. Without hesitating, Olive reached through the gap in the pine boughs, grabbed the edge of the blanket, and began to tug it toward the back of the hut, dragging the paladin's sword with it. As soon as she could get her fingers on the sword, Olive pulled the weapon through the gap in the wall. The scabbard slid off the blade and flopped back on the blanket.

Deciding that the paladin wouldn't need his scabbard in the battle to come, the halfling let it lay. She opened the invisible sack she'd been carrying on her shoulder. As she slipped the sword into the sack, the weapon vanished from sight.

Olive was just about to hurry back to the edge of the woods when a familiar voice stopped her in her tracks.

"Nice hovel you have here. Not much profit in resurrecting dead gods, is there?"

Finder! Olive thought excitedly. She turned around and pressed her eyes back against the gap in the pine boughs.

Coral stood inside her hut with the bard. The saurial sat down on the blanket, not seeming to notice that it was in a different position. Her tail fell across Dragonbait's scabbard, but she didn't notice the missing weapon. Finder sat down opposite her. Though he did not speak aloud, the bard was gesturing with his hands. Olive realized he was speaking with Coral in saurial.

Sweet Selune! Olive thought. He's not trying to make a deal with her like he tried to do with Xaran, is he? He can't be!

In a loud, surprised voice, the bard said in Realms common, "Akabar's blood? You mean that's the seed you've been looking for?"

Then Olive saw the flower in Finder's ear, its tendrils wrapped around his hair. She pulled away from Coral's hut as if it had scorched her and took off for the forest where Alias, Grypht, and Akabar were waiting.

* * * * *

Alias touched Grypht's arm and pointed at the light stone

beacon the moment after Olive placed it in front of Dragonbait's hut. Grypht nodded and began to move off so he could get a better view of the hut. He disappeared into the darkness. Alias and Akabar waited anxiously for Olive to return. A few minutes later, though they couldn't see her, they heard her running toward them. They could also hear her sobbing.

Please, Tymora, no! Alias thought. Don't let anything be wrong with Dragonbait.

Fifty pounds of invisible halfling slammed into Alias's legs and clung to her like a child. "They've got him!" she cried.

Alias knelt down and managed to get hold of Olive's invisible shoulders. "Olive, try to keep calm," the swordswoman said, though her own voice rose alarmingly. "What have they done to him? Is Dragonbait all right?"

"Dragonbait is fine," Olive hissed. "It's Finder. He's been possessed. He's one of the minions!"

"No!" Alias whispered in shock.

"Yes," Olive sniffed. "He's got a flower coming out of his ear, and he's sitting in Coral's tent right now. We've got to get out of here."

"No," Akabar said. "Finder doesn't know our plans, and if we carry them out quickly, he won't have time to prepare them for our attack."

"No, Akabar!" Olive said. "You don't understand. Your blood is the seed! I heard Finder say so. If they catch you, it's all over."

"Akabar's blood can't be the seed," Alias said. "Coral told Dragonbait they were going to resurrect Moander tonight. How could Coral say that if she didn't even know where Akabar was?"

"Alias, she's the Mouth of Moander," Olive said. "She says whatever Moander wants her to say. She lied to upset Dragonbait, just as Moander lied to you when you were its prisoner."

Alias nodded thoughtfully. Moander took great delight in causing people grief and fear. The god would say anything to achieve that goal.

"I am not the seed," Akabar snarled.

"Akabar," Alias argued, "Moander had plenty of opportunity to put its power inside you and taint your blood. All its minions have been looking for you, trying to capture you. Olive must be right."

Akabar's eyes narrowed into slits and his head shook with

anger. It had taken him a long time to forget his shame and fury at the way Moander had used his body to harm his friends. He couldn't deny that he'd been powerless in the god's control, and there had been times when he'd been unconscious and could have been violated with some foul magic. "Then it's the god's justice that I have been sent to destroy Moander," the mage said, his voice like steel. "I must stay."

"Akabar, be reasonable. We can't risk having you get captured. We have to get you out of here!" Alias insisted.

"No!" Akabar said stubbornly, "I am not fleeing."

"Akabar, suppose Moander's enchanted you to come here. By staying, you're simply doing its bidding," the swordswoman pointed out.

"It's too late to cancel our plans now," Akabar said "There's no way to alert Grypht. He's relying on us to do our parts."

"All right," Alias sighed. As unwise as she felt it to be, she had no choice but to give in to the mage's logic.

"What are you going to do about Finder?" Olive asked anxiously. "You can't hit him with a cone of cold. It could kill him."

Akabar knelt beside Alias and laid his hand beside the swordswoman's on the halfling's shoulder. He gave Olive an encouraging squeeze. "Dragonbait is a paladin. He can cast a cure disease spell on Finder."

Olive nodded, though since she was invisible, the others couldn't see it. She pulled Dragonbait's sword out of the invisible sack and held the weapon out so Alias could see it.

Alias took the sword and whispered "Toast" in saurial. The sword glowed, then burst into flame. Olive drew a torch out of her knapsack and ignited it over the saurial's magical weapon.

"Good luck," Alias whispered to the halfling as the light from the torch, held by the halfling's invisible hand, bounced around the edge of the clearing.

"The light stone's gone out," Akabar whispered.

Alias heard a twittering noise coming from the inner huts. "There's the alarm."

From the center of the camp came a shout in saurial. "There's Dragonbait!" Alias said, spying the paladin running toward them, weaving his way through the huts of the saurial camp. "Get ready."

Akabar pulled out a feather from one of his robe pockets and began chanting a spell that would enable him to fly.

Alias gasped suddenly as the vines that fastened the pine boughs to the huts lashed out from the huts and tangled themselves around the paladin's legs. Dragonbait fell to the ground, trying desperately to pull the vines from his legs, but more vines began tangling around his arms and waist. Between the huts, a white saurial in white robes gestured in Dragonbait's direction. Vines began wrapping around the paladin's throat.

"No!" Alias shouted, rushing forward. Before she could reach the paladin's side, however, other vines lashed out at her from huts at the edge of the clearing. Alias hacked through the vines with Dragonbait's flaming blade, but more vines kept coming at her.

As suddenly as they had appeared, the vines dropped to the ground, motionless. Akabar must have dispelled the magic that animated them, Alias thought. The swordswoman looked toward where Coral had stood to see if she was casting another spell at her, but the white saurial was nowhere in sight. Alias ran to help Dragonbait, only to find the vines surrounding him had also lost their enchantment and the saurial paladin was already pulling himself free.

"Are you all right?" she asked her companion in saurial.

"Yes," The paladin replied. With a remorseful scent of mint, he added, "I was stupid to get captured. I'm sorry."

"I'll yell at you later," Alias said, handing him his flaming sword. She grabbed the lizard's hand and pulled him back to the edge of the clearing, where Akabar was waiting.

"You might have been captured out there. What were you thinking, woman?" Akabar demanded.

"Sorry," Alias said. "Thanks for dispelling those tangle vines."

"I didn't do it," Akabar said. "It must have been Grypht."

"But he should be on the other side of the camp by now," Alias said.

"Alias, we haven't got time for discussions. Hold still so I can cast a flying spell on you," Akabar ordered.

Akabar repeated the chant for the spell he'd already cast on himself, brushing Alias's arms with a second feather. Instantly the feather burst into flame and disappeared.

"That's it?" she asked. "What do I do, flap my arms?"

"If you want to. However, it's not necessary," Akabar said. He turned to Dragonbait and explained hastily. "Olive is starting fires in the brush to the south of the clearing. Grypht will cast a

SONG OF THE SAURIALS

wall of fire on the west side. You must use your sword to start igniting the forest on this side while Alias and I begin burning the huts. We're trying to drive the saurials out of the vale into the mountains to the east. Once the fires are all lit, Grypht and I will fly to the east to cast cones of cold at the saurials as they flee from the vale; Alias will be our lookout. You'll have to deal with any saurials who aren't panicked by the fires and are still acting on Moander's behalf."

Dragonbait nodded. He ran his finger down Alias's sword arm, whispering "Good luck" in saurial. As Alias and Akabar soared upward and off toward the huts, the paladin hurried to begin setting fires along the north edge of the vale.

* * * * *

Grypht paused a moment in midflight to look down into the camp. The sight of all the tribe's spell-casters bursting out of their huts, catching their toes on the halfling's trip wires, and sprawling on the ground might have been amusing in other circumstances. The wizard tried not to dwell on the thought that if his plan worked, most of these people would be dead before morning. He reminded himself of all the other lives at stake. He thought, too, of the desperate cry for release Coral had made in Alias's soul song. Even if it meant Coral's death, Grypht knew the priestess would accept anything rather than serve the Darkbringer.

He could see Coral's white hide standing out in the dusk. A dark figure stood beside her. The wizard squinted, but he had trouble making out much detail in the gathering darkness. He couldn't discern which of their tribe it was. Then the dark figure disappeared in a flash of light. The sight unsettled the old wizard. Who was the spell-caster, and where had he gone? Grypht wondered.

The sight of small fires burning below brought the wizard's mind back to the task at hand. He soared to the west side of the clearing and began to chant the words of his wall of fire spell.

* * * * *

From her vantage point high in the air, Alias saw the shimmering violet wall of flames to the west of the vale and whistled in awe. "It's nearly three hundred feet long," she breathed.

Hovering beside her, Akabar concentrated on rolling the flaming sphere beneath him into another hut before he stole a glance westward at Grypht's handiwork. "We're fortunate to have so powerful an ally," he said, then concentrated on moving the flaming sphere once more.

Beneath Akabar and Alias, the saurial workers had begun to smell the smoke and emerge from their huts. Just as Grypht had predicted, not even the Darkbringer could control the instinct of the saurials to flee from fire. Although the small flying saurials might have fled in any direction they wanted, they followed the rest and flew east toward the mage and swordswoman.

"Fliers," Alias warned. "Ten of them, at least."

Akabar looked up and pulled out Grypht's wand of frost. He flew across the path of the fliers twice, luring them into following him. Alias remained, hovering near the ground until she saw no more fliers passing by. Then she followed them, keeping out of range of Akabar's wand.

The mage flew low over a patch of brush. It was important that the fliers didn't fall too great a distance when they fell into their torpor. The wand's cold might kill their possessing vines and leave them unharmed, but they couldn't survive a crash to the earth from any great height. With a sudden twist, Akabar faced the fliers coming at him and hovered in place.

The lead flier was only five yards from Akabar when the mage pointed the wand of frost at it, and only three when he gave the whistle that approximated the saurial word to trigger the wand. Motes of white crystalline ice blasted out of the tip of the wand in a cone sixty feet long. The flying saurial in the lead was immediately covered in a rime of frost and dropped to the ground. Another eight, also whitened by the wand's magical cold, fell after him.

Two fliers had been beyond the reach of the wand's cone, however. Now they dived down upon Akabar with their sharp beaks open.

Akabar headed for a higher altitude to evade the attackers, but one managed to tear through his robe and leave a gash in his side. The mage cried out and clutched at his side.

Alias flew to the side of the injured mage. As the two remaining fliers turned and swooped down on them, Alias drew her sword. One creature called out in saurial, "Look out! She has a weapon!" and pulled up, but the other couldn't stop its dive in time. Alias's blade tore through the saurial's wing, and the creature spun helplessly to the earth. Alias chased the remaining flying saurial as Akabar flew down toward the injured one.

Grypht had told Alias that the flying saurials could fly with the grace and speed of eagles. Alias might never have caught up with this one in ordinary circumstances, but the creature was exhausted from its day's labor and had lost much of its maneuverability because of Moander's possessive vines. Since Alias's flight was magical, the swordswoman was not in the least winded by her chase. She swooped down on the last winged saurial, grabbing it by the vines that grew from its back and wrapped about its waist.

The creature struggled frantically, and its vines began wrapping around Alias's arm. The swordswoman soared earthward and landed beside Akabar. Quickly the mage sliced the vines off near the saurial's back. The little saurial began to slash at Akabar's arms with its beak, but the mage grabbed it by its throat and held it fast while Alias tied its wings behind its back with a length of rope. Then they laid the trussed flier alongside the injured one by the side of the trail leading west out of the vale. Finally they stood and waited for the saurials who were coming up the trail on foot. It had been Akabar's idea to drive the saurials eastward, so they would have to climb uphill, slowing them down so it would be easier to cast magic on them.

Alias could hear the approaching saurials shouting, and she could smell the violet scent of their fear rising up the vale with the smoke of the fires. "Are you all right?" she asked the mage beside her. He was bleeding from the gashes in his side and his arm.

Akabar nodded and held out Grypht's wand. "It'll hurt more later, when I have time to think about it," he said.

The approaching saurials were somewhat larger than the fliers, and Akabar didn't wait till the last minute to fire the wand at them. When they were twenty feet away, he whistled the wand's command word. The lead creatures were struck by the blast of freezing ice, but they kept coming for several seconds before they were stopped by the cold. At least twenty fell to the ground, but others behind them kept coming.

Akabar flew over the fallen saurials and fired off another

blast from the wand. Many more saurials dropped. A few, too large to be affected quickly by the cold or with some resistance to magic, ran on up the hill. Alias took to the air to get out of their path.

"I could get to enjoy this flying thing," the swordswoman said, turning a somersault in the air. She sheathed her sword and landed back on the ground, then began dragging saurials off the path so they wouldn't be crushed by any that followed.

Akabar was intent on the remaining saurials charging up the hill. He already had his wand pointed at them. The Turmish mage whistled out the command word, but as the wand fired its icy cone, it crumbled in Akabar's hand, its power spent.

Suddenly, from the air above her, Alias heard chanting. She looked up to see two saurials of Dragonbait's type looking down on Akabar. Spell-casters, she realized, with fly spells like our own! The Turmish mage couldn't hear them, so he was oblivious to their presence.

"Akabar! Above you!" the swordswoman called out in warning, but Akabar still didn't move. He was frozen in the same position he'd been in when he pointed the wand. The saurial mages held him fast with their magic.

Alias drew her sword and flew up into their midst, shouting a battle cry in saurial and blasting the scent of her anger in their direction. The mages quickly flew off in separate directions. Alias turned back to Akabar, only to discover that a third flying saurial had snatched up the paralyzed mage in a net and was now flying back toward the camp with him.

Alias flew after Akabar's captor. Slowed by his burden, the saurial couldn't keep ahead of the furious swordswoman, but Alias had forgotten about the other two mages. She heard a chanting just above her, and suddenly she felt as though she were flying through jelly. Her flight had been slowed with magic. Akabar's captor burst ahead of her. The other saurial mages swooped down on her with another net, and she couldn't dodge out of the way in time. They closed her up in the net and wrenched her sword from her hand. Then they flew after Akabar's captor, toward the looming pile that would become Moander's new body.

* * * * *

Olive tossed the stub of her spent torch into the burning brush. "I sure hope I don't run into any treants or druids tonight," she muttered. She looked eastward at Grypht's wall of fire. Olive had never seen a blaze so big.

It was getting terribly hot in the vale, and the halfling noticed steam rising from the pile that was to become Moander's body. She knew the fire's main purpose was to herd the saurials toward Akabar's and Grypht's cones of cold, but she couldn't help wishing they'd get extra lucky and manage to burn the wet pile of hacked forest as well, despite the magic that protected it from fire. She would never be comfortable until she was sure Moander's waiting body was gone for good.

She had begun to move eastward, out of the vale, when she noticed something moving near the top of the pile, something white. Olive shook her head in surprise. It was Coral, climbing to the top of her god's potential body. She must be pretty far gone to hang around a burning vale, Olive thought. Then she saw another figure about halfway up the pile, also climbing toward the top. The halfling gasped. It was Dragonbait!

"Stupid paladin!" Olive growled. "After I specifically told him that Alias didn't want any dangerous heroics. He'd die up there, Olive realized, if she didn't get him to climb back down. With an irritated sigh, she moved toward the pile and began climbing after the paladin.

* * * * *

Grypht threw a cone of cold at a group of saurial stragglers moving up the hills away from the burning vale. He landed beside a cluster of saurial bodies lying on the ground. It was getting warm from the fire's heat; the fallen would rise out of their torpor soon, but many of them would be too weak to move without the rotting vines providing energy to their bodies. He walked through the bodies until he found a perfect candidate to help him—one of the large saurials with the sharp, diamond-shaped plates of armor running down his back.

The wizard bent over the saurial and shook him. "Sweetleaf," he called, "snap out of it." Grypht forced a danger scent from his glands to help bring the other saurial around.

"Wh-what?" Sweetleaf said, opening his eyes suddenly.

"You've been under the Darkbringer's power. Cure your disease quickly. We have a lot of work to do."

"I—I remember now. I was possessed," Sweetleaf muttered.

"Fortunately, since you were a stranger in the tribe, none of the others knew you were a cleric, or you would have been possessed sooner and in no shape to help us now," Grypht said. "Now cure yourself so we can be sure no more of Moander's spores taint your body. Then we can begin to rescue the rest of our unfortunate brothers."

Akabar had done a good job, the saurial wizard noted privately, looking up the hill at the number of saurials the mage had felled with the wand. Grypht was too busy worrying about his own people, though, to wonder where the mage was at the moment.

* * * * *

Akabar lay on the very top of the pile of dead vegetation that Moander intended to make its new body. He could hear Alias screaming and struggling with the saurial mages who had captured her. She was only a few yards away from him, but magically held as he was, he was powerless to help her. He knew he was frightened, but he had his faith to support him. Alias, on the other hand, must be terrified, he realized. She had tried to convince him to flee to avoid exactly this situation. To be honest, he had hoped to avoid it, but fleeing was not an honorable option.

Zhara had told him that he would be responsible for the god's death forever, and he had accepted the honor with pride. His priestess wife had been unable to tell him, however, if he would live through the experience. At the moment, he suspected he would not. His blood, from the wounds in his side and his arm, hissed and sparkled as it dripped onto the greenery beneath him. That certainly wasn't a good sign, but if Moander had to be resurrected to be destroyed, so be it, he thought.

In the moonlight, he could see a white saurial moving toward him. It was Coral, Moander's high priestess. She knelt beside him. A potpourri of conflicting emotional scents poured from her. Moander could force her to feel its evil pleasure, but the god did not, or could not, prevent her from expressing her own grief and fear.

Coral held up a large, luminous mushroom, which she shoved into Akabar's mouth. The acrid taste made the mage feel violently ill, but he was unable to spit it out. He felt his mouth grow numb. Next Coral drew out a dagger carved from a giant thorn and pressed the tip of it against the artery in his neck. Akabar closed his eyes, certain he was about to die, but he felt no more than a prick in his neck. He opened his eyes again. Coral held the dagger up to the moonlight. There was a single drop of his blood on its tip, and before Akabar's eyes, the blood crystallized into a brilliant, rounded gem. Coral plucked the gem from the dagger, spat on it, and pushed it into the pile of greenery beneath them.

Just as Akabar was beginning to hope he might not actually be killed, the mage felt the pile shift beneath him, and he began to sink into it. His skin began to sparkle everywhere the greenery touched him. The red and white robe he wore began to rot away from his body, exposing more of his flesh to the magic of the pile. Since he could do nothing else, the Turmish mage began to pray.

❦ 19 ❦

The Weapon

Held by four saurial mages, Alias could do nothing but shriek and cry as Coral chanted foul prayers over Akabar, declaring his blood the seed of Moander's resurrection. As the Turmish mage was sucked into the rotting mess the saurials had built for Moander, the swordswoman began to shake uncontrollably. This was her worst nightmare—the one she forced herself to forget whenever she woke from it. In it, she inevitably watched her friend being absorbed by the Darkbringer just as she had been. Now, though, there was no waking up.

Akabar should have gone back to the cave as soon as they found out that he was the seed, she thought. She should have knocked him out and dragged him away. And Zhara never should have let him come north. There had to have been some way to prevent all this.

Suddenly the swordswoman's arm began to burn as if it were on fire. The blue brands on her arm glowed brighter than lantern light. "No," Alias whispered.

"Yes," a voice said in saurial. Alias looked up into the face of the saurial who once was Dragonbait's lover. Her duties with the seed complete, the priestess had moved to the swordswoman's side. She studied Alias's arm eagerly. "The symbol of Moander is returning to her arm," she announced.

Dragonbait, who had nearly reached the top of the pile, didn't need to hear the Mouth of Moander's words to know what was happening to Alias. He could feel it himself in the brand on his chest that bound him to the swordswoman. There, reasserting itself in his own scales, he could see the tattoo of a blue glowing mouth of fangs set in a human palm.

When the pain had subsided, he finished climbing up the side of the pile of greenery. Crashing through the soggy, rotting vegetation, he cried out the trigger word to set his sword aflame. He stabbed one of the mages through the heart and the corpse fell into the pile. As if the pile had an insatiable appetite, the body was sucked into it almost instantly.

Before the paladin could attack again, Coral finished chanting another entanglement spell. A vine rose up from the pile, wrapped itself around Dragonbait's waist, and pulled him away from Alias. A second vine lashed itself around his legs and held him fast. He couldn't hack at the vines without slashing himself.

Coral stepped up to the paladin, a ceremonial dagger in her hand. "Champion," she whispered, "you know what must happen now. Your sacrifice will bind the servant's will to Moander."

"Coral, no. You can't do this. This isn't you. Fight it, please," the paladin urged.

"You have your sword," the white saurial whispered.

Dragonbait held his sword beside Coral's head. The flames of the blade were reflected in her white scales.

"Either I will kill you, or you will kill me," Coral said.

Dragonbait watched as Alias struggled with the three remaining saurial mages. If he were the only one to die, he wouldn't even consider killing Coral. He would let her take his life. But Alias was his sister, and Coral was the Mouth of Moander. He couldn't let Moander have Alias. Still he hesitated.

Coral raised her dagger. Tears shone in her eyes, and the smoke-laden air was heavy with the scent of her grief. "How can you condemn me to be your murderer?" she growled at the paladin. "I thought you loved me."

Dragonbait swung his blade, and Coral's body and head tumbled into the pile. There was no bloodshed. Nothing but rotted vines and dust spilled out of the priestess's severed neck. The pile didn't even try to suck her into it for nourishment. There was nothing left of her.

Immediately the vines that held Dragonbait fell away from him as if the magic in them had been dispelled. The paladin presumed the magic had died with Coral and began to move cautiously toward the mages who held Alias. One began to chant a spell and gesture in the paladin's direction, but the words died on his lips, and he tumbled forward with a dagger in his back.

Now held by only two people, Alias threw her weight to one side, knocking one of the mages to her knees. Dragonbait rushed the remaining mage and sliced him in two. Like Coral, this mage was nothing but dust and rotted vines inside. With her bare fists, Alias throttled the female saurial beside her until the mage fell at her feet.

"Dragonbait, your sword!" the swordswoman shouted. "Give me your sword! "

Confused, the paladin let Alias take his sword from his hands. She began to slice into the top of the pile, looking for Akabar.

A dark figure landed beside Dragonbait and wordlessly pulled the dagger out of the mage who had tried to cast a spell over the paladin. The figure stood up and sheathed his blade. It was Finder Wyvernspur.

The pile shifted suddenly, knocking Dragonbait and Finder to their knees. The massive heap wasn't merely settling, the paladin realized; it was coming to life. He struggled to his feet as Alias began hacking at the vegetation more frantically, screaming out Akabar's name.

As the paladin helped him to rise, Finder shouted, "We can't stay here!"

Dragonbait was inclined to agree, but when he saw the wild-eyed look in the swordswoman's eyes, he was sure he'd never convince her to leave. The smell of her grief for Akabar permeated the air.

"Akabar is gone!" Finder shouted. "There's no hope for him! If you don't help me get Alias away from here, she'll die!"

Dragonbait nodded. He took the hand the bard offered him and moved toward Alias.

"Sister," he called out, "give me your hand."

Alias looked up at her saurial brother, confused. She didn't question him; she simply reached up and grabbed his paw. Dragonbait clenched her fingers with all his strength. Then Alias saw Finder standing behind the paladin. The bard held the finder's stone in his hand.

"No!" Alias shrieked.

Finder sang to the finder's stone, and the three adventurers glowed brightly for an instant, then disappeared. When they reappeared in the Singing Cave, Alias was still shrieking. She jerked her hand away from Dragonbait's and pointed the paladin's flaming sword at the bard's heart.

Finder dropped Dragonbait's hand. "I'll be back," he said. Then he sang to his magic stone again and vanished.

* * * * *

By the time Olive reached the top of the pile, it was beginning to tremble alarmingly. She wasn't sure if it was her imagination or not, but it seemed to be moving toward the east side of the vale. The halfling looked around at the dead bodies and the shaking greenery and started to shiver.

Olive screamed out Dragonbait's name, trying to discern in the darkness if he was one of the corpses. A vine sprang up from the pile right in front of the halfling. An eye was visible on the end of it, round and glassy, like a fish's. Olive gasped and took a step backward. More vines began popping out of the surface of the pile all around the halfling, each tipped with some sort of eye—a saurial's eye, or a wild cat's eye, or a bird's eye. Then more vines appeared with mouths on their ends—fanged lizards' mouths, birds' beaks, a beaver's mouth. The mouths all began calling out Moander's name in a cacophonous chorus that set the halfling's heart pounding with fear.

Olive moved cautiously away toward the edge of the pile. She'd slide down somehow; even falling to the ground would be preferable to becoming part of those eyes and mouths. A feline-mouthed vine lunged toward her, and the halfling shrieked.

Before the vine could strike her, strong hands grabbed her and lifted her off the top of the pile.

Olive gasped from the shock, then sighed with relief. She swiveled her head, expecting to see Akabar or Grypht. Her eyes widened in astonishment at the sight of her rescuer.

"Didn't I tell you that you had to be more careful, little Lady Luck?" Finder Wyvernspur said as he soared northward with the halfling wrapped in his arms.

* * * * *

Grypht looked up from the exhausted form of a small flying saurial at the cleric, Sweetleaf, who stood over him anxiously.

"Excuse me, High One," the cleric said, "but we have a problem in the vale. The—"

"I'll set a backfire soon to keep the fire from spreading," Grypht said. "There's time yet. Don't worry, Sweetleaf."

"It's not the fire, High One," the cleric explained. "It's Moander. It's been resurrected."

Grypht stood up and looked into the vale. Sweetleaf was right. Moander had been resurrected, and it was heading eastward, straight toward them.

The wizard had never really believed that rescuing Dragonbait and recovering the saurial workers would halt Moander's resurrection. If anything, he had realized, it would precipitate the event, but since the Mouth of Moander had the seed and intended to use it that night, there hadn't seemed any reason to put off the inevitable. Grypht had hoped, however, that he would have had more time to get his people back on their feet.

The mountain of greenery slid slowly but steadily across the ground, pushed along by some unseen magical force. Grypht shuddered to think just how much power Moander expended on movement. As the god moved slowly over the fires set in the vale, the flames were instantly smothered by its damp mass. Boulders caught in its path were crushed into gravel. Whenever it came across an especially large tree that the saurials had cut down but had been unable to haul, Moander sucked it into its body, where it was immediately splintered into smaller pieces.

Now that the saurials were free from the god's possession and no longer served him, the wizard had no doubt what use Moander would have for them now. Moander would consume the saurials whole. The wizard looked up and down the hillside for Alias, Dragonbait, Olive, and Akabar, but they were nowhere to be seen, despite the fact that they had agreed to meet him here. Grypht began to grow alarmed. What could have happened to them?

The sound of Moander's approach, cracking trees and smashing rock and rumbling earth, now reached the wizard's ears. Above all those sounds came a cacophony of singing from the hundreds of mouths that grew from the god's body. The Darkbringer was chanting its own name over and over again in victory.

"High One, what should we do?" Sweetleaf asked nervously.

Grypht was about to scoop up as many of the small fliers as he could carry and teleport away with them and Sweetleaf when suddenly Moander changed directions and began heading northward, toward the mountain slope and the Singing

Cave.

"It's following that flier!" Sweetleaf cried, pointing to a dark shape moving northward through the air with the smooth movement of a mage using a fly spell. "Who is it, High One?" Sweetleaf asked.

Just before the shape disappeared into the Singing Cave, Grypht caught sight of the yellow glow the finder's stone gave off in the dark. "Can it be . . . the bard?" Grypht asked uncertainly.

Suddenly Grypht remembered the dark shape he'd seen standing in the camp beside Coral when they'd begun their attack. Finder had returned in time for the battle after all. With his magical stone, the bard could have teleported to the Singing Cave. Could it be that he was deliberately leading Moander away from the saurials? Did he know what had happened to the others?

He had to discover what the bard was up to, the wizard decided. Perhaps Finder could help move the unconscious saurials. "Do what you can for our people, Sweetleaf," Grypht ordered the cleric. "I'll return as soon as I can." The saurial wizard clutched his staff and teleported to the Singing Cave.

* * * * *

Finder drifted into the mouth of the Singing Cave and landed smoothly among the ferns.

"Don't move!" Alias growled, waving Dragonbait's sword at the bard's chest.

Dragonbait knocked the swordswoman's hand aside. "Alias, he's holding Olive. You'll skewer her," the paladin warned. He could see the invisible halfling with his heat sight.

"What are you talking about?" the swordswoman demanded. "His arms are empty."

"No, they're not," Olive piped up. She wished herself visible, and suddenly she was. She looked back up at the bard. "How come you could see me when I was invisible?" she demanded.

"When you get to be my age, Olive, no beautiful woman is invisible," Finder said.

Olive began to smile at the bard's flattery, but she caught sight of the flower in the bard's hair and shuddered nervously.

Sensing her unease, Finder set the halfling down on the floor.

Olive scurried toward Alias.

Grypht appeared behind the bard. He could smell the anger and the fear permeating the air around him. "What's going on?" he demanded.

"Finder's been possessed by Moander!" Alias declared. Her voice cracked with pain and sorrow.

"See the flower in his ear?" Olive chirped.

In the cave lit by Dragonbait's flaming sword, the finder's stone, and the magical blue sigils of Moander glowing on Alias's arm and Dragonbait's chest, Grypht had no trouble picking out the flower growing from the bard's ear and the mossy growth on his chin.

"Champion can use his power to cure disease on him," Grypht said.

"No!" Finder said, stepping back. "I don't need to be cured. I know it appears as if I've been possessed, but I'm not. Alias, you didn't see me do it, but I was the one who dispelled Coral's entanglement vines earlier. I also rescued you and Dragonbait from Moander's grasp. Would I have done all that if I was one of the god's minions?"

"You kept me from rescuing Akabar!" Alias cried. "You let Moander swallow him!"

Grypht felt his heart sinking when he learned the mage's fate. He had admired Akabar's courage and been moved by his concern for the saurials, who weren't even his own people.

"Alias, there was no way you were going to reach Akabar," Finder said. He took a step toward her with his arms extended.

Alias again pointed Dragonbait's sword at the bard's chest. "Don't move!" she ordered him again.

"Moander is heading up the mountain even as we speak," Grypht said, "led here by the bard—"

"I was trying to lead Moander away from your people," Finder protested.

"Olive, check to see how close it is to us," Alias told the halfling. Olive hurried to obey.

"We could use your help, but we can't trust you unless you let Dragonbait cure the disease within you," Grypht said to Finder.

"I cannot cure him, High One," Dragonbait said. "I wasted my power trying to cure Coral. I have used my shen sight on the bard, however. I still sense no evil in him."

Although Grypht realized that Finder was the sort of man

who wouldn't bow to any master, the saurial wizard had never seen anyone resist Moander's possession once the Darkbringer's disease had begun to manifest itself physically. "How is this possible?" he asked the bard.

"Xaran shot a burr of possession at me in the orc lair," Finder explained. "It exploded its spores in my face, but nothing happened. I presumed its magic had failed. I'd forgotten that two hours before it happened I had swallowed magical potions that slow and neutralize poison. I believe the potions' magic must have affected the spores so that they grew more slowly and altered the vines so Moander can't use them to take hold of my body or mind."

"Moander's just reached the mountain slope," Olive reported from the cave's mouth. "The incline's slowing it down some, but it's still coming."

"If you aren't possessed, what were you doing in Coral's hut?" Alias asked, unconvinced by Finder's story. "Olive saw you there."

"Trying to find the seed in order to destroy it. I was hoping that Coral and Moander would believe I was possessed. I got them to tell me where the seed was. I knew Olive was outside, looking into the hut. I made sure she heard that Akabar's blood was the seed they were looking for, and I said it in Realms common so Olive was certain to understand me."

"Olive heard you," Alias admitted. Finally convinced that Finder had tried to help, she lowered Dragonbait's sword from the bard's chest and spoke the command word to extinguish the blade's flame. "She told Akabar and me," the swordswoman whispered.

"Then why didn't you get Akabar away from here?" Finder demanded.

"He refused to leave," Alias sobbed. "He insisted on fighting Moander, whatever the risk."

"The fool!" Finder muttered.

Grypht shook his head. "Akabar did what he felt he must. If you aren't possessed," the wizard asked Finder, "why were you so anxious that Dragonbait not cure you? The vines of possession will eat away at your insides."

"But the vines won't kill me," Finder said. "Their magic will make me immortal."

Grypht shook his head, appalled at the bard's acceptance of

so bizarre a life. "We need Finder's help to teleport my tribe out of the vale. For the time being, I'm prepared to trust him."

"Moander has reached the uncut forest!" Olive said, hurrying back into the cave. "I think it's time we got out of here."

"I'll teleport us all back to my keep," Finder said. "We'll be safe there for the time being."

Anxious to leave before Moander got any closer, Olive forgot her earlier fear of Finder and was prepared to accept his offer immediately. She reached up to take his hand.

"What about the saurials?" Alias asked the bard angrily.

"I can make several trips back for them," Finder replied. "The stone's power is endless."

"And what then?" Alias demanded. The rage that had been boiling up inside her ever since Akabar had disappeared into the pile spewed out at the bard. "What happens when we've all fled and Moander starts crossing the mountains? Do we begin to evacuate the dales?" the swordswoman demanded. "And after the dales, the Elven Woods? Cormyr? Can you take the Realms to a safe place, Finder?"

Tears began to stream down Alias's cheeks as her voice rose. "Akabar is inside that creature, and it's your fault. If you had used the para-elemental ice in your silly stone to put the saurials into a torpor, then Akabar would never have gotten near that pile. He'd be here with us now, and all the saurials would be safe. But your stone was more important than people. You never loved anyone but yourself. Now that you have your precious immortality and your magical stone, why bother to help us? You don't need us. We mean nothing to you."

"Alias," Finder whispered, "that's not true. I love you with all my heart."

"No, you don't," the swordswoman declared. "You don't understand the first thing about love."

Finder was silent for a moment, too ashamed to argue further. All the things Alias had said were true except one. He did love her, even enough to admit he was wrong. "I'm sorry," he said. "You're right. I should have used the stone before. It's too late now, I know, but I'm sorry."

"Prove it! Release the ice from the stone!" Alias replied vehemently. "Use it to stab Moander through the heart and freeze it to death! Then we can rescue Akabar!"

"I'm . . . not sure that will work," Finder said hesitantly.

"It just might," Grypht interjected hurriedly, "if we can attach the para-elemental ice to something that can withstand that much cold . . . a magical weapon or staff, perhaps."

Dragonbait took his sword from Alias and offered it to the wizard, hilt first.

"Para-elemental ice on a magically flaming sword?" Grypht said dubiously. "I wouldn't recommend it."

Finder looked at Alias's tear-stained face. Now he had some idea how she had felt when he had scolded her for the heresy of changing his songs. The bard struggled against an uncontrollable desire to make her smile again. In the end, he lost the struggle. He drew out his dagger. "This belonged to my grandfather," he said. "It has certain power against evil creatures."

"That should do nicely," Grypht said. "Now, do we break the stone to get at the ice?" he asked.

"Can you levitate the stone?" the bard asked, holding out the finder's stone.

Grypht nodded and pulled out a tiny golden wire from the pocket of his robe. As he concentrated on summoning the magical power to him, the smell of fresh-mown hay began to fill the cave. "Rise," he said, shaping the wire into a scoop and lifting it into the air. The wire glittered and vanished as Finder's magical stone drifted out of the bard's hands.

From outside came the sound of splintering wood as Moander made its way through the forest below the cave, ingesting the trees into its body.

Finder tapped on his magical stone with the tip of his dagger until he had positioned it so that the long axis was perpendicular to the floor. "Olive," the bard said calmly, "I need your steady halfling hands and your sweet halfling voice. Are you still wearing that ring I gave you?"

"Yes," Olive said. "Do you want it back?"

"No. I want you to be wearing it for protection. Take this one, too, to keep the chill off." The bard slid a second ring from one of his fingers and slipped it on Olive's finger beside the one he'd given her earlier.

He looked up at Alias. "I need you to sing a high C," he said, "on cue. Hold it until I motion for you to stop."

Alias nodded.

"Olive, a high G for you, and hold it." Finder motioned for the two women to begin. As their voices blended in a chord, the bard began singing a series of random atonal notes. Then he motioned for the women to stop. He tapped his dagger on the side of the Finder's stone, and a tiny crack appeared at the center of the stone along the facet lines.

From outside, the sound of the toppling trees and the rumbling of the ground as Moander advanced grew so loud the adventurers had to raise their voices to be heard. They could hear Moander's cacophonous chanting of its name clearly now. Dragonbait moved to the cave entrance to keep an eye on the god's progress.

Handing his dagger to the halfling, Finder ordered her, "Hold it so the blade is level to the ground." Olive held the dagger out with both hands.

The bard lifted the top of his magical stone away from the bottom. A terrible cold filled the cave instantly, causing their breath to steam. The water droplets on the walls of the cave froze; the ferns on the ground turned gray and brittle, and the swallows nesting in various nooks and crannies began twittering in alarm. Alias's arms began to turn blue and she started to shiver uncontrollably. Grypht moved toward the mouth of the cave, where the air was warmer. Protected by Finder's ring of cold resistance, Olive didn't notice the chill. Finder simply ignored it.

"Alias, take this," the bard said, handing the swordswoman the top of the stone.

Alias took the piece of crystal gingerly, expecting it to be cold, too, but it felt as warm as Finder's hand.

Sticking out of the center of the bottom of the stone, like a needle in a pincushion, was a sliver of ice as clear as glass. Finder held his hands beneath the stone and ordered Grypht to release it from his levitation spell.

"Done," the wizard replied from the mouth of the cave.

Finder knelt down in front of Olive. He huffed once on the tip of the dagger blade to cover it with moisture. "Steady now, Olive girl," he said. He tilted the stone so that the tip of the ice needle touched the dagger's groove. As he slipped the stone away, the needle of ice fell into the groove, with the end of the needle hanging out over the tip of the dagger. Finder breathed on the blade once again to freeze the needle of para-elemental ice to the dagger's blade.

The bard stood up and tossed the bottom of the finder's stone in his hand. "There may just be enough power in this piece to light my way to Akabar," he explained to the swordswoman. "If I succeed in destroying Moander but fail to come out of the pile, you must try to use the top half of the stone to locate the mage."

"Can't you put both halves together again?" Alias asked.

Finder shook his head. "Never again," he said.

Suddenly Alias realized that Finder's immortality might not protect him from death at the hands of a god. He might never come back to her. She'd asked him to sacrificed his stone, but she didn't want him to sacrifice his life.

"Let me take the dagger," the swordswoman said. "Moander is as much my enemy as anyone's."

Finder shook his head. "No. This is my responsibility," he said firmly.

The walls and floor of the cave began to shake from Moander's approach. The swallows in the cave abandoned their nests and swarmed outside, fleeing from the quaking mountain.

"Set the dagger down carefully, Olive," Finder ordered. "Then I'll have to ask for my ring of cold resistance back. Keep the ring of protection. As careless as you are, you need it."

Olive laid the dagger down in the frozen ferns. Finder took back the ring of cold resistance and slipped it on his finger. Hastily Olive pulled out the silver Harpers pin Finder had given her. As the bard bent over to pick up the dagger, Olive fastened the pin to his tunic, saying, "Wear this for luck."

"But I gave you that pin. It's yours," Finder objected.

"Then you'd better bring it back to me, hadn't you?" the half-ling said with a wink.

"Take care, little Lady Luck," Finder whispered, kissing her gently on the forehead. He stood and looked into Alias's eyes. "Remember, no matter what happens, I love you," he said. Touching the sigil of Moander on her arm, he promised, "I will rid you of this."

"Moander is starting to move faster!" Dragonbait shouted. "You must hurry!"

Finder kissed Alias's cheek and rushed to the mouth of the cave. The pile of greenery was only a hundred feet away, and the top of the pile was now level with the cave entrance. Eight long tendrils, tipped with fanged mouths, snaked out from the god's body toward the cave.

Grypht drew back into the cave and began chanting.

Dragonbait drew his sword, prepared to fend off the god, but Finder pushed the paladin back inside the cave. "Look after Alias," he shouted over the din.

Three of the tendrils snaked out and grabbed Finder, pulling him from the cave entrance. The remaining tendrils reached into the cave after Grypht and the others, but the slimy vines slammed into an invisible wall of force cast by the wizard. The saurials and the two women were safe for the moment, but they could only watch helplessly as the bard was drawn toward Moander's body.

As Moander constricted its tendrils around Finder's limbs and torso, the bard forced himself to remain calm. There was a protective enchantment on the sliver of para-elemental ice that helped insulate the ice. He still needed to dispel that enchantment. The tendrils drew Finder to the top of Moander's body, which now stood several hundred feet above the ground. The decaying greenery steamed about the bard, giving off a pungent, earthy smell. Hundreds of tendrils tipped with eyes and mouths waved over the surface of the god. One tendril, tipped with the eye of a deer, snaked toward him, studying him curiously. "You are possessed by my vines," its mouth declared. "Why don't you obey?"

Finder laughed. "Because I'm not your servant, Darkbringer! I'm your doom." The bard sang out a shrill note, dispelling the enchantment about the para-elemental ice, leaving it completely exposed to the air. Cold shot out from tip of Finder's dagger in a blast of icy wind.

The mouths shrieked as the tendrils supporting them froze and turned as brittle as glass. Finder slashed at the constricting vines with his dagger, and they shattered into pieces.

Moander realized immediately it had made a mistake. The god had instructed its minions to channel most of its power into protecting it from fire, leaving it vulnerable to freezing. The para-elemental cold emanating from the tip of the bard's dagger was a dangerous threat. The god abandoned the idea of capturing the bard. Survival had higher priority.

As Finder hovered above the god's body, holding out half of his magical stone, he thought of Akabar Bel Akash. The arguments the two of them had had over the finder's stone brought the Turmish mage's face readily to the bard's mind. A beam of bright light sprang out from the piece of the stone, aimed at the center of the the pile of rotting vegetation.

The eyes at the end of the tendrils blinked shut in the light. Without warning, a whole tree shot out from the god's body, aimed right at Finder. The bard dodged to one side—right into an ambush.

Finder suddenly found himself pelted with spears fashioned from the trunks of sapling trees. Several struck him glancing blows, then bounced away, but one pierced his thigh. The bard eased the spear out of his flesh. It was time to stop being a target. With his dagger held out before him, Finder plunged toward Moander, following the beacon light from the piece of magical stone.

The vegetation on the surface of the god's body shriveled as the bard approached it and crackled like glass as he shot straight through it into Moander's interior. The bard could hear the mouths of the god's body shrieking in pain. As the pile shifted and tumbled, Finder was slammed about like a die rattling in a cup. With every tumble, he crashed through frozen branches and vines and corpses of wild animals.

Suddenly the tumbling stopped. Finder pulled himself together and began to follow the light from the finder's stone once again. The deeper he moved into the god's body, the warmer it became, so the cold from the para-elemental ice took longer to freeze the vines that tried to choke and entangle the bard. Finder was forced to expend more and more energy slashing and hacking with his dagger to clear his path.

The bard began to feel weak from exhaustion and the blood he'd lost from the wound in his leg. Just as he began to consider abandoning his quest, the beam from the piece of the finder's stone struck a patch of darkness it couldn't penetrate. Finder halted in surprise and fear.

The patch of darkness was shaped like a doorway, and Finder recognized it immediately. It was the gate between the Lost Vale and the plane of Tarterus, the gate that Moander had used to transport its saurial minions to the Realms. The entire body of the god had been built around the gate.

Moander's normal abode was the Abyss, but one could reach the Abyss from Tarterus. Moander must have sucked Akabar through the gate, through Tarterus, to its abode in the Abyss.

A small, brilliant gem near the base of the gate caught the bard's eye. He picked it up to examine it more closely. It was the shape and color of a drop of blood, and it felt warm in his hand. Very warm. It seemed to throb with great power. Could it be the seed that had resurrected Moander? Finder wondered. What would happen to the god's new body if it was separated from the seed by a gate?

The bard tried to toss the gem through the gate, but it bounced back. It would have to be carried through by a living person, he realized. Finder retrieved the gem and slipped it inside his boot. He approached the gate, but he hesitated before stepping through it.

In his youth, the bard had visited the ethereal and astral planes a number of times. As an older man, he'd investigated several of the elemental and para-elemental planes. As a prisoner of the Harpers, he'd been exiled to the region between the positive energy plane and a quasi-elemental plane. The thought of stepping through a gate leading to an outer plane, though, filled him with horror—especially so fell a region as Tarterus, where, the sages said, creatures from the Abyss and from Hades constantly fought one another for control of the land, foul and poisonous as it was, and enslaved any beings they discovered.

Dragonbait had leaped through such a gate into Tarterus to stalk evil creatures; that was how the paladin had come to be captured by the fiend Phalse and brought to the Realms. The paladin had suffered greatly at Phalse's hands, but he had emerged from Tarterus alive. Moander's saurial minions had survived their forced march through the plane, as well. The bard chided himself aloud for his trepidity. "Surely Finder Wyvernspur can brave its dangers." It would be easier than facing Alias without Akabar at his side, he decided.

Finder took a deep breath and flew through the dark hole, following the light of the piece of finder's stone.

*　*　*　*　*

As Alias, Olive, Dragonbait, and Grypht watched Finder dive into Moander's body, they were filled with hope. The god cried out in agony and lost its balance on the mountain slope, tumbling down the slope into the vale, shedding great chunks of its body. Then it lay still. The adventurers emerged from the cave and for a long time continued their vigil over the god's fallen body, but neither Finder nor Akabar emerged from the mass of greenery.

Alias was beginning to consider climbing into the vale to do battle with the god herself, when suddenly she felt as if a burning brand had touched her sword arm. She looked down at her arm and shouted with joy, "It's gone! Moander's sigil is gone! The god is dead!"

Dragonbait clutched at his chest from the pain the disappearing sigil had caused him, then embraced the swordswoman.

"Finder's destroyed Moander!" Olive shouted with glee.

"No . . . he has only destroyed the body Moander occupied in this world," Grypht reminded the others, and his words cast a shadow of foreboding on their elation.

✿ 20 ✿

Finder in the Underworld

Once he'd passed through the dark gate inside Moander's Realmsian body, Finder found himself hovering a few feet over a bog bordering a river. The soil from the bog glowed a dull red, bathing the surface of the plane about him in a hellish light. The plants of the bog lay on their sides, withered and brown. He was grateful his flying spell hadn't worn off yet, for he would just as soon not touch the soil or the plants. The river was as black as night and flowed fast and smooth. Although the bard had never been to Tarterus, he knew enough about the plane to realize that the river was the Styx, and that to touch or drink from it would bring complete oblivion.

The air of the plane might have been warm before he arrived, but around his freezing dagger it remained chill. In the sky overhead, he could see a line of receding spheres, like pearls spread out on an invisible string, all glowing a dull red. There was a different sphere of Tarterus for every world in the prime material plane. He was on the sphere connected to the Realms, and somewhere out there was the sphere of Tarterus that was linked to the saurial's home world. There was air between the spheres, and he could fly from this sphere of Tarterus to the saurials' sphere of Tarterus, but that was not his destination.

The light from his half of the finder's stone glowed much more dimly in this place, like a candle burning in a nearly airless room. The bard could just barely pick out the trace of the beam of light indicating Akabar's direction. Finder flew along its path. The light led to the river's edge and stopped.

He would have to take a boat, he realized. If he tried to travel by himself, he would attract the attention of the myriad of evil creatures that dwelled in this plane, creatures like Phalse, who captured fools like Dragonbait and himself who traveled where they shouldn't. Even if he could keep from the notice of such creatures, he could easily get lost in this place and wander for centuries.

He had only a vague idea of how one went about summoning Charon, the Boatman of the Styx. It required some magical spells that he didn't possess. In lieu of that, Finder decided to try the only other magic he had beyond the broken finder's stone and the dagger he might still need to use to wrest Akabar from Moander's grasp. He pulled the horn of blasting from his belt. If it failed to bring Charon, it might at least hail one of the lesser boatmen who carried passengers along the river.

Finder didn't trigger the instrument's destructive magic, but blew into it as he would a normal horn. He blew a fanfare he'd once composed in honor of a legion of soldiers who had all been killed in a single day in battle. It seemed an appropriate tune for this place. Then he waited.

In less than a minute, the black water began to churn and froth; then a heavy, sparkling silver mist appeared upriver and drifted downstream with the current. As the mist drew closer, Finder could just barely make out the pointed bow of a boat shrouded within it. Then suddenly the boat, as black as the water of the Styx, emerged from the silver mist, and the mist dissolved into nothingness.

A single boatman stood in the back of the boat and steered it toward the shore with a pole. The boat halted beside Finder, and the boatman held it stationary without any apparent effort, despite the swift current that flowed around it. Finder's eyes widened at the sight of the boatman. It was Charon himself, not one of his helpers. The Lord of the Styx wore a full-length hooded cloak of black silk, trimmed with ermine. Beneath the hood, his face was haggard and his eyes glowed a fiery red. The hands that held the pole were nearly skeletal. The figure stood in the boat without speaking.

"I'm Finder Wyvernspur," the bard explained. "I'm seeking Akabar Bel Akash. He has been taken by the god Moander, who dwells in the Abyss."

Charon held out his palm.

"Will you take this horn in payment?" the bard asked.

Charon motioned for Finder to blow the horn again.

Finder repeated the fanfare for the dead legion of soldiers.

Charon nodded and held out his hand. Finder laid the horn in the boatman's palm, taking care not to touch his flesh.

Charon set the horn down at his feet and motioned for Finder to come aboard. The bard floated over the boat and took care to settle himself down into it gently, but he was still surprised that the boat didn't rock at all from his weight. The boat was completely dry inside and empty save for him, the boatman, and the horn. Finder sat facing forward so he wouldn't be forced to stare at Charon, whose eyes made him feel uneasy. The sensation of bobbing on the water or of air flowing by was completely absent, even as Charon pushed the boat away from the river's edge into the faster-moving water in the middle of the stream. The boat seemed so still that Finder began to feel as if he'd seated himself in a coffin buried in the earth.

The river steamed around them, in the chillness of the air Finder created with his sliver of para-elemental ice. The bard glanced back at Charon to see if the cold made the boatman uncomfortable. Charon seemed completely oblivious not only to the cold, but to the bard's presence as well. Finder recalled then that the boatman traveled through regions of the outer planes that would make Icewind Dale seem temperate.

The bard turned his attention to the scenery, but the bogs which stretched out from both banks of the river were a depressing sight. Dead, brown marsh grasses covered the ground as far as the eye could see, and the monotony of the flatland was broken only occasionally by stunted, leafless bushes. Despite the warmth and moisture of the soil, nothing grew. Only after great storms, when the rain had temporarily washed away the poison of the soil, could any plant survive in this region of desolation.

In an effort to take his mind off the bleak scenery around him, Finder tried to think of Alias and Olive. He tried to remember their faces and how they had sounded when they sang together in the Singing Cave and the feel of their hands on his own, but the memories wouldn't come to him. The river Styx, he recalled, drove away memories of the living.

The bard found himself dwelling instead on memories of Flattery and Kirkson and Maryje. It seemed he thought of nothing else for hours as Charon steered his boat through twisted paths of the river. A desire to throw himself in the river, so that he could forget the evils of his past life, grew stronger with every passing minute.

Finder shook himself with sudden alarm, remembering that the river would rob him of all his memories, good as well as bad. He would forget his songs . . . Olive . . . even Alias. Whether the allure of oblivion was due to some enchantment of the dark water and depressing landscape or his own weakness, the bard knew he had to fight it off somehow. A song, he thought. I should sing a song.

Uncertain how the boatman would react to any other music, Finder began by humming "The Tears of Selune." When Charon gave no indication of annoyance or displeasure and nothing leaped out at the boat from the banks, the bard began to sing the words. Halfway through the song, he began wondering if Olive had been right, that Selune's Shards sang it as a duet. He started the song from the beginning, and for the first time since he'd written them three centuries ago, he began changing the lyrics so that they would work better as a duet. By the time Charon pulled his boat over to the opposite shore, the bard felt as though he'd changed his whole life. He thanked the boatman for the ride, though he had paid for it with the horn, and Charon acknowledged the bard's gratitude with a nod.

Finder hovered out of the boat and flew the few feet to solid ground. While he'd been concentrating on his music, he hadn't noticed the change in scenery, but now he surveyed the new landscape with repulsion. The bogs of Tarterus hadn't been half as horrible as his first sight of Moander's realm in the Abyss. The shoreline was encrusted with slimy brown muck; the banks were heaped with piles of rotting carcasses and decaying vegetation, and a noisome odor filled the air. Finder turned back to Charon, uncertain if he really wanted to journey any farther into this oppressive region, but the boatman and his boat were gone.

Grateful yet again that his fly spell hadn't worn off, the bard held out the broken finder's stone, which put out a feeble light pointing away from the river. The stench beyond the banks of the river was unbearable, but he had no choice. Flying over the fields strewn with debris and the mountains of refuse, Finder wondered if Moander's realm was the repository for all the garbage of the other six hundred and sixty-five layers of the Abyss.

The bard hadn't flown far when, from the corner of his eye,

he thought he spied a huge gem, but when he landed and bent over to pick it up, it proved to be a piece of rotten fruit. Likewise, his eyes were deceived into seeing a silvered sword, which turned out to be the slime-encrusted bone of some great beast. When he tried to salvage a gilded, leather-bound tome and found himself holding a rotted log alive with larvae, the bard realized that all these illusions were calculated to keep him from his quest. He flew on, ignoring all the other riches he imagined he saw, no matter how enticing they looked.

As he continued on, following the light of the broken finder's stone, Finder passed several of Moander's minions. Although most of the minions looked like humans or elves, some appeared to be beasts—elephants, horses, cats, rats, hounds, deer, hawks, sparrows—or magical creatures like dragons and treants. A few must have once been creatures from other worlds, for Finder didn't recognize their kind. Yet every minion had in common the tendril vines growing from its body, controlling its actions and making it subject to the Darkbringer. Finder realized that if it hadn't been for his possession by the vines, he wouldn't be passing through this realm without being challenged.

The light of the finder's stone led the bard to a great hill, as large as the mound on which the city of Yulash stood. At first Finder thought the hill might be Moander's stronghold. As he drew closer, however, Finder realized that the hill was in fact Moander's true body, the one that held the very essence of the god's being. Unlike all the other shells it possessed in all the worlds of the prime material plane, if this body were destroyed, the Darkbringer would cease to exist completely and forever.

Moander's Abyssal form was another pile of rotting vegetation, but it was easily five times the size of the body the god had possessed in the Realms. Thousands of tendrils ending in eyes and mouths waved from the pile, and orange rivers of poisoned water flowed down its slopes. Yet for all its vast size, the true body of Moander seemed to tremble from the cold coming from the dagger Finder carried.

At the foot of the hill that was Moander stood Akabar Bel Akash. He was tethered about his ankles with slimy tendrils, and his wrists were likewise bound. His eyes were closed, and he did not speak.

"Hold, Nameless Bard!" a chorus of voices cried from the mouths of Moander.

Finder halted.

"You were a fool to come here," the mouths of Moander declared. "For destroying my body in the Realms, you have earned my everlasting enmity. Yet despite your crimes against me, I must admire your resourcefulness. I think that I will let you live on as my servant. Now, hand over the seed of power that you stole from my Realmsian body."

Finder slipped the broken half of the finder's stone into his boot and drew out the tiny blood-red gem he'd discovered lying before the magical gate inside Moander's Realmsian body. Apparently, by stepping through the gate and separating the gem from the Realms, he had indeed robbed the god of its power to exist in that world. The gem, Finder suspected, held not just power but some attribute that made it possible for Moander to return to the Realms.

If he smashed the gem, Moander might never regain that power, and the Realms would be safe from the Darkbringer forever. Yet if he gave the gem to Moander, it might take years for the god to find a way to build yet another body in the Realms, and the people of the Realms would have all that time to prepare some other defense against the Darkbringer.

"I'll give you the seed, Moander," Finder said, "in exchange for Akabar Bel Akash and safe passage from your realm. I'll even let you keep your everlasting enmity." He grinned maliciously.

"Arrogant fool! I could slay you where you stand," Moander's mouths snarled.

"I suspect not," the bard said. "If you could, you would have killed me the moment I stepped into your realm, but you can't, can you? You've been using too much of your power these past few months, possessing saurials and forcing them to do your bidding. You must be feeling a little weak. Your true body is also susceptible to cold, isn't it? I can see your tendrils shivering from the icy air that surrounds my dagger. I, on the other hand, could crush your precious seed in a moment. Release Akabar now, and I will return the seed," Finder ordered.

"No," a voice said, a voice that sounded like Akabar but couldn't have been, for the mage's lips never moved. Finder watched with surprise as a white mist slid from Akabar's body and drifted over toward him.

"No!" Moander's mouths shouted.

The mist coalesced into a translucent form shaped like Akabar.

"Akabar, is that you?" Finder asked the misty figure.

"This is my spirit and soul," a voice from the mist said. "Moander holds my body and mind in thrall, but it cannot tether this part of my being. Finder, I cannot allow you to bargain for my life. I will soon be finished with living. I am prepared to dwell now in another plane."

"But Alias wants me to bring you back," Finder objected.

"Yes," the mage's spirit form replied with a smile. "Alias was always very demanding. Finder, I have abided by this monster's side only long enough for your arrival. In my dreams, the gods of light told me that I was to instruct you. Now, at last, I know what it is I must teach you. First, understand this," the spirit form said, using the formal tone of a Southern scholar. "This body behind me is Moander's true body. If it is destroyed, Moander's essence will be destroyed forever, completely, in every incarnation in every world."

"Akabar," Finder said, "I know that already. I don't care about it. I only came here to get you."

"Now know this," Akabar's spirit continued. "You have the power to destroy Moander's true body. You were right—its true body is weak now. Cling fast to the seed of power, Finder Wyvernspur, for with it in your possession and your dagger of cold, you can destroy this god."

"Destroy me! Destroy the mage! Destroy yourself!" the voices of Moander sang, but their tone held a hint of panic.

"You may indeed die in the attempt," the spirit said to Finder.

"I didn't come here to kill Moander," Finder protested. "I came to bring you back. Moander, release Akabar's body and mind, and I will leave here without injuring you."

"Promise?" the mouths of Moander asked eagerly.

"No!" Akabar's spirit cried angrily. "Finder," he said hastily, "I realize this is not the fate you had in mind for yourself, but if you do not destroy Moander now, you will be throwing away the only opportunity creation has ever had to rid itself of this monster. Finally learn this," the mage's spirit said, concluding his instruction, "This is how an unselfish man dies."

Akabar's spirit form raised his arms as high as he could and called out in Turmish to the gods of light he venerated. Finder recognized many of the gods' names, though most of what Akabar's spirit said was not clear to him. The spirit's last words were a Turmish prayer that the bard did recognize.

"Gods of my heart, claim your faithful servant," Akabar's spirit cried, and a white light, as bright as the desert sun, encased the mage's spirit form. The light glowed so brightly that Finder had to turn his back and close his eyes.

Moander's mouths shrieked with fear and rage as the god's eyes were blinded and it sensed it was being robbed of its hostage.

The light vanished, and with it took Akabar's spirit and soul. Akabar's body crumbled to dust.

Finder shook with awe. There was no way he could ignore Akabar's sacrifice and turn around and go home. Only a fool would accept all the luck that Tymora had thrown in his path these past two days and give nothing in return. In one hand, the bard clenched the seed, created from Akabar's blood and Moander's power, and in the other, his dagger, tipped with para-elemental ice. He flew up above the body of the god.

"Destroy me! Destroy yourself!" Moander's mouths shrieked hysterically.

"Only my body, Moander," the bard said. "Not my soul." Finder veered and dove toward the god's body with his dagger of para-elemental ice extended. As he struck the Darkbringer's exterior and broke through to the god's interior, he was plunged into complete darkness and oblivion. His eyes saw nothing, his body felt nothing, and his mind went completely blank.

❧ 21 ❧

New Lives

Back in the Lost Vale, Alias, Grypht, Dragonbait, and Olive waited for over an hour, watching the pile of rotting greenery for some sign of Finder and Akabar. When the two men failed to appear, Alias's anxiety grew unbearable. "We have to find them!" she declared, heading for the path that led down into the vale, but Grypht put a restraining hand on her shoulder.

"Use the stone," he said softly.

"What?" Alias asked in confusion.

"The half of Finder's stone that he left you. Use it."

Alias pulled the stone from her cloak. "Akabar," she said, thinking of the mage, but the stone didn't even glow. Alias's hands began to tremble.

The wizard took the stone from the swordswoman's hands. "I'll try the direction of Sweetleaf, as a test," he said, thinking of the saurial cleric he had rescued earlier. The stone lit up and sent a feeble beacon toward the eastern slopes of the vale.

Next Grypht spoke the bard's name, concentrating on Finder's face, then his voice, and finally his songs. There was no reaction from the stone.

"There could be many reasons why it will not locate them," the wizard said. "Because they are possessed, or enchanted with a misdirection, or—" Grypht halted.

"Or dead," Alias said flatly. There was no sense denying it. She felt completely numb. Finder had saved the Realms from Moander, but it had cost his life and Akabar's.

"We should look after the living," Grypht said after a moment. "There are saurials who need our help."

Alias nodded, but as the adventurers trekked down to the east side of the vale, the air around them grew heavy with the scent of roses and the sounds of Alias's and Olive's weeping.

* * * * *

In the early light of dawn, Olive climbed back up to the Singing Cave. She had spent the rest of the night nursing saurials until she was sick of looking at their scaly hides. She needed to sleep, but more than that, she needed to be alone. Now she sat in the mouth of the cave, watching the sun rise over the Desertsmouth Mountains and listening to the wind whistle around her, weeping silently.

Someone in the cave behind her cleared his throat politely and asked, "Mistress Ruskettle? Are you all right?" Olive looked around listlessly. Breck Orcsbane stood in the cave; assembled behind him were Elminster, Mourngrym, Morala, Zhara, and three young saurials.

"You're a little late," Olive said. "We already took care of Moander—Finder did, that is." With a wave of her hand, she indicated the trail of frost-covered vegetation strewn down the mountainside, ending in a large, frozen mass of greenery.

Lord Mourngrym whistled in awe. "How did he do *that?*" he asked.

"He broke open the finder's stone and used the piece of paraelemental ice that was inside," Olive said.

Elminster and Morala exchanged surprised looks. "Where is Finder now?" Elminster asked.

"He went into the god's body to find Akabar," Olive said, "but he never came out again. Alias has a broken piece of the finder's stone she's been using to locate missing saurials for Grypht, but when she tried to locate Finder and Akabar, nothing happened." Olive choked back a sob and forced herself to say what she didn't want to admit: "They're both dead." The halfling looked up at Zhara. "I'm . . . sorry," she said to the Turmish priestess.

Zhara lowered her head. "I knew already," she said softly. "My husband's spirit visited me in a dream last night. He is with our gods, and his soul is at peace."

Olive looked at Zhara with surprise. "Did he say anything about Finder? " she asked hopefully.

Akabar's wife shook her head.

Olive turned her head, as if she were looking at the vale below. The vale blurred before her eyes as she blinked back more tears.

"I've brought Grypht's apprentices," Elminster said. "They're anxious to see him."

Olive wiped her eyes on her tunic sleeve and turned again to speak with the others. "Grypht'll be glad to see them, too. He can use all the help he can get. Most of the saurials are pretty sick from being possessed. Moander's vines of possession didn't leave them time to get enough food to eat or heal any injuries."

"Morala and I have brought magic to help them," Zhara said. "Take us to them, please."

Olive led the others out of the cave and down to the eastern slopes of the vale, where the saurials were recovering from their ordeal.

Elminster and Grypht's apprentices hurried forward to meet with the saurial wizard, while Morala went to Alias's side. The elderly priestess looked up at the swordswoman. "I'm sorry that you lost your friend Akabar . . . and Finder, too," she said.

Alias acknowledged Morala's sympathy with a nod. Tossing her head proudly, she said, "Before he died, Finder told me about Flattery."

Morala looked down at the ground, and Alias could see that the priestess's eyes were moist. After several seconds, Morala looked back up at her. "Then I am doubly sorry for your loss," the old woman whispered.

"Thank you," Alias said sincerely, though she was a little surprised to discover that Morala appeared to grieve for a man she'd once condemned. "Did you know that Finder destroyed the finder's stone to try to rescue Akabar from Moander?" Alias asked.

The priestess nodded. "The halfling told us," she said. "She seems quite upset by his death."

Alias watched as Olive bent over an injured saurial and checked his bandages. "Finder and Olive were a good influence on each other. Olive's in the habit of behaving herself now, but it's not the same to her without knowing it will please Finder. I'll always feel empty whenever I sing, wishing he were there to hear."

A saurial nearby chirped for water, and Alias excused herself to tend to the creature.

Once she'd picked up the basics about the saurials' physiology, Morala took charge of the work to be done. She dismissed Alias, Dragonbait, and Olive, ordering them to get some rest, and the three adventurers gratefully obeyed. Next the white-haired priestess mustered Zhara, Breck Orcsbane, and Lord Mourngrym and set them to work making a comfortable camp-site for the hundred or so saurials that remained, most of whom were too weak to care for themselves, let alone one another. By the time Alias awoke four hours later, Morala had cleaned, fed, and sheltered every saurial in sight. She and Zhara had also healed and cured diseases in as many of them as their power and potions could handle in one day.

The swordswoman joined Grypht, his three apprentices, and Elminster for a meal of bread and fruit under the shade of an old oak tree. The five mages had just finished tracking down those saurials who had escaped the cones of cold the night before. Grypht was beginning to look exhausted, but he wouldn't sleep until he had finalized arrangements for his tribe's welfare.

Grypht explained to Alias, "My people and I could return to our world today, but the land that belongs to our tribe has been poisoned by Moander's minions. It will be years before any plant or creature could live there. Our whole tribe would become homeless vagabonds at a time when they are already very weak. Elminster thinks we should stay here in the Realms, in this vale. We can work at healing the scar Moander forced us to put on this land. What do you think?"

"I think that would be wonderful," the swordswoman replied.

"Wonderful? Why wonderful?" Grypht asked.

"Because then Dragonbait could be with his people, but I wouldn't lose him entirely," Alias explained.

"You are Champion's sister and a singer of soul songs for our tribe; we are your people as well. Will you stay with us awhile?" the wizard asked. "We could use your advice."

"Yes, of course," Alias agreed. The emptiness that the deaths of Akabar and Finder had created in her heart lifted slightly with the realization that someone else needed her, that she had a new family and new duties.

"You are certain that no one will contest our occupation of this vale?" the saurial wizard asked Elminster. "In our world, a place like this would be envied by many tribes."

Elminster shook his head. "This vale was once the home of elves. They left long ago. It has been hidden magically for so long that few know of its existence. Should ye have any problems, the Harpers and the Lord of Shadowdale are eager to become thy allies and help defend thy tribe until ye are able to defend thyselves again."

Grypht nodded. "That is enough. If the people agree, we will stay. Now I will sleep," he said. Then he rose to his feet and went off to rest, his apprentices following him.

When they were alone, Alias asked Elminster, "Where have you been? Why didn't you return right away from Grypht's world after his transference spell took you there? Mourngrym said you can always get back home no matter where you go."

"I assure thee, Alias, I didst try," the old sage replied, "but unbeknownst to Grypht, Moander had cast a powerful lock spell that prevented anyone from escaping Grypht's world by teleportation or worldwalking. Grypht managed to escape only because he used a transference spell that Moander had not foreseen to include in the lock spell. I might have cast a transference spell myself, but I could not use it on Grypht's apprentices and I didst not wish to abandon them. The four of us began trekking overland, trying to reach a gate to Tarterus."

"But when Morala scried for you, you were alone," Alias said.

"Nay. Grypht's apprentices traveled with me, but I made them invisible to keep them safe," Elminster explained. Olive and Dragonbait came up to them at that moment and sat on either side of Alias. Dragonbait stroked Alias's sword arm once, and she smiled up at him, grateful to have her brother with her. Olive began playing with the fruit and bread laid out on the ground, but she didn't feel tempted to eat any of it.

"And when you reached the gate to Tarterus, what happened?" Alias asked Elminster.

"We did not reach the gate. It was another two days' journey. Fortunately I was finally able to cast a worldwalk spell to take myself and Grypht's apprentices to Shadowdale when Moander's lock spell failed." The sage stressed the last four words so strongly that Alias realized immediately there was something unusual about Moander's failed spell.

"So why did it fail?" she asked.

"Because not only has Moander's body in the Realms been destroyed this past night, but someone killed Moander's true body in the Abyss. The god has been destroyed forever."

"Akabar?" Alias asked with astonishment. "He said the gods

told him to do just that."

"Partly," Elminster replied. "Remember last year when I told thee of the old prophecy that ye would free the Darkbringer?"

Alias nodded wordlessly.

"There was another prophecy that went with it: 'When the good man teaches wisdom to the fool, the Darkbringer will die.' "

"Akabar and Finder," Alias whispered.

Elminster nodded.

"But how did they get to the Abyss?" the swordswoman asked.

"There is a gate to Tarterus in this vale. The saurials built Moander's new body around it. Akabar and Finder must have passed through the gate and arrived somehow in the Abyss."

"So they've saved everyone from Moander, not just the Realms?" Olive asked.

"Yes," Elminster replied.

"You don't look too happy about that," Olive said.

"I am not unhappy, only anxious," the sage answered. "When a god's existence ends, something or someone else is always ready to snatch up its powers. There is no knowing whether the power will go to a good or evil being."

Morala, Breck, and Mourngrym walked up to the old oak tree where Elminster and the two adventurers sat.

"We wanted you to know that Lord Mourngrym has taken Kyre's place as the third Harper in our tribunal, and we have come to a decision," Morala said, "regarding the Nameless Bard."

"Finder Wyvernspur," Alias reminded the priestess.

"Exactly," Breck said. "We've voted to rescind our decree banishing his name and songs and pardon him for his crimes."

"Sort of a case of closing the gate after the cows have escaped, isn't it?" Olive asked.

"There is a principle involved here, Mistress Ruskettle," Morala said.

"We understand that it won't make up for his loss, Alias," the Lord of Shadowdale said. "But the truth will be told about him, and everyone will know he died a hero."

"Thank you, Mourngrym," Alias replied. "I appreciate it. Finder would appreciate it, too."

"Finder would rather be alive," Olive muttered.

Olive felt something tug at one of her curls, and she heard Finder's voice whisper in her head, Don't sulk, little Lady Luck. It doesn't become you.

The halfling looked around suddenly, her eyes wide.

"What's wrong, Olive?" Alias asked.

"Did you hear something?" Olive asked. "A voice?"

Alias shook her head.

"And since Finder is no longer a Harper in disgrace," Breck Orcsbane said, "we must welcome his choice of candidates to our ranks."

Olive, struggling to understand why she had suddenly heard Finder's voice so clearly when no one else had, was oblivious to the fact that everyone's eyes were on her.

Dragonbait signed subtly to the halfling in the thieves' hand cant. They mean you, rogue.

"Me?" the halfling said. "What about me?"

"I told them," Alias explained, "that Finder gave you his Harper's pin."

"Pin?" Olive asked slyly, suddenly aware that if she didn't watch her step, she could end up an official snooty, goody-goody Harper, complete with responsibilities to live up to and rules to follow. "I haven't got any pin," she insisted. It was true, since she'd fastened Finder's Harper's pin to his cloak before he'd gone off to fight Moander. She tossed her hair defiantly.

Something slid down her hair and landed on the ground directly in front of her. There was no mistaking the glittering silver harp-and-crescent-moon pattern of the pin, which had seemed to dislodge itself from behind her ear.

Elminster reached over and held up the pin. "Yes . . . this is Finder's pin," the sage said. "I saw him give it to the halfling last year after she freed him from Cassana's dungeon, then helped him rescue Akabar, Alias, and Dragonbait."

"Actually, we've been looking for someone just like you for a special project," Breck Orcsbane said, "so we're lucky you came along."

Olive sighed. She didn't know how he'd done it, but she suspected that Finder had once more gotten her mixed up in some crazy adventure.

* * * * *

The bard chuckled and leaned back against the frozen corpse of Moander—the Darkbringer's true body. He was very tired— nearly exhausted, in fact. Scrying on and sending a message to Olive and teleporting his silver Harper's pin to the Realms had expended more energy than he could really afford. Still, it had been worth it, just to see the look on the halfling's face when she discovered herself inducted into the ranks of the Harpers.

Alias would be fine with Dragonbait, but since the bard wasn't sure when or if he'd ever find the power to return to the Realms, he had decided that the Harpers would have to look after Olive for him.

In the meantime, he'd have to find a realm of his own somewhere else in the outer planes. Just because he'd managed to wrestle the Darkbringer's powers away didn't mean he had to dwell in the former god's abysmal abode. The bard rose to his feet and began humming a new song as he flew down to the banks of the Styx to catch a ride to his new home . . . wherever he decided to make it.

FORGOTTEN REALMS
FANTASY ADVENTURE

THE MAZTICA TRILOGY
Douglas Niles

IRONHELM

A slave girl learns of a great destiny laid upon her by the gods themselves. And across the sea, a legion of skilled mercenaries sails west to discover a land of primitive savagery mixed with high culture. Under the banner of its vigilant god the legion claims these lands for itself. And only as Erix sees her land invaded is her destiny revealed.

VIPERHAND

The God of War feasts upon chaos while the desperate lovers, Erix and Halloran, strive to escape the waves of catastrophe sweeping Maztica. Each is forced into a choice of historical proportion and deeply personal emotion. The destruction of the fabulously wealthy continent of Maztica looms on the horizon. Available now.

FEATHERED DRAGON

Forces of terror rack Maztica, destroying cities and forcing whole populations to flee for their lives. The one hope for survival is the promised return of Qotal, the Feathered Dragon. Erixitl of Palul holds the key to that return, but only if she succeeds in her final and most difficult quest.

FORGOTTEN REALMS
FANTASY ADVENTURE

The **Dark Elf** Trilogy

HOMELAND
R.A. Salvatore

Strange and exotic Menzoberranzan is the vast city of the drow. Imagine the world of the dark elves, where families battle families and fantastic monsters rise up from the lightless depths. Possessing a sense of honor beyond the scope offered him by his unprincipled kinsmen, young Drizzt finds himself with a dilemma: Can he live in a honorless society?

EXILE
R.A. Salvatore

Exiled from Menzoberranzan, the city of the drow, Drizzt must find acceptance among races normally at war with his kind. And all the while, the hero must look back over his shoulder for signs of deadly pursuit—the dark elves are not a forgiving race.

SOJOURN
R.A. Salvatore

Drizzt makes his way to the surface world, finding even more trouble than he imagined. Available in May 1991.

BUCK ROGERS
XXVc
THE 25TH CENTURY
BOOKS ™

THE INNER PLANETS TRILOGY

Book One:

FIRST POWER PLAY
John Miller

As the New Earth Organization rebuilds an Earth shattered by the Martian Wars, NEO sympathizer Kemal Gavilan receives a corpse and a cryptic message from the asteroids. The Mercurian prince sends master pirate Black Barney to find out what he can, but the answer is hot: they've uncovered a weapon that can focus the sun's energy for global annihilation! The Martian and Venusian powers insist they're innocent. Kemal is forced to rejoin the royal family he once rejected to learn the awful truth.

Book Two:

PRIME SQUARED
M. S. Murdock

Having discovered his own family's plans for a colossal laser device, Kemal prepares to head back to Earth to inform NEO. The prince learns, however, that Ardala Valmar has snared a prototype of the weapon. Kemal is compelled to stay and destroy the greater of two evils—his family's nearly completed full-scale model. The Mercurian prince maneuvers through one double-cross after another, trying to keep his uncle, the reigning Sun King, from uncovering his true allegiance.

Book Three:

MATRIX CUBED
Britton Bloom

Kemal unravels instability in the Sun King empire and finds himself thrust into daunting circumstances. His problems are compounded by the fact that others—including RAM—may have developed remarkably similar laser projects. Available in May 1991.

EXPLORE AD&D® COMPUTER FANTASY ROLE-PLAYING LIKE NEVER BEFORE!

Introducing **EYE OF THE BEHOLDER**, volume 1 of the first graphically based AD&D® computer fantasy role-playing saga – THE LEGEND SERIES!

Stunning 3-D graphics and explosive sound deliver mesmerizing face-to-face combat and encounters! Easy "point-and-click" commands and 3-D point of view create a "you are there" feeling throughout your entire adventure. Everything you experience, including movement, spell-casting and combat, is from your point of view! AD&D® computer fantasy role-playing has *never* been like this!

Available for: IBM, AMIGA.

Visit your retailer or call 1-800-245-4525, in USA & Canada, for VISA /MC orders. To receive SSI's complete catalog, send $1.00 to:

STRATEGIC SIMULATIONS, INC.®
675 Almanor Avenue, Suite 201
Sunnyvale, CA 94086